M000190232

FREEDOMLAND

CHRISTOPHER JACKSON

FreedomLand by Christopher Jackson

https://www.facebook.com/authorchristopherjackson

this is a work of fiction. Names, characters, places, and incidents either are the product of the author's imagination or are used fictitiously, and any semblance to actual persons, living or dead, business establishments, events, or locales, is entirely coincidental.

copyright © 2019

All rights reserved.

No part of this book may be reproduced or transmitted in any form or by any means, electronic or mechanical, including photocopying, recording, or by any information storage and retrieval system without the written permission of the author, except where permitted by law. Purchase only authorized editions.

Print Book ISBN: 978-1-09838-029-8

Ebook ISBN: 978-1-09838-030-4

Cover Design by Laura Spector

www.LauraSpector.com

For Naoko
Thirty Years Living in Ten Cities on Four Continents
One Epic, Lifelong Road Trip
One Strong, Brave, Beautiful, Brilliant Companion

CHAPTER ONE

Watching two lawyers from the Jubblies Corporation shoot his friend Bud Roy Roemer in the left clavicle deepened Gage Randolph's respect for the cutthroat nature of the restaurant business.

Shocked into immobility, Gage could do nothing but sit in the cab of his 1985 Ford Bronco and stare, openmouthed, as Bud Roy sank slowly to the sidewalk outside his restaurant. The sharp crack of the 9mm pistol announcing the abrupt conclusion to a surprisingly contentious intellectual property dispute between Bud Roy and Jubblies still hung in the air. While a deputy sheriff had pulled the trigger, Gage knew it had been at Jubblies's bidding.

Bud Roy's sin, in Jubblies's eyes, was opening a restaurant named Knockers Bar and Grill across the street from a well-established Jubblies branch in Fayetteville, North Carolina. "You can't do that," the Jubblies manager had told him. "It's illegal and," the man had added without a shred of irony, "it's offensive to women."

Bud Roy, as conversant in intellectual property law as he was supportive of the #MeToo movement, was unmoved by the man's argument. Having failed in his appeal to Bud Roy's sense of chivalry, the manager sent Corporate Jubblies a photo of the garish sign bearing the name of Bud Roy's restaurant. Much aggrieved at the inelegant assault on Jubblies's brand image, Corporate Jubblies had fired off a series of stern cease-and-desist letters insisting he change the name of his restaurant to something "non-breast-related."

But a man with a dream, even a misogynistic one, is difficult to dissuade. Despite the threats, Bud Roy and his sign stood tall. Having run out of patience with their stubborn foe, the Jubblies execs went to the mattresses. This was a rash decision. Had Jubblies waited a week, Bud Roy would have folded on his own. The restaurant business was tough enough without limiting prospective clientele to "men who were hoping Knockers was Jubblies, but with naked chicks." Teetering on the brink of insolvency, Bud Roy's remedy had been to open at 6:00 a.m. to capture the mammary-obsessed market for the one meal of the day that Jubblies did not serve. The results had been disappointing.

"We told you to cease and desist," a shaken Jubblies attorney said as Bud Roy squirmed on the pavement outside of his restaurant, vainly trying to stem the flow of blood from his left shoulder.

"You were ruining the good Jubblies name," the second attorney added, swallowing hard to force the vomit rising in his throat back to his stomach. Yale Law School had not prepared him for bare-knuckled enforcement of intellectual property law.

"They're *breasts*," Bud Roy hissed through clenched teeth as the immediate shock of getting shot wore off and the pain introduced itself. "You can't *own* them."

Jubblies, for once on the side of women everywhere, disagreed. "The law begs to differ," the first attorney said as Cumberland County Deputy Sheriff Samuel Aucoin, his sidearm still drawn, rushed up to provide first aid to the man he had just shot.

"Damn it, Bud Roy," Sam said as he holstered his weapon and applied a compress to the man's bleeding shoulder. "Pulling a gun was bad enough. Why'd you go and discharge it?"

"He didn't have no gun!" Gage protested as he appeared behind Sam, having run in from the parking lot to help his stricken friend. "All he had was a cordless phone. See?" He pointed to the phone lying on the ground just beyond Bud Roy's outstretched hand.

"Shit!" Sam said as he frisked Bud Roy to confirm there was no weapon. He grabbed the phone and held it up in wonder. "How old is this fucking phone? It's the same size as a goddamn .44 Magnum. And what was that shot I heard?"

"That was my Bronco backfiring," Gage said. "She always has a little intestinal distress when I start her up."

"Fuck, fuck, fuck!" Sam said, unable to summon a better description of his current predicament. He looked at Bud Roy. "Don't any of your customers drive cars built in the twenty-first century?" Receiving a grimace in reply, Sam radioed for an ambulance and backup.

Bud Roy Roemer, like any good American who had suffered misfortune at the hands of both a large corporation and the government, could see past the pain to a potential financial windfall. He beckoned Gage Randolph nearer and whispered into his friend's ear, "Call Linus McTane."

Then he passed out.

"What I don't get," Bud Roy Roemer said the next day in his hospital room where he lay recovering from clavicle repair surgery, "is how Jubblies can shoot a fella for havin' a restaurant called Knockers. Don't seem fair they get to lay claim to all the good restaurant names." Making sure only to move his eyes, the sole remaining items in his physical inventory he assessed didn't hurt, Bud Roy looked at his attorney and then at Gage Randolph.

"Yeah, what kind of bullshit is that, Linus?" Gage asked, reinforcing Bud Roy's question in case McTane did not understand its importance.

McTane looked over at the two men from his perch on the windowsill of the room. "It's the kinda bullshit you shoulda let me deal with, Bud Roy. You did yourself no favors not seeking legal counsel. Intellectual property disputes are no simple matter."

Bud Roy's choice of lawyers was a good one. McTane possessed a gifted legal mind and very few ethical redlines. He looked and sounded like a lawyer ought to, equipped as he was with a sonorous baritone voice and a broad, open face topped by a luxuriant head of thick silver hair that suggested both competence and honesty. McTane was also fat. Bud Roy didn't know why, exactly, but he thought fat lawyers were better than skinny ones.

"Well, I'm lawyered up now. And we're way past intellectual property," Bud Roy said. "I may've been worked up, but that was no cause for a deputy representin' the fine state of North Carolina to shoot me in the only left clavicle I have. Do I have a case?"

McTane smiled. Bud Roy's payday was also his. "We'll sue the county for shooting you. That should be easy money. My guess is they'll settle quickly. Police shoot people all the time. They know how to make it go away. But the real money, as any plastic surgeon will tell you, is in Jubblies."

Gage Randolph and Linus McTane watched Bud Roy Roemer's smile as the fentanyl kicked in and he drifted off dreaming of Jubblies money.

During the trial four months later, Linus McTane did the best he could with a jury composed of seven women, all of whom looked with disfavor upon Bud Roy Roemer's choice of restaurant name, and five men who intuitively sensed they should shut the hell up and let the women sort this one out. Recognizing the lack of sympathy in a jury he considered populated with seven angry women and five cowering eunuchs, McTane tried to turn the dispute into one of David versus Goliath. And the strategy might have worked had the lawyer not made a fatal error during his closing argument.

The jury members leaned forward with rapt interest when McTane, grasping the railing of the jury box in his best imitation of Atticus Finch, told them that the Cumberland County deputy had drawn his weapon "for no good reason and subsequently discharged said weapon for the even less good reason of supporting two corporate slicks in their attempt to bully a small businessman." But they slumped back in their seats when McTane succumbed to the siren call of locker room humor and the worst angels of his nature.

"Although," he added with a wink that made his next words even more abhorrent, "in the deputy's defense, this was not the first time messin' around with jubblies led to an accidental discharge."

McTane's misguided summation destroyed the painstaking progress of his earlier legal tradecraft and did the impossible: he made a large corporation with a business plan based on exploiting women to sell overpriced, underspiced hot wings into an object of sympathy.

"Apparently, these rich folks here want you to believe there ain't room in Cumberland County, North Carolina, for Jubblies *and* Knockers," McTane said before sending the jury off to decide how many millions to award Bud Roy. "But I think you know differently."

It was not 1963, however, and the jury did, indeed, know differently. After a remarkably brief deliberation, they ordered Jubblies to pay the hospital bill of the uninsured, Obamacare refusenik Bud Roy Roemer and a further sum of one dollar in punitive damages.

"What the fuck, Linus?" Bud Roy inquired on the courthouse steps after the verdict. The two were flanked by Bud Roy's fiancée, Shelley DeWeese, and Gage Randolph, who had attended the trial to witness his friend's big moment.

"Can't win 'em all, Bud Roy," McTane answered.

"Well, asshole, maybe you should have told me that when I hired you. Maybe you should have that on the fucking window of your fucking office." Bud Roy made a grand gesture with his arm and said, "Linus McTane: Attorney Who Can't Win 'Em All." Thin and wiry, standing five feet ten with short brown hair, an angular face, and deep-set green eyes that had seen more disappointment than success since they had first opened almost thirty-five years ago, Bud Roy Roemer radiated equal parts anger and resignation about his lot in life.

"I know you're upset," McTane said as he started down the steps. "The jury just didn't break our way. That sometimes happens."

"No shit!" Bud Roy said, not feeling nearly as stoic as McTane. "I thought I had a right to trial by a jury of my peers. That jury's estrogen count was through the roof. And that was the men. The pussies. And there were also six blacks. Blacks. Women. Black women. How the hell are they my peers, Linus? I'm white and have a penis."

"Well, technically, you're the plaintiff and not the one on trial," McTane said. "And remember, the county has already coughed up one point eight million for shooting you. That's more than your restaurant would ever have paid you. You did not walk away from this empty-handed."

"Linus, I got shot in the fucking clavicle! Which, by the way, hurts like a motherfucking bastard. I didn't know I even *had* a clavicle until Barney Fife pumped a 9 mil Silvertip into it. Now, the *only* body part I am aware of is my clavicle. You want to know what your fucking clavicle is attached to, Linus? Fucking everything. I can't walk, talk, take a shit, or get a blow-job without somehow hurting my fucking clavicle." Bud Roy turned to his fiancée. "Ain't that right, Shelley?"

Shelley DeWeese was also angry with the verdict. After Bud Roy had banked a substantial settlement from Cumberland County, she had found she enjoyed having money. And now that she did, she wanted to have a lot more. Shelley believed she had been robbed, and Bud Roy finding a way to both make himself a victim *and* publicly announce she was giving him blowjobs did little to improve her mood. Her brown eyes shot daggers at him, and her already thin lips practically disappeared as she compressed them in anger. "I can't speak to whether you find blowjobs painful now, but I can promise you it won't be a problem in the future."

McTane smiled, Gage winced, and Bud Roy rolled his eyes.

Gage offered his support before Shelley could continue. "I've heard you complain plenty, Bud Roy. Although not about blowjobs," he added with a haste he instantly regretted when McTane and Shelley looked at him strangely.

"Thanks, Gage," Bud Roy said. "See, Linus, I'm suffering, and you couldn't deliver a verdict." He drove home his point. "All you did was settle with the county and further piss off a jury of women who already hated both of us. I coulda done that all by myself. Yet you still walk away with about half a million."

McTane sighed. A New England Yankee who had headed south after law school and never looked back, he preferred his southerners quiet, resentful, and accepting of their fate. He found his client's verbosity taxing. "Well, I suffered through law school for the privilege, Bud Roy."

To McTane's great relief, the quartet's descent of the courthouse steps traced the ebb of Bud Roy's anger. By the time they reached McTane's Lexus SUV, his client's outrage and disappointment was a spent force.

"Linus, that place was my life. It wasn't much, sure. But it was mine. I owned it. I was the boss. Now I don't even have that." Bud Roy knew Jubblies would sue him if he reopened, and his heart was not in it if his place couldn't be Knockers.

Sensing this was a moment for a client and his lawyer, Gage and Shelley moved off toward Bud Roy's brand-new Ford Expedition, purchased with some of his clavicle money.

McTane looked at Bud Roy. "No. You don't have your restaurant. But you do have over one million in the bank after I take my cut…"

"Not really," Bud Roy said. "We just bought the Ford. That was over fifty. I also owe some to a plastic surgeon. Shelley got some work done."

"I noticed some changes in her," McTane said. "But a gentleman never asks."

"Seemed like a good idea."

"So did the Civil War," Linus McTane said. "Get some rest, stay off your clavicle, and take a little time to think about what comes next.

What came next for Bud Roy Roemer was a weeklong fishing trip with Gage Randolph on the Little Tennessee River. Since Gage was unemployed, he had the time. Since Bud Roy was paying, Gage had the means.

Shelley DeWeese had remained in Fayetteville, coming to terms with being a just barely millionaire by fulfilling her burning ambition to buy an African leopard. This quest had unsettled Bud Roy.

"A leopard?" Gage asked from the front of the canoe as the pair drifted with the current. "Can't you just get her a big tomcat?"

"Trust me, that was my very first thought," Bud Roy said as he expertly cast his fly near a log that looked promising. "She flat-out rejected my offer to get her the biggest, meanest fucking cat at the pound."

Bud Roy snapped his line a fraction too early as a good-size bass broke the surface in a play for the fly. He cursed. Being distracted by the ramifications of imminent leopard ownership had caused him to miss a fish he normally would have boated. After casting again, he said, "I told her buying a leopard was a big deal. Said I wasn't ready for that. Then Shelley told me if I didn't get her a leopard we were through."

"She ain't one to bluff," Gage said. "But why a leopard?"

Bud Roy spit some tobacco juice into the river and watched the current carry the dollop of spittle away. "She's obsessed with that *Chomp!* TV show on basic cable. Her favorite big cat is the leopard. She can watch 'em for hours." He shook his head at his predicament. "I fail to see the attraction myself. Damn channel runs nothin' but programs of giant cats killin' the livin' shit out of anything that moves. Either that or shows with bugs fuckin' to Mozart for a solid hour. I tell ya, Gage, it don't do much for a man's self-esteem when he can't last as long as a dung beetle."

Gage laughed as he finished tying off a fly. "So what are ya gonna do?"

"Well, it looks like we're buyin' a leopard," Bud Roy said with a sigh. He dipped his paddle in the river and aligned the canoe with the current. "And we're also buyin' the fencing that's needed to hold the damn thing so it don't eat us," he continued after stowing the paddle. "That costs even more than the cat."

"I guess ya got plenty of clavicle money to burn."

"See, that's what Shelley thinks," Bud Roy said. "I said we need to make this money last. Told her that, while I might have another clavicle to cash in, it ain't like goin' to the ATM. I also ain't terribly enthused about getting shot again. She said buyin' a new SUV was wasteful. I told her we couldn't ride a goddamn leopard to the grocery store." He watched as Gage teased his fly into a promising spot near the bank. "Ya know," he said once Gage stopped casting, "we been poor our whole lives. We're so used to not being able to spend money even on things we need that, when we somehow finally get some, we go batshit insane and buy things we can't possibly use."

"Well, I suppose you could say a leopard is ideal for home defense." Gage fished for a few minutes while he pondered his friend's predicament. He, too, was a *Chomp!* devotee. While not a professionally trained naturalist, hours spent consuming the show's celebration of carnivorous African megafauna had taught him enough to spot a bad wildlife-related idea when he saw one. "Bud Roy, you don't want a leopard. Little cats are assholes. A big one? Shit, you might as well hire a serial killer to do odd jobs around the house."

"Shut up and fish, Gage," Bud Roy said, his face a puddle of worry.

CHAPTER TWO

At 9:50 a.m. on a Friday, unshaven, reeking of vodka sweat, and sourly contemplating unemployment, Bill Spark arrived at the FM radio station where he worked to fill his four-hour sliver of Cincinnati's airwaves for the last time.

Picking his way through a jumble of cubicles and administrative assistants with the overly purposeful strides of a man clinging tenuously to bipedalism, he entered his usual sound booth, locked the door, and kicked off his last show with Twisted Sister's "We're Not Gonna Take It." Backed by the fierce urgency of Dee Snider's growling baritone, the soon-to-be unemployed radio jock launched into the epic rant that would make him famous.

"Yes, I am inebriated," he declared. "Drunk on freedom, high on personal responsibility, stoned on hard work."

So moved by his own eloquence that he forgot it was radio, Bill Spark stood up.

"I'm mainlining the same smack our Founding Fathers OD'd on when they conceived a nation where, if you work hard, pay your bills, and don't screw up, the government will let you alone and you can be all you can be. A land where you tend to your own and your neighbors do the same, and if they don't, well, that's their problem, not yours. I know it must be a dream because it sure as hell isn't the land I see outside my window," Bill said, waving his hand dramatically at a calendar of Kate Upton, the sole feature on the windowless beige walls of the sound booth, hung there in defiance of management's prohibition against "sexist office adornments" by the station's *Morning Menace* shock jock duo of Tweeter and the Deek.

An hour into Bill Spark's diatribe, the station manager suggested cutting the power and kicking him off the air. Higher-ups demurred. Remarkably, the renegade DJ was still running ad spots for boner medicine, laser hair removal, hemorrhoid relief, guilt-free end-of-life care for aging parents, and the other necessities that people who had come of age on eighties music were beginning to require. Bill Spark's ravings were, at worst, revenue neutral. There was even an unspoken yearning by some in management for an on-air suicide; radio was a medium where that could work, especially if he used a gun.

A format change at his station and an inability to find another job in an industry that was changing in ways Bill could neither anticipate nor comprehend had driven him to straddle the fine line between outrage and insanity that so often leads to fame and fortune in the internet age. The final straw had come in the form of his sole job offer from a small station in the village of Umiujaq, nestled on the northern shores of Hudson Bay in a part of Canada so bitterly cold and remote even Canadians didn't go there. Bill had thought updating the four hundred-odd Umiujaqians on the latest polar bear mauling or emceeing the annual seal-clubbing festival would be a waste of his talent. Out of options, he had called in sick and gone on a three-day bender that provided the magic elixir of self-pity, sleep deprivation, anger, despair, and Ketel One needed to fuel his transformation from amiable mid market disc jockey to right-wing radio firebrand.

Unaware that his diatribe was going viral, Bill worked his shift; offered a populist, if not altogether paranoid four-hour thesis on what ailed the United States; and bid farewell to Cincinnati at 2:00 p.m. on the button: "This is Bill Spark, signing off to go look for the America we all deserve."

He cut to commercial and left the studio. On his way out, he told the station manager to go fuck himself.

Immediately afterward, the now jobless DJ hailed a taxi, went home, turned off his phone, stumbled to the toilet, urinated continuously for a single minute, then went to bed and slept for eighteen straight hours. He awoke the next morning with a massive headache, a wispy sense of being pissed off at Kate Upton, sixty-three missed calls on his cell phone, and two Cincinnati TV news trucks on his lawn.

Running through his voice mail—some from concerned friends, many from reporters, three from Sean Hannity's booking agent, and more than a few from radio stations wanting to discuss a job, including the station that had just let him go—he discovered that the impossible-to-remember final four hours he had spent on the air in Cincinnati had made him famous. Searching his own name on the internet, he found it trending on Twitter and running amok on Google. The most popular videos on YouTube were highlights of his four-hour rant, dubbed the "It Must Be a Dream" speech, set to stunning vistas of the Rocky Mountains, bald eagles in flight, men walking on the moon, men storming the beaches of Normandy, men going to work in factories, and men plowing endless acres of corn and wheat. Bill idly wondered as he watched these hastily made homages to American greatness where all the women were. But he figured that most, if not all, of the people who had made these videos were men with no jobs, no girlfriends, and no prospects of landing either in the foreseeable future.

For reasons Bill could not quite understand, one video also flashed pictures of Millard Fillmore at regular intervals. The only reason he knew it was Millard Fillmore was because big block letters jumped off the screen proclaiming, "MILLARD FILLMORE." While this helpfully put a name to the face, it did not answer the larger existential question he voiced to the empty room: "Who the hell is Millard Fillmore?"

A quick internet search told him that Millard Fillmore was the thirteenth president of the United States. It also left him feeling uneasy that somehow his performance had made him into, in the eyes of the creator of the video at least, the twenty-first-century standard-bearer of the Know Nothings.

With the video on pause and Millard Fillmore sternly gazing upon him, Bill realized he had tapped into something important. He had resonated with an audience far greater than he had ever known. Bill Spark had gone national. He had done so unconventionally, for sure, but he sensed his potential was even greater because of it.

He concluded he had an opportunity in front of him. But he also realized that he had a limited shelf life. He needed to leverage his newfound fame in exactly the right way, for in a week he would be old news.

Finding the constant digital deluge overwhelming, Bill Spark turned off his phone, shut his laptop, closed the drapes, sat quietly in his favorite chair cloaked in the semidarkness, sipped the fifth of Johnnie Walker Blue Label he kept on hand for serious thinking, and tried to figure out what came next.

What came next was harder than Bill Spark had thought it would be. Eschewing standard offers from stations looking to capitalize on his newfound fame to energize their own tired formats, he foreswore all contractual entanglements and moved to Richmond, Virginia. There, he founded his own internet broadcast site, *The Firebell*, so called because he wanted everyone to wake up, and sought to monetize his epic rant.

The immediate difficulty was that Bill Spark sober could not quite bring himself to say the things that seemed to flow so easily from the lips of Bill Spark drunk. To overcome this unforeseen problem, he considered doing all of his shows liquored up. After trying this approach for a week, he figured it was not a long-term solution in that it would likely kill him.

The answer to his dilemma came in the form of a blonde, blue-eyed, twenty-two-year-old Richmond college intern from Minnesota named Sierra

Dahlin—"Call me Sierra Darlin'…everyone does!"—a staunch believer with political views just to the right of Joe McCarthy. Sierra had been so moved by Bill's famous diatribe that she sported a tattoo reading "It Must Be a Dream" on her right inner thigh. He hired Sierra hoping to see more of her inner thigh, which quickly came to pass. But she also proved to be net savvy, something he was not and which had been a major impediment to his objective of becoming an internet mogul. While Bill struggled to bottle the lightning of those four magical hours in Cincinnati, Sierra kept his internet site alive.

With the screen name Sierra Darlin' and an avatar featuring her in a low-cut V-neck and push-up bra, Sierra nurtured *The Firebell*'s growing, vibrant internet community, composed mainly of young to middle-aged white males disenchanted with life in the United States but quite enchanted with her. A firm disciplinarian, Sierra dispensed online justice in a manner reminiscent of Judge Roy Bean. A gifted polemicist, she raised topics that generated a torrent of posts and rabid discussion. She had a knack for making pronouncements—such as "The only trigger warning we need to respect is the sound of a .357 Python being cocked"—that pissed off devout liberals and sent orgasmic waves of pleasure through conservatives.

Since Bill had spent no time on internet comment boards unrelated to the tragicomic flailing about of Cincinnati's professional sports teams, the posts of Sierra's online flock, ranging from the cogent and closely reasoned to the unhinged, were a revelation. In them, he realized he had found his voice. To prepare for his next broadcast, Bill mined the boards for the comments and topics that he felt resonated with his audience. He wove them together into a seamless patter that people mistook for his own. Ratings soared, clicks multiplied, and the ad revenue from gold vendors, gun makers, televangelists, and survivalist outfitters poured in.

With the online community feeding him the very bile he repackaged and regurgitated for them in daily four-hour broadcasts, Bill decided the next step was to go live. He armed himself with Sierra's most dyspeptic rants, put-downs, and ripostes—the ones she brandished to slay liberal trolls on the comment boards—and used them to bait callers on his live show.

This, too, proved to be a spectacular success. *The Firebell* became what Bill had always hoped it would be: a source of relatively easy money. He put his show on television and enhanced viewership by bringing Sierra into the studio with him. She rose to the challenge and loudly took on anything or anyone that pissed her off…which turned out to be quite a lot. Bill often wondered what someone so young and hot had to be mad about. But molten resentment mixed with generous doses of cleavage generated revenue, so he decided solving her problems was not in his best interest.

But Bill's strategy with *The Firebell* had a problem. He quickly discovered you couldn't dole out the Apocalypse in sensibly sized servings. This forced him to "amp up the crazy," as he thought of it. If a Democrat was a socialist one week, he or—even better, she—was a commie crypto fascist the next. If the government was coming for your guns on Monday, by Wednesday, the audience expected to hear that Washington, DC, was building concentration camps to house gun owners.

Bill realized his listeners *wanted* things to get worse. It justified their pain and confusion. It warranted their rage. Although not a Bible-reading man, he figured it wasn't the Apocalypse that was so bad; it was the days leading up to it.

But a bobsled run directly to the back of the Bible was not what Bill wanted. He desired a much shallower glide path to the abyss, one that would allow him to milk the site for a few years, bed Sierra as often as possible, stash a lot of cash, and then go live off the interest in Costa Rica.

Unfortunately, the IRS interfered with his plans by launching an aggressive audit triggered by his use of a controversial tax preparation software that not only maximized existing deductions but seemed hellbent on creating entirely new ones. If Bill had had lingering moral qualms about what he was doing, a sudden and most unwelcome IRS audit of the manner by which he shielded his rapidly growing nest egg from the government's gaping maw generated actual anger. Suddenly, the voice he usually had to fabricate from the grievances of others naturally welled out of him. For the first time since that fateful morning in Cincinnati, he was pissed off, perfectly positioned to do something about it, and stone-cold sober.

Growing angrier by the broadcast, Bill Spark one day told his listeners that America had failed them and that there was only one conclusion any sane patriot could reach. In retrospect, he would admit he didn't mean it. But that didn't matter to Gage Randolph, who was listening in North Carolina. And it was the final straw for rabid *Firebell* fan Jacob Kelley, who was tuning in from Banks County, Georgia.

CHAPTER THREE

Three weeks after Bill Spark's metaphorical call to arms, Jacob Kelley pulled into a rest stop outside of Richmond. In the trunk of his stolen car were twenty-five pounds of pipe bombs packed with homemade explosives and wired with blasting caps. He did not want to stop in Richmond, so close to Sierra Darlin' he could practically taste her. He feared doing so would distract him from his mission. But sixty-four ounces of Coca-Cola purchased at a 7-Eleven on I-85 outside of Dinwiddie, Virginia, made the Richmond pitstop a necessity.

Who knows? he thought as he hotfooted it to the john. *If I pull this off, maybe the next time I come through here, Sierra will know who I am and want to see me.*

The Firebell broadcast a few weeks ago had resonated with Jacob, a sporadically employed welder straddling the poverty line in Banks County. A fanatical Sierra Darlin' devotee and member of South of the Line, a hardcore Civil War reenactor group, Jacob felt—no, *knew*—he had to do something dramatic to call attention to the problems plaguing America. He might not lead the rebellion, but, like those patriots at Fort Sumter, he could fire the first shot.

Upon hearing Bill Spark's antigovernment and antitax call to arms three weeks earlier, Jacob knew he wanted to send a message to the IRS. A sporadic churchgoer, he scoffed at those who stood up and announced that God was speaking to them. But now he wasn't so sure. Although *The*

Firebell had inspired him, Jacob believed there was a greater voice urging him to fulfill his destiny. He was no longer a sometime welder whose only hope for a brighter future lay in winning the Powerball. He would speak out, be heard, and make a difference. For the first time in his life, Jacob Kelley believed he mattered.

You cannot have my money, and you sure as hell can't spend it in ways that do not benefit me, he thought with no sense of irony as he guided his car back onto the publicly funded network of roads conveying him to Washington, DC. That he rarely made enough to pay taxes was of no matter. What little he did pay was too much. Bill Spark was right. Taxation was theft. This was a message he felt compelled to deliver to the hated Feds in Washington.

But he hadn't been sure how to deliver it. Jacob's discovery that divine revelation did not automatically follow divine inspiration had disappointed him. But maybe that was what Google was for. There was, after all, no need for God to talk to people through a burning bush as long as they had a wireless connection.

And sure enough, one evening, the internet spoke to Jacob as he practiced what, for him, was multitasking: perusing Google while sitting on the toilet. The idea came to him fully formed. He knew what he had to do. The result was in the trunk.

What Jacob did not know was how loud his voice would be. He was no explosives expert. While twenty-five pounds of explosives sounded like a lot, would it really bring down an entire building? He didn't think so. At the very least, he wanted to blow out the windows and maybe take down a wall.

Jacob reached Washington, DC, in the early evening. He drove by the White House and felt his frustration grow. No matter who sat in the Oval Office, things never really changed—at least not for him. He still couldn't find a full-time job. When he did work, he thought he was laboring solely to fund FICA, whatever the hell that was. Waiting for the city to empty, he killed time glaring at the statue of Abraham Lincoln and gazing wistfully at Robert E. Lee's house across the river in Arlington Cemetery.

What should have been…

At midnight, with the streets finally cleared of tourists and with a certainty that all government workers had gone home, Jacob parked down the street from the Internal Revenue Service Federal Building, which was a more formidable structure than he had expected. He took his duffel full of pipe bombs out of the trunk; hefted them, feeling their weight; and concluded they were too puny to do much damage to the massive edifice that protected the IRS from the oppressed American citizenry.

But Jacob Kelley pressed on. Duffel in hand, and screwing up his face at the smell that emanated from within it, he walked around the corner and headed for the main entrance on Constitution Avenue.

John Markham was settling into his twelve-to-eight shift in the security office at the IRS when he glanced at the bank of CCTV monitors at his station and noticed a medium-size Caucasian man loitering at the Constitution Avenue entrance. The man was under six feet, Markham judged, slope-shouldered, and with a slight paunch, dressed in blue jeans and a yellow T-shirt. Locks of dirty-blond hair sprouted around the rim of his Atlanta Braves baseball cap like crabgrass growing in a crack in the sidewalk. He was carrying an orange duffel bag.

Markham sighed. He really wanted to dig into his reheated takeout from Ben's Chili Bowl, but he had worked at the IRS long enough to know it attracted more than its share of disgruntled citizens. These things were best dealt with quickly.

Markham grabbed a hand radio from the charging rack and asked for DC police to do a drive-by as he made his way to the front. In his experience, these folks moved along when asked to do so, especially if a police cruiser pulled up. They were angry, probably crazy, but not willing to spend time in jail.

"Sir, excuse me. Can I help you?" Markham asked in a loud, confident voice as he opened the door and came face-to-face with Jacob Kelley. He knew that immediately asserting authority reduced the chances of a physical altercation. Standing six feet six and weighing 245 solid pounds reduced the chances even further.

Jacob jumped. He was not expecting a guard to approach him so quickly. His initial look of surprise turned into a glare he could not mask. *Some big black guy thinks he can tell me what to do?*

Markham read the thoughts lurking behind Jacob's pale-blue eyes, charitably gave him the benefit of the doubt that the man had used the descriptor *black guy* in his head, and suppressed both a smile and a sigh. Things were changing, but not fast enough and not without a fight. "Sir, can I help you?"

"Nah. I was just waiting for the bus."

"Buses don't run this late. Neither does the Metro. You should get a taxi or an Uber or something. And I must ask you to wait down the street, sir. Away from the doors of the building."

"Sure, Officer," Jacob said in a manner that communicated compliance but not respect. He moved off.

Markham wrinkled his face at the lingering odor. "Damn," he muttered to himself. "If you're sick, go to the hospital."

Markham watched the man amble to the street and felt sorry for the cabbie who would have the misfortune of picking him up. *Will take a helluva lot of those pine tree deodorizer things to make that right,* he thought.

As he made his way down the hall, his radio crackled with DC dispatch asking if he still needed a drive-by. Markham was about to decline the offer when he looked back down the block-long corridor and saw the stranger back on the steps, this time removing what appeared to be a bundle of cylinders about two feet long from the bag and placing them on the ground.

"Damn!" Markham yelled into the radio as he broke into a sprint back toward the entrance. "Send him now and send him fast. Possible bomber. Entrance on Constitution."

Markham could never explain why he ran toward the suspect and not away. It was not to protect the IRS building, as he figured the bombs he saw wouldn't do too much damage. And it was not to disarm the bomb. He didn't know how to do that. In later retellings to his friends, he said it all boiled down to see bad guy, chase bad guy.

For a big man, Markham moved quickly and covered the distance with a speed that surprised Jacob. He burst through the door and grabbed the man's arm before the would-be bomber could retreat down the steps.

"Lemme go!" Jacob yelled.

"What's in the bag?" Markham asked as he hustled the man down the steps two at a time. A DC radio car pulled up with lights flashing, and a cop Markham knew well got out.

"Backup is on the way, John," Officer Oscar Simmons told Markham. "Whaddya got?"

"What I got is a probable bomb about forty feet away, and this guy put it there."

Simmons drew his weapon. "Cuff him, and let's move across the street right now."

Jacob Kelley had come too far to fail. He did not want to die, but he definitely had no desire to serve time for an *attempted* bombing. As Markham reached for his handcuffs, Jacob pressed the remote control hidden in his clenched fist, which sent a wireless signal to the simple, but reliable, detonator in the bomb. The detonator did exactly what it was supposed to do.

Later, bomb squad and law enforcement experts would conclude Jacob Kelley was more of an ideas man than a details man. An analysis of his internet search history revealed he had but a cursory interest in the physics behind the effective construction and detonation of a bomb. He had displayed far more fascination with photos of Sierra Darlin'.

Jacob did not understand that making a fertilizer bomb was more complicated than merely "hot-wiring a turd," as one professionally offended bomb squad tech described his effort. Explosions pursue the path of least resistance, which is why it is a good idea for pipe bombers to seal their pipes at both ends. Jacob's bombs were, more accurately, a set of fertilizer mortars.

Unfortunately for Markham, Simmons, and Jacob, the mortars were aimed at them. The detonation showered the three men with the pipes' contents as they stood in front of the Internal Revenue Service Federal Building on Constitution Avenue at 12:45 a.m. on a Thursday morning.

"Shit!" Markham and Simmons shouted correctly as they began wiping furiously at their faces.

"Shit!" Jacob also exclaimed, but more because the bomb did not work as he had intended. He recovered his wits faster than the other two men, who were now gagging and vomiting. Momentarily freed from Markham's iron grip, he sprinted down Constitution Avenue for his car parked around the corner on 10th Street.

Keys in his hand and Georgia on his mind, Jacob Kelley was in the car and barreling across the Potomac River before the first responders to Oscar Simmons's frantic call for help could stop laughing.

John Markham and Oscar Simmons scrubbed themselves down in showers lasting over an hour before they were coaxed into a debriefing.

"Please tell me you got the guy," Markham said. "I've been washing fecal matter out of orifices where no fecal matter should ever be."

Simmons shuddered in assent.

FBI Special Agent Peter Carlson, who had been called in because law enforcement had designated the attack an attempted act of terrorism on federal property, brought them up to date. "We got video of the incident off the IRS security cameras, including a shot of the perp's face that may just be good enough to release to the public if we clean it up. And we got the plate number of his car, a 2003 Ford Taurus. Turns out the it was stolen out of a used-car lot in northern Georgia. Also, there were no fingerprints on the devices, so the bomber was thinking about not getting caught, if nothing else."

"Damn," Simmons said. "I wanted to shoot him in both testicles and one knee before I went home tonight."

"Not leaving me much," Markham said.

"I figured you were more hands-on, big guy," Simmons said. "He would still be alive for you to crush his skull."

"We're gonna get him," Carlson said. "We're tracing cell phones active in the area at the time the shit…um…I mean, this event hit the…uh…the event occurred."

Simmons and Markham glared furiously around the room full of law enforcement professionals, daring anyone to laugh.

"Anyway, we have narrowed it down to a few numbers, and one in particular, belonging to a Jacob Kelley from Banks County, Georgia, former home of the aforementioned stolen auto. The phone's trace shows Kelley was heading south on 95 before going dark. We are shifting our resources in that direction. We've compared Kelley's driver's license photo to the photo from the video and believe we have a match."

"Just so I know," Markham asked, "what kind of fertilizer was it? Manure? Something this Kelley asshole bought at Home Depot?"

"Well, you see…" Carlson paused, unsure how to give Markham the bad news. "We have conducted a preliminary analysis of the, uh, substance in the bombs."

Markham and Simmons looked up at him.

"It was, indeed, fecal matter…"

"I coulda told you that," Simmons said.

"But, see, um, it appears to be human and not animal. We assume it is Kelley's own personal, uh, load."

No one knew why, but this disclosure made Simmons and Markham's experience much worse. Certainly to Simmons and Markham. Everyone else in the room picked a spot on the wall to examine with great care, studiously avoiding eye contact.

"We can trace the DNA, though," Carlson said, "and because this bomb used a biological, uh, agent, Kelley moves to the top of the most wanted list for attacking the IRS with a WMD." He gathered his notes. "I gotta go brief the press. They're gonna love this."

John Markham and Oscar Simmons both found little comfort in Jacob Kelley's upgraded status. They got up without a word and headed back to the showers.

Later that afternoon, having laid low for a few hours, Jacob Kelley pulled his second stolen car of the week into a rest stop on southbound I-95. He figured he needed to get off the major roads and keep stealing cars to avoid the police. But first he needed new clothes. Despite his efforts to clean himself up, he reeked.

As he walked toward a kiosk selling *Virginia Is for Lovers* T-shirts, he stopped when he saw his face on the TV screen behind the vendor. The scrawl at the bottom noted he was a person of interest in an attempted bombing of the IRS.

Committed to improving his aroma, Jacob bought a T-shirt and a pair of pants from the vendor, who seemed in an understandable rush to complete the transaction. Jacob also retrieved a razor from his overnight bag and headed to the restroom to clean up and transform his appearance as best he could.

Thirty minutes later, clean-shaven and newly bald, Jacob risked turning on his phone for a quick scan of the headlines. Although he knew from the movies the government could trace his phone, and he had visions of satellites overhead shifting into position to target him, he needed to see what the press was saying.

The initial media response was brutal and, he thought, very unfair. "Asshole commie lame-stream media," Jacob muttered as he read headlines written by editors overly pleased with their own cleverness: antitax movement explodes: GEORGIA MAN SUSPECTED OF FECAL BLAST IN FRONT OF IRS trumpeted *The Washington Post. USA Today* ran with: WMD! WEAPON OF MASS DEFECATION USED AGAINST IRS! The *New York Post* was more succinct with its headline, which screamed HOLY S%&T! in three-inch letters on the front page and dubbed Jacob Kelley "the Unacrapper."

"Unacrapper," Jacob Kelley muttered. "Figures they wouldn't understand." But the realization he was now a hunted man enveloped him like a cold fog. How had the Feds tied him to the crime so quickly? Fingerprints? Nope. He had worn gloves, that was for goddamn sure, when making and handling his pipe bombs. DNA? The last one intrigued him. He risked a quick Google search before getting rid of the phone for good.

John Markham and Oscar Simmons were still at the station, glistening from the latest of several showers, when Peter Carlson gave them an update.

"We think we got Kelley located. He turned on his phone at a rest stop south of Richmond to run a Google search. Would you like to know what his search string was?" Carlson asked with a grin.

"Would it be too much to hope it was 'How to eat shit and die'?" Markham asked, his sense of humor slowly returning.

"Sadly, that wasn't it," Carlson said. "It was—get this—'Do my turds have DNA?'"

Simmons leaned back in his chair and looked at Carlson for several seconds. "Do *my turds* have DNA?"

Carlson smiled. "Yes. 'My turds.' He was very specific."

Simmons rubbed his temples as if he were pondering an equation proving string theory. "Bet even Google's not seen that one before. Well, that should narrow the list of suspects."

"If it doesn't," Markham said, "something is seriously fucking wrong in downstate Virginia."

Peter Carlson moved toward the door. "Virginia State Police are there now. It should be just a matter of time."

"Come to think of it, Officer, I did see this guy," the kiosk vendor told the Virginia state trooper holding a blowup of Jacob Kelley's Georgia driver's license photo. "He bought a T-shirt," the vendor said, pointing at the stack of *Virginia Is for Lovers* souvenir shirts. "And a pair of sweats. I'll tell you, he smelled something awful. Like he'd been swimming in a septic tank."

"Did you notice what kind of car he was driving?" the trooper asked. An unsuccessful search for the stolen car made police suspect Jacob had switched vehicles.

"Sorry, sir, I did not."

At that moment, Jacob Kelley was on a back road in yet another stolen vehicle, heading south. While everything else had not worked out according to plan, his surprising gift for automobile theft had manifested itself at the right time. An hour earlier in the parking lot at the rest area, he had deposited his cell phone in a car with Massachusetts plates on the assumption it was heading north and would draw law enforcement, at least temporarily, away from him. He knew they would look for him in the South, but he had nowhere else to go.

He pulled into a secluded wooded area off the two-lane and sat back to await nightfall.

"Likely you won't be able to shoot Kelley in the balls today," Peter Carlson told John Markham and Oscar Simmons five hours later. "He has gone to ground. Kelley's stupid but has apparently watched all the Jason Bourne movies. He dropped his cell phone in the car of a guy from Boston headed home with his family. The Jersey staties pulled them over on the Garden State Parkway. They had no idea the phone was in their car."

"You checked them out, I suppose," Markham asked more out of reflex than anything else.

"Oh yeah," Carlson said. "Reputable. Father teaches history at Tufts. Mom works in advertising. Driving back from vacation in Florida with two small kids. Orlando to Boston in a Honda CR-V. No doubt the father is capable of homicide at this point, but not smearing the IRS building with his own feces."

"Fucking *CSI* TV shows. Fucking Mark Harmon on fucking *NCIS* and the fucking spy movies making moron perpetrators smart. It pisses me off," Simmons said.

"Me too. You two go ahead home and get some sleep. You've had a shitty day." Carlson smiled as he caught their dead-eyed stares. "Too soon?"

"Right now, Agent Carlson, I ain't particular 'bout who I shoot," Simmons said.

CHAPTER FOUR

"Jesus Christ. He ate the whole chicken in one bite," Bud Roy Roemer said. "I hope Costco delivers, or I'm gonna spend my entire life just keeping the damn thing full so he don't come after us."

The leopard had arrived.

"Oh, it won't be that bad," Shelley DeWeese said as she gazed with affection at the 137-pound African leopard she had named Howard. Having consumed an entire chicken as if it were a meat-flavored Tic Tac, Howard the Leopard was now exploring his new floodlit enclosure in the Roemer-DeWeese backyard. "Here, let me feed him," she said. She took a T-bone from Bud Roy and tossed it into Howard's pen. Howard pounced and consumed it in under ten seconds.

Once he had determined Shelley was serious about leopard ownership, Bud Roy had consulted Linus McTane in the hope there was a North Carolina law against owning a pet that could and would kill you in your sleep. Or at any other time of its choosing. However, the North Carolina State Constitution was disturbingly silent on the matter. This was an oversight by the state's Founding Fathers that Bud Roy had found unforgivable.

"It's your land, and there aren't any legal restrictions to keeping a leopard on your property," McTane had told him. "Get the license, and then all you have to do is keep it in a proper enclosure and not abuse it. I am sure a leopard is like any other animal. Just show it who's boss."

Bud Roy now tried to follow McTane's advice and looked the animal in the eye. Howard returned his gaze with an implacable contempt fueled by the evolutionary memory of countless generations of Howard's ancestors chasing down and consuming Bud Roy's. Howard was the boss, and he knew it. So did Bud Roy.

While the big cat seemed happy enough in the backyard, Shelley, who had somehow bonded with the animal, was not. She wanted Howard to come in the house.

"It's dark outside. He's by himself. He'll get cold and lonely," she said.

"It's a fucking *leopard*," Bud Roy pointed out. "It's supposed to live outside. You ask any African what their worst fucking day in Africa was, and I bet every man jack one of them will say, 'The day a leopard got into my hut.'"

"Bud Roy," Shelley said, "when you came to me and said your lifelong dream was to open a restaurant named Knockers, I didn't say nothin'. In fact, I was supportive. Men have more self-destructive desires than that, believe you me. And then when you wanted me to get these ridiculous things installed," she said while pointing at her silicone-enhanced breasts, "I went along with that, too, even though it's me who has to carry them around all the time while all you do is drop by when the mood strikes to fiddle with 'em."

Bud Roy knew any reply would make things worse. He remained silent.

"By the way," Shelley said, "did you ever think about how you wanting me to get these things made me feel? I'll tell ya, since you obviously did not. It made me feel like shit. Like I wasn't good enough for you."

"I'm sorry," Bud Roy said.

Shelley looked at him for a long moment. "You might just mean that. Well, you've got what you want, and now it's my turn. This is my dream; having a leopard. Maybe you think it's silly, and maybe it is. I don't care. You should be more supportive."

"Shelley, this damn cat wants to eat me," he said.

"I'm gonna bring him into the house, Bud Roy, and that is all there is to it unless you don't never want to see these again," she said, cupping her breasts and stopping his further protests while they were idling in his throat. "It won't be a problem. I bet he's house-trained before you know it."

"Housebroken? For God's sake, woman, this ain't no tabby cat. What are you gonna use for a litter box? The bathtub?"

Zacharias Townsend settled his long frame into the Eames chair in his study as Bill Spark and Sierra Darlin' opened their show with an homage to the traditional American pastime of hating the IRS.

The developer of a bulletproof database and software operating system for major corporate and government platforms, Zacharias Townsend was worth $68 billion. Having made $68 billion, he was keen to make $68 billion more. As such, he was very reluctant to part with any portion of his fortune. Carnegie, Gates, Buffett: these guys were misguided, he believed. The assets of the rich were best deployed to create jobs and generate more wealth, especially for the wealthy.

Even more than charity, Zacharias loathed the notion of the government taxing income. In particular, his income. He hated the government's powers of taxation so much that he had started a new software business—a passionate, well-funded hobby of the type in which only the superrich can indulge—dedicated to starving the IRS and the United States government of its citizens' money.

ElimiTax didn't just help taxpayers maximize deductions; it recommended ways to create new and often questionable ones. "TurboTax helps you pay your taxes," went one popular ad for the product. "ElimiTax helps you avoid them entirely." Not content with simple evasion, ElimiTax's parent company also took the offensive. It had mustered an army of lawyers to help users fight off the threatened IRS audits of anyone using the software and an army of lobbyists to ensure Congress cut funding so the agency couldn't afford to conduct audits anyway. Zacharias could think of no better way to use $1 billion or so of his $68 billion than by fomenting taxpayer revolt.

His current residence was the most visible manifestation of Zacharias's loathing for taxes and government. *Freedomland* was a sumptuously refurbished, self-propelled, semisubmersible exploratory oil rig repurposed for private use and kept slightly outside the territorial waters of the United States at all times. Upon its christening, Zacharias had promised, "*Freedomland* will usher in a new era in mobile personal sovereignty solutions for the discriminating, ultra-high-net-worth individual."

Zacharias's mobile tax haven could ply the seas at up to seven knots while the mogul kept tabs on his business empire via a state-of-the-art communications system. On *Freedomland*, he influenced politicians with lavish weekend policy retreats focused on creating laws that would favor him, plotting to destroy his competitors, and working to prevent the United States government from having enough funds to do anything but finance the military-industrial complex in which he had substantial investments.

After self-enrichment, Zacharias's other defining passion was collecting Civil War memorabilia. Displayed throughout *Freedomland*'s endless corridors and vast living and working spaces, his collection was the most extensive in private hands. He took a particular interest in the Confederacy and identified with the South's struggle against a tyrannical national government. Self-aggrandizing even in his hobbies, Zacharias believed he was taking up the fallen banner of the Confederacy and was intent on proving the Lost Cause was justice delayed.

He looked over at an empty display case in his office awaiting his latest acquisition and lit a cigar in anticipation.

CHAPTER FIVE

"**R**ebel, goddamn it! Stop chewing on Stonewall Jackson's arm."

Gage Randolph took his hand from the steering wheel of his ancient Ford Bronco and gave the part-Rottweiler, part-something-from-the-forest mixed breed a chop across the muzzle. With a small yelp, Rebel the Hound hove his considerable mass to the floorboard of the SUV.

Gage felt remorse for smacking his best friend on the nose, but he was now the custodian of a priceless Confederate artifact. It wouldn't do to have his dog eat it. It also wouldn't get him paid.

Gage was a dedicated Civil War reenactor and member of South of the Line. SOL, as its members referred to it without irony, celebrated the Confederacy. On the SOL website, he had met an anonymous, wealthy collector of Civil War artifacts interested in far more than minié balls, belt buckles, and the odd pistol or saber. The man was rich, motivated, and without apparent concern for the law.

In a private chatroom, the collector enticed Gage with an offer of $50,000—far more than his yearly salary as a mechanic in Fayetteville—to dig up Stonewall Jackson's arm, reputed to be buried in Locust Grove, Virginia. Gage initially had declined. Some sense of honor overcame the lure of fifty large, mixed with doubts that the arm even existed. The buyer was remorseless, however, and said he knew for a fact the arm was really there and that he just needed a guy he could trust, a "patriot with the stones for this kind of work," to go dig it up.

Ultimately, providence and economic dislocation were working in favor of the buyer and against Gage. The day Bill Spark had inspired Jacob Kelley to blow up the IRS building, he also had railed against leftists impugning the honor of the South. "Our Southern history is being rewritten," the Ohio native had said. "Our heritage is being destroyed, and the very essence of who we are as a people, as a nation, is being reworked and replaced. We need to rise up, become the true custodians of our past, and stand steadfast and unapologetic in defense of our ancestors and how they built this great nation. If we don't, we are doomed."

That same day, Gage had been laid off, and the offer of fifty grand, especially harnessed to an act of Southern patriotism, looked a lot better. *Why let Stonewall's arm be erased along with his honor and military reputation?* he thought. *Stonewall would want me to do this.*

Surprisingly, the arm was where the collector had assured him it would be. In a rusted box, protected by layers of oilcloth now brittle and dry, lay the shattered limb. Now the macabre artifact lay in repose on the front seat of his Bronco. If he could just keep his damn dog from ingesting it, his bank balance would look better than it ever had.

He gripped the wheel and kept one eye on the undulating two-lane road and the other on Rebel the Hound. Nervous the police would be out in force due to the attempted bombing on the IRS hours earlier, Gage wished he had picked a different day to carry out the theft. Acutely aware he was now a grave robber and acting as guilty as he felt, Gage stayed off the main I-95 to I-85 thoroughfare to Fayetteville as he cut through the countryside on back roads. *Much like the original owner of the arm did all those years ago*, he thought.

Monica Bell was lost. But she was making good time barreling through either Virginia or North Carolina as she did battle with Sierra Darlin' via cell phone.

On vacation from her television and radio shows, the popular liberal pundit was driving her way up the East Coast on a weeklong college speaking tour. Unafraid to step into the arena with any conservative, Monica had taken Bill Spark up on his invitation to discuss the Unacrapper story, unaware Sierra would also be on the show. Had Monica known, she would have pulled over. Sierra Darlin' made her so mad she forgot what she was doing and where she was. Not good when driving a car.

Distracted by the verbal jousting, Monica had blown by her exit and now found herself on a back road. Not one to pay for the same real estate twice, she trusted the GPS to guide her north and protect her from hillbillies while she continued to pummel the conservative nitwit for her idiotic defense of the Unacrapper.

"No, Sierra," Monica said, "real Americans do not sympathize with this sick and disturbed individual. There are plenty of Americans who pay their taxes and do so out of a sense of thankfulness and obligation for all that this nation provides. We do so because we know we're stronger acting together than we are keeping to ourselves."

"Maybe you fancy New Yorkers think that, and maybe you convinced the three or four actual fans of your little radio and TV shows, but down here in the real America, we don't agree," Sierra replied. "We're tired of Washington taking what's ours, and we understand the rage that drove this fella to do what he did."

"Who is this 'we' you're talking about?" Monica asked. "My state is a net contributor of tax dollars. And those dollars flow south to states like whichever one I might be in tonight as I drive, I hope, toward Charlottesville. So don't complain about how hard it is to row when you don't even put your oars in the water." She was unsure if that made sense, but she thought it sounded homespun and thus might resonate with *The Firebell*'s audience. "And as for my radio and TV shows, the audience is growing faster than yours."

"Oh yes. What's the name of your show again?" Sierra asked. She knew how to push Monica's buttons.

"You know damn well what its name is, Sierra," Monica Bell said with a calm she did not feel.

Monica Bell's radio and television shows bore a rather pedestrian, if accurate, title: *The Monica Bell Show.* She was popular because she was smart, informed, opinionated, and so gorgeous she could stop traffic on a freeway. For television, she knew the last one, sadly, might have mattered the most.

Before Monica became a media figure, she had been a professor of comparative politics at a large university in Oklahoma. She was known as a tough grader and a brutal cross-examiner of students, no matter their political viewpoints. This did not put her in good stead with most of her pupils, nearly all of whom had reached the conclusion that higher education was about confirming their self-worth rather than developing critical thinking skills. College was something you did to get a job, not a place to educate yourself.

The dean of humanities counseled her after his office received a raft of complaints from much-aggrieved students, many of whom cited their stellar high school grade-point averages as proof of their intellectual horsepower. He had received even more complaints from the parents, who were not, as they universally observed, paying enormous tuition bills to have the beliefs of their children challenged by a mere professor.

But Monica persisted. The end came when the dean spent a very uncomfortable half hour talking to a prominent conservative benefactor of the university whose son had received a D- on, as Monica described it, a "lame and unoriginal defense of the policies of Ronald Reagan." The oilman made it clear he would not fund a new library if Monica were around to use it. Soon after, the dean called her into his office and strongly hinted that perhaps she was better suited for punditry than academia.

"The writing is easier," he told her. "No need to fact-check, near as I can tell, nor do you need to sustain a coherent argument."

Frustrated that success in teaching seemed to be measured by customer satisfaction, which in turn was based on the students not having to work very hard, Monica agreed it was time to leave the ivory tower and pursue fame and fortune while educating the masses. She soon gained a reputation as an able defender of the liberal viewpoint, unafraid to go toe-to-toe with anyone on the Fox News channel.

Her star rose quickly. Monica would have preferred that her popularity be based on her piercing intellect, academic credentials, and ability to present cogent arguments with concision and eloquence. Yet she knew that was secondary. While she understood her good looks were a significant reason she was on television, a discussion with her own network over the name of her show drove home the difficulty of moving past the "distractingly busty and sloe-eyed" label bestowed upon her by a television critic she no longer spoke to.

It was well-known industry gossip that *The Firebell* had been the working title of her show. By happenstance, Bill Spark had gone public with it days before her debut broadcast. Faced with having to come up with a new name and graphics within a week, an unimaginative coterie of male network executives ran down a list of proposed titles that confirmed her worst fears about why they wanted her on the air.

"How about *Bell's Curves*?" asked one, staring openly at her breasts.

"I get it. Wordplay on my name and the Gaussian distribution? Perhaps suggesting my show would be fact-based, reliant on statistics, and intelligent. But, at the same time, you are reminding prospective viewers I have a great rack. Why don't we just call the show *Monica's Tits*?" she snapped.

"*Saved by the Bell*?" suggested another.

"Have you ever watched TV?" she asked.

"How about *Bell-i-Cose*?" proposed a bald man with a degree from Wharton.

"Too Italian-sounding, too cutesy, and too stupid," she said.

"*Bell Bottoms*?" the first one tried.

"Just what the hell is that supposed to convey?" Monica asked. "Maybe we should just give me a porn name while we're at it."

Monica shot down every idea they had and then said, "Fuck it. It's my show, and that's what we'll call it—"

"*Fuck It*?" the bald man interrupted, radiating panic and confusion in equal parts. "I don't think that will pass muster with programming."

"Jesus," Monica Bell said. "I wish I could call it that. No, I meant we'll call it *The Monica Bell Show*. It may not be very catchy, but you can't say it's misleading. It's almost as honest as *Fuck It*. And the better to remind you pubescent nitwits who's calling the shots around here."

"Well," Sierra Darlin' said, taking Monica Bell's momentary silence as a sign she had drawn blood, "here at *The Firebell*, we believe all we should pay Washington for is a strong military and a high wall."

Monica Bell had expected this sound bite and was ready to pounce. However, at that moment, she came upon a curve in the two-lane road she was traveling on just a shade too fast.

"I'll be damned," Jacob Kelley muttered when he closed the gap with the vehicle in front of him enough to read the bumper sticker on the back of the old Bronco. "*S-O-L*. Maybe my luck is turning."

Once darkness had fallen, Jacob Kelley had started moving south, doubting the wisdom of sticking to two-lane blacktop roads rather than I-95 to I-85. He felt both concealed and conspicuous at the same time. Seeing the old Ford Bronco up ahead with a South of the Line bumper sticker featuring the Stars and Bars had given him hope. An SOL brother would help him.

He flashed his high beams to signal the Southern patriot in front of him.

"Ha. Sierra Darlin', you tell that damn commie," Gage Randolph said. He was enjoying what was, from his perspective, another sound thrashing of Monica Bell. He thought she was as misguided a liberal as one could find outside of Europe.

Gage noticed Rebel the Hound making another play for Stonewall Jackson's arm and reached over to swat his snout. At that moment, the car behind him hit its brights. The reflection in the rearview mirror dazzled Gage, who jerked upright, hit the brakes, and swerved to the left while going into a curve.

"Asshole!" he yelled.

Then he noticed the car coming at him.

Monica Bell was about to skewer Sierra Darlin' with a perfect rejoinder when she glided into the curve too fast, hit her brakes, and noticed a large, ungainly vehicle taking up half of her lane. Instead of annihilating Sierra's sound bite, she only had time to exclaim, "*Yaaah!*"

Monica pulled her wheel to the right while she braked. Her BMW 7 Series did everything a car of German origin should, gripping the pavement and following orders with precision and without question. Unfortunately, her overcorrection guided the Beemer toward a ditch on the side of the road.

"Yaaah!" Gage Randolph also yelled.

He, too, stomped on his brakes and pulled his wheel to the right. Like an ocean liner struggling to avoid an iceberg off its port side, his old Ford Bronco listed heavily and drifted with neither urgency nor purpose as he helmed it to starboard.

Because he was not in as much immediate danger, Jacob Kelley enjoyed the luxury of eloquence. "Fuck!" he yelled as he saw a wall of careening vehicles suddenly materialize ahead of him.

Too late, he slammed on his brakes, sending the nose of his stolen Toyota into the back end of Gage Randolph's Bronco. Fortunately for Gage and Monica Bell, the extra boost provided by Jacob Kelley's car propelled the rear quarter of the Bronco to the right just enough to miss the BMW on its journey to the drainage ditch, where it bottomed out and came to rest on the far bank with its nose pointed at the sky.

"Monica? Monica, are you still with us?" Bill Spark's voice called out from the radio in Jacob Kelley's car, the front end of which was caved in and smoking after the collision with Gage Randolph's SUV. The Bronco looked no worse than it usually did.

Gage got out and walked back toward Jacob's wrecked car, still furious about the high beams. "What in Christ's name were you trying to do?" he yelled as Jacob, shaken but none the worse for wear, exited his vehicle.

"Sorry, sir," Jacob said, trying to placate him. He needed this guy. He couldn't afford to hang around waiting for the police. "I saw your SOL bumper sticker and just wanted to get your attention so we could have a chat."

With the mention of South of the Line, Gage calmed down. He was always happy to meet a fellow Lineman, as they called themselves. Besides, he had his own reasons for avoiding an interview with the highway patrol or the sheriff.

"Monica?…Well, Sierra," Bill chuckled over the airwaves, "it looks like you drove Monica off the air."

"She needs to drive herself back to New York where she belongs," Sierra Darlin' said.

Despite appreciating Sierra's snappy rejoinder, Jacob reached in the car and switched off the radio.

"You a fan of *The Firebell*, too?" Gage asked him. "My name's Gage Randolph," he said, offering his hand.

Jacob took it but did not give his name. "Oh yeah. You're also a reenactor, right? We might've met at a couple of battles."

"No kid…" Gage suddenly remembered the BMW. He looked over at the expensive German sedan, clinging to the far side of the drainage ditch, its headlights projecting twin halogen columns into the night sky. "We better see 'bout the other driver."

They jogged over to the side of the road and capered across the ditch to the BMW.

Monica Bell wasn't dead, but she was out. Her unconsciousness was due less from the impact than from the assault perpetrated by various airbags deploying with Teutonic force and precision to save her head from something worse.

Jacob said, "Look, I know all about bein' a Good Samaritan and all. But I have to be honest, Gage. I can't hang around and wait for the police…"

Gage shifted his gaze from the driver of the BMW—she looked familiar—to the bald fellow standing next to him. He looked familiar, too. "I don't believe I caught your name."

Jacob took a breath. If he was going to get Gage's help, he would need to come clean. "Jacob Kelley."

"Jacob Kelley?" Gage took a step back. "The same Jacob Kelley who tried to blow up the IRS? The Unacrapper?"

CHAPTER SIX

Later that night, Bud Roy Roemer sat in his underwear at the kitchen table, his phone crooked in his left ear as he ate a piece of cherry pie and drank a glass of milk. He was having trouble understanding how his friend Gage Randolph had ended up with Monica Bell, Stonewall Jackson's arm, and the Unacrapper in his Ford Bronco.

"Tonight, I dug up Stonewall Jackson's arm for a collector," Gage explained. "I was driving home on back roads because I was afraid the cops would put out a dragnet…"

"For Stonewall Jackson's arm?" Bud Roy asked.

Bud Roy's befuddled voice, tinny and brittle when filtered through the cheap speaker in the cell phone sitting on the dash of Gage's Bronco, struggled to compete with the engine's growl. Gage shot a quick glance at Jacob Kelley sitting next to him. Jacob was busy repelling Rebel's persistent advances on Stonewall Jackson's arm while keeping an eye on Monica's prone form in the back seat.

"They might think it's important," Gage said.

"But why would they think it was you who stole it?" Bud Roy asked.

"I don't know," Gage said. He was growing exasperated with the grilling. It all made sense to him until he said it out loud. "But what if they closed down 95 to search every car?"

"For Stonewall Jackson's arm? That nobody knew for sure was buried up there in Virginia?"

"Yeah," Gage said, leaping once again to a conclusion Bud Roy could not reach. "What would I say? 'Oh, Officer, this is an entirely different one-hundred-and-fifty-year-old arm'?"

Bud Roy remained silent.

"Anyway," Gage continued, "a short ways before the state line, I was in a three-car collision. This is somewhat ironical since we were the only three goddamn cars on the entire road."

"OK," Bud Roy said, putting Stonewall Jackson's arm out of his mind for the moment. "And in the other two cars were…"

"…the Unacrapper and Monica Bell," Gage finished.

"I'm pretty sure I prefer Jacob to Unacrapper," Jacob offered.

"And Monica Bell was on the radio," Bud Roy said. "I was listening to Sierra Darlin' kick her ass when…"

"She and I almost had a head-on," Gage finished.

"And the Unacrapper?" Bud Roy asked.

"Jacob," Jacob said.

"Rear-ended me," Gage said.

"But why are they all in your car?" Bud Roy asked.

"The Unacrapper's car was totaled, and he can't exactly call Uber. Monica Bell was hurt. We couldn't just leave her there," Gage said.

"Because grave robbin' and tryin' to blow up the Internal Revenue Service with a twenty-five-pound butt burrito are both OK," Bud Roy summed up, "but ya'll draw the line at leaving the scene of an accident?"

"You had to be there to understand," Gage said.

"Not even then."

"Anyway," Gage continued, "I thought she looked familiar, so we checked her ID and discovered who she was. We figured since she was famous we couldn't leave her there."

"Why?" Bud Roy asked.

"I don't know. I guess being famous made leaving her somehow worse than if she was not famous. It was kinda like we knew her. So the plan is to drop her off at the nearest emergency room—outside, of course—and then keep driving."

"Lemme get this straight," Bud Roy said between bites of pie. "After a long night of grave robbin', you thought the best way to reduce your chances of gettin' caught was to add a famous liberal TV pundit and America's most wanted domestic terrorist to your carload of Confederate general arms?"

"Bud Roy, things was happening fast, and maybe we weren't thinking..."

Just then, Monica's eyes opened. She groaned and sat up and looked around. Then she realized she was in an ancient SUV with two strange men and something that might have been a wolf. Then she screamed.

"What the hell was that?" Bud Roy asked.

"I think Monica's awake," Gage said.

"Lady, don't be alarmed. We're takin' you to the hospital," Jacob said. He reached his hand back to reassure her, which was a mistake. Monica darted as far away as the confines of the Ford Bronco would allow, curled into a protective ball, and then kicked him in the face with both feet.

"Ow! Jesu Quwist! I dink she boke by nobe!" Jacob yelled, covering his nose with both hands as blood ran down his face.

"What's going on?" Bud Roy asked.

Gage provided the play-by-play. "Bud Roy, Monica Bell woke up and kicked the Unacrapper...I mean, Jacob, in the face. Right in the conk."

"You're Jacob Kelley? The Unacrapper?" Monica asked, reloading for another kick.

"Goddabbit, Gade," Jacob said as he ministered to his wounded nose with one hand and dissuaded Rebel from sniffing his bloody face with the other, "do you hab to idebify ebbyone in da car? Why don you intoduce her to dis fuggin' houn while you're ad id?"

"So the driver is Gage and the guy on the phone is Bud Roy," Monica said as if running down a mental checklist.

"For fuck's sake, Gage," Bud Roy said, "why don't you just give her my Social Security number?"

"Everyone shut up for a second!" Gage yelled. "It would seem that dropping Ms. Bell here off at the hospital is now out of the question. We need a place to hole up and think. And you know where I mean."

Bud Roy sighed. His friend had somehow found trouble. He would help him. That's what friends did. "You have a key. The utilities are still on. Get in before dawn."

Monica had different plans. "I'm not going anywhere with any of you!" she yelled. "Let me out right now!"

In a seamless transition from grave robber to kidnapper, Gage reached over and took a blue-steeled .357 Magnum with a four-inch barrel out of the glove compartment. He handed it to Jacob, who pointed it at Monica.

"Ma'am," Gage said while looking at her in the rearview mirror, "I'd be most appreciative if you would be quiet for a spell and just do what we say."

An hour later, Bud Roy Roemer found himself in a late-night argument with Shelley DeWeese.

"Shelley, he's my friend and he's in trouble. We'll keep them at the restaurant for a few days until we can figure out what to do. As for the Unacrapper, he'll be moving on soon."

"And why're you telling me this?" she asked. "I was having a pleasant dream about Howard. Now you tell me Gage Randolph has kidnapped a famous TV person *and* the Unacrapper? Jesus, Bud Roy, just me hearin' that is probably illegal. I ain't going to jail just 'cuz you woke me up to tell me Gage is in trouble. That ain't exactly breaking news."

Bud Roy was questioning the wisdom of sharing Gage's predicament with Shelley. But he was in it now, and, by definition, so was she. Marriage through thick and thin. Well, here was a little of the thin. And they weren't even married yet.

"Gage is in trouble. He needs help, and if it were me in trouble, he would have my back. No questions asked," Bud Roy said.

Shelley thumped her pillow as much in frustration as in a bid to get more comfortable. "Honey, Gage dug up Stonewall Jackson's arm and then kidnapped Monica Bell and the Unacrapper. At several points during his evening, he could have opted *not* to commit a felony, and he blew past all of 'em."

"He didn't kidnap *both* of them. He was only tryin' to help Monica until he *had* to kidnap her when she woke up and kicked the Unacrapper in the face."

"You say that like it should make sense." Shelley propped herself up in bed, abandoning her hopes for a quick return to her dream about Howard. "Any one of those actions might be called regrettable. But all three together suggest Gage Randolph is walkin' around dead and don't know enough to lie down. Why didn't they just drive off and call the police after they were out of the area?"

Bud Roy hated Shelley's perfectly reasonable questions. Questions he himself had been asking not too long ago. Questions with no good answers, but questions that were now moot.

"Look, this has got to be done, and I need your help. Besides," he added, "have I ever complained about Howard?"

"Hourly," Shelley said.

The two abandoned cars on the two-lane blacktop road went unnoticed for three hours after Gage Randolph, Jacob Kelley, and Monica Bell had departed the scene. Local law enforcement contacted the Virginia State Police, who paid attention once they ran the plates and discovered one car was stolen and the other belonged to Monica Bell. A string of car thefts occurring in a progressively southern direction suggested the driver of the stolen vehicle was Jacob Kelley. Two hours later, a crime scene technician arrived, lifted several prints, and got a hit on Jacob, who was in the system for a drunk-and-disorderly in Banks County, Georgia, five years earlier.

"What do we know?" a Virginia statie asked. "He collided with Monica Bell and then took her hostage? Did they walk out of here?" He walked over the road with the crime scene technician while shining a powerful flashlight on the surface. "Take a gander at this," he said to the tech. "You see what I see?"

"Different tire prints. Looks like maybe there were three cars," the tech said as he took photos. "My guess is an SUV."

"Try to get a match on the tires," the patrolman said. "I'll put out a call to all hospitals within a one-hundred-mile radius. See if they've treated anyone for injuries consistent with an auto accident."

"Will do," the tech said. "I love it when you use words like 'radius.' Makes me feel like I'm in one of those *CSI* shows."

"You're too ugly for TV," the patrolman said. "Also, look over the area where the Beemer is. See if we can get an idea of how many people besides Bell and Kelley are involved."

As the tech moved off to the drainage ditch to process the scene around the BMW, the patrolman got on the radio. "Put on the captain," he told the dispatcher. "He's gonna love this. He always wanted to be a TV star."

CHAPTER SEVEN

The next afternoon, Bill Spark was in the zone.

"So poor little Monica Bell gets chased off the air by the impenetrable, unassailable, incontrovertible, ironclad, locked-down logic of our own Sierra Darlin'. Then, rather than admit to herself and her loser liberal fan base that Sierra opened up a major-league can of whup ass on her, she *stages* an accident in the heart of real America and tries to shift the blame to the eternal boogieman of the left...*southerners!* Mark my words, loyal listeners: she is setting all conservatives up to take a fall!"

There was a pause as Bill tried to bookend his theory in a way his audience could understand.

"My best guess is that she is now kicking back for a few weeks on the Isle of *Lesbos*, sipping mai tais with Amelia Earhart—who, by the by, set the cause of women drivers back fifty years by not listening to the guy with the map. Meanwhile, the Feds kick in the doors of every self-respecting southern family within two hundred miles of the supposed accident, scaring children, bullying old folks, and reminding us once again why government is the problem."

He sat back and took a breath, both pleased and appalled with himself. He liked Monica and hoped she was OK. But talk radio was a leave-no-man-or-woman-alive arena. "Let's go to the phones. We got Andy callin' in all the way from Tomball, Texas."

Bill's producer stabbed a button on his blinking phone bank.

"Yeah, Bill. You nailed it. All the evidence points to a libtard conspiracy. The way the police processed the supposed crime scene means they were in on it. Prolly Feds in disguise."

"Thanks, Andy," Bill said. "You are thinkin' hard out there in Tomball. Watch out for armadillos; they will mess your truck up something fierce." He made the cut sign. He loved this part. All he had to do was suggest something wasn't as the media made it seem, and his rabid army of listeners created an alternative reality.

"OK, we got James from Chicago, Illinois, up to bat. Jimbo, what's on your mind?"

"It's James, not Jimbo. Yeah. Look, are you seriously suggesting Monica Bell anticipated the argument that took place on your show—which she clearly won—and then, to frame conservatives, staged an accident and her disappearance in the middle of nowhere? Perhaps you've never heard of Occam's razor, which suggests that the simplest explanation is the most likely..."

Bill leaned back in his Herman Miller high-backed office chair, placed his size-twelve black Chuck Taylor All Stars on the desk, and smiled through the glass at his producer. *"Occam's razor?"* he mouthed. Jimbo from Chicago was gold. For the next hour, the army of *Firebell* listeners would fall upon this Poindexter like hyenas on an injured wildebeest. He could practically take the rest of the show off.

"...also, a rudimentary Google search will tell you Amelia Earhart, a feminist icon and deservedly so, would be well over one hundred years old had she not perished over the Pacific. She would be in no condition to sip mai tais on Lesbos, or anywhere else. You treated her poorly, and she is an American heroine. Every woman, metaphorically, was her copilot on a fateful journey to..."

Bill leaned forward to the microphone. His producer jabbed at the console, and the remainder of Jimbo from Chicago's peroration, like Amelia Earhart's final resting place, remained known but to God.

"Well, ooooooookaaaaay, Jimbo from Chicago. I'm amazed you made it that long into the phone call without getting shot, given what that city is like. Talk about a failed argument for gun control. Apparently, you prefer to let the lame-stream media do your thinking for you. If I want to hear the rest of your half-baked theory, I'll tune in to Anderson Cooper on CNN and let him finish it for you. Perhaps you should take that Occam's razor you were yackin' about and shave off your hippie beard and go get a job. But be careful. Good old American health care doesn't cover melted snowflakes, bruised feelings, or shaving nicks suffered by the unemployable when they are trying to pass for presentable."

Bill caught his producer's attention and did the I-need-to-pee dance. The producer jumped down the queue to a frequent caller who could expound on any topic for at least five entertaining, if not entirely logical, minutes.

"Our old friend Bobby from Lone Jack, Missouri, is on the line. Watcha got for us today, Bobby?"

"Hi there, Bill. First, thanks for setting that idiot from Chicago straight so I don't have to. Gotta be a Cubs fan. Your theory makes sense. If you unnerstand how the Virginia State Police process a typical crime scene…"

Bill removed his headset and stepped outside the sound booth while his producer injected an "uh-huh" and a "hmm" every thirty to forty-five seconds as Bobby from Lone Jack educated *The Firebell* listening audience about the investigatory procedures of the Virginia State Police. After taking care of business, Bill strolled back into the sound booth.

"…now all of this makes sense if you consider how many illegal immigrants and Muslims Obama salted away in the Deep State to make the United States government more Kenyo-centric…"

Bill hit the mute button when a light flashed on his console indicating his producer wanted to talk. "Kenyo-centric?" Bill said when he picked up the phone.

"Yeah, he is really off his meds today," the producer said. "Listen, you aren't going to believe this, but Zacharias Townsend is on the line and wants to speak privately."

"You're right," Bill said, "I can't believe it. Just one question, though. Who is Zacharias Townsend?"

"You don't read much, do you?" the producer asked. "Townsend is one of the richest guys on the planet. He's amassed about eleventy billion metric fucktons of wealth. Sails around on his own private luxury oil rig."

"Oh, *that* Zacharias Townsend. Did he say what he wants?"

"No. I don't think guys like him feel the need to explain themselves to guys like me. Line seven."

Bill pressed the correct button and said hello.

"This is Zacharias Townsend. I listen to your show. I think I can help you."

"How's that?" Bill asked, trying not to laugh at the pretentious Bond villain self-introduction. He also reminded himself not to show unseemly excitement over possibly getting his hands on even a single metric fuckton of Zacharias Townsend's money.

"As you are likely aware, I am not a fan of the government taking what I have earned and giving it to those who are neither as smart nor as hardworking as I am."

"You and me both," Bill said. "That's why I used your ElimiTax software. Of course, now I got the IRS crawling up my ass with a blowtorch."

"Which is why I'm calling," Zacharias said.

Bill made a rolling motion with his hand to tell the producer to keep Bobby talking. "Mention Benghazi," he mouthed.

"If you can get the IRS off my back," Bill Spark told Zacharias Townsend, "I'm all ears."

"Man makes sense," Jacob Kelley said from his perch on a barstool at the recently defunct Knockers Bar and Grill as he listened to Bobby from Lone Jack, Missouri, tie Benghazi to Vince Foster, Jimmy Carter, communists, atheists, and water fluoridation.

"Just how many hits of Oxy have you had today?" Monica Bell asked from the stage where topless dancers used to entertain the Knockers clientele. She was thankful for the fuzzy pink padding on the handcuffs chaining her to a stripper pole running from the base of the stage to the ceiling. "That guy is a mixture of Alex Jones, the *National Enquirer,* and Glenn Beck all rolled up into one lard-assed ball of stupid. The only positive thing to say about the fuckwhistle is that his cholesterol count puts him in the ground within a year."

"You're just mad 'cuz Sierra Darlin' beat you so bad on the air you staged your own disappearance," Gage Randolph said from the bar. He took a pull from a long-necked Budweiser.

"*You* made me disappear! You and the Unacrapper…"

"Jacob," Jacob said quietly.

"You were there when it happened, for God's sake," Monica continued, ignoring Jacob's automatic correction. "Are you seriously going to tell me, even though you were on the road that night and *know* the truth, that you buy into the demonstrable fucknuttery of a guy you never met from Jackoff, Missouri…"

"Lone Jack," Gage corrected her. "I visited there once to take part in a reenactment of the Battle of Lone Jack. It was a Confederate victory in the Civil War. And you shouldn't make fun of a town just because it's small and has an odd name. People call it home." He looked at Monica and downed the rest of his Bud. "Besides, Bill Spark and Bobby have a point. How do we know you didn't take advantage of our being on the road last night and pretend to have an accident? *I* was in my lane. *You* were the one who veered out of control. Could be that me and him"—Gage pointed the neck of his empty Bud at Jacob—"are the real victims here. There is plenty of blame to go around. Blame on both sides."

"Two hundred and fifty years of quotes by American presidents to draw on, and you go with that one? Jesus." Monica snorted, rattling the handcuffs for effect. "I'm chained to a stripper pole, and you and the Unacrapper…"

"Jacob," Jacob said. "And you did kick me in the nose. It hurt. Still does."

"…are the victims? I guess this must be one for the bucket list, too. You got me chained up in your little man cave here so you can act out a Princess Leia in Jabba the Hutt's lair fantasy. How about it, Crapper…"

"Unacrapper," Gage corrected her.

"Jacob," Jacob corrected Gage.

Monica smiled at the point she had scored. "How about it? You want to run down to Walmart and see if they got a gold bikini for me?"

Both Jacob and Gage were silent as they contemplated Monica in a gold bikini. Monica was silent as she commended herself for taking charge of the situation.

"Earth to wanted felons: let's get back to reality. First, think about it all you want, but know it'll never happen. Second, you better figure out a way to get me to the little strippers' room, or we're all gonna be victims," she said as she rattled the handcuffs on the pole. "These Jubblies hot wings you keep feeding me are not sitting right."

CHAPTER EIGHT

Craving fish tacos and a side of fries at 11:15 p.m., Deputy Sheriff Samuel Aucoin guided his Ford Police Interceptor into the parking lot of Jubblies restaurant. The pickings were slim at this time of night, but Jubblies could set him up.

Sam got out of the car and adjusted his duty belt, repositioning his gun in a microscopic gesture universal to cops everywhere and which years of repetition had made as natural to him as breathing. He went into the restaurant to place his order.

Emerging fifteen minutes later, Sam glanced across the street at the darkened hulk of Knockers Bar and Grill, where his rapid ascent through the ranks of the Cumberland County Sheriff's Department had taken a slight detour when he had shot Bud Roy Roemer in the left clavicle. The all-too-familiar shape of Gage Randolph's ancient Ford Bronco sat near the entrance to Knockers, illuminated by a single lonely vapor light. Sam stood looking at it, reliving every moment from drawing his weapon to discharging the fateful clavicle-shattering 9mm round. The incident replayed in his mind with high-definition clarity. He recalled the ancient and enormous cordless phone Bud Roy had carried when he had confronted the Jubblies suits outside of Knockers. As big as it was old, the fucking thing had looked like a large-caliber handgun in the glare of the afternoon sun.

As Sam had tried to monitor the heated verbal exchange among the three men, he had mistaken the phone for a handgun, neither a rarity in Fayetteville nor on the person of open-carry permit holder Bud Roy Roemer.

Sam had drawn his weapon while saying, "Bud Roy..."

Then Bud Roy had pointed his phone at the Jubblies lawyers while proclaiming with great emotion, "Hands off my Knockers!" At the same time, Gage had started his Bronco, which backfired, causing Sam to send a round into Bud Roy's left clavicle.

Sam forced himself back to the present as he stood in the parking lot holding his fish tacos and fries, looking at the Bronco. What was it doing there? Was it like a trail horse that knew its way home?

He got in his patrol car and picked up the radio. "Dispatch, this is Bravo 12."

"This is Dispatch, Bravo 12." There was a pause, and then, "10-20?"

Sam swore silently. Dispatch was asking for his location. But he knew damn well where Sam was from the GPS locator in his vehicle. Dispatch just wanted the deputy to reveal over the radio that he was at Jubblies. He responded by giving the street address.

"Copy, Bravo 12," Dispatch came back. "Confirming your 20 at Jubblies. How are the fish tacos?"

Given the number of mike squelches on the network, the law enforcement night shift in Fayetteville and beyond was enjoying the dispatcher's game. Sam took the high road. "Dispatch, Bravo 12, 10-37," he said, giving the address of Bud Roy's former restaurant and announcing his intention to investigate a suspicious vehicle.

"Bravo 12, what's the make and number of the vehicle?"

Sam steered his car across the street and behind the automobile. "It's an early-model Ford Bronco." He read off the familiar license plate number, dreading what would come next.

The dispatcher ran the number. "Copy, Bravo 12. This particular 1985 Ford Bronco is registered to a Mr. Gage Randolph. Is this not the same Ford Bronco that provoked you into shooting one Mr. Bud Roy Roemer, resulting in none of us getting raises this year so the county could pay off the lawsuit?"

"Affirmative." Sam sighed.

"Maybe you should leave this Bronco alone before you end up shooting the mayor or drilling a nun hugging an orphan who's holding a kitten."

He took a breath. "Dispatch, the car is sitting in the parking lot of a shuttered business. I'm gonna take a closer look."

"Copy, Bravo 12. Please exercise extreme caution. This vehicle is known to be loud and possibly upsetting."

Another chorus of mike squelches signified the continued pleasure of Fayetteville's finest.

Sam took his five-cell flashlight in his left hand, unfastened the safety strap on his holster with his right, and walked up to the vehicle, shining his light in the windows. It was empty. Coming up to the front, he placed his hand on the hood. The engine was cold. The Bronco had been in the stable awhile.

Proceeding to the front door, Sam shined his light into the entryway of Knockers Bar and Grill. He could see nothing, and the doors were locked. A cursory check of the remaining windows and the rear door revealed they were locked, too.

Reporting situation normal, Sam Aucoin departed with his dignity intact and his midnight snack still warm.

Inside, Gage Randolph, Jacob Kelley, and Monica Bell, sedated by chicken wings, beer, and exhaustion, dozed undisturbed and unaware of their brush with the law.

CHAPTER NINE

"We can't kill her," Gage Randolph told Bud Roy Roemer over biscuits and sausage gravy seven hours later at a Cracker Barrel on the outskirts of Fayetteville.

"Well, I don't want to," Bud Roy replied through a mouthful of biscuit. "But she's seen you, she's seen the Unacrapper, and she knows my first name thanks to your helpful play-by-play over the phone a couple nights ago. Just how do you propose we get out of this mess without killing her?"

Gage looked sheepish. "To be honest, Bud Roy, she knows your full name. When we, uh, brought her to Knockers, she asked, 'What *is* this place?' in the way them snotty northerners have. I told her, 'Knockers is a restaurant owned by my friend Bud Roy Roemer, and he worked real hard to make a go of it.' I was just trying to stand up for you."

"Jesus, Gage!" Bud Roy hissed. "You told her my *full* name?"

"Sorry."

Just to be doing something, Bud Roy stabbed a piece of breakfast ham and chewed it without pleasure. "You know," he said, "I think you have some criminal version of, uh, whatchamacallit, the Tourette's syndrome." He snapped his fingers. "That's it exactly. You suffer from criminal Tourette's. You blurt out vital information while committing felonies. Information law enforcement professionals will find useful for throwin' your ass in jail. And mine, too, most likely."

"I've been thinking about what to do," Gage said.

"Does it involve you, me, and the Unacrapper standing in a circle and shooting each other?" Bud Roy asked. "Because that seems to be our best play."

"I've spent a couple of days with Monica now," Gage said. "I don't think she hates us, and I don't think she wants to press charges."

"Correct me if I'm wrong," Bud Roy said, removing his Carolina Hurricanes ball cap and rubbing his head, "but you are guilty of the following, uh, transgressions against this person who you think does not bear us ill will: you ran her off the road, kidnapped her…" By now, he was counting off on his fingers. "…had America's most wanted terrorist point a .357 Magnum at her while she was in the back seat of your car with a skeleton arm and a dog the size of a mule deer, took her to an abandoned restaurant, chained her to a stripper pole, and have been feeding her Jubblies hot wings three meals a day." He waggled his upheld fingers at Gage for effect. "You think this was just another night out for her?"

"I think she's in what you call the first stages of Helsinki syndrome."

Bud Roy rubbed his left clavicle, which he noticed now gave him trouble when he was stressed. "What? I think you got a pronoun problem there, Gage. *I* don't call nothin' 'Helsinki syndrome.' *I* don't have a clue what *you* are talking about. Are you now *diagnosing* your hostage? Did you graduate from medical school last night, Dr. Randolph?"

"Helsinki syndrome," Gage repeated.

"And is this a disease? Cancer or something else useful that will kill her for us?" Bud Roy asked with more hope than he knew was warranted.

"Nah. I remember this from the first *Die Hard* movie," Gage said. "The TV guy was interviewin' a hostage expert, and he was tellin' the TV guy that the hostages would start identifyin' with the hostage takers. Called it Helsinki syndrome."

Bud Roy waited. He knew there was more. At least, he hoped there was more.

"Now all I need to do is give her *more* Helsinki syndrome," Gage concluded.

Bud Roy looked at Gage as he tried to process what his friend was thinking. He failed. "That was a movie. I don't know if there even *is* a Helsinki syndrome. I think I've heard of a Stockholm syndrome. But whaddo I know? And who the hell knows if we can give Monica Bell *more* of it, whatever it's called? By the way, we're Hans Gruber in this production, not John McClane. You and me, my friend, are gonna end up doin' a Peter Pan right off Nakatomi Plaza."

"Do you have a better idea? 'Cuz I am open to suggestions."

Shaking his head like he was fighting off a pesky gnat, Bud Roy said, "Well, I guess we oughta be glad your favorite movie ain't *Silence of the Lambs*. Although that movie offers up a clear solution." He sighed as he toyed with his ball cap. "No, Gage, I don't have any ideas, much less a better one. But if my dating life has taught me anything, trying to seduce a woman while you have her chained to a stripper pole ain't likely to be successful."

He looked out the window just as Deputy Sheriff Samuel Aucoin pulled his police cruiser into the Cracker Barrel parking lot. *This, we don't need*, he thought. "But we better come up with something fast," Bud Roy said.

Sam Aucoin was on his way back to the station at the end of his shift when he noticed Gage Randolph's Ford Bronco outside the Cracker Barrel. Curious and also hungry again since it had been seven hours since the fish tacos, he swung his cruiser into the parking lot. Exiting the car, he hitched his gun belt and strolled into the restaurant.

While hoping to find Gage and ask him why his Bronco had been outside of Knockers a few hours earlier, he was unsettled, although unsurprised, to see Gage with Bud Roy Roemer. Those two were as thick as the low-level thieves Sam suspected them to be. Still, he would have preferred to avoid any encounter with Bud Roy, who understandably nursed a grudge along with his shattered left clavicle. Committed to this course of action, however, Sam strolled up to the pair's table.

"Gage. Bud Roy," Sam said, "how are you both this morning?"

"Fair to middlin'," Bud Roy said. "My left clavicle's been acting up."

Sam ignored Bud Roy and looked at his companion. "Gage, I noticed your truck in the parking lot of Bud Roy's old restaurant last night. I checked it out. What's wrong? Did it break down?"

Gage looked at Bud Roy for a long second and then up at Sam standing in front of the table. "Nope. The Bronco's fine. I parked it there when I met Bud Roy. We been out on the town and are now finishing up with some breakfast."

"Out on the town? All night? In Fayetteville?" Sam asked. "Maybe I oughta Breathalyze you two before I get breakfast."

Bud Roy wanted this conversation to end before it could get started. He feared Gage's criminal Tourette's would kick in and his friend would confess to the litany of felonies he had committed and Bud Roy had abetted in the past twenty-four hours.

"I still own the property, Deputy," Bud Roy said before Gage could speak. "I gave permission for Gage to park there. Is that against the law?"

"No," Sam said.

"Well, unless you've come here to shoot me in my right clavicle so I can have a matched set, why don't you leave us be? We're just tryin' to have breakfast."

Sam smiled briefly, as if to himself. "Gentlemen," he said, and turned to find a table.

After Sam left, Gage said, "That was a close one. We dodged a bullet there."

Bud Roy offered him a withering look. "Dodged a bullet? You just linked me to the trainload of felonies you've been rackin' up, the *least* of which is partial grave robbing. You just made me an accessory."

Gage looked down at his coffee. "I thought we could be each other's alibi..."

"What, you mean like Bonnie was Clyde's alibi? Or Butch was Sundance's?" Bud Roy shook his head. "Dodged a bullet? It was more like you said, 'Oh, here comes a bullet. Let me grab my good friend Bud Roy Roemer and place him di-freaking-rectly in its path.'" After polishing off his final biscuit, he took a swig of Coke. "We need help. I'm gonna talk to Linus."

Neither Bud Roy Roemer's mood, nor his clavicle, were much improved by the time he and Shelley DeWeese met with Linus McTane later that afternoon. Bud Roy had intended to raise the matter of Monica Bell and the Unacrapper living at his bar. But he never got around to it, as he was much aggrieved to learn that $600,000 of his settlement from Cumberland County was taxable. He sought additional information and clarity. "What the fuck, Linus?"

McTane had known this conversation was coming, and he had not looked forward to it. Shelley's presence was not helping. She was even tougher than Bud Roy when it came to money.

"Yeah, Linus. What the fuck?" Shelley DeWeese clarified. "Why does Bud Roy have to pay taxes on money the state had to pay *him* because *they* shot *him* in the clavicle? Why is left-clavicle money taxable?"

McTane waited a moment until they both had quit speaking. "There was a subtle but crucial bit of information left unclear in the suit's resolution. The authorities, in their unending quest to stick it to the average citizen, have decided to exploit the issue and levy taxes on ya'll," McTane said. He shook his head sadly. "See, our original suit had both punitive and personal injury claims. Now, the settlement said all claims were resolved, but there was not a distinction on the manner in which they were. The government is making noises that a portion of the settlement is a reward for punitive damages and another is for personal injury."

McTane waited while they processed this and then continued. "Now for the hard part: personal injury awards are not taxable. Punitive damages are, however." He sipped some iced tea from a glass perspiring on his desk. "If the state carries the day with its argument on the structure of the settlement, you could owe taxes on the portion, six hundred thousand dollars, they claim was assigned as punitive damages."

"What's the hit?" Bud Roy and Shelley asked together.

"Given your income last year, and the six hundred grand," McTane said, dropping the hammer, "I figure you will owe a shade over two hundred thousand dollars."

They both erupted, their obscenities canceling each other out and enveloping McTane in a miasma of profane white noise. He sipped his tea as the couple continued their tirade.

"…shoot you in the clavicle and then a few months later have the IRS kick you in the balls," Bud Roy concluded when Shelley took a breath.

"Look, you two," McTane said, "if someone had told you last year you were going to make so much money that your *tax* bill would be two hundred thousand dollars, you would have been jumping for joy. Why can't you focus on what you have instead of what you don't?"

Shelley pounced. "Because, Linus, what we *have* at the moment is two hundred thousand dollars more than what we will have after the government screws us."

"You're missing the point," McTane said.

Shelley stood up, followed by Bud Roy. "Linus, don't think for a minute you've heard the last from us."

"I never do," the lawyer replied.

"Jesus, Bud Roy," Shelley DeWeese said as her fiancé pulled out of the parking lot of Linus McTane's law office, "Linus has fucked us so many times I think we oughta marry him."

Long experience with his fiancé had taught Bud Roy Roemer the value of saying nothing. Instead, he glanced at his watch, noted it was time for *The Firebell*, and switched on the radio.

"Good afternoon to all you real Americans tuning in," Bill Spark said. "Today, I am declaring my independence. As you all know, the IRS and I disagree about how much of my money—money I earned—I should get to keep."

"Welcome to our world, Bill," Shelley snapped.

"I figure after I pay to support the troops, the police, and the firefighters, I have done my share. That's all I need from my government, and I don't think I should have to pay for anything else. I did not ask Uncle Sam for a helping hand in the pursuit of happiness. I used my own hand."

Bill Spark paused for several long seconds as he tried to find a way past the unfortunate phrasing.

"Try getting shot in the clavicle," Bud Roy said into the momentary dead air. "Talk about a hard way to make a buck."

Bill regrouped and plunged ahead.

"Yesterday, I got a call from Zacharias Townsend. Y'all may know him as the founder of Acropolis software and the Janus database software suite that powers just about every major corporation and a lot of the internet. But he is also a patriot. A patriot intent on resisting an oppressive government."

Having just learned they had $200,000 worth of reasons to side with him, Bud Roy and Shelley nodded in agreement as they drove through Fayetteville listening to Bill Spark.

"Zacharias Townsend is putting his money where my mouth is," Bill continued. "He wants to help me fight Washington. And he is providing me a platform to do it. An oil platform, that is."

Bud Roy turned to Shelley. "Isn't that a line from the *Beverly Hillbillies* song?"

"Hush," she said. "This guy is singin' my tune right now."

"Listeners, Zacharias Townsend is purchasing a stake in *The Firebell*. Next week, I will broadcast live from *Freedomland*, Townsend's floating middle finger to Washington, DC. We will sell ad time as we always do, but any money I make out there stays with me because I will have earned it outside of Uncle Sam's grubby clutches. I've moved past ElimiTax to refusing to pay tax. And Zacharias Townsend has promised me the best legal team money can buy to defend me when Washington bureaucrats come for what isn't theirs."

Shelley turned down the radio. "Bud Roy, *The Firebell* and this Townsend guy could be the answer to our problems."

"How so?"

She looked at him. "We need to get ElimiTax to protect our clavicle money. Then we need to tell our story to the world and to Townsend. If we do, I bet he'll throw his lawyers between the government and our nest egg."

Bud Roy shrugged. But it was an eloquent shrug suggesting more than simple agreement with her thinking. *I haven't heard a better idea today*, he thought, remembering Gage Randolph's plan to give Monica Bell Helsinki syndrome.

He turned up the volume again so *The Firebell* could ring loud and clear.

CHAPTER TEN

Gage Randolph switched off the radio as Bill Spark finished discussing Zacharias Townsend's investment in *The Firebell*. "Wow. A whole oil rig floating around just outta reach of Uncle Sam," he marveled. "What would it be like to have that much money?"

Jacob Kelley said, "Spark's radio show a few weeks ago, where he was complainin' about taxes and losing our identity? That's when he inspired me to take action."

"Be sure to tell him that when you meet him in jail," Monica Bell said from her nest on the stage, chained to the stripper pole. "If he can talk you into doing something that stupid over the *radio*, there's no telling what he'll be able to make you do when you're sharing an eight-by-six-foot cell with him."

Jacob looked up from a laptop computer he had borrowed from Gage to follow the latest news about the manhunt for him. "I'd be nicer to me if I was you. No one knows where you are."

"Jacob," Gage said, "why don't you take the computer back to the office? You ain't helping things out here."

Jacob looked at Gage and then at Monica. He flipped the laptop lid down with more force than was good for it, slid off the barstool, and clomped down the hall to the office in back.

When Jacob was out of earshot, Monica asked, "What are you gonna do with me, Gage? I don't think you want to kill me. And you can't let me go."

Gage looked down at the bar and then back up at her. "Hell, I don't know. I'm still tryin' to figure out how we all ended up here."

"I ended up here because you and the Unacrapper kidnapped me. How you two ended up here could keep a team of psychiatrists busy for a decade—although I would attribute it to our failing schools and a concerted effort by the Republican Party to make our citizenry dumber than dirt."

Gage got up from the bar with a Budweiser longneck in each hand. He walked over to the stage and handed Monica one of the Buds as he sat down.

"Firstly, let's save the punditry for your elite liberal buddies. You know, I was just tryin' to help you out. I recognized you right away in your car." Gage took a swig of beer. "I was afraid you were hurt. I told Jacob to help me get you in the Bronco so we could take you to the hospital. Told him that was my price for givin' him a ride."

"You really didn't know the Unacrapper until that night?"

Gage rubbed his forehead. "Honest to God. We…all three of us…met the same way, trying not to kill each other on that damn highway."

"So what's the deal with the skeleton? Or part of it, anyway."

"Stonewall Jackson's left arm. He lost it at the Battle of Chancellorsville. Shot by his own men. They amputated his arm and buried it behind Ellwood Manor. I dug it up so's I could sell it to a wealthy Civil War memorabilia collector."

"I would've thought," Monica said, "you would be the last person to do such a thing, given your passion for the Civil War." She had spent much of her time in captivity listening to the two men discuss their mutual experiences as Civil War reenactors.

"Why shouldn't I?" Gage said. "I mean, goddamn. Look how they're tearin' down statues of Confederate heroes all over. Why shouldn't I give Stonewall's arm to someone who 'preciates it? If we leave it in the ground, it won't be long before a bunch of liberal do-gooders decide the grave hurts their feelings and they dig up the arm and throw it in the garbage." He took another swig from the bottle of Bud. "And if I get a little money for preserving Southern heritage, what's the harm?"

Monica Bell had definite opinions on honoring the memory of the leaders of the Confederacy, but she did not think sharing them with Gage Randolph would be conducive to securing her timely release.

"Gage, your desire to do the right thing is commendable. You're a good man, and you know what the right thing to do is."

Drawing on every exploitative sexist beer commercial she had ever seen, Bell took a long, sensuous drink from her Bud longneck. She leaned toward him as if to suggest they were sharing intimate confidences and perhaps more. *He's not a bad-looking man*, Monica thought as she sized him up. Over six feet. In shape the way a man gets through hard work and not by a gym membership. She looked into his hazel eyes and drew closer to his handsome face topped by a mass of unruly black hair.

Pulled in by Monica's gaze, Gage looked into her coffee-brown eyes. He wet his lips with his tongue and leaned closer to her. Then his eyes widened as if someone had jabbed him in the crotch with a cattle prod.

"Jeeeesuuuuus Christ!" Gage said and slapped his forehead with his non-beer-holding hand so hard it made Monica wince. "Here I am trying to give you Helsinki syndrome, and you're doin' the same damn thing to me! Well, give it up 'cuz I seen *Die Hard* plenty, let me tell you."

Monica took another pull from her Budweiser as she attempted to retrace the thought process by which Gage had seen through her attempt to co-opt him. Somehow he was smart enough to have divined her intentions but stupid enough to have done so using *Die Hard* as the metric for analysis. She thought, *Die Hard? What the hell is Helsinki syndrome? Why is it that men can somehow navigate every life challenge by applying lessons from a movie?*

"Gage," she said, "I have no clue what you're talking about. I mean that sincerely. I think I saw *Die Hard* once on DVD when I was in college. What's it have to do with us right now? Is this some weird southern man thing?"

"Like hell you don't know what's going on. You was Helsinki-in' the livin' crap out of me. Almost worked, too."

"OK, you got me," she said. "But you still don't know what to do. Face it: you're going to have to let me go. It will be easier if you did it now."

"Ma'am—" Gage said.

"Ma'am?" Monica interjected. "You have me chained to a goddamn stripper pole, and you're calling me ma'am?"

"No need to be rude just 'cuz I got ya chained up," he said. "Way I was raised. Momma would slap me upside the head if I disrespected a woman."

"Your mom insisted you use polite forms of address with women you chain to stripper poles? Now that's some good parenting right there."

Gage ignored her. Arguing with Monica opened up many avenues of exploration. He needed to remain on task. "Now, as I was sayin': you could walk out of here right now and be back on the air tonight if I could just make you believe I didn't intend for any of this to happen."

"OK," Monica said. "I believe you."

"Just 'cuz I talk slow don't mean I'm stupid," he said.

"No, you being stupid means you're stupid," she snapped. "Just how do you think you can prevent me from going to the cops?"

"I'm workin' on a plan," Gage said. "Well, me and Bud Roy are. Maybe *you* stole Stonewall Jackson's arm. And maybe you don't want the police knowing about it. So maybe what we got is a…whaddyacallit? A Mexican standoff."

"Right," she said, drawing out the word and slathering it with sarcasm. "I gave a speech in Durham the night of the, uh, armed robbery. I drove up to Virginia, stole Stonewall Jackson's arm, drove *back* to North Carolina, and then turned north again. All this while doing a phone interview with that idiot Bill Spark and his bleached-blonde pit bull." She drained the last of her Bud and waggled the empty at Gage to signal she was up for another round.

"I ain't got all the angles just right yet," he said as he popped open two more Bud longnecks for them. "Maybe you used your feminine wiles and sexually enticed me to do your dirty work. How about that?"

"Feminine wiles? Sexually enticed? Jesus Christ, Gage. Do you secretly read Harlequin Romances? Who talks like that?"

Gage shrugged but did not answer. Sometimes it made sense to hunker down and let the storm blow itself out.

Monica wasn't done. "You have got to be the worst kidnapper in Creation. Or maybe just the nicest. Not everyone intending to implement a kidnapping and blackmail scheme runs it past the victim so she can spot all the holes."

"Well, Ms. Bell," Gage said, stressing the *ms.*, "I ain't the only one with a vote in this operation. Others got, what are they…equities? Yes, others got them, too. And maybe we're gonna get a little legal advice. Bud Roy is good friends with Linus McTane, who's one helluva…" He stopped talking, hoping his divulging of yet another coconspirator in her kidnapping had escaped Monica's notice.

She laughed out loud. "So Linus McTane is, I take it, an attorney? And he is advising you on the legal ramifications of chaining me to a stripper pole against my will? Anything else you care to share?"

"Bud Roy says I can't shut up on account I got criminal Tourette's," Gage mumbled.

CHAPTER ELEVEN

The next morning Bill Spark concluded he preferred working with Isaac Newton, not against him. He was not happy to find himself in a helicopter, a machine he believed only stayed aloft by beating the laws of physics into submission.

"A plane I can deal with," he told Sierra Darlin' over the intercom. "It has wings. Birds have wings. Wings keep you in the sky. There are no wings on this. Only a big fan on top. It's not natural."

"I think it's way cool," Sierra said. "A private helicopter to a private offshore oil rig. This is the life."

"It's only 'the life' if you're around to live it," Bill said. "We're being kept in the air by about ten thousand moving parts assembled by a guy who hates his job. If just one of them fails, we're going into the ground like a fucking dart."

"More like a rock," the pilot said, joining the conversation. "A dart has a certain aerodynamic elegance to it. We'll just plummet into the drink. There won't be nothin' pretty about it." The pilot smiled. He enjoyed people who didn't like to fly.

"Really?" Bill asked, gripping the armrests of his sumptuous leather-covered captain's chair so hard his knuckles turned white. "Can't you do that autorotation thing?"

"Nah. Just a term we invented to give passengers like you hope in your last few terrifying seconds on Earth. Might as well spend that time reliving your sex life or something. Besides, we're over the Atlantic. Even if we survive, there are the sharks…"

Bill looked out the window expecting to see nothing but a swirling mass of dorsal fins knifing through the water. But cowardice gave way to avarice as he glimpsed *Freedomland* looming out of the slate-gray Atlantic, backlit by the morning sun. "Wow!" he said.

Zacharias Townsend had spared no expense. The former oil rig looked like a cross between a lush tropical island and a giant layered wedding cake. Several stories of terraces and balconies culminated in a rooftop playground sporting at least three pools, gardens, what appeared to be a driving range, and three helipads hanging off the sides. Once, Bill had visited the Vanderbilt mansion, Biltmore, in Asheville, North Carolina. He had figured that that was the epitome of wealthy excess, but Zacharias Townsend appeared to have one-upped George Washington Vanderbilt. His Biltmore could float. As the helicopter's landing gear gently kissed the helipad, Bill Spark vowed to become Zacharias Townsend's new best friend.

"Did you see the bathroom?" Sierra Darlin' asked as they explored their quarters, which were bigger than any house Bill Spark had ever lived in. "I bet you could swim laps in the tub."

"Yeah, sure," he said, ignoring Sierra's monologue on the wonders that awaited him in the bathroom. He was studying a framed and faded letter written by Robert E. Lee. He recalled the passageways leading to his room were filled with Civil War artifacts: all genuine, and all Confederate.

Zacharias Townsend entered the room after giving a sharp, perfunctory rap on the door. Bill assessed it was the mogul's way of signifying he didn't mind observing social niceties but also that he didn't feel bound by them. He introduced himself as he offered his hand. "I'm a big fan of your radio show."

Bill, a tall man himself, was three inches shorter than Zacharias, although heavier. Where Zacharias was angles and sharp edges, Bill was rounded and soft. They both had eyes set too close together, but Zacharias's gray-blue ones projected a predatory, hard-edged glint that bore into Bill's skull. Bill held the billionaire's gaze for as long as he could and saw…nothing. It was like looking into the eyeballs of a shark.

"Nice to meet you, Mr. Townsend," the talk radio host said, although he was not altogether sure that was accurate. Zacharias Townsend had more money than Scrooge McDuck, and he seemed willing to help Bill Spark get some. However, and allowing that he was acting on a fleeting first impression, Bill thought the guy was pure evil in human form.

Zacharias shifted his gaze to Sierra. Her taut, compact frame; blonde hair; flawless, tanned skin; and cornflower-blue eyes had their usual impact. As he watched, Bill detected something—nothing more than a glimmer—but definitely something in Zacharias's eyes that had not been there before.

He wants her, Bill thought.

"And you must be the amazing, and truly stunning, Sierra Darlin'. Your reputation proceeds you. You demolished Monica Bell so thoroughly I don't think there is any trace of her left," Zacharias said as he held on to Sierra's hand for, Bill thought, much longer than necessary.

Yep, he wants her.

Sierra cranked up the wattage of her already radiant smile. "I have heard so much about you, Mr. Townsend…"

"Please, call me Zack. All my friends do."

I didn't get a "Call me Zack," Bill thought. *I guess I'm not at the friends stage yet. Looks like Sierra is blowing right past it, though. Five more minutes, and she'll have her bra off.* He looked at an antique rifle mounted on the wall and idly wondered if it was loaded.

"Oh, gosh…Zack," Sierra stammered. "Thanks so much for having us out to *Freedomland*. It's amazing. *You* are amazing," she said.

72

"I'm inclined to agree with you on both counts," Zacharias said with what he probably thought was a smile. "I'd love to stay and hear more about how great you think I am, but I have a few things to do before we meet for dinner tonight."

Zacharias Townsend turned at the door to look back at Sierra Darlin' and eventually, as if an afterthought, Bill Spark. "In the meantime," he said, "make yourselves at home. Enjoy all that *Freedomland* has to offer. I look forward to discussing my business proposition with you both."

Several hours later, as they made their way through the labyrinth of corridors toward Zacharias Townsend's private quarters, Bill Spark and Sierra Darlin' revisited the argument that had been occupying them since their initial meeting with the billionaire.

"For Chrissake," she said. "What are you so insecure about? Didn't we just have a fight and then some hot makeup sex?"

"All I'm saying is that thirty seconds after meeting him you were ready to join in a game of the Fox News anchor and the intern."

Sierra paused in front of the massive oak doors to Zacharias's quarters. "We've got a chance here to do something great. Don't blow it just because someone might want to get in my pants. Believe me, a *lot* of guys want the privilege. At the moment, only you have access. But that'll change if you act like you own me."

"Fine."

Bill pressed a button he presumed was the doorbell. Ten seconds later, a young woman in an honest-to-God maid's outfit opened the door.

"Good evening. Mr. Townsend is expecting you. Please follow me," she said.

"You bet!" Bill said with more zest than the situation warranted. "Can't wait to see Zack!"

Sierra shot him a quick glare.

The Townsend's cavernous apartment appeared to occupy an entire half of the third deck, and they had spared no expense in furnishing and decoration. Yet, for all that, the space was much like the man himself: spare, functional, stripped of anything not essential, and devoid of any human touches.

The maid ushered them into a dining room with an expanse of glass looking out over the darkened ocean. In the center of the room was a twenty-person table with chrome legs and an obsidian surface. Bill thought it had all the charm of an exam table in a doctor's office. Four place settings were at the far end of the table, closest to a fireplace large enough to consume an entire Christmas tree.

Zacharias entered the room from a recessed door on the far wall. Trailing behind him was a brunette woman sporting a golden tan so perfect and even it could not have been natural. She exuded sensuality, physicality, and detached contemptuousness in equal measure and must have scared the hell out of anyone not worth billions of dollars. She certainly scared Bill. Even Sierra seemed tense. Bill realized the woman was much taller, possibly over six feet, than she had first appeared when she stood next to the angular, narrow, six-foot, seven-inch Zacharias.

"Welcome to our home. This is my wife, Barbara," Zacharias said.

Barbara Townsend said, "Pleased to meet you," in a manner suggesting she was not, in fact, terribly pleased to meet them.

"We're thrilled to be here. I just love what you've done with the place," Sierra said as if she were commenting on new wallpaper in the dining room of a three-bedroom ranch house in suburban Richmond rather than a $750 million custom-built oil rig.

"Thanks. We were hoping you'd like it," Barbara said. Her gaze drifted over them without apparent interest to a full bar running down the far wall. A Filipino bartender caught her eye and nodded, setting to work on whatever libation she required to get through the evening.

"Enough with the small talk. Let's sit down and eat," Zacharias said. He pulled out a chair for Sierra and then sat across from her, leaving Bill to replicate the gesture for Barbara after an awkward interlude where he had begun to seat himself while she stood looking at him.

The barman brought Barbara a vodka martini with four olives. This seemed like a lot of olives to Bill, but it did not seem prudent to say so. The barman took orders for the rest of the table, retreated to his station and set to work as servers appeared from yet another recessed doorway bearing the soup and salad course.

Dinner proceeded well, with a comfortable and effortless discussion about *The Firebell*, out-of-control government, and the unnecessary burden of taxation. Even Barbara grew more animated, although that may have been due to her ingesting several martinis. Bill thought, despite the rocky start, that the evening was going to end as a success.

Then Barbara extended one of her very, very long legs underneath the table until her bare foot and surprisingly prehensile toes gained a purchase in Bill's groin.

Unfortunately, the radio host was at that moment working with great enthusiasm to crack an uncooperative lobster claw as he half listened to Zacharias hold forth on the evils of progressive tax rates. Understandably shocked to be on the receiving end of such intimate podiatric ministrations from the haughty Amazonian wife of a software billionaire, he reacted with a spasm that rocketed the lobster claw diagonally across the table and into Zacharias's right eye.

"Fuck!" Zacharias screamed in a voice two octaves above normal. He slapped both hands over his injured eye to protect it from further incoming crustaceans.

"Ohmigod! Zack! Are you OK?" Sierra asked, half rising out of her chair.

"No!" Zacharias yelled. "I just had half a fucking lobster penetrate my eyeball!"

Bill sat in stunned, uncomprehending, slack-jawed silence. He looked briefly at Barbara, who gave him a wink.

"Zacharias, I'm…I'm…I am so sorry," he finally managed to stammer. "It just…the claw was slippery…I didn't mean to shoot it into your eyeball."

The waitstaff and Barbara, who could not quite contain her smirk, moved to assist Zacharias. His eye was welded shut and watering profusely.

"Honey, let's get you to the doctor. I'm sure he can fix you right up," Barbara said.

"Aaaah," Zacharias said as he stood up, still holding his eye. "This is the last time lobster will be on the menu. I'm still gonna have the cook buy lobsters and boil the fuckers alive…but then into the trash they go."

Jesus, Bill thought. *I wonder what he wants to do to me?*

Barbara Townsend took her husband's arm and led him out of the room. A waiter returned to tell the visibly shaken Sierra Darlin' and ashen-faced Bill Spark that dinner was over and they could return to their quarters.

"Jesus Christ, Bill. What the hell happened back there?" Sierra Darlin' asked once they got back to their apartment.

"You will not believe this," Bill Spark said as he flopped into an expensive, modern, and very uncomfortable chair in the living room. "Barbara Townsend tried to give me a, uh, a hand job…but with her foot."

He was right—Sierra did not believe him. "Give me a break. She was hardly coming on to you. Hell, it was obvious she didn't want to be in the same room with either of us," she said. "You're still mad about Zack flirting with me. You did it on purpose!"

"You think I practice shooting lobster claws across the table just in case I get mad at someone during a surf-and-turf dinner?"

Bill got up and poured himself a glass of Craigellachie Centenary whiskey from the sideboard. He marveled at the taste for a moment, wondering what it cost. "Listen, I was minding my business and thought, like you, the dinner was going great." He took another gulp of scotch. "I was working on the lobster claw, and suddenly, her foot was in my crotch. And she has got some truly talented toes. She could do origami with those toes. Probably make one of those paper cranes with them."

Sierra's eyes narrowed until they looked like the slits in a machine gun nest. "That bitch. I'm gonna knock her flat."

Bill found himself both pleased that Sierra was mad and aroused at the thought of her wrestling with Barbara. He forced himself to return to the moment. "Listen, babe, I think you are tougher than barbwire. But had the four of us fought to the death in that room, I'm positive only Barbara Townsend would have walked out."

"You don't think I could…"

"She could kick *my* ass," Bill said. He was flustered to see his pronouncement did not carry the appropriate weight with Sierra.

"I just hope you blinding Zach with a lobster claw didn't put an end to our deal," Sierra Darlin' said.

It didn't. Two hours later, Zacharias Townsend knocked twice and once again let himself in. Barbara Townsend was with him. Upon seeing this, Bill Spark reflexively covered his groin with his left hand, his right holding yet another glass of expensive scotch. Sierra Darlin' shot a brief glare at Barbara before focusing on her husband. "Oh, Zack. Is your eye hurt?" she asked, looking at the black eye patch that only enhanced Zacharias's palpable menace.

"Just a scratched cornea. Doctor says I have to wear this for a few days," Zacharias said. "I just wanted to drop by to say there are no hard feelings. I know it was an accident." He extended his hand toward Bill.

Bill clasped Zacharias's hand with the fervor of a man being pulled from a burning building. "Zacharias, thank you so much. I was worried this accident had ruined our friendship."

Everyone in the room knew that Bill meant "deal" instead of "friendship." But Zacharias Townsend was too good a businessman to allow a partial blinding by lobster impede a desired acquisition. "Not at all," Zacharias said. "I'm looking forward to your first broadcast from *Freedomland*. We're going to change this country."

"So what's the next step?" Sierra asked.

Bill was only partly following the conversation as he watched Barbara slip her left foot out of her shoe and bunch up the silk area rug she was standing on with her toes, all the while making unbreakable eye contact with him.

Zacharias answered Sierra's question. "We have a state-of-the-art broadcast studio here. We're going to stream the show on the internet and beam it to several stations I own. And we're going to tell the government to keep their hands off your profits and their nose out of your business."

"And what do you want from us?" Sierra asked. She looked over at Bill, who seemed fixated with Barbara's bare left foot.

"I want only five percent of the show, plus rent," Zacharias said. "That is more than the government will leave you with. But money is secondary. We need to push the envelope. I also need you to become citizens of *Freedomland*. You will be the first two citizens after Barbara and me. You will join us in seceding from the United States."

CHAPTER TWELVE

*W*e *had a DEAL!*

Zacharias Townsend stabbed the send button, hurling his message through cyberspace to the recipient waiting in the private chat room on the South of the Line website. He was furious that the seller of Stonewall Jackson's arm was doubling the delivery price to $100,000.

> *The deal has CHANGED! If you want the arm, you need to come up with an extra fifty large. If you won't pay, I'll find someone who will.*

From Bud Roy's desk in the office at Knockers, Gage Randolph smiled as he sent his secure message back to the buyer. He did not have to wait long for a reply.

> *You think you can find another buyer for the arm of Stonewall? Just how are you going to do that? And just what will your fellow SOL members think once I tell them you stole the arm?*

After his earlier encounters with Sam Aucoin and Monica Bell, Gage was conscious of the need to keep his criminal Tourette's under control. Gage typed in reply, *I guess I'd be scared if you knew who I am. But you don't, and I'm not going to tell you my name or anything else about me except that I want 100k for the arm.*

Suddenly, the video camera on his laptop came on, and a cadaverous-looking man with an eye patch glared at him from the middle of the screen.

"Your name is Gage Randolph," the man said. "My name is Zacharias Townsend."

Gage stabbed at his keyboard with no apparent effect. After realizing his computer was frozen, he looked back into the camera. "Who're you? How'd you do that to my computer?"

"Software billionaire," Zacharias replied, answering both questions. As he did so, his Wikipedia entry opened on Gage's screen.

"The rich oil-rig guy?" Gage asked after reading a few lines of the Wiki. "The guy who's helping Bill Spark screw Uncle Sam? I heard him talking about it the other day on his show. Well, that I like." He paused as his brain caught up with what his gut was telling him. "That also means one hundred thousand should be nothin' to you."

Zacharias took a breath. This was not going the way he had thought it would. Usually, his name frightened people. He thought the eye patch he was now wearing would've enhanced the effect. *There should be some upside to taking a lobster claw to the cornea*, he thought.

Zacharias concluded he needed to bypass Gage's avarice to jump-start what appeared to be the man's seldom-used instinct for self-preservation. Making a flurry of internet pages open in Gage's browser, he said, "Take a few minutes to look those over."

The first headline on Gage's computer was from *The New York Times*: STONEWALL JACKSON'S ARM STOLEN IN GRAVE ROBBERY. *USA Today* went with: (DIS)ARMAGEDDON! The *Huffington Post* thought ARMAGEDDON was pun enough and referred to the thief as the ONE-ARM BANDIT. The ever-reliable *New York Post* ran with: THE CONFEDERACY DISARMED! FIRST THE UNACRAPPER, NOW THE ULNAGRABBER!

"Fake news," Gage assessed. "Ulnagrabber? That there's a flat-out lie. I didn't take no lady parts. Just Stonewall's arm." He sounded displeased, as if the press were questioning his professional grave-robbing ethics.

Zacharias rested his head in his hand for a moment and then looked back into the camera. "The *ulna*," he said, "is a bone in the human forearm. You seem to be confusing it with the *vulva*, which—and historians are unanimous in this assessment—Stonewall Jackson did not have one of."

"Who cares?" Gage retorted.

"I would assume any woman you have sex with might," Zacharias observed. Still, he made a mental note to pay some attention to Barbara's forearms the next time they made love on the off chance he was missing something.

"So what does this have to do with me?"

"Um, everything," Zacharias said. "A few more mouse clicks, and the Feds will be at your door. Or I could really work you over. I know a few of your SOL friends who would be happy to get their hands on the fella who desecrated the grave of a great Confederate general. Have you been over to the message boards lately? They're really pissed."

"You're threatening me?"

Zacharias thought the question somewhat unnecessary. "I'm trying to," he said. "Most people pick up on it faster than you, though."

"Well, Mr. Computer Genius," Gage said. "Go ahead and call the Feds. There are plenty of computer records of you talkin' to me in this chat room. Must be a log or something tracking what we said. I will bring you down with me and sell you for a carton of Luckies when we hit the pen."

Zacharias gave Gage credit for having a spine but did not think it was attached to a functioning brain stem. He felt like he was trying to explain a card trick to a dog. "Gage," he said with the slow cadence of a man focused on practicing a patience he did not possess, "I am going to, again, repeat two key words…*software billionaire.* It is important you understand what those two words mean."

"So you're rich. So what?"

Zacharias sighed. This was going to be a heavy lift. "Rich does not even scratch the surface of what I am. The 'so what,' Gage, is that I have hacked this site so thoroughly that the chat room records will show what I want them to show. They will show you came to me trying to sell the arm and that I, a responsible steward of our history, strung you along and contacted the proper authorities."

Zacharias drank some scotch. He thought the eye patch and the scotch added to the image he was trying to convey. Gage Randolph, he assessed, required visual cues. He hoped these would suffice before he was compelled to resort to sock puppets. Placing his glass carefully upon a coaster, he continued. "The other 'so what' is that I am rich and respected, and everyone will believe me. And I have an army of lawyers to obliterate anyone who doesn't. What do you bring to the fight?"

Gage paused for a moment, considering the question. Then he turned away from the camera. He appeared to be talking to someone. Or, more accurately, something, because shortly thereafter, the jowls of an enormous dog appeared next to him, sniffing the desktop for any food within range of its lengthy tongue.

"I got two things, Mr. Townsend. One, I got the arm. And, number two, I got this here dog. His name's Rebel. Now, you may be asking yourself what one has to do with the other. Let me explain it to you in simple words, like you used for me." He took a swig of Coke and, after doing so, set it carefully upon an empty Cheetos bag, mocking Zacharias's mannered performance with the scotch.

"See, Rebel here—well, he wants nothing more in life than to eat Stonewall Jackson's arm." Gage reached off camera to retrieve a box. He opened it and revealed the contents to Zacharias. "This arm, as a matter of fact."

Zacharias reached toward the screen as if to touch the morbid treasure. Rebel the Hound made his own attempt to get hold of it, earning him a rebuke from Gage.

"Goddamn it, Rebel. Not yet!…So," Gage said, "if I were to walk out of the room for a few minutes and leave Rebel here alone with the arm… well, I bet it wouldn't be too long before it became dog food. Rebel don't show no mercy to no bones, believe me."

Gage polished off his Coke and belched. "Call the police," he said. "Send your doctored-up internet files to the Feds. But in less than five minutes, I can have Rebel destroy the evidence, and shortly after, it will be just another pile of dog shit on the street."

Zacharias sat back and stared into the camera with grudging admiration. He was so used to intimidating people because they had a lot to gain, he was unprepared to fail at bullying someone with nothing to lose.

Keep your focus on what is important, he thought. *Stonewall's arm is worth more than beating this dipshit in a negotiation.*

"Fine," Zacharias said, surprised at how difficult it was to speak the next words. "One hundred thousand it is."

"No," Gage said. "One hundred thousand was the price before you made fun of me and tried to scare me by sayin' how rich and powerful you was. Now that you've reminded me of how much money you got lyin' around, the price has gone up. I want two hundred and fifty thousand."

"Fuck me!" Zacharias spat.

"Now look who's changin' the terms," Gage replied, grinning broadly. "That particular request will cost more. I ain't sayin' it's a deal killer, mind you. But if you want me to get up close and personal with your…uh, ulna, or your vulva, we will need to come to terms."

Zacharias took a deep breath. The rest of his night was shot. He would spend it reliving this discussion and trying to understand how this semieducated, Toby Keith-listening-to shit heel had bested him.

"You don't know me; not really," Zacharias said, the menace in his tone unmistakable. "You think I've always been rich?"

"Oh, I'm sure you built your empire all by yourself," Gage said. "With nothing more than a million-dollar loan from your old man."

Zacharias gave a small snort. "Don't confuse me with some whole other body, Mr. Randolph. First, I actually am a billionaire. Second, I am a self-made one. My dad didn't have ten dollars to loan me, much less a million. I grew up poor, Gage. So don't think I'm some soft trust-fund shithead. I built my empire a brick at a time. I overcame my enemies because I knew what being poor was like and was determined I never would be again."

"Yeah, yeah," Gage said. "You're the American Dream come to life."

"No, I'm not. I'm a fucking American nightmare. I'm not a predatory capitalist. I'm viral. I kill the host."

Gage looked into the monitor for ten seconds before speaking. "Mr. Townsend, I'm sure I should be scared, but I'm not. I don't think you can hurt me more than life already has. Now, it's getting late, and Rebel is feeling a might peckish. Two hundred and fifty grand is what it costs to get the arm. Do you want it or not?"

Zacharias sighed. "OK. You have a deal. When do I get it?"

"I'm thinkin' we swap money for bones at the reenactment of the Battle of Bentonville this Saturday. It seems fitting, that bein' the place where the South stood tall one last time."

"Fine," Zacharias said. "I was going to go anyway. I'll wire the money when you give me the arm."

"Nah," Gage said. "I want cash. With all your threats of how you can make a computer do anything and how scary and tough you are, how am I supposed to believe you won't just pretend to send me the money and then drain my bank account altogether after I give you the arm?"

Zacharias was annoyed, as that was exactly what he was planning to do. "Fine. Cash for bones. This Saturday, in Bentonville."

"From one tycoon to another," Gage said, "it was a pleasure doing business with you."

Zacharias Townsend cut the feed and pondered the many horrible things he might do to Gage Randolph once he got the arm. It wasn't a matter of killing the man. Of course he would. How he killed him…well, that was a matter worthy of consideration.

"How're you with discussing…uh, whatchacallems…hypotheticals?" Bud Roy Roemer asked Linus McTane the next morning over breakfast at a local diner.

"Hypothetically," McTane said as he liberally doused his biscuits and sausage gravy with salt and pepper, "I am just dandy discussing hypotheticals."

"We got a couple of doozies for ya," Gage Randolph said. "Bud Roy, which of our hypotheticals should we start him off with?"

"Well," Bud Roy said as he buttered a piece of toast, "let us suppose, hypothetically, two guys might know where Monica Bell and the Unacrapper are. What should they do?"

McTane stopped chewing and looked at Bud Roy and Gage for a long moment. Then he said, "You know, I was really enjoying my biscuits and gravy. The current Mrs. McTane…well…she insists I eat only granola and fruit for breakfast. I guess because she has mistaken me for a fucking blue jay. I hardly ever get the chance to eat a proper southern breakfast. But now," he said, pushing the plate to the side, "I'll just go straight to the antacid. What in the name of Christ have you boys been up to?"

"It's a long story," Gage said.

"Why not hit me with the high points?" McTane suggested. "I take it you have information on the whereabouts of the Unacrapper and Monica Bell? If so, and with you both being, hypothetically, good and upstanding citizens of Fayetteville, North Carolina, might I suggest you turn this information over to the proper law enforcement authorities?"

"Now, see, this is where it gets a skidge complicated." Bud Roy took a sip of coffee.

"I'll bet it does," McTane said.

Gage took over from Bud Roy. "I was sorta tricked into helping the Unacrapper kidnap Monica Bell after we all ran into each other on a back road in Virginia. Now they're hiding out at Knockers."

"That goddamn bar," the lawyer said. He pulled his biscuits and gravy back in front of him and attacked with renewed vigor. McTane figured he would come out ahead if he died of clogged arteries before this conversation ended. Against his better judgment, he sought clarification. "Why on Earth is Monica Bell, whose politics make Bernie Sanders look like Jefferson Davis, hiding out with the Unacrapper at Knockers?"

"Technically, only the Unacrapper is hiding out," Gage said, removing his Mack Truck ball cap to run his fingers through his thick black hair. "Monica is, uh, chained to the stripper pole until we can make her understand that we didn't mean to kidnap her."

"At some future point, I am sure I will want to hear how one gets tricked into taking hostages," McTane said between mouthfuls. "But let me cut to the chase and give you my best unvarnished legal advice." He paused for another mouthful of biscuit and sausage gravy. Bud Roy and Gage peered at him across the table.

"You both appear to be royally fucked," McTane pronounced.

"Hell, Linus. We came to that conclusion on our own," Bud Roy said. "We were kinda hopin' you might be able to give us something more, you bein' a lawyer and all."

"Well, just what kind of legal advice do you think biscuits and gravy at a truck stop is gonna buy you?" McTane rubbed his temples. "Perhaps you want me to get up in court and cite temporary insanity for you, Bud Roy, because your clavicle bone is connected to your brain bone?"

"Is temporary insanity some kind of, uh, precedent?" Gage asked between mouthfuls of pancake as he tapped into legal terminology he had grown familiar with while watching film adaptations of John Grisham novels.

"It is for you two!" McTane said, louder than he intended. Nearby diners gave the group a brief look before returning to their food.

"Now, calm down, Linus," Bud Roy said. "Gage really was just trying to help Monica, and things got out of hand. It's surprisingly easy to move from helping someone to aiding and abetting a domestic terrorist and kidnapping."

"So I am learning this morning," McTane said. "Just what the hell were you doing on a back road up in Virginia anyway, Gage?"

"Well, now," Gage said. "Your question leads us to our second hypothetical. I suppose you've heard by now that Stonewall Jackson's arm is missing."

"Missing?" McTane said. "Are you saying the arm wandered away from the rest of Stonewall's corpse while it was visiting the mall? Is it now featured prominently on a carton of milk?" He shook his head and held up his fork as Gage started to reply. "Lemme guess: you made a pilgrimage to Virginia to pay homage to a Southern hero and got caught on the slippery slope that has driven so many innocent tourists to grave desecration and body-part theft. Am I correct?"

"To be truthful, I went there to steal Stonewall's arm," Gage said. "I have a buyer, a really rich guy, and I need your help in making sure he don't rip me off. I'm also hopin' he can help me in some way with our first hypothetical."

"By doing what?" McTane asked.

"I dunno. Whatever it is rich people do to get out of being punished for all the shit rich people do," Gage said.

"What about the Unacrapper?"

"Well," Bud Roy said, "we figure if we can get Monica Bell not to press charges, we can then tell Mr. Kelley he needs to be movin' on."

"I'll bite," McTane said before draining the last of his orange juice. "Who's the buyer?"

Gage and Bud Roy exchanged looks, and Gage said, "Zacharias Townsend."

McTane raised his eyebrows in both surprise and admiration. "Well, you two are runnin' with the bulls now, ain't ya?" He paused for a moment, his formidable legal brain crunching the data he had been fed. "Look, I still think you're both screwed and should hightail it to Canada. But you might have a very slim chance at getting out of this. Against my better judgment, I'm gonna let you buy me this breakfast, which I will consider a retainer for my legal services." He finished the last of his coffee and continued. "I need to think about this. In the meantime, please don't go and make this worse. I would think you couldn't possibly do so, but I have gained a new appreciation for your ability to dig any hole you find yourselves in deeper still. Just lie low, and let me figure out the next move. If there is one."

Linus McTane slid his bulk out of the booth, placed the check in front of Bud Roy Roemer, and left.

CHAPTER THIRTEEN

Who knew there were so many kinds of tampons? Gage Randolph thought three hours later as he pondered the selection in the feminine care section of the CVS Pharmacy in downtown Fayetteville. He was there because Monica Bell had issued a dire warning that Gage must buy certain provisions required for extended captivity. Among her demands was that he give her a longer leash. A visit to the local hardware store to purchase thirty feet of quarter-inch steel cable and some time in his personal machine shop fashioning a manacle for Monica's ankle solved that problem. The new restraint allowed her to visit the bathroom at will but still kept her away from the windows, doors, and telephones.

With the Unacrapper monitoring her in his absence, Gage first went to Marshalls to buy a bra, panties, and other essentials. He now felt as if he knew her as well as any man in her life. Maybe better.

Gage was pondering buying Monica a box of maxi pads when Sam Aucoin, off duty and in street clothes, came up behind him.

"Morning, Gage," Sam said as he peered into the man's basket. "Shopping for a girlfriend, or just trying something out?"

"Very funny, Deputy. I'm just pickin' up some notions for a woman I know."

"Must know her darn well," Sam said, studying the basket's contents. "You seem to have a full array of women's stuff in there. I didn't have you pegged as the sensitive type. Hell, I've been married for almost eight years, and my wife still doesn't trust me to do this type of shopping. You sure this all ain't for you? No shame in it. Takes all kinds. That's my philosophy."

"A lot you don't know about me, Deputy. Maybe I got me a girlfriend, and maybe she's laid up. And maybe I'm helpin' her out. Any problem?"

"A lot of maybes in there, Gage. Makes me wonder what you're up to."

"And what I wonder is why you're wonderin' what I'm up to. Maybe you're still mad at me 'cuz you blame my Bronco for makin' you shoot Bud Roy. What I'm up to, Deputy, is shoppin'. I would like to get back to it, if you don't mind."

"Not at all, Gage," Sam Aucoin said. "You take care." He moved off with a last glance in the basket.

"There's something going on with Gage Randolph," Sam Aucoin told his wife when he got home.

Rebecca Aucoin leaned her lithe frame against the center island in their expansive kitchen. "Sam, you need to let this go. You're gonna get sued by him and Bud Roy for harassment. And they might just have a case."

"Becks, I swear I'm not trying to make up for what happened. You need to know Gage Randolph." Sam grabbed a Brooklyn East IPA from their large stainless-steel fridge. He opened it with a well-practiced twist using his wedding ring as an opener and took a healthy swig before continuing. "There is no way in hell he would go shopping for feminine products unless he had to. It's at odds with everything I know about the man."

Rebecca plopped a slice of lemon and a sprig of mint into a club soda she had grabbed while her husband had been rooting for a beer and took a sip. She looked at Sam for a moment, taking him in as if they had first met. A shade over six feet, big and in shape, as a cop should be. He was, in fact, everything a cop should be. On their first date their sophomore year at Wake Forest University, he had told her of his desire for a career in law enforcement. He had double majored in psychology and finance, and she in education. Sam Aucoin could've been a lot of things. He had a genuine talent for investing, which had allowed them to buy their spacious house in Fayetteville. But that was a hobby. Being a cop was what he loved. And he was very good at it. So good that his career, while momentarily slowed by shooting Bud Roy Roemer in the clavicle, was still moving in a positive trajectory. Sam just needed to be patient.

"Don't you think you're focused on him because of the shooting?"

"No," her husband said too quickly. He saw her face, nodded at what it told him, and tried again. "I know it could seem that way. And believe me, all I want to do is take that moment back. I shot a man armed only with what later turned out to be a cordless phone the size of a salami. And now I doubt myself every time I go out on patrol. I hate that feeling."

"I know," Rebecca said as she put her arms around him. "I don't want you doubting yourself out there, either."

"Well, here's something I don't doubt," Sam Aucoin said as he bent his head slightly to kiss his wife, who was nearly as tall as he was. "Gage Randolph is not a man who would buy feminine hygiene products for his girlfriend if he had one. Or, if he *had* a girlfriend, he's not the kind of man whose girlfriend would use…and I'm quoting from memory here…Hydra Zen Neurocalm Detoxifying Moisturising Multi-Relief Anti-Stress Gel Essence."

"What the fuck is in this teeny tiny tube?" Gage Randolph asked Monica Bell as he delivered the last of her requested supplies. "It cost over sixty dollars all by itself. At the CVS! God knows what you must pay for it in New York."

"Skin care's important when you're on high-definition TV. Even more so when the chief reason you are on TV is that you look as good as I do," Monica said with more than a little derision as she took the precious item from Gage.

"Well, if the secret ingredient ain't unicorn tears and diamond powder, you got ripped off. I spend less on groceries in a week than you do regeneratin' your hydra, or whatever you call it."

"Given that hot wings and Ding Dongs comprise your diet, the comparison doesn't mean much." Monica picked up her purse, took out her wallet, and handed Gage five $100 bills. She sensed the outlay to keep her comfortable would stress his finances and he would be too proud to admit it. Something in her did not want to do that to him.

I'll be damned. Maybe there really is a Helsinki syndrome, she thought. *I'm paying my damned kidnapper for room and board.* She considered asking Gage to download *Die Hard* for them to watch.

From his perch at the bar, Jacob Kelley observed the exchange. "If you got cash to spare, why don't you send some my way?"

Monica looked at him. She did not like it when Gage left her alone with him. He leered at her body. The stress of being America's most wanted and most mocked terrorist was taking a toll on him. A man like Jacob—equal parts bitter, stupid, and mean—could not be a punch line for long without snapping.

"That's the last of my cash. Would you like to use my ATM card?" Monica asked innocently.

"No, he would not," Gage answered. "We get them *CSI* shows down here in Dixie, too."

"Maybe you can pay me some other way," Jacob said, his gaze resting heavily and obviously on Monica.

She glared at Jacob. Before she could speak, Gage said, "Now, Crapper…"

"Jacob," Jacob said automatically.

"You are a guest here, and an unwelcome one at that, if you must know. For the moment, we're givin' you a roof and a bed and some food while you figger out your next move. I offer that because you're a fellow southerner, a brother in SOL, and because we're sort of in this together. But if you touch her, or ever again suggest you might, I will shoot you right in the dick. Frankly, I got too much gun for the job." Gage touched the .357 resting on his hip in an open-carry holster.

Without a word, Jacob walked back to what had been Bud Roy's office, where he had set up camp.

"Thank you," Monica said.

"Figurin' a way out of this most surely is complicated," Gage said. "But how we treat you while we do isn't."

"Other than chaining me to a pole, you mean."

"Well, yeah. There don't seem to be much way around that. But you gotta admit I'm trying to make you as comfortable as possible," Gage said.

"Oh, I do. I'm going to give you a rave review on Yelp."

Monica gathered the various articles he had purchased for her and headed for the bathroom. She had discovered one pleasant benefit of being held captive in a former strip joint: there was an honest-to-God bathroom with a bathtub and shower. Gage had purchased enough chain to allow her to use it on her own. There was no window, no other exit, and nothing she could use to cut through her shackles. But Monica Bell was slowly earning Gage Randolph's trust, and it was just a matter of time before he slipped up.

"Bud Roy, we're *millionaires*. Just barely, sure, but we are. It means something," Shelley DeWeese said while gyrating astride Bud Roy Roemer. "I just can't, I mean I just cannot, go back to being a, uh, *thousandaire*. We gotta do something."

"Christ, Shelley," he grunted from below. "Lord knows I'm tryin'. If you would just…stop…talkin' about money for a moment and…concentrate…"

She did as asked, and Bud Roy, wanting to assume some control of the situation, executed what he believed to be a masterful move that left him charging confidently for the finish line atop an amenable, if not altogether ecstatic, Shelley DeWeese.

Bud Roy's sprint in the final furlong, however, was interrupted by Howard the Leopard. The big cat—having proven he could spend a few hours a day in the house without eating anyone—had been napping in the hallway. But the thrashing, undulating mound on the bed, making sounds that registered in his tiny cat brain as a wildebeest in distress, triggered primal hunting instincts that had been rendered dormant, but not extinct, by a constant supply of steak and chicken. Howard the Leopard was a tawny blur as he leaped eight feet from the door of the bedroom to the bed, executed a perfect four-point landing, and sank 137 pounds of fur, muscle, claws, and teeth into Bud Roy's ass.

"Jesus H. Christ!" Bud Roy screamed, flailing furiously at the leopard before the cat could remove an entire posterior cheek for consumption.

"Oh, Buuuud Roooooy!" Shelley screamed in ecstasy, confusing her fiancé's powerful, Howard the Leopard-assisted thrust and subsequent panic-stricken gyrations for a sexual prowess on his part heretofore unknown to her. In her orgasmic throes, she mistook Bud Roy's invocation of the Son of God as confirmation of his own sexual bliss.

Howard the Leopard, assessing that Bud Roy's protestations indicated a dissatisfaction that might imperil a chicken or flank steak being thrown his way in the near future, retracted his claws, withdrew his fangs, and sinuously moved to a neutral corner.

"Goddamn it, Shelley!" Bud Roy said as he moved off her and gingerly probed his butt for puncture wounds. "Didn't I tell you we can't have that fucking homicidal leopard roaming free in the house?"

"He was just playing, honey," Shelley said as she slowly realized the true source of her bliss. "He didn't mean nothin' by it. You're not bleedin'. It was just love nibbles."

"Tell that to my ass," Bud Roy said as he ran a finger over a dimple created by one of Howard's fangs. "Talk about a boner-shrinker. Try keeping it up while a leopard is attempting to eat your butt cheek." He gave silent thanks the comforter had borne the brunt of Howard the Leopard's blitzkrieg.

"Honey, you should be thankin' him. Lord knows I am. That was just… the best ever. I may have another one just *thinkin'* about it."

"Well, I regret I have but one ass to give for your orgasm."

"Oh, hush. You're not in danger of dying," Shelley said as Bud Roy stood in front of a mirror trying to check for damage. "No blood. In fact, the only hemorrhaging takin' place is in our bank account."

Bud Roy sighed and padded back to bed, careful to give Howard the Leopard a wide berth as he did so. Neither sex nor giant cat attacks would long deter Shelley from worrying about their tax burden.

"You know what gets me," Shelley said as, much to Bud Roy's disappointment, she covered her torso with the comforter, "is that we'll pay all this money…and for what? I mean, what benefit do we get? It'll probably go to schools, but you and me don't have no kids. Or some stupid social welfare program. Or, knowing the government, to some program denying citizens the right to own a leopard."

If only. Hell, even I'd vote for a Democrat if they'd deliver on that, Bud Roy thought as he watched Howard the Leopard industriously lick himself in a post-kill grooming session. "I'm not sure what to do about it," he said, refocusing. "My guess is if we try to fight the IRS, they'll take everything. We can't win."

"Well, not by ourselves. But what if we had a powerful ally? What if we had someone back us in our fight? Someone so powerful even the government might back down?"

"Oh Lord. Are you back on that Zacharias Townsend kick again?"

"It makes sense, Bud Roy. He hates the government, and he hates taxes. Hell, he's even a Confederate Civil War buff. Now that Gage is sellin' him Stonewall's arm, we should go with Gage to meet Townsend and then tell him our tale of woe. Who knows? Maybe we could even get on *The Firebell*," Shelley said.

Bud Roy knew that this fight, like the one over Howard the Leopard, was one he would lose. Shelley DeWeese, when she wanted something, was a force of nature. Besides, being on the radio with Bill Spark and Sierra Darlin' appealed to him.

"OK. I'll talk to Gage and make us part of the package. But after that, no promises. Rich people don't give a damn about the problems of other people. They resent us for even thinkin' we have problems."

"*We're* rich people," Shelley said. "And I aim to make sure we stay that way." She flopped down the comforter to expose Dr. Curtis DeLong's exquisite handiwork. "What say we see if we can top the last time?"

"OK," Bud Roy Roemer said. "But if that damn cat's gonna stay in here, you're on top."

CHAPTER FOURTEEN

"This is much, much, much worse than a helicopter," Bill Spark croaked after barfing into a large bucket that Captain John Purdy kept on the bridge of his seventy-foot Hatteras Sportfish. He was returning to terra firma with Sierra Darlin' to conduct a round of media interviews to hype their show, tout their move to Zacharias Townsend's floating tax haven, and, as Zacharias had put it, "stir the pot."

However, and Bill thought Zacharias had done it on purpose as retribution for his eyeball laceration, the helicopter was down for repairs. Zacharias had contracted with small boats up and down the East Coast to make taxi runs to *Freedomland* for supplies and to transport guests as his mobile wannabe nation-state moved along, always thirteen miles offshore. Purdy had received the call to fetch the two.

Unfortunately, the boat was running over seven-foot seas, stirred up by a rare early-season hurricane pushing its way north. While a seventy-foot boat had sounded like a lot when Bill was told that would be his conveyance back to the United States, it seemed terribly small and fragile as it pounded its way home.

"This is nothing, sir," Purdy said. A squat, barrel-bodied, African American man with a dusting of gray hair clinging to his scalp, he looked at home behind the helm. "This is a helluva boat. It can handle a lot worse. And I've been in worse. Just try and relax; we'll be ashore in no time."

"I dunno; this seems awfully rough," Bill said as he widened his stance near the bucket. He did his best to look nautical, casting what he thought would pass for a knowing, seasoned eye at the roiling seas around them.

"I been out in thirty- to forty-foot seas in cutters not much bigger than this," Purdy, a retired coast guard captain, said. Unlike a lot of coasties, who had spent so much time on an angry ocean that they never wanted to see it again after retirement, Purdy loved the sea. He also had married well, and his wife's inheritance hadn't even felt the pinch when she had bought him a brand-new Hatteras GT 70 upon his retirement. He had christened her the *Marlinspike*, and now he ran a successful charter service that allowed him to treat his military pension like fun money. He loved his boat about as much as he loved his wife and split his time equally with both.

"Maybe I should go below and lie down," Bill said.

"I wouldn't recommend it, sir," Purdy said. "First, you're better off out here, keeping your eye on the horizon and the wind in your face. You go inside, the motion is just going to feel ten times worse." He paused to correct his course. "Second, if you miss the bucket inside, you'll ruin my day and yours because I will insist you help me clean it up. Just last week, I had a guy puke all over my new flat screen below. He was pissed off when I handed him a rag and some Windex. But this boat is often my home and always my place of business. I'm understanding of seasickness, but only if you follow my orders."

Bill looked out at the ocean again and tried to concentrate on the horizon, just like Purdy had recommended. "I guess it's better out here. I'll say this, though: they never show these types of seas in the photo spreads in yachting magazines."

Purdy laughed. "I had a long and distinguished career saving rich assholes who had more boat than brains. Most of 'em should've stayed tied up at the pier drinking martinis and making up sea stories to impress the mistress."

Bill smiled. When he got yacht money, he would follow Purdy's advice.

Purdy looked around. "Where's your lady friend?"

"She went below to call into *The Monica Bell Show*. She tries to mess with them every day." He was a little annoyed Sierra was unaffected by the rough passage to the mainland.

"She's a pistol, for sure," Purdy said. "Good sea legs, too."

"You got satellite reception here on the bridge? Or even better, a TV? They do a simulcast," Bill said. "We can listen to her kick ass."

"Bill, this thing is loaded. I even got extra cupholders." John Purdy flipped a switch, and the satellite TV built into the bridge console came to life. He turned up the volume as they found the right station.

"You cannot be serious," an Academy Award-winning actress, the latest in a string of liberal luminaries sitting in for Monica Bell during her absence, said to Sierra Darlin'.

"Until proven otherwise, my theory is as good as any other," Sierra replied, unfazed by the dripping disdain from a cinematic legend.

"You really believe Monica Bell faked her own disappearance?"

"Why not? She's been trailing behind us in the ratings. She couldn't beat us on brains and talent, so she had to cheat the way liberals always do. She had to get people to feel sorry for her."

"And you have proof of this accusation?" the actress asked.

"Do you have proof it *didn't* happen?" Sierra retorted.

"That is the stupidest—"

The actress was unable to finish her sentence as Sierra jumped back in. "Look, maybe it happened, maybe it didn't. But until we know for sure, my theory is just as sound as anyone else's."

"You're making unfounded accusations," the actress said.

Sierra was ready for the charge. "We have plenty of proof she's wrong. We have plenty of proof she's a liberal. We have plenty of proof that every time she tries to take on me, or Bill Spark, or anyone else who has a conservative viewpoint and a brain, she loses. It doesn't take much to follow this logic to its inevitable conclusion. Monica Bell was tired of losing and is now trying to make America's snowflakes feel sorry for her."

"Well, you're right about one thing," the actress said.

"I'm glad you agree—"

"No, no. Let me finish. You are right: It doesn't take much to arrive at your conclusion. It doesn't take much intelligence. It doesn't take much compassion. It doesn't take much in the way of common sense to create the scenario you just did. And it requires no character whatsoever."

Sierra Darlin' was undeterred. "Well, if you want to indulge in personal attacks, as the left is so fond of doing, let me return the favor. I bet Monica Bell was high the night she disappeared. I recall it was even easier than usual for me to refute her idiotic arguments. Likely drugged up because she was so frustrated that I kept kicking her butt. She couldn't take it anymore, parked her car, and wandered off to cry and hug a tree. I bet she wishes she had a gun about now. The woods must be scary to a New York City limousine liberal like her."

"I've gotta be honest," John Purdy said to Bill Spark as the actress told Sierra Darlin' she was the embodiment of all that was wrong with America. "I don't much agree with Sierra's politics, or yours. Or anyone's. But there is no surrender in the young lady. She just doubles down."

"She is somethin'," Bill replied.

"I'm not sure I meant it as a compliment," Purdy said. He throttled back the two big diesels on his boat as Wilmington, North Carolina, pierced the horizon. Purdy settled his gaze on Bill. "Set aside how I might feel about someone pining for the good old days of the Confederacy—"

"That's not what we're talking about," Bill interrupted, looking equal parts contrite, embarrassed, and uneasy. Wilmington was still too far to make by swimming.

Purdy waved him off. "Don't worry. I'm not interested in having that discussion. Even if we crossed the Atlantic, we wouldn't have enough time. All I meant was that for someone with a good job, great looks, and no apparent reason to be so angry, she seems awfully mad."

Bill looked at Purdy. "To be honest, Cap'n, I agree with you."

"So what's she mad about?"

"I think she was born mad. Rage fuels everything she does." Bill looked out at the Port of Wilmington and absently rubbed his shoulders, scratched bloody by a vigorous coupling with Sierra during their last night on *Freedomland*. "Sometimes I like it, but other times, she scares the hell out of me."

"She's like the ocean," John Purdy said. "Beautiful, but don't turn your back on her."

"Damn it, Ponce," the network executive told the producer of *The Monica Bell Show*, James "Ponce" DeLeon, four days later, "if I'd known you could work this kind of miracle, I would've had that ball-busting harridan kidnapped a long time ago."

"I wouldn't be doing my job if I couldn't solve problems, Bill," DeLeon said with what he calibrated was the correct mixture of humility and confidence.

When the host of an eponymous cable news show disappears, that can be problematic. But the media hype surrounding Monica Bell's disappearance, coupled with DeLeon enlisting a wellspring of liberal Hollywood stars offering to sit in for her, meant ratings had never been higher.

"You wouldn't *have* a job," Bill Parsegan said.

DeLeon just smiled. It wouldn't be a normal day in the testoster-one-fueled world of cable news if a higher-up didn't flop his pecker on the table so his underlings could gaze in awe. Trouble only occurred when someone forgot the dick measuring was metaphorical. A few months earlier, Parsegan narrowly had avoided being fired after misinterpreting a casual conversation in the hallway with Monica. She had thought she was saying good morning and asking him how his weekend was. He had thought their quick chat indicated an interest on her part in seeing a photo of his penis, which he subsequently sent to her brand-new Apple iPhone in all of its high-definition glory.

In reply, Monica had sent back a photo of a small, lonely Cheez Doodle, made even less significant by lying in repose on her expansive desk blotter. *Mine's bigger*, read the accompanying text. A subsequent message announced: *And now I own your ass.* The next week, a crew began installing a new, expensive set for the TV version of her radio show.

Before Parsegan boarded the elevator to return to his aerie on the thirty-fifth floor of the New York City skyscraper the network called home, he told DeLeon, "We got a good thing going. But it won't last. Either she comes back and we have to figure out how to hold the numbers, or she doesn't and we have to hold the numbers. Either way, you need to deliver."

DeLeon sighed after parting ways with his boss. He considered Monica to be a friend. He also considered her to be incredibly hot, and he had not yet been successful in his own attempts to get her into bed. So he hoped she was OK. But her disappearance had been a boon to the show, and he also hoped she would remain in mortal peril for a while longer so he could capitalize on a ratings bonanza driven in equal parts by Hollywood glitz and morbid curiosity.

Some might have considered DeLeon's thinking cynical. A good many people might have even ventured he was a selfish asshole. Fortunately for him, he was a cable news show producer: being a cynical, selfish asshole was widely seen as career enhancing.

DeLeon assessed his situation. Today, he was solid. He had yet another Academy Award-winning actress slated to guest host the show. He hoped she would have a sense of humor, although initial signs were not encouraging. DeLeon believed comedians were better suited for the format. You had to be smart and informed, but you couldn't take cable news too seriously. One ponderous actor who had helmed the show after Monica's disappearance seemed to believe that because he had once *played* the president of the United States his opinion was of equal value to that of an actual president. Then again, with the lines between entertainment and politics becoming increasingly blurred, DeLeon thought, maybe there was no distinction.

DeLeon walked back to his office while mulling over his next step. He needed to keep winning. Parsegan hadn't forgotten the Cheez Doodle episode, and it was clear he would be more than happy to clean house of anyone associated with his digital emasculation. As he sat at his desk, DeLeon pondered the ten-minute bit he set aside in each broadcast for updates on the search for Monica. He had decided a simple recitation by law enforcement officials of the status of the case would not keep his audience hooked. Therefore, he had added a segment where a panel indulged in conspiracy theories and graphic Ned Beatty-in-*Deliverance*-type scenarios involving Monica and banjo-playing hillbillies. Those spots were helping to boost the numbers and generate publicity, but they were not a long-term solution.

"Monica, I hope you turn up soon," Ponce DeLeon said to himself as he swung around in his desk chair to take in Manhattan's skyline. "We need to move on, one way or the other."

CHAPTER FIFTEEN

"Fayetteville 911," the operator said the next morning. "How may I assist you?"

"He ate my Sprinkles," Alma Spivey said. "And he's not even sorry."

"Ma'am? I don't understand. What is your emergency?" The operator sighed. He was closing out a very long shift.

"Sprinkles. He ate Sprinkles," Alma repeated.

"Sprinkles? I'm sorry, ma'am, is this a baking- or snack food-related dispute? This is the 911 operator. This line is for actual emergencies. Maybe you dialed us by mistake."

"I did not dial you by mistake!" Alma yelled. "I'm reporting a crime. My beautiful pet is gone forever because he ate it."

"Ma'am, I'm sorry. We don't handle missing pets. Please call Cumberland County Animal Control."

"My pet is *not* missing," Alma said. "I know where my Sprinkles is. He's...he's...been *eaten* and is currently in the stomach of...of...they call him Howard."

"Ma'am?" the operator inquired, feeling a bewilderment he found surprising because he thought he had heard it all after fifteen years on the job, not to mention seven hours into his latest shift. "Are you saying a man named Howard ate your, uh, ate Sprinkles? What is...or was...Sprinkles? A fish of some sort?"

"A fish? No! Do you think I'd give a damn if someone ate my fish?" Alma squeaked with great indignation. "Sprinkles was a beautiful seven-year-old standard poodle."

"A *standard poodle?*" the operator asked, incredulous. "Those things weigh in at...what? Fifty? Sixty pounds?"

"Sprinkles was fifty-seven pounds," Alma said.

"Jesus!" The operator waved his colleagues over, indicating he had something new on the line. "So you are reporting that a man named Howard ate a fifty-seven-pound standard poodle?" he recapped for the benefit of his colleagues.

What the fuck! a coworker mouthed as she stood by the desk, listening to the call.

"Christ, that's a new one," the operator told Alma before she could reply. "Did this fella...Howard...did Howard eat the poodle in one sitting? I mean, with all due respect, that is a shitload of poodle. Did he cook it? Or did he just dig right in and have a, oh, I dunno, a poodle tartar? You know, like a kind of Hannibal Lecter. But with dogs."

"I...oh my...what?" Alma sputtered.

The operator stopped for a moment, realizing his morbid curiosity over the technicalities of Sprinkles's demise had made the woman even more distraught. He regrouped and asked, "What's Howard's last name, and where does he live?"

"Howard's not a man. He's a leopard," Alma said, having recovered from the barrage of questions. "And he lives in the house of my neighbor, Bud Roy Roemer."

"So you're saying Mr. Roemer has an exotic pet? And this animal attacked and, uh, consumed your poodle?" the operator asked, relieved he had not discovered yet another depth to which humanity could sink.

"Yes," Alma Spivey said. "Now please send someone over here immediately to shoot the leopard. And shoot Bud Roy, too, for all I care. It won't be the first time for him."

"Why me?" Sam Aucoin asked the dispatcher when he got the call to investigate the improper housing of an exotic pet at Bud Roy Roemer's residence.

"Sorry, Bravo 12," the dispatcher said. "You were free and you were closest. Try not to shoot Roemer again. Or the leopard. Unless either tries to bite you."

"Copy," Sam said. "What seems to be the problem with the leopard?"

"Other than Bud Roy Roemer having one, you mean?"

"No law against it if he has a proper enclosure. What people are keeping in their backyards around here would surprise you."

"Apparently," the dispatcher said, reading from the complaint, "the leopard ate a standard poodle."

"Not sure that's against the law, either, Dispatch. I hate those things. They always get those stupid haircuts. Like Edward Scissorhands is their groomer. A standard poodle?" Sam asked as he turned his cruiser into the driveway leading to Bud Roy's split-level ranch house. "Why in hell would anyone want one of those things?"

"No accounting for taste, Bravo 12."

"OK, I'm on the scene. Before you say it, just let me assure you my weapon is in its holster and I intend to keep it there...unless I see a standard poodle. All bets are off if I run into one of those."

"Well," the dispatcher said before signing off, "if the 911 call is accurate, you won't."

Sam remained in his car until a Cumberland County Animal Control officer pulled her big panel van in behind his idling cruiser ten minutes later.

"Mornin', Amy," he said as they both exited their vehicles. He and Amy Harris had worked together several times, cornering mad dogs, rabid raccoons, escaped pythons, and once a black bear that had consumed twenty-four Pabst Blue Ribbon beers after chasing off a group of picnickers.

"Well, at least it ain't a big-ass lizard today," Harris said as she leaned in for a brief hug from Sam. "A dog-eatin' leopard is an agreeable change of pace."

"If we got to take it in, you sure the van'll hold it?" Sam asked, pointing at her animal control unit.

"It'll do. I'm gonna trank the damn thing until it's higher than Snoop Dogg kickin' back after a concert. I'm not escorting a mad leopard anywhere."

"Speaking of ornery wildlife," Sam said as he spied the short figure of what he presumed to be the complainant, Alma Spivey, clad in her housecoat and slippers, coming toward them. "This must be the former dog owner."

Alma Spivey appeared to be in her mid-sixties. She didn't walk so much as bat the offending atmosphere aside with short, purposeful strides as she made her way across her yard. The woman seemed propelled by anger, fueled by spite. Short and plump and still dressed for bed, wearing a fine pink hairnet over large blue curlers in her gray hair, Alma pulled her teal-and-yellow quilted housecoat around her to ward off the morning chill as she drew up to Sam and Harris. Gazing at the mishmash of bright pastel colors clinging to her squat frame, Sam thought it looked like Easter had thrown up all over Alma Spivey.

"Good to see you finally made it," she snapped before Sam and Harris could offer introductions. "I see you brought guns. Good. Let's go shoot that horrible animal right now."

"Just hold on, ma'am," Sam said. "Officer Harris and I are not here to shoot anything…or anyone," he added as if to remind himself. "We need to first understand what happened. Then we are going to assess the animal's enclosure and how the owners handle the leopard. When we have the facts, we will determine whether the animal can remain on this property. Shooting is not on the schedule for today if we can avoid it."

"He ate Sprinkles," Alma said. She glared up at him through black-and-tortoiseshell horn-rimmed glasses embossed with silver butter-flies at the end pieces.

"We heard," Sam said. "Now let's go talk to the owner and see if we can't resolve this matter."

Together they walked up to Bud Roy's front porch, where Sam rang the bell. Two minutes later, Bud Roy appeared in his doorway, still clad in the boxers he slept in. Although bleary-eyed at six thirty in the morning, the sight of Deputy Sheriff Sam Aucoin standing on his porch with who Bud Roy mistakenly believed to be an African American female police officer jolted him wide awake. Bud Roy was afraid this visit had to do with his guests at his restaurant. What he couldn't figure out was why his annoying neighbor, Alma Spivey, was with them. *Damn busybody wants to watch them arrest me*, he thought.

Bud Roy looked at Sam. "Well, if it ain't Deputy Aucoin. Have you come to show your new partner how to shoot an unarmed man in the clavicle? Hang on. I'll go get my phone so we can do a proper reenactment."

"No one is getting shot today," Sam said. He was tiring of Bud Roy's references to the shooting but also could not fault him.

Harris took over, introducing herself and explaining the reason for their visit. "Your neighbor here, Ms. Spivey, has lodged a complaint that you have an exotic pet on the premises. She says your failure to confine the animal properly has resulted in the death of her dog."

"We want that vile creature disposed of immediately!" Alma demanded.

"You talkin' about Howard? Or Shelley?" Bud Roy asked. He grinned and absently scratched his gut underneath his tattered Carolina Panthers T-shirt. He was finding his footing now that the reason for the visit was clear.

"What? You have *two* of them now?" Alma asked. "Well, then I want them both shot. Especially the one that ate Sprinkles. That damn cat is a menace and belongs in a zoo. Or back in Africa."

"I guess we're talkin' about Howard and not Shelley. Unlike Howard and the deputy's partner here," Bud Roy said as he nodded toward Harris, "Shelley most definitely is not African American." He smiled, although no one else found that observation amusing. Sam gave a sidelong glance at Harris to see if she was moving to shoot Bud Roy with a tranquilizer dart. He wouldn't have blamed her, but he did not want to be associated, even indirectly, with yet another ballistic assault upon Bud Roy's person.

After a moment, Bud Roy continued. "Well, ma'am, Howard is what ya call a carnivorous type of cat. He don't care for dessert. I doubt he would have any interest in sprinkles, or chocolate, or anything that wasn't actual meat and didn't cost upward of four dollars a pound."

"Sprinkles is a dog, you idiot. My dog. And he's missing. And I know damn well your leopard had something to do with it," Alma said while jabbing a fat index finger into Bud Roy's chest.

"Well, Alma," Bud Roy said, drawing out her name and stressing both syllables, "our leopard lives in a secure state-certified enclosure that more than meets all the requirements for keeping an exotic pet." *Unless he's in our house shredding the furniture and trying to eat one of my ass cheeks*, he silently added.

"That thing is a menace to the neighborhood," Alma said. "And the police are here to shoot it."

"As I told you, we're not shooting anything," Sam said.

Bud Roy looked at Alma. "And as I said, we keep Howard in a secure pen. And my backyard is secure, too. Cost me a goddamn fortune in hard-earned clavicle money to fix it up. Looks like a medium-security prison back there. So I can assure you Howard did not get out, hunt down, and eat your damn dog, Ms. Spivey. If he ate it, then dinner came to Howard last night."

"May we see the enclosure, sir?" Harris asked.

Bud Roy gave a theatrical sigh as he pretended to think about complying with what everyone knew was a demand put forward in the manner of a polite question. "Go wait at the gate on the right side." He pointed to the far end of the house. "I'll come around and let you in after I get some clothes on."

Bud Roy closed the door, and his visitors listened to his footsteps recede as he clomped back to his bedroom. Sam turned to Harris and said, "Thanks for not shooting him with a dart when he made that crack about you and the leopard being African American."

Amy Harris looked up at Sam Aucoin. Her gaze held equal parts bemusement and sadness, and carried the weight of a history and personal experience he could not fathom. "Sam, if I shot every person who said shit like that, I wouldn't have any darts left for the animals."

Shelley DeWeese was awake when Bud Roy Roemer returned to the bedroom. "Who was that?" she asked.

"Alma Spivey; Sam Aucoin, who apparently did not drive out here to shoot me again; and some black woman from animal control." Bud Roy made a sour face as he fished his pants off the floor.

"What does that old bat Spivey want now?" Shelley asked, a worried look on her face.

"She thinks Howard ate her dog, Sprinkles." Bud Roy slipped his jeans on over his boxers, grabbed some socks out of the dresser, and sat down on the foot of the bed to put on his shoes. "I think if you name your dog Sprinkles, you are kinda condemin' it to one of your lower levels on the food chain."

Shelley was quiet, looking down at the sheets. Bud Roy looked at her for a moment, noticing for the first time the concern on her face.

"Uh-oh," Bud Roy said. "Howard ate Sprinkles, didn't he?"

"It was an accident," Shelley said in a small voice, tears welling out of her eyes and snaking down her cheeks. "I was gonna tell you. But we'd had such a good day with him I didn't want to have a setback. You and Howard have bonded."

"Howard bonded with my ass, Shelley. If we was in prison, I would be his bitch. Now, what the hell happened?" Bud Roy asked, rubbing his sore clavicle.

"Well, I was walkin' him back to the pen last night, like I always do after he visits us. And he followed just fine, like he always does."

"Yeah, you carryin' five pounds of beef no doubt had something to do with that. Fuckin' cat eats better than anyone I know. Would it kill him to eat a bucket of Tender Vittles or something instead?"

"Well, you don't want to have a hungry leopard in the house, do you?"

Bud Roy conceded the point. Shelley continued with her story.

"He saw something move, and...damn it...it happened so fast, I only sorta saw it. He must've jumped like fifteen feet." Shelley shook her head in wonder as she recalled the big cat in action. "Whatever he got didn't make a sound. I don't think Sprinkles, if it was Sprinkles, knew what hit it. And then Howard took it in his pen and up in the tree faster than I could believe. I didn't get a good look...honest to God, it was over in less than ten seconds, but whatever he killed was good-size. I was hopin' it was a deer. We get them sometimes. But I guess it coulda been her dog."

"Well, if it was Sprinkles, he had it comin'," Bud Roy said. "Before we got the fence, that damn dog never shit in his own yard. Always came over here. I complained to Old Lady Spivey, but she never stopped it. She musta fed the fuckin' mutt bran and Metamucil."

"I don't even know how he got in," Shelley said. "We got that Howard-proof pen plus the Howard-proof fence."

"Yeah, I know. That damn fencing cost me more than my first seven cars combined," Bud Roy said. He paused a moment, thinking back to last night, and let out a big breath. "Truth be told, I might've left the gate open a crack when I took out the garbage. Sprinkles coulda got in."

Shelley began to sob. "Howard ate a dog, and now they're gonna take him away…"

Bud Roy Roemer sat on the bed next to her and put his arm around his fiancée. He decided at that moment that he loved Shelley DeWeese more than he hated Howard the Leopard. This was, he had to admit, a considerable amount.

"No, they won't. If it was Sprinkles, then he was trespassing. Howard just did what any self-respectin', home-ownin' leopard would do. He ain't goin' nowhere."

"Here's what I surmise happened," Bud Roy Roemer said ten minutes later. He, Sam Aucoin, Amy Harris, and Alma Spivey stared openmouthed at the unconsumed left haunch of a standard poodle nestled in the branch of a sturdy elm tree in Howard's enclosure. "I accidentally left the gate open *ever so slightly* when I took out the trash last night. In the *teeny tiny* amount of time it took me to take my trash to the curb, as all responsible citizens do, Sprinkles must've snuck in to use the toilet, so to speak."

Bud Roy looked at Alma, rendered mute by the macabre evidence of Sprinkles the Dog's demise.

"That dog had a thing about doin' his business in my yard," Bud Roy continued. "Used to do it all the time 'fore we got the fence. Bet he'd been savin' it up for just such an opportunity." He looked at Sam and Harris, surprised that they seemed to believe him. "It just so happened that all of this, uh, coincided with Shelley cleaning out his enclosure." Bud Roy fudged this part, as he did not want to reveal that Howard had been in the house.

"Sprinkles came into the yard at the precise time the gate was open. Howard just reacted to something that looked like game." He gave an eloquent shrug and delivered his summation. "No one's at fault. Sprinkles was doin' what came naturally to him. And Howard did what he's programmed to do."

Alma remained silent, staring at Sprinkles the Dog's leg. Howard the Leopard rested in the elm's shade. He was the picture of feline serenity as he napped, secure in the knowledge that a poodle thigh, aging nicely, awaited him in the tree should he feel peckish later.

Sam looked at Harris. "Amy?"

"Well, this is about the best enclosure money can buy," she said.

"Tell me about it," Bud Roy muttered.

"And the yard fence is more than adequate. The animal seems well cared for, the paperwork is in order, and they appear to be handling it responsibly. Maybe need to refine the procedure for opening the enclosure." Harris looked at the three of them and then addressed Alma. "Ma'am?"

Alma snapped out of her trance and looked at Harris.

"Ma'am, this enclosure is more than adequate for securing this animal. And the owners are proper in their care and handling of the cat. Sprinkles just had terrible timing. There is nothing left to do other than say how sorry I am for your loss."

At those words, Alma Spivey recovered the faculty of speech. "What? Are you insane? Look up in that tree. All that's left of my pet is a single leg. Kinda hard to walk that, don't you think? This thing," she said, pointing a quivering finger at Howard, "ate Sprinkles. And all you can say is 'I'm sorry'?"

"You heard her, Alma," Bud Roy said. "Me and Shelley are responsible leopard owners, and we keep Howard locked up properly."

"Ma'am," Harris said, "they did not break any laws. Sprinkles was in the wrong place at the wrong time. You should've kept him leashed or in a fenced yard."

"So it's my fault?" Alma screeched, eyes wide behind her horn-rimmed glasses.

"Yes," Bud Roy said at the same time Amy Harris said, "No."

"Bud Roy..." Sam said.

"Well, damn it, it is," Bud Roy said, rising to the big cat's defense. "All Howard did was stand his ground like any good Second Amendment-loving American leopard should. Sprinkles picked the wrong goddamn yard to lay some cable." He had grown tired of his neighbor complaining about what he was doing on his property and resentful of these government agents—as he thought of them—presuming to pass judgment on whether he had exercised his right to leopard ownership responsibly. Howard the Leopard would get the best defense that Bud Roy Roemer could muster.

"I want my Sprinkles back!" Alma yelled at him.

"Fine," he said, glaring back at her. "Give Howard another hour, and I'll bring Sprinkles home in a bucket."

"You horrible man!" Alma looked ready to strike Bud Roy.

"Officer Harris, why don't you take Ms. Spivey home while I talk to Bud Roy?" Sam suggested.

"You better do what this fellow says, Alma," Bud Roy said. "At your age, a shattered clavicle will kill you just as fast as a busted hip."

Harris put her arm around Alma and steered her back home, telling her that once she had finished grieving for Sprinkles the animal shelter had plenty of loving dogs in need of a good home.

Sam looked at Bud Roy. "You coulda been more understanding. Her dog met a rather gruesome end. I'm sure she's in shock."

"You're right," Bud Roy said. "Normally, she's not this pleasant."

Sam looked over at Howard the Leopard and then back at Bud Roy. "That's a whole lotta cat."

"More leopard than I need, but not as much as Shelley wants."

Sam shifted gears. "I've been meanin' to ask, what's going on at your old restaurant? I see Gage's Bronco parked outside there more often than not."

Bud Roy gave him the answer he had been working on since their encounter a few days ago during breakfast at Cracker Barrel. "I still own the place, and Gage is doin' some work for me. Fixin' it up. Maybe I'll sell it, or maybe I'll give it another go. Still decidin'. Anyway, Gage is out of a job at the moment and needs the money."

"You're not goin' to reopen Knockers, are you?"

"Nah. At least, not under that name. Those people at Jubblies got no sense of humor at all," Bud Roy said. "Good ribs and wings, though."

"Fair enough." Sam took a big breath, exhaled, and adjusted his gun belt. "You know, I ran into Gage at the CVS. He was buying a bunch of women's products. Is he seeing anyone?"

"You lookin' to ask him out?" Bud Roy replied, arching an eyebrow. "Deputy, if you want to know who Gage is seeing, ask Gage."

As soon as the words were out of his mouth, Bud Roy regretted them. He figured Sam would do just that. Then Gage's criminal Tourette's would kick in, and Gage would say he was wooing Monica Bell back at Knockers and the Unacrapper was his wingman.

Bud Roy pointed to Howard with his chin. "Are we OK about the cat? Shelley's worried we're gonna lose him."

"You're fine. It wasn't your fault. Anyone can see you've tried to give Howard a nice home."

"Indeed we have, Deputy. Shelley will spend every dime we have to make sure of that."

CHAPTER SIXTEEN

"Thank God I could talk you out of leftover wings for breakfast," Monica Bell said as she bit into an Egg McMuffin. "But if you don't get me some veggies soon, you'll kill me even if you don't mean to."

"You oughta be happy we're feedin' you at all," Jacob Kelley said.

"What's this 'we' stuff?" Monica asked before taking a welcome sip of McDonald's coffee. "Seems to me Gage here is doing all the work and spending all the money."

"Well, I can't exactly go out and show my face around town, now can I?"

"Maybe you shoulda thought about that before you tried to blow up the IRS building with your, uh, homemade bombs," Monica said.

"I was makin' a political statement."

"Spare me the patriotic speech, Crapper."

"I'm tellin' you for the last time, my name is Jacob," he said. "And I don't 'preciate you suggesting to Gage here that I'm freeloadin'. Gage knows I'm good for it."

"I think your new nickname fits you. Besides, what do inmates make in prison? How many license plates do you think you'll need to make to pay Gage back for all those Jubblies hot wings you put down every night?"

"You better watch your mouth, lady," Jacob said. "I don't let anyone talk to me like that."

Gage Randolph watched them spar. He was tiring of Jacob and hoped he would move on. Perhaps Monica could push him into doing so. She excelled at pissing off people.

"Crapper," Monica said, "you let everybody talk to you like that. That's why you're angry, why you think the world owes you, and that's why you're a racist and a misogynist. It's simple." She continued over Jacob's attempted reply. "Deep down, you know you're a loser. I knew it the night I kicked you in the nose. I'd call you a pussy, but that's a fantastic thing, which you might learn one day. Although you'll have to pay for it."

Monica stared straight at Jacob until he looked away. "You better shut her up," he said to Gage.

"Don't think I could even if I wanted to," Gage replied. "Maybe it's time for you to be headin' wherever you need to get to next. You can't stay here forever. Have you figgered out your next move?"

"I'm workin' on it, but the timing ain't right," Jacob said. "But I'll be leaving soon enough. In the meantime, keep her out of my face."

He got up from the bar and made his way back to the office, where he monitored the manhunt on the computer and fumed over the Unacrapper label. Even *The New York Times* was using the name.

"He's a real charmer, don't you think?" Monica asked after Jacob sulked his way to the back room.

"He's got his reasons, I suspect, for bein' surly," Gage said. "It's hard to get to a certain point in life and realize you'll never be more than you are. If you ain't much to begin with, it can beat a man down."

Monica looked at Gage for a moment. "You know, despite being the world's most inept kidnapper, you can be insightful."

"Oh, I don't know. Maybe my own disappointments give me a window into what he's feelin'. I've had my own dreams that I can quite seem to reach. It's frustrating."

"And what, besides staying one step ahead of the law, is your dream?"

Gage looked at the ceiling for a moment before deciding to trust his captive with such sensitive information. "I've always wanted to run my own restaurant."

Monica's face registered her surprise. "Coming from a man who seems to be Jubblies' best customer, this is a revelation."

Gage laughed. "Truth is, Jubblies ain't my favorite. I could certainly improve their ribs. I really wanted to be Bud Roy's cook here and turn this place into a genuine eatery, but he had his heart set on it being what it was." Monica looked around the seedy, empty room. "He should've listened to you. I hope your dream will come true someday. And thank you for giving me a bit of insight into the Crapper. People are never only one thing."

"Oh, I don't know," Gage said, smiling, "sometimes people are just assholes."

Monica laughed and looked at him with genuine warmth. "And sometimes a man listens to the better angels of his nature."

Gage raised his paper cup of coffee in her direction. "That may be the nicest thing you've ever said to me."

Monica returned the coffee cup salute. "Don't let it go to your head. Or any other part of you."

"Morning, Deputy. You want your usual? A large coffee and two chocolate glazed with sprinkles?" the Krispy Kreme clerk asked Sam Aucoin.

He blanched. The all-too-recent image of Howard the Leopard's midnight snack had put him off his preferred doughnut. *Might be some time before I can go back to those*, he thought.

"You know what? Let's mix it up and make it a large coffee and four original glazed, please," he told the clerk.

Sam took his haul to a window table, along with the morning paper. He had finished his shift and changed into civilian clothes but wasn't ready to go home. Despite the early hour, Rebecca was already at work, preparing for another day with her third-grade class. Sam didn't want to sit around an empty house with a jumble of thoughts running through his mind.

He took a bite of doughnut, happy that Sprinkles the Dog's grisly end had not put him off doughnuts entirely. But a breakfast like this would mean an extra hour in the gym. Just as well. He had a lot on his mind. Scarfing down doughnuts and pumping iron were his usual methods for working out a problem. He took another bite, followed it with a sip of coffee, and looked down at his copy of *The Fayetteville Observer*. SEARCH FOR MONICA BELL CONTINUES ran the headline.

Sam had seen too many missing persons cases to think after so many days this one was going to end well. Still, it was strange someone this famous could just vanish. He gazed for a moment at the headshot of Monica that accompanied the article, a close-up of her perfect features and large brown eyes framed by medium-length brown hair.

Aucoin thought of Gage Randolph at the CVS buying women's makeup and other items. He thought of Gage's SUV parked outside of Bud Roy Roemer's old restaurant.

Could he have kidnapped Monica Bell? Could he be holding her captive at Knockers? He laughed out loud. *Christ, they'd send me to the shrink if I went to command with that theory.*

Sam had another bite of doughnut and thought about it some more. He concluded, as he went back to his paper, that for all of his faults, Gage Randolph was a decent, if somewhat misguided, man. He just didn't seem like a kidnapper. Or, to be more accurate, Gage did not seem like a *successful* kidnapper.

Gage is acting funny and is definitely up to something...but not kidnapping.

Sam reached for another doughnut and returned to his paper. An article next to the one about Monica caught his eye. THE HUNT IS ON FOR STONEWALL JACKSON'S ARM, the headline read. Aucoin scanned the article. *Now, that sounds like Gage Randolph,* he thought. What struck him was that the arm was stolen the same night that Monica had disappeared.

Gage is up to something…

Knowing that he was acting on nothing more than the wisp of a suggestion of the possibility of a suspicion, he pulled out his iPhone. He opened his map app and entered Locust Grove, Virginia, until recently the resting place of Stonewall's arm. While it was not a direct route back to Fayetteville, Sam noted the road on which Monica was last seen was a route home from Locust Grove. If you wanted to go the long way. Maybe to avoid the law if you were feeling guilty about something.

More out of a desire to squelch what he considered an unformed and ill-considered hunch rather than to buttress it, he called up an acquaintance in the Virginia State Police and asked what they had discovered at the scene of Monica Bell's disappearance. Forty-five minutes and three phone calls later, Sam Aucoin left the restaurant deep in thought. Two doughnuts remained untouched at his table.

"Damn it, Bud Roy," Linus McTane said three hours later, "I'm still thinking about what to do. 'Deep' does not begin to describe the exquisite level of crapola you boys are in. The fix for this isn't simple, and every solution I come up with seems to involve committing several additional felonies. Some of them quite serious."

"Things are progressin' a tad faster than we want 'em to, Linus," Bud Roy Roemer said as he slouched in one of two client chairs on the far side of McTane's expansive oak desk. A midmorning sunbeam negotiated its way through the half-open curtains on the window to Bud Roy's left and splashed onto the dark-blue rug in the middle of McTane's office.

Gage Randolph, who had found a home in the other chair, spoke up. "Deputy Aucoin, the one who shot Bud Roy here in the clavicle—"

"We all know who Sam Aucoin is," McTane interjected. He heaved a seismic sigh. "You know, I'll bet I went the first fifty years of my life never once saying or hearing the word *clavicle*. Now," he spread his arms before dropping them to the desk, "not a goddamn day goes by where I don't hear it or say it multiple times. For Pete's sake, just the other day, I walked into a restaurant where a guy was playing a clavichord." McTane shook his head in disbelief. "In Fayetteville, North Carolina. A clavichord."

Gage and Bud Roy looked at McTane with puzzled expressions.

"You know—one of them itty-bitty European keyboards. Kinda sounds like a piano on helium. It lacks the balls to be a real piano, I guess. Sorta like the way a Yorkie ain't a real dog."

Gage and Bud Roy remained nonplussed. It was familiar territory for them.

"I guess what I'm sayin'," McTane said while making a fluttery gesture with his hands to show frustration, "is I can't escape the word *clavicle* or even words that remind me of *clavicle*. Such as the aforementioned clavichord."

Gage waited a beat to make sure McTane was finished. "Well, Aucoin saw me shoppin' for wimmin's things at the CVS. Now he's askin' 'round about whether I got a girlfriend. We're afraid he's gonna start snoopin' with more...uh...earnestness."

"I suppose you actually having a lady friend, so we can give Aucoin a simple and truthful explanation, is too much to hope for," McTane said.

"I'm workin' on it," Gage replied.

"On tryin' to get a girlfriend?" McTane asked.

"He's wooin' Monica Bell," Bud Roy said.

"The one ya'll got chained to a stripper pole at Knockers?"

"As opposed to the women we got chained to stripper poles elsewhere?" Bud Roy asked.

"With you two, I've learned to request specificity."

"He's tryin' to give her Helsinki syndrome," Bud Roy said. "It's a *Die Hard* thing."

"Of course," McTane said, unfazed. "Well, I'm more of a *Godfather* man myself. But we should keep the Corleone family approach as a last resort. Then again, John McClane's method of problem-solving was rather direct."

"Damn right," Gage said.

The conversation lulled as McTane's secretary brought in three Cokes and three glasses of ice on a tray. The glasses had a twist of lemon in them. Bud Roy and Gage looked at the lemon with suspicion. They were purists.

After the secretary left the room, McTane decanted his Coke and asked, "How is the relationship developing, Gage?" He watched the Coke settle in the glass. "You kidnapping the object of your affections and chaining her to a stripper pole in a bankrupt restaurant has slowed your, uh, wooing some, I would imagine."

"Well, I don't think she hates me," Gage assessed. He set his lemon delicately to the side and sipped his soda.

"Yeah, that comes after you're married," said McTane, who was on his third wife.

"I don't think she wants to put me in jail. But she don't like the Unacrapper. He definitely complicates things. That's why we need to get him on his way." Gage knocked back a quarter-glass of the Coke. "But he feels kinda safe at Knockers. I don't think he wants to leave."

"I hear ya," McTane said. "Getting a young terrorist to leave the lair and take his first tentative steps out into the big, scary world can be a challenge. I'm sure you and the missus are up to it, though."

The three sat quietly, sipping Cokes and watching dust motes dance in the sunbeam. Bud Roy broke the silence. "Linus, ya got any ideas that aren't all smart-ass and don't involve us surrendering to the local authorities? Like I said, things are movin' along."

McTane leaned back in his desk chair. Finally, he said, "Boys, I have spent some considerable time pondering our present vexation. I have concluded your best hope lies with Zacharias Townsend and getting him, Monica Bell, and the Unacrapper all in the same room. Only a rich SOB with no scruples has the heft to fix your problems." He leaned forward and smiled. "Gage, it all depends on your upcoming, uh, illegal arm transfer. Lemme tell ya what I'm thinkin'."

CHAPTER SEVENTEEN

Sam Aucoin swung his new Honda Pilot into the parking lot of Marse Robert's. The restaurant occupied a low-slung brick building with an incongruous portico glommed on to the entrance to evoke—unsuccessfully, he assessed—Robert E. Lee's house in Arlington, Virginia. Sam was there because of Gage Randolph's and Bud Roy Roemer's membership in South of the Line, which had made Marse Robert's its unofficial headquarters.

Sam braced himself before going in. Like his wife, he had moved southeast for college, she from California and he from New Mexico. Both Aucoins had grown to like North Carolina, and they thought of it as home. But he didn't like what he termed the *knuckle draggers* in the state who didn't know Strom Thurmond was dead. That Jesse Helms was dead. They grudgingly acknowledged that Jim Crow was dead, but seemed eager to reanimate the corpse. Sam believed most of North Carolina was ready to move on. But not everyone. And certainly not those who had found a home in SOL.

After talking to the Virginia State Police, Sam had called his friend Hollis Turnbull, a successful financial planner and investment advisor as well as an enthusiastic Civil War reenactor. "You wanna know about SOL?" Turnbull had asked. "Meet me for lunch at Marse Robert's. You gotta see it to understand it."

I see it, Sam thought as he took in the faux antebellum portico on the otherwise unremarkable rectangular building with a gravel parking lot in front. *But I'll never understand it.*

A hostess decked out in what he presumed was a period costume greeted Sam in the lobby. He was thankful she was not fanning herself and beginning her sentences with, "I do declare..." She directed him to Hollis Turnbull, who occupied a space at the long, L-shaped oak bar in the main dining room. A heavyset man wearing an expensive gray suit and a powder-blue power tie, Turnbull had his polished black ECCO dress shoes hooked on the brass footrail for balance. He had started without Sam and was several rounds into a liquid lunch.

"Sam, my boy," Turnbull said, greeting him with a wave and a smile. His face had a healthy, happy flush. "Have a seat. What's your pleasure?"

"I'll have what he's having," Sam told the bartender as he slapped the well-lubricated Turnbull on the shoulder. "I just won't be having as much."

"A double of Colonel E.H. Taylor single barrel coming up," the bartender said.

"Christ," Sam said. "Sounds like I'll need to work overtime to afford that. Whatever happened to Old Grand-Dad?"

Turnbull smiled. "You and I both know you can afford it," he said. "Besides, I wouldn't wash my boots in Old Grand-Dad."

"Too bad," Sam said as the bartender delivered his glass. "Old Grand-Dad is right for the job." He gave Turnbull a long look, and the cop peered through. "You got a ride home, Hollis?"

Turnbull smiled. "Uber. Best thing for the three-martini lunch since olives." He shifted his ample bulk on his stool to give himself a three-quarter view of Sam. His florid face still showed plenty of Scottish ancestry, as did his sandy hair and blue eyes. "So, what's up?"

"Tell me about SOL," Sam said. "What kind of people belong to the group? What do they do? How serious are they about the Civil War? And, I guess, *why* are they serious about the Civil War?"

Turnbull swirled some of his whiskey in his tumbler, taking in the aroma. "Well," he said, "first you need to know I wouldn't join SOL if you put a gun to my head. Also, I think you need to understand that the Civil War attracts all kinds of people. Reenacting groups are a genuine economic melting pot. Wealthy, intellectual, professional-class snobs, such as yours truly," Turnbull said, pushing his index finger a knuckle deep into his gut. "You know: doctors, lawyers, bankers. But there are just as many blue-collar types." He took in a deep breath and then let it out. "The Civil War bug," he said, "afflicts all kinds for a variety of reasons."

"So you all are passionate?" Sam asked.

Turnbull laughed. "Passion would be a, one might say, prerequisite for spending money a lot of 'em don't have on wool sack coats and hobnailed shoes—just to look the part—and then traveling hundreds of miles to walk about in that getup in the summer heat to try and connect with the past." He shook his head as he thought about his hobby. "And don't get me started on weaponry. Christ, that will really set you back. Yep, *passionate* is a good word."

"Passionate enough," Sam asked, "to dig up Stonewall Jackson's arm?"

Turnbull ruminated as he drained the remaining whiskey from his glass and signaled the bartender for another double with a water back. Sam had known him long enough to understand Turnbull did not rush his conversation. He was deliberate in everything he did. Sam desired this quality in an investment advisor, accepted it in a golfing partner, and tolerated it when pumping the man for information. He enjoyed his own whiskey and let the silence run its course.

"I read about that," Turnbull said at last. "No true reenactor would desecrate a grave, northern or southern, any more than you would dig up Washington's corpse."

"You don't seem to lump SOL members in with most reenactors," Sam noted.

"No, I don't. But you know what another word to describe a lot of Civil War aficionados, especially those fixated on the Confederate experience, would be?"

Sam shook his head.

"*Trivial,*" Turnbull said, nodding as the bartender placed his order in front of him. "They fixate on trivia. Check out the websites. Heated debates on the proper loads for muskets, the correct weave and cloth for shirts and pants during a given year in the war, endless disquisitions about the food they ate, what the buttons on their uniforms looked like." He took a handful of nuts from a bowl on the bar. "They hide from the truth in a forest of trivia."

"So these guys know a lot about the, uh, minutiae of the war. What's that have to do with Stonewall's arm?"

Turnbull laughed. "To say they know a lot is an understatement." He toasted Aucoin with his new round and resumed. "Why, I've seen guys who didn't graduate high school correct professional historians, people who've spent their entire career studying the Civil War, on some technical point about weaponry or a minor issue about this brigade or that. And you know something? The amateurs were right. And they used their grasp of the unimportant to distract from the real discussions about the war. It's as if you told a weatherman that, because he was off by a degree of temperature, the entire forecast of 'partly sunny' was incorrect."

"It might be this hundred-proof bourbon," Sam said, "but I don't follow."

Turnbull placed his hand on the bar. It was clear he had given this topic some thought. "These guys know everything there is to know about everything that doesn't really matter. Interesting, yes. But not important. Trivial. And mastering trivia is what amateurs do when they don't want to tackle the tough questions. The ones that require thought, years of study, and, uh, intellectual rigor."

"They are buffs," Sam said. "Not interested in what the war meant or still means?"

Turnbull slapped the bar. "The SOBs in the SOL fascinate me. They also scare the hell out of me. So I spend time here tryin' to understand 'em. Why, entire weeks can go by with SOL members discussing the war, and not once will they utter the word *slavery*. It's like somebody trying to understand the Middle East and not using the words *oil* or *Islam*."

"They probably don't get a lot of African American families in here to lend their perspective to the discussion," Sam observed as he scanned the sparsely populated dining area.

Turnbull shook his head. "Ya think? Name like Marse Robert's?"

"Kinda like holding a Holocaust discussion group at Hitler's Bar and Grill. You're going to limit participation to a certain point of view."

"Believe it or not," Turnbull said with a wry smile, "a lot of African Americans are not big fans of Robert E. Lee. No matter how nice Lost Causers say he was to his slaves."

"And you a southerner," Sam said.

"Owning another human being takes 'nice' right out of the equation, don't you think?" Turnbull shook his head. "Don't get me wrong. I love reenacting. And I love the Civil War. I find it all fascinating, even the, what did you call it? The minutiae? Hell, on a certain level, it's important."

"How do you figure?"

"If you are asking why General So and So didn't do *X*, the answer may lie in understanding how those boys lived day to day. Maybe *X* was beyond their means." Turnbull shrugged, popped a few more nuts from the bowl on the bar into his mouth, and took a sip of whiskey before continuing. "SOL strongly leans pro-South, neo-Confederate, and even neo-Nazi. Very different from those of us who believe that reenacting provides, I guess, a tactile connection to the subject matter."

"So you think the SOL crowd is too wrapped up in symbols and the Lost Cause bullshit?"

"What I think," Turnbull said, "is these SOL yahoos goin' out there dressed in butternut and shootin' blanks at one another has more to do with how pissed off they are that they got a hundred bucks to their name and no prospects. They hate the blacks. They hate the feminists. They hate the liberals. They hate their place in the America they have and want to bring back the America their great-great-grandpappy lost." Turnbull turned his glass on the bar as he considered Sam's initial question. "Now someone who would dig up Stonewall's arm? That is a man with a very unhealthy reverence for a past best left dead and buried."

Sam sipped his whiskey. Turnbull added a splash of water to his.

"OK. Let me be more specific," Sam said. "Would Gage Randolph steal Jackson's arm?"

Turnbull shrugged. "Gage is being buffeted by forces he doesn't comprehend."

"Him and about three hundred million other Americans. Would SOL be a good fit?"

"I don't know. Gage is not an asshole. He's definitely not like those slack-jawed mouth breathers walking around with the fucking Nazi flags. I've seen him get up and leave when the talk turns ugly. He doesn't make a show of it. And he doesn't try'n stop it. He just doesn't seem to want to be around it."

"Not being evil is not the same as being good," Sam said.

Turnbull nodded, "So I've been told." He paused to tie his impressions together. "Gage strikes me as a decent man at a loss for decent friends. He's searching for someplace to belong, like so many of us are from time to time. It's like he's trying on a suit and thought he found one he liked. But the more he looks at himself in the mirror, the less he likes what he sees. I think Gage Randolph is reaching the conclusion that gray just isn't his color."

"So he wouldn't have reason to do it," Sam ventured.

"Someone else would have to supply the reason," Turnbull said.

"Fair enough. How about Bud Roy Roemer? Could he be that some-one else?"

Turnbull smiled. "You got a history with him, don't you?"

"I shot him in the left clavicle."

129

"The left clavicle? Just what the hell were you aiming at?"

Sam grinned at the *True Grit* reference. "The left clavicle."

Turnbull laughed and then turned serious again. "Bud Roy is racist. He's got no problem looking in the mirror and liking what he sees. He was bred for it. His daddy was in the Klan. Being an asshole is a preexisting condition for Bud Roy. But don't make the mistake of thinkin' he's stupid. We like to think that about racists. It's comforting and convenient. But it isn't always true." He took another sip from his glass and continued. "Bud Roy is not at all stupid. Even has some college. Had to quit when his daddy drank the tuition money. Sorta been downhill for Bud Roy ever since. It's like there just wasn't enough of him to get off the canvas one more time. He needed to blame someone for his lot in life, and his daddy's lessons in that regard were just the thing."

Sam raised an eyebrow. "Just because the parent is a fuck-up doesn't mean the kid has to follow suit. My dad couldn't keep it in his pants. But I would never step out on Becks."

Turnbull smiled and slapped the top of the bar with a thick hand. "Nor should you. She's more than you deserve or should expect to have."

Sam smiled back. "True enough. So Bud Roy's a racist asshat," he said, getting the conversation back on track.

Turnbull took a sip of whiskey. "He's not strong enough to be anything else. He finds it easier—and more fun—I should add, to go along with what his daddy taught him. You know how people say racists aren't born, they're made? I don't think that's true. Saying something's 'made' implies completion. Racists aren't complete. Bud Roy is, for lack of a better phrase, an unfinished human. And he's too lazy and too angry to take on the tough work required to finish the job."

Sam looked at Turnbull. "I dunno. Maybe the job's never finished. Most of us spend all our energy trying not to fuck up the same way twice. Leaves us open to fucking up in new and spectacular ways we never saw coming."

He shook his head. "We keep driving forward with our eyes locked on the accident in the rearview mirror."

"Tell me about it," Turnbull said. "Shit, I got more to overcome than most. Jesus, I dress up as a Confederate general for a hobby. To quote Patton, 'I love it. God help me, I do love it so.'"

"I'm pretty sure you quoted George C. Scott. But I see your point. I doubt Bud Roy is that self-aware."

"He isn't. But his assholery is what you might call latent. His more objectionable traits are activated, so to speak, by a proximity fuse."

"A lazy racist?"

"Would you prefer him to be an energetic one?"

"Fair point."

Turnbull slapped the top of the bar again, signaling that the conversation had run its course. "Samuel, Colonel E.H. Taylor and his merry band have breached the kidneys and are storming the bladder. I gotta go piss. But I'll tell ya what: you wanna know more about these boys and what makes them tick, drive up to Bentonville this weekend. SOL is taking part in a reenactment of the Battle of Bentonville. I'll be there leading my group and will introduce ya around. You can see Gage Randolph fall in the re-creation of Mower's Charge."

Sam looked at Turnbull. "Gage is gonna pretend to die?"

Turnbull slid off the barstool with practiced ease and steadied himself on the bar's brass rail as if being introduced to the basic laws of physics. "Gage always dies. Every battle. Even if the Confederates win. He says it's his way of honoring those who fell. And I'll tell ya something else," he said over his shoulder as he moved in the general direction of the men's room, "Gage Randolph is the best damn bloater I've ever seen."

CHAPTER EIGHTEEN

"Don't feed him hot wings," Gage Randolph told Monica Bell. "They give him gas."

"You talking about the Unacrapper or Rebel?" she asked.

"Jacob," Jacob Kelley said. "And shut up."

Gage said, "Last time you fed Rebel wings, I had to walk him four times that night. It was like I was livin' with my grandpa again."

"Well, serves you right for eating at Jubblies three times a day," Monica said as she fended off another advance from Rebel the Hound.

"Food's passable," Gage said mildly.

"It's not just the food, and while it doesn't suck, it is hardly world-class," Monica said. "It's what the damn place represents. It's demeaning to women."

Gage remained silent. He hadn't given either a critique or a defense of Jubblies much thought. He didn't think now was a good time to peel back that onion.

But Jacob was game. "Maybe it's a celebration of women. Maybe the men who go there love and respect women."

"Get real," Monica said. "The place is called *Jubblies*, not *Women*. It's about tits. It objectifies women. Hell, not even that. The place fixates on a particular body part. What Jubblies does *not* do," she said while glaring at Jacob, "is celebrate women." She glanced over at Gage. "At least when your pal Bud Roy named *this* place, he had the courage of his convictions."

"Well, Bud Roy, now, he's been arrested a few times. But I don't think he's ever been convicted," Gage said.

"What I meant was…"

Gage laughed. "I know what you meant. I just like pullin' your chain."

Jacob chimed back in. "Don't see why that threatens you. You would look damn good in a Jubblies outfit. Most feminazis wouldn't."

Gage may not have read any Simone de Beauvoir, but he knew a mistake when he heard one. He leaned forward on the table, chin in his hands, his face open and interested, his eyes unblinking, awaiting Jacob's imminent beatdown.

Monica licked hot sauce off her fingers before answering. She had to admit the sauce wasn't bad.

"Crapper, you've just made my point. But you're too stupid to realize it. Rather than explain it to you, lemme ask you this: how would you feel if your girlfriend—were she real and not of the inflatable variety—told you she was going to eat lunch at a place called Pecs and Schlongs? Would you be OK with that? Would you want her guzzling margaritas while ogling her waiter, a shirtless bodybuilder wearing crotchless chaps and sporting a foot-long dong?"

"I'd be fine with it," Jacob said. He smiled triumphantly. "Because I'd be working there, too."

Monica snorted. "I said the place was called Pecs and Schlongs, not Man Boobs and Nubbins."

Jacob flushed red. "Don't matter. The foot-long schlong is a mythical creature anyway, like unicorns and, uh, ocelots."

Monica laughed, then drove the knife in deep with a twist. "Dream on. Just because one's not attached to you doesn't mean big dicks aren't out there."

Gage winced as he witnessed Jacob's verbal castration. Monica reveled in Jacob's discomfort for a few long seconds as she ate some coleslaw. *Closest thing to vegetables I've had in almost a week, and it's probably got more calories than an apple pie*, she thought. She then continued her vivisection of Jacob before he could regroup.

"The difference between me and you, besides a shitload of IQ points and a bank balance that requires the use of commas, is I believe what the body part is attached to is far more important than the body part itself. Best sex I ever had was with the entire man, not just his wang." She let them process that observation and then said, "Now, you, Crapper—all you care about are the tits. Makes you a sexist asshole and makes you destined to spend life alone. Or it would if you weren't headed to prison. Either way, enjoy your Jubblies, both the food and the tatas. You may not see their likes again."

The Unacrapper stabbed at his food but wisely remained silent.

Despite his reluctance to swim in such perilous waters, Gage ventured a mild criticism. "Well, what about them Chippendales guys and the wimmin throwin' their underwear while the men grind away on some stage. How's that different?"

Monica nodded her approval. "Not bad, Gage. One difference is that the women don't go to work the next day and grab the crotch of their male secretary. They don't go to lunch and talk about men like they were a collection of body parts, and even if they did, they don't act on it. One difference, besides maturity, is power."

Jacob said, "Spare me, Ms. Millionaire. You think we got power?"

Monica looked at him for a long moment. "You think I do? There aren't enough hours in the day to tell you about what I go through just to *get* to work, not to mention what happens when I'm there. Besides, just who the hell do you think is chained to a goddamn stripper pole at the moment?"

Rebel the Hound made another play for one of the hot wings. Monica was too quick for him. "Rebel seems to think it's time to talk about something else." She stood up, gave the dog a pat on the head to ease his disappointment, and asked, "We got anything stronger than Coca-Cola?"

"Jim Beam's behind the bar. I'll get it. Your chain don't go that far," Gage said. He looked at Jacob moping at the table. "You wanna snort, too?"

"Yeah, I'll have one."

Gage brought the half-full bottle and three glasses back to the table and poured a round of generous servings.

"I'm gonna have to leave you two alone tomorrow," he announced. "Me and Rebel are goin' to reenact the Battle of Bentonville. I'm gonna fall beatin' back Mower's Charge."

Jacob made a sour face and drank some bourbon. He would have been going to Bentonville, too, if every law enforcement agency in the United States hadn't been searching for him. He looked forward to reenacting almost as much as he looked forward to sex. Reenacting, at least, occurred with some measure of frequency. "Think anyone would notice if I showed up?" Jacob asked.

"You're the Unacrapper," Gage said. "Everyone will notice if you show up. SOL is already taking a lot of heat because you were a member. The last thing we need is for you to appear in our ranks at Bentonville like it was part of your social calendar."

"Whaddya mean 'were a member'?" Jacob asked. "Have they kicked me out?"

"Well, not yet," Gage said. "But there is plenty of pressure bein' put on the leadership to renounce you."

"They're cowards if they do," Jacob said. "The Confederacy didn't run away from the boys that fired on Fort Sumter. They embraced 'em for a job well done."

"The boys that fired on Fort Sumter didn't fling their feces at the Union forces like a bunch of enraged baboons," Monica said. "Maybe the SOL folks don't mind what you did; they just mind how you did it. You would know better than me, Crapper, but I assume even racist morons have criteria for acceptable behavior. Something like 'Don't shit where you hate.' Am I right?"

Gage redirected the conversation before Jacob could respond. "Anyway, I'll need you two to behave and get along." His gaze bore into Jacob. "And I expect everything and everyone to be the same when I get back."

Jacob Kelley shrugged and drained the last of his glass. "I'm gonna catch *The Firebell* and let you and the smart-ass liberal ballbuster here yack it up." He collected the laptop and moved off toward his quarters in the office in back of the bar.

"Why *Die Hard*, Gage?" Monica Bell asked when Jacob Kelley had gone.

"Huh?"

"You were talking about *Die Hard* and Helsinki syndrome earlier. Why did you draw on that movie for your master plan to manage this accidental kidnapping?"

Gage Randolph smiled. Monica's use of the word *accidental* implied progress. "Me and John McClane. Wrong goddamn place at the wrong goddamn time. 'Sides," he said as he added more bourbon to each glass, "I like movies. I watch a lot of them."

Monica said nothing. She just gave him her full attention.

Gage continued. "Thing about a well-done movie, no matter what kind of day you've had, it can transport you somewhere else for a couple of hours. It's, uh, rejuvenating, I guess."

"You like to escape for a while, right?"

"Well, sure. I don't know if you've ever been poor, but it can grind on you, just wear you down. If you can forget you're poor for even a little while, pretend you're somewhere else or someone else, or just watch someone else live a life you can't imagine..." Gage shrugged. "I guess someone in your income bracket would say it's like goin' to a spa."

"So let me guess: tomorrow you're gonna dress up and play soldier. Be someone else." Monica reached down to scratch her ankle where the manacle was chafing her.

"It ain't dress-up," Gage said. "We're serious about it. We study everything from uniforms to how they made camp, and we even cook traditional food. Because of us, people understand what the soldiers went through."

Monica shook her head. "It's edutainment, Gage, not history. It doesn't ask you to think, and it doesn't challenge you. No one who goes to watch these things learns anything about the Civil War other than it was hot and loud and they served funnel cakes and beer down by the parking lot after the battle."

"This from a cable TV and talk radio host. Really?"

"Touché." Monica sipped some bourbon. "You know, I used to be a professor. But I valued education more than either my university or my students did. At least with my current career, I don't have to pretend."

"I watch you from time to time. Although if I'm tellin' the truth, it's more because you're really hot. But sometimes I learned something. Didn't agree much." Gage stretched and then said, "But it wasn't a waste of time."

"The contradiction of TV in America: you must look a certain way to get a job, and that prevents people from taking you seriously when you do."

Gage snorted his contempt. "Yeah, I'm having a hard time identifyin' with your, uh, predicament there, Monica. You hate being good-looking, rich, and on TV?"

"No, I like all of those things. What I hate is not mattering. If I could do it over, I would try to find another university and teach again. I guess I was happiest when I was good-looking, upper-middle class, and standing in a classroom."

Gage looked around the empty bar. It was a place he had become too familiar with. "Ain't none of us matter all that much, I guess. Hell, one reason I reenact is that people watch us, ask me questions, and treat me like I'm somethin' rather than nothin'."

"And you're going to be a Confederate?" Monica asked.

"Nothing wrong with that," Gage said.

"You mean other than the treason and slavery thing?" Monica wanted to stress test the Helsinki syndrome bond she and Gage were developing.

"The war was about states' rights, not slavery," Gage replied. "Those men were fightin' for their homes and the right to live as they saw fit. I'm tryin' to honor that."

"Gage, you are—despite kidnapping me, chaining me to a stripper pole, and force-feeding me Jubblies three times a day—a good man. But what you just said is flat-out wrong. The war was about slavery."

"Most southerners didn't even own slaves. So how could it be about that?"

"Because most southerners wanted to. If you put their aspirations in a speech, it would be called the 'I Have a Really Fucked-Up Evil Dream' speech."

"No way." Gage knocked back a slug of bourbon. "They were fighting government overreach. Just like we are today. They believed in that enough to die for it." He reached for the bottle in the middle of the table and poured two more shots.

"They believed in their right to own human beings enough to kill for it," Monica said. "We've been working out so-called states' rights issues since the country began. And we still are. But slavery? That called for more than agreeing to disagree."

"You East Coast elites livin' in your bubble don't even know what you're talkin' about. How could you possibly unnerstand who we are and what we're facing?"

Monica rolled her eyes. "First, whatever grievance you think you have today is not remedied by erasing the sins of yesterday. And second, give me a break. I live in New York City. I have to navigate about a dozen cultures and languages each day as soon as I set foot on the street. New York is many things. One thing it is not, however, is a bubble."

Monica took another sip and moved to friendlier territory. Their relationship seemed legitimate. She had something to work with. She smiled her best smile at Gage and said, "Christ, I once caught a cab on the Upper West Side driven by a guy who, I swear, spoke in clicks. You know, that language in Africa..."

"Xhosa," Gage said.

Monica looked at him, too stunned to finish her story. "How the hell do you know that?"

"Movies. The bushmen spoke something like it in *The Gods Must Be Crazy*. Also, it's the language of Wakanda in *Black Panther*."

Monica shook her head. "You surprise me at times."

Gage sighed. "Look, even if I wanted to go to college, I can't afford tuition. And I damn sure don't have the money to go to Africa. Or anywhere else, come to think of it. So I take advantage of what's in reach. Got a library card, too. Although I'll be honest, I watch movies more than I read. Maybe, Monica, it don't matter so much how the world comes to you. Just so long as you let it in when it does."

Monica looked at him as if conducting a thorough reappraisal, but said nothing.

After a moment, Gage asked, "So, what was the problem with that Xhosa-speaking cab driver?" He knew she had been working on a joke, and he still wanted to hear it.

Monica smiled. "The car was hot, but I didn't open my jacket because I was afraid the sound of the snaps would tell him I wanted to go to the airport."

Gage laughed. It was damn hard not to like her. But that didn't mean he wanted to surrender. "You livin' in New York don't mean you unnershtand what's goin' on here," he said. The bourbon was making his tongue thick.

"True," Monica agreed. She was speaking carefully, too. The absorptive capacity of hot wings was not up to the challenge posed by several shots of Jim Beam. "But you seem to have a chip on your shoulder about folks who went to college. Being educated should not be a bad thing, Gage. Speaking intelligently about current events, or science, or, well, anything should be the aspiration of a good citizen."

"See, there ya go," Gage said. "You're educated; I'm not. You're smart; I'm dumb. We get that all the time from y'all."

Monica looked at him for a moment and considered taking another drink of bourbon, but abstained. She needed to remain conscious, if not sober. Their trust, established over several long conversations and small but important gestures, had survived a difference of opinion on a topic central to Gage Randolph's identity. She could make the bond stronger if she played her cards right. *I gotta Google this Helsinki thing when I get free*, she thought. *Gage just might be onto something. Die Hard. Who knew!*

"Gage, I don't think you're dumb. You've said a lot of smart things tonight. I do think kidnapping me and holding me hostage at a bar called Knockers is fucking moronic. But the Unacrapper makes us all dumber, and you've spent more time with him than most."

"Well, thanks," Gage said. "I'm doin' the best I can with the whole kidnappin' thing."

"I realize that. As kidnappings go, this is more than I could have asked for. But you are misinformed about many things and completely off the boil"—she belched slightly—"about what constitutes a proper diet."

"Just because I don't agree with you don't make me ignorant. We just see things differently is all. But you lefties, you like to make it seem like we're all stupid."

Monica nodded. "Education can create occasion for unwarranted arrogance. And it seems the narrower the education, the more likely the presumption of universal knowledge."

He looked at her and smiled. *Smile ain't half-bad*, she thought.

Gage said, "Let's assume I have no clue what that meant and that it's your fault I don't."

She laughed. "Sorry, I was in NPR mode. Let's say, for example, some guy gets a PhD because he wrote a thesis on French poetry between the years 1721 and 1732. Now this guy thinks he's qualified to comment on anything. He spent years studying one tiny thing and believes that makes him smart about everything."

"In my high school, we used to take kids like that and stick their heads in the toilet."

"Once they get tenure, you can't do that anymore," Monica said, shaking her head. "Anyway, despite being several Jim Beams past the legal limit, here I am trying to understand you."

"Well, you would be the only one," Gage said as he leaned back in his chair. He fished his cell phone from his shirt pocket, checked for messages, and then set it on the table in front of him before continuing. "You liberals look at us and think we're stupid and think we vote against our own interests because we don't know better."

Monica remained silent. She knew where he was going and would be waiting when he arrived.

Gage placed both hands on the table and leaned over to emphasize his point. "Lemme tell you somethin'. We know exactly what's happenin' to us. We're getting royally, spectacularly screwed. And we're getting it from both sides. Democrats fuck us. Republicans fuck us. Blue-collar folks are bein' passed around like the new guy in prison."

Monica Bell winced at the analogy. Gage Randolph made good points in a bad way.

He continued. "The difference is that Democrats pretend they want to help us but screw us over anyway. And what's worse is they mock us while they're doin' it. Mock our culture, mock our diet, mock our guns, mock our religion. Now, why would I, or anyone, want to vote for that? At least after the Republicans have their way, they leave us be."

"No, they don't. They'll only leave you be when there's nothing left to take."

"Maybe. But help from either side has been a fucking goat rope." Gage shook his head. "You got your people who don't care we're poor and think that's the way things ought to be. That would be your Republicans. Or you got folks who want to help but make it worse. Democrats are great at that." He took another swig before continuing. "They're like some well-meanin' neighbor who stops by to help you jump-start your car but accidentally sets your house on fire. Sure, your car might be runnin' when they finish helpin', but now your fuckin' house is on *fire*. So while you try to save your burning house by bailing water from the kiddie pool out back—which, by the way, you were usin' to ice down your Pabst Blue Ribbon so you could enjoy a quiet fuckin' Sunday afternoon for the first time in two months—they stand around congratulatin' themselves for fixin' your car."

Gage looked at Monica and gave her a rueful smile. "After all is said and done, you know what their help leaves you with? A shitty car, a pile of ashes where your house used to be, and a six-pack of warm beer."

Monica laughed. Not simply because she appreciated the humor, but because she understood the pain behind it. Sometimes the only thing you could do was laugh.

Gage paused for a moment, enjoying the feeling of making a beautiful, intelligent woman laugh. The commercial was right; some things really were priceless. Then he concluded his assessment of what ailed America. "Finally, you got some epic assholes who want to make it even worse than it is already. I'm startin' to believe this group consists entirely of pundits. No skin in the game, but they get paid plenty to recommend shit they don't have to take responsibility for."

Monica nodded as if in agreement, despite the last criticism hitting a little too close to home. But she thought his analysis ignored America's chronic illness. "Gage, you've addressed the symptoms. But the disease marches on. We will never get better until we realize our problem is people who don't care how bad they have it as long as someone else has it worse. Imagine how much hate and fear it takes for folks to accept the second-lowest rung on the ladder so long as they can keep someone else on the bottom one."

Gage reached for his glass and drained the remaining bourbon in a long pull. The conversation was over. He slapped the glass back on the table, pushed himself up, and said, "Excuse me, but things are percolatin'. I gotta use the john. You may be right about all them hot wings. It might be time to mix up the routine." He smiled at her as if to suggest there were no hard feelings and moved toward the bathroom.

Dulled by the bourbon, it took Monica Bell a moment to notice his phone was still on the table.

CHAPTER NINETEEN

"**G**o for Ponce."

"Hope I didn't catch you on top of somebody," Monica Bell said when James "Ponce" DeLeon answered his phone.

"What? Of course not," DeLeon said, managing to sound outraged. Scared straight after Roger Ailes, Bill O'Reilly, and Charlie Rose had gone down, he now kept his sex life confined to Manhattan's singles scene and out of the office. "Who is this?"

"It's Monica."

"Ohmigod! Monica! Where are you? Are you OK? I've been sitting here worried sick about you!"

"Well, when you're the producer of *The Monica Bell Show* and Monica Bell goes missing, I bet that makes you worry about where the next paycheck's gonna come from."

"I can worry about lots of things at once," DeLeon said. "That's why I'm a good producer."

"Shouldn't we be talking about me right now?"

"Oh, of course. Where are you? Did the police find you?"

"No. Believe it or not, I'm calling from Fayetteville, North Carolina. In a sure sign God is a thirteen-year-old boy, I'm being held captive in a bankrupt topless bar called Knockers. I've spent the better part of the week chained to a stripper pole. I got one of the kidnappers drunk, and he left his phone within reach."

"God, what a story. This will bring in killer ratings."

"I'm fine, thanks. Your concern is touching."

"I'm concerned about you," DeLeon said. "That goes without saying. But just think of the ratings when you come back to tell your story. Through the roof!"

"Listen, dummy. It gets better," Monica said, listening for the sound of a flushing toilet and also for footsteps in case Jacob Kelley returned. "The Unacrapper is one of the kidnappers."

"Fuck me," DeLeon said.

"Not in my job description, thank God. Now, can you stop channeling your inner Weinstein and focus on the problem at hand?"

"I didn't mean it like that."

"I know. But I enjoy keeping you on your toes."

"I'll call 911 right now and get you out of there. You could be on the air tonight. Both radio and TV," DeLeon said.

"If I wanted the police here in five minutes, I would've called 911 myself."

"Well, what do you want?"

Monica was silent for a moment. She looked around the dark, forlorn space that had been her home for several long days. A big U-shaped bar jutting out into the middle of the room. Cheap wooden tables scattered across the floor, some still bearing the standard restaurant-issue sugar and salt and pepper dispensers. A few even had bottles of Tabasco sauce. And then there was the ridiculous stage and the brass stripper pole to which she was tethered. She was ready to go and shook her head in disbelief at what she was about to say. "See, this is where it gets a little complicated. One of the kidnappers is a decent guy. Comes across a bit dopey but really isn't. Politically, he's somewhat to the right of Tucker Carlson's most racist grandfather. But he was only trying to help me, and it turned into a kidnapping."

"How does 'trying to help' turn into kidnapping?" DeLeon asked, not unreasonably.

"I know. It sounds crazy. And there is no way to explain it. But there you go. I don't wanna get this guy in trouble." *Goddamn it, Die Hard. What are you doing to me?* Monica thought.

"What about the Unacrapper?" DeLeon asked.

"Him I want put away. No one who shits out their own bombs should be walking the streets. He's a fucking loon and creepy to boot."

DeLeon got up from the sofa and paced toward the windows that comprised the back wall of his twenty-third-floor office. He admired the view for a moment before speaking. "So you want to stay? You're not in danger?"

"I didn't say any of those things. I am chained to a stripper pole. I am being held against my will by two men, one of whom is number one on America's Most Wanted List and a world-class asshat. No, I don't want to stay..." Monica paused. She was unsure where she was going with this.

DeLeon remained quiet. He knew Monica was smart. He knew she was smarter than he was. She was working toward something, and she didn't need any help getting there. They both sat for a moment, he in his plush Midtown office in Manhattan, she chained to a stripper pole in Fayetteville, North Carolina. He let the ambient noise of New York City traffic waft up from the street and fill the distance between them.

Finally, Monica said, "I want to figure this out and avoid getting the one guy in trouble while making sure the other guy does time. In addition, there's some kind of story here. Not sure what, exactly, but in between bouts of colitis brought on by the horrible food, I am learning something."

"You're not beginning to identify with them, are you? I've heard that can happen."

"No, I don't have Helsinki syndrome."

"What's that?"

"What, you've never seen *Die Hard*?"

"The movie? Nope."

"I'll be damned," she said. "I thought every guy had."

DeLeon was silent as he tried to figure out how *Die Hard* related to Monica's disappearance. Then he gave up and retreated to his safe harbor in moments of confusion: he started talking about himself. "Are you sure this isn't a test of my character? Are you saying you want to stay put because you want to see if I will tell you you're crazy and that I'm calling the police as soon as I hang up?"

"Ponce, I already know you're a narcissistic asshole. That's why you're such a good producer."

"Thanks, Monica," DeLeon said, touched. "That means a lot to me."

"You're welcome. Now the question before us is, how do we accomplish this without me getting killed?"

"You think you're in that much danger?"

"The Unacrapper feels trapped and threatened. Also, I might be, uh, pushing his buttons. I kicked him in the face and suggested he's got a small penis."

"Men generally don't like that. Maybe you should stop," DeLeon offered.

"We both know the answer to that. He is everything worth hating wrapped up in one convenient package of Crisco and stupid."

"Well, if we can't save you from yourself, we need to give you a way to communicate. I suspect you can't keep drinking your captors under the table every time you want to make a phone call." DeLeon paused, staring out the window. Finally, he said, "It's Friday. I'm flying down to Fayetteville tonight. I assume one can fly to Fayetteville?"

"Lose the attitude when you arrive. They already don't like us for the Civil War, and most everything that came after."

"OK. I'll get there. I'll find this Knockers place, and then we will just have to figure out what's next. I'll get a phone for you. At least then we can talk, and you can reach out if you feel you're in danger."

"That sounds like the start of what might be a plan. I can't reach any of the windows or the doors here. You might have to break in. There are only two of them, and I'm hoping at some point they will have to leave me alone."

"You sure this is the way you want it to be?" DeLeon asked.

"I think so. I'll sleep on it."

"OK. In a few hours, I'll be just down the street."

"Thanks, Ponce," Monica said, meaning it.

"I know I'm a jerk. But I'm also your jerk."

Monica heard the toilet flush in the back room. "OK, jerk," she said. "I gotta go."

She ended the call and put the phone back on the table where Gage had left it. With no time to figure out how to delete the number, she just had to hope he wouldn't notice. Monica hurried over to the stage and feigned being passed out. Given the amount of bourbon she had consumed, it wasn't difficult.

Gage stopped to look at her. He reached over and gently covered her with the blanket. Then he moved over to the table and saw his cell phone. He looked back at Monica Bell sleeping and then again at the phone.

Picking up the phone and putting it in his pocket without looking at it further, Gage Randolph headed toward the back room to talk to Jacob Kelley. He had an idea.

CHAPTER TWENTY

"This is our last broadcast from the Commonwealth of Virginia," Bill Spark said. "Tomorrow, we are doing a special show from Bentonville, North Carolina. After that, *The Firebell* is moving to *Freedomland*. Freedom from taxes, freedom from ridiculous government regulation, freedom from political correctness, and freedom from government bureaucrats. You think I've been a voice of clarity and reason before? Wait till you get a load of me coming to you from Zacharias Townsend's beacon of hope floating thirteen miles offshore. The future of America. The future of humanity."

"That's right, Bill," Sierra Darlin' chimed in. "We can't lead when we're mired in the muck and mire."

Bill grimaced behind his microphone at Sierra's awkward phrasing. She was good, but she had moments when her lack of polish was jarring.

"So we're gonna lead the revolution from the Promised Land. And we're going to fight for each of you. We're gonna jump-start democracy, hot-wire freedom, and give liberty a turbo boost. And to start this revolution off right, tomorrow we're going to broadcast live from the reenactment of the Civil War Battle of Bentonville. We're gonna relive the last stand a group of patriots made for liberty, for states' rights, and for small government. Come and join us. All of us. The visionary and patriotic Zacharias Townsend will be our special guest."

"OK," Bill said, "let's go to the phones. Let's hear from the megaphone of freedom, the loudspeaker of democracy, and the bullhorn of liberty that is *The Firebell*'s listening audience. Time to roar, people!"

"It looks like we got Ralph from Booneville, Mississippi, on the line," Sierra said. "What's on your mind, Ralph?"

"Yeah. Hi, Bill. Hi, Sierra. Am I on?"

"Yes, Ralph, you're on with Bill Spark and me, Sierra Darlin'. What's bothering you about America today?"

"It seems to me certain groups of people are not appreciative enough of their bein' allowed to live in America. Takin' a knee durin' the national anthem. Disrespectin' the troops. Spittin' on the police. Sayin' only black lives matter. Protectin' the rights of them thievin', rapin' illegals. Perhaps we need to return to the days when everyone knew their place."

Bill jumped in before Ralph's blowing of the racial dog whistle turned into an unambiguous call for a return to slavery, or at least Jim Crow. He had become a practiced hand at letting his audience voice just enough of their worldview without permitting them to follow their train of thought to its inevitable destination.

"Yeah, Ralph. If I understand what you're sayin', and I'm sure I do, we need to focus on what unites us and return to the old-fashioned values of blind patriotism and simple, unquestioning respect for everyone who wears a uniform."

"That's not exactly…"

"We hear ya, Ralph. Thanks for callin'. You have a fine day in beautiful Booneville, Mississippi. I tell ya, old Dan'l Boone really got around, didn't he, Sierra? He must have a city or town named for him in half the states."

"Also, he was a damn good-lookin' man. I've got a thing for a man in buckskin and a coonskin cap," Sierra purred into the mike.

"Looks like raccoons just went on the endangered species list," Bill chortled. "By the way, it's a crime we still have that list. If you can't adapt, you shouldn't be here. Man is part of nature. Government should not interfere with nature or with progress. Who's our next caller?"

"Well, Bill, we got a fella named Jacob on the line. He must be a big fan of Dick Cheney because he says he's callin' from an undisclosed location," Sierra said.

"Hey, Jacob. I don't blame ya for not wantin' the government to know where you're at," Bill said. "You and I both know we've got 'em worried. And a worried government is a dangerous government. What can Sierra and I do for you today?"

"Yeah. Uh, hi. Am I on the air?"

"You are, Jacob," Bill said.

"Wow. I can't believe it. Me on the air with Bill Spark and Sierra Darlin'. Hi, Sierra. I'm a huge fan. You're so pretty and smart."

"Aren't you sweet, Jacob. What's on your mind today?" Sierra asked. Like Bill, she realized that about half of talk radio's interaction during the call-in portion was the jock confirming to the caller that he or she was on the air.

"Yeah, I wanna talk about a guy I think is an American hero. A misunderstood man. I wanna talk about Jacob Kelley."

"Ah, the Unacrapper," Bill said.

"Jacob. His name is Jacob."

"Like you," Bill said.

"Uh, yeah,"

"OK, Jacob. What did you want to say?"

"Look, people seem to be makin' fun of how Jacob Kelley struck a blow for liberty, but no one is focused on the why. We oughta be explorin' why he felt compelled to make the statement he did, which is a, uh, whaddyacallit...a metaphor?"

"Yeah, sure, Jacob. A metaphor. Or is it a simile? Sierra, do you know which it is?"

"Maybe it's an allegory?" Sierra ventured.

"Aw, hell, let's go with metaphor," Bill said. "We don't get too wrapped up with technicalities here on *The Firebell*. What you call somethin' ain't nearly as important as callin' it the way you see it."

"OK. Yeah, a metaphor. A metaphor for how people feel 'bout bein' overtaxed, overregulated, and underrepresented."

Bill shrugged at Sierra, giving her the chance to weigh in first.

"You know, Jacob. You share more than just a name with the Unacrapper..."

"Jacob."

"Jacob. Yes, you're right. The nickname is just the lame-stream media's way to diminish the brave and noble acts of a patriot. They would challenge George Washington's honesty if he were alive today. That's how much they hate America."

"That's right, Sierra. Jacob Kelley is a patriot. An American hero. He was strikin' a blow for liberty when he did what he done."

"Wow. What a passionate defense. Thank you for speaking up. You really seem to identify with him. Maybe you *are* him," she said in jest.

"Well, in fact..."

Over their headphones, Bill and Sierra heard a door open. Then they heard another voice say, "Crapper? What the fuck..."

The phone went dead, and the engineer hit a button on the console to prevent the F-bomb from the unknown voice hitting the airwaves. He cut to Sierra and Bill. Bill looked at Sierra and mouthed the words, "Holy shit. It might have been *him!*"

"Well, we seem to have lost Jacob from an undisclosed location," Bill said. "It sounded like he was about to tell us something important. We might speculate on who the caller was, but what we know for sure is he's made some good points about Jacob Kelley, the Unacrapper, and his motivation for placing a, uh, homemade bomb in front of the IRS building."

Bill paused as the engineer made the sign to cut to commercial.

"OK, folks, we're gonna take a quick break so our friends at Pale Rider Survival Center can tell you all about their huge discounts on the purchase of bump stocks. Don't be the only one in your neighborhood limited to shooting only as fast as you can pull the trigger. Visit Pale Rider and get your bump stock today. Hell, get two. Surely you got more than one gun. And if ya don't, Pale Rider can help ya fix that problem, too."

Bill cut to commercial. He turned down the sound as the voice-over intoned: "You are all that stands between your family and some thug in a hoodie carrying a 9 mil he bought on the street..."

"You think it was him?" he asked the engineer.

"I think we're gonna get a visit from the FBI today," the engineer said.

"Save the file," Bill Spark directed. "I'm already givin' Uncle Sam the finger. I don't want to poke him in the eye with it, too. And stay around for a while in case they call. Me and Sierra gotta hit the road for Bentonville. You come after."

"What the hell were you thinking?" Gage Randolph asked after Jacob Kelley abruptly disconnected his call to *The Firebell*.

"I was thinkin' that I'm tired of people callin' me the Unacrapper. Or Crapper for short," Jacob said.

Gage was furious. "Well, maybe you shoulda thought of that before you took the mother of all dumps to make your fucking turdageddon device. If I hadn't a come back here to talk to you, you'd still be talkin' to them and pretty soon we'd both be talkin' to the FBI."

"I used a burner phone I bought at a 7-Eleven before I, uh, ran into you. They can't trace the phone because I blocked the outgoing number. 'Sides, I doubt the Federals are a big part of *The Firebell*'s listening audience." Jacob grinned. "I bet NPR is more their speed."

Gage took a chair, the stress of the past few days descending upon him all at once. He took a deep breath and then looked at Jacob. "The Feds are lookin' for a guy who hates the government and loves Sierra Darlin'. Don't you think they might be, you know, monitoring *The Firebell*? Because you're an antigovernment type but also because they know you are, uh, obsessed with Sierra."

"I don't think I'm obsessed," Jacob said.

"For Christ's sake," Gage said. "I saw in the paper that your internet search history was about two percent related to bomb making and ninety-eight percent related to Sierra Darlin'. That is not a healthy balance if you are, in fact, aimin' to make an explosive device."

"I'm interested in her philosophy," Jacob mumbled.

"Then you must think she stores her philosophy in her cleavage," Gage said. "Because that was what you were most interested in. But forget about that. Gimme that damn phone right now."

Jacob handed the cheap cell phone to Gage, who dropped it on the floor and stomped it to pieces.

"You better fuckin' hope they didn't track this thing," he said. "Now I know you're goin' stir crazy. So I got an idea to get you out of here and on your way. Matter of fact, I been workin' on it for a while now. I had to get things right with Monica before I could move on it, though."

"What is it?" Jacob asked.

"Before we get to that, you need to understand the risk I'm taking. You mess this up and I will shoot you, nurse you back to health, and shoot you again."

CHAPTER TWENTY-ONE

The next morning, Barbara Townsend was not pleased. "I hate this," she fumed as she looked out the window of the luxurious Sikorsky S-76C helicopter flying her and Zacharias Townsend from *Freedomland* to Bentonville, North Carolina, early on a Saturday morning. To make matters worse, the same storm that had made Bill Spark's voyage to the mainland so miserable was battering the Sikorsky. "Why do I have to go with you to this stupid fake battle in this stupid fake town?"

Zacharias sighed and rubbed his one good eye. "Look, I have some sensitive deals to wrap up. You are exceptional publicity, and you make men stupid. I need both superpowers from you today. Can you do that for me?"

His wife stretched extravagantly. "I was going to go to the gym today, have a nice massage, and then ball you until you begged for mercy." She reached over and caressed his face. "Now guess which one I won't have time for?"

"Just as well," Zacharias said. "This eye patch screws up my peripheral vision. When you're on top, all I can see is one boob and half your face. It's like I'm fucking a Picasso."

"Even half of me is better than all of someone else," Barbara said. "Or do you think I didn't notice you flirting with that little blonde Fox News wannabe the other night at dinner?"

"All business," Zacharias said. Then he turned so his working eye looked into hers. "Is that why I look like Rooster fucking Cogburn right now? You thought I was flirting with Sierra, so you gave Bill one of your patented toe jobs while he was fiddling with a lobster claw?" Barbara arched her eyebrows as her husband continued. "I saw you stretch out your leg under the table the other night. In fact, it was the last thing I saw before I took a lobster claw traveling at ninety miles an hour right in my eyeball."

"Timing is everything," Barbara said with a grin. "But I'm glad there's no permanent damage." She looked at her diamond-encrusted Cartier watch. "How much longer until we get to Mayberry R.F.D.?"

"Twenty minutes," he replied. He traced his fingers gently over the length of her left forearm. "Maybe we can find a way to pass the time."

"Dream on, Rooster."

"So much for the ulna," Zacharias Townsend muttered. He turned to look out the window as the storm-battered North Carolina coast came into view.

"I look ridiculous," Jacob Kelley said.

"I can't believe it, but this pinhead is right," Monica Bell said. "He looks ridiculous."

"I think it's an accurate depiction of what someone who might have suffered a terrible facial wound in the Civil War might look like," Gage Randolph said.

He and Jacob stood before Monica in full Confederate regalia. Gage bore the chevrons of a first sergeant on his butternut jacket. He had a slouch hat on his head, a coarse shirt that looked homespun, high-waisted pants, canvas gaiters, and hobnailed shoes. The uniform looked hot and uncomfortable to Monica. Gage carried a three-button canvas haversack, a powder horn, and what he told her was a replica 1862 C.S. Richmond .58-caliber musket.

Jacob wore similar attire, except his hat was perched atop a dirty gray wig and his face was swathed in grimy bandages. The enormous tip of a glued-on walrus mustache protruded out of the bandages on the right side. He had altered his appearance further by stuffing two bath towels under his jacket, giving him a prodigious beer belly.

"We'll say you're suffering from powder burns," Gage said.

"And pregnant," Monica added.

"I don't know," Jacob said. "Maybe this isn't such a good idea. Who ever heard of a fat Confederate soldier? They was all skinny and half-starved."

"Well, I do have to agree with Gage. You don't look like you're the Unacrapper anymore," Monica said. She had been delighted to find out that Gage wanted to take Jacob with him to the reenactment. She didn't want him to back out now. If Ponce DeLeon was in town and staking out Knockers, then she needed them both to go so she could make contact.

To prepare for leaving Monica unguarded, Gage had removed everything from her reach that she could use as a tool. He had even gone outside a few feet from the building while Jacob emitted a serious of ludicrous high-pitched screams he figured approximated Monica yelling at the top of her lungs for help. Satisfied no passerby could hear her, Gage was comfortable leaving his hostage alone for the day.

"OK, Crapper..."

"Jacob," the other man said.

"That's another thing," Gage said. "You ain't Jacob Kelley today. As a matter of fact, you ain't Jacob anyone today. Today, you are Bob Smith, up from Atlanta to help in the reenactment. You also ain't an SOL member. Got it?"

Jacob nodded his assent.

"OK. Get your stuff together and let's get moving."

Jacob shuffled off, and Gage turned to Monica. "Look, this is almost over. I would take it as a personal favor if you didn't escape today. If I can get rid of him, then you and I can work out what comes next."

"Well, it doesn't look like you're giving me much choice," Monica said as she surveyed the barren area around her. "I'm sitting here in the big empty."

"Yeah, well, it wouldn't be natural to not try and escape, now, would it? I know you might get bored, so I downloaded a few movies for you to watch on this laptop." Gage handed her his computer. "But I turned off the Wi-Fi, so there isn't any internet."

"Thanks. Have a good battle. Remember what side you're on so you don't accidentally move us toward a more perfect union."

"Oh, I almost forgot." Gage reached into his satchel and, with a sheepish look, withdrew a book. "I thought you might like to read. I went to the bookstore. I don't know what you like, but I thought maybe this would interest you." He held out the book.

She took the book from Gage and raised her eyebrows in surprise as she saw the title. *Emma*.

"Jane Austen, Gage?"

"Well, to be honest, I was just gonna go in and get you a *People* magazine. And maybe a news magazine. But I told a clerk I was lookin' to buy a book for a friend. She asked what you were like. After I described you..."

"Probably told her you were a ball-busting bitch," Jacob said as he returned.

"If I am, that shouldn't threaten you any, Crapper," Monica retorted. "You got nothin' to bust."

"Anyway," Gage said, "she recommended this."

Monica smiled at the thought of him buying a Jane Austen novel. "Well, I haven't read it since college. But since two rednecks in Civil War costumes have me chained to a stripper pole, a novel about a strong woman rebelling against nineteenth-century sexist idiocy seems appropriate."

Gage Randolph smiled, knowing that, despite her sarcasm, he had done well. He turned to Jacob Kelley. "Let's get a move on," he said, twirling the keys to his Ford Bronco around his index finger. "There're Yankees afoot that need shootin'."

"Just why are we spending a valuable Saturday going to watch a bunch of goobers shoot muskets, eat beef jerky, and remind me why I'm glad I live in the twenty-first century?" Rebecca Aucoin asked her husband as he drove them to Bentonville, North Carolina.

"Well, I don't think they're *all* goobers," Sam Aucoin said. "Matter of fact, I spent some time researching these reenactors, and most of these groups are very serious. Some of them may be *too* serious, but the majority are into their hobby the way someone would be into, say, skydiving or something. But there are some idiots out there. Hard-core neo-Confederates, like the South of the Line members. Those clowns believe *Gone with the Wind* was a documentary."

Rebecca stretched and yawned in the right-hand seat as Sam guided the Honda Pilot up the highway. Like all cops, he drove fast, with confidence and skill. The forty-mile trip would not take long.

"Fine. But why the sudden interest? Don't tell me you're gonna give up golf. Highlight of my week is ogling the golf pro at the club while you and Hollis struggle to break 150."

Her husband took in a deep breath. "To be honest, Becks, I'm going up there to get a look at these SOL guys. Maybe see what Gage Randolph is up to."

"You can't be serious…"

"I have a sneaking suspicion he stole Stonewall Jackson's arm. He might even have something to do with Monica Bell's disappearance. Bud Roy Roemer might be involved, too. But for obvious reasons, I'm being very cautious about pursuing that angle."

Rebecca glared at him, although it was a look of exasperation mixed with deep affection. "Samuel Aucoin, you are going to get yourself sued, fired, and run out of North Carolina...and maybe not even in that order. You've got five miles to convince me you aren't crazy. If you can't, you're never going to see me naked again."

Sam grinned and gave her a pat on the leg. "Stakes are damn high."

As he drove, he laid out his suspicions and the evidence, albeit some of it circumstantial, he had amassed. He finished by saying he had heard that renowned Civil War memorabilia collector and "all-around douchebag billionaire" Zacharias Townsend would be there, too. "Something isn't right," he concluded.

Rebecca nodded. "OK. You convinced me with a mile to spare. I don't think you're right, but it's worth a trip to Bentonville to find out. And," she said as she put her head on his shoulder, "maybe tonight you'll get to see me naked."

Sam Aucoin glanced at his wife and smiled. "Hell, that would be worth two trips to Bentonville."

"Can't you control this mutt?" Jacob Kelley asked, irritated by Rebel the Hound's repeated attempts to lick the fake blood off the bandages swaddling his face.

"Rebel ain't used to company on a drive," Gage said. "He's just showin' you he's glad you're with us."

"Why's he even comin' along?"

"Me and Rebel do most things together. And it's historically accurate. Both sides had dogs as mascots."

Rebel gave Jacob's bandaged face another lap, leaving a big, slobbery stain.

"I heard that in Vicksburg food was so scarce the soldiers ended up eatin' dogs. Maybe you and Rebel ought to go to that reenactment next," Jacob groused.

"Rebel can be much less nice if I tell him," Gage said with an edge in his voice.

"Sorry," Jacob said quickly. A lifelong fan of country music, he adhered to the genre's core philosophy that it was unwise to sleep with another man's wife, dent his truck, or threaten his dog. "I'm worried and got a lot on my mind."

Gage said, "Look here, Crapper..."

"Jacob."

"We're both wrong. Remember, today you are Bob Smith, up from Atlanta. This is your first reenactment, and you wanted to take part but not mess things up. It's why you're playing a wounded private."

"What if someone asks me what I do?" Jacob asked, warming to the acting job ahead.

"I dunno. What do you want Bob Smith to be?"

"How about a taxidermist?" Jacob offered.

"Really? That's kind of out there in left field," Gage said. "Do you know anything about taxidermy?"

"Not really," Jacob admitted. "I had a fish mounted once."

Gage took the statement in stride. He figured anyone who would stuff his own shit into a pipe was a few bubbles off plumb to begin with. "Then why don't you stick to somethin' you know?" he advised. "With our luck, the first person you'd run into would be an off-duty policeman with a passion for taxidermy."

Both men remained deep in thought for a few miles. Then Gage said, "Paper said you was a welder. Why don't you be the owner of an auto body shop? You can pretend to be successful and still talk about what you know."

Jacob frowned at Gage's observation that he would have to pretend to be successful. But he brightened at the prospect of being something other than a semiemployed welder on the run from the law because he had tried to blow up the IRS. "Do you really think we can get Zacharias Townsend to take me to *Freedomland*?"

"He wants Stonewall's arm so bad he's willing to do almost anything," Gage said. "Our lawyer thinks he can talk him into it. So does Bud Roy."

"Worth a shot, I guess. Not sure what other options are out there." Jacob gazed out the window as they passed through a blip of a town called Newton Grove.

"Believe me, Bob Smith from Atlanta, it's your only shot."

CHAPTER TWENTY-TWO

Gage Randolph pulled his Bronco into the parking area at the Bentonville battlefield. He spied Bud Roy Roemer's new Ford Expedition in the lot next to Linus McTane's Lexus, with Zacharias Townsend's helicopter nesting in a grassy field farther back. They reminded Gage that there was rich, and there was *really* rich.

"OK," he said to Jacob Kelley, "looks like the gang's all here. Stay quiet and let us do the talkin'. I think we got an excellent shot at getting you out of here today."

They exited the Bronco with Rebel the Hound and made their way to an enormous campaign tent serving as Zacharias's shelter for the day. McTane, Bud Roy, and Shelley DeWeese were waiting nearby.

McTane greeted them as they walked up. "Gage," he said. "And I take it this here is Bob Smith from Atlanta."

Kelley nodded to the group.

"OK," McTane said. "Let's make a deal."

They walked toward the tent. Two large men wearing sunglasses despite the overcast weather stopped them. The pair had earpieces connected to walkie-talkies on their belts. The bulges in their jackets underneath their left arms told everyone they weren't ticket takers to an exhibit.

"Sorry, folks," the lead bodyguard said as he eyed Rebel the Hound uneasily. "This is a private area."

"Mr. Townsend is expecting me. The name's Gage Randolph." He handed the man his driver's license.

The guard took it, looked at the photo, and then back at Gage. "We were told to admit only you, Mr. Randolph."

"Well, these folks are with me. Either we all come in or none of us do. And I turn around and leave with the item Mr. Townsend wants."

The bodyguards exchanged looks. They wanted to tell the group to take a hike, but they knew it wasn't their call. "Hang on," one said and went into the tent for a few moments. When he reemerged, he reluctantly told the group they could enter.

Gage went in first. A large camp table with several expensive chairs arrayed around it sat in the middle of the tent. The Townsends, it seemed, were never uncomfortable. The hum of a generator explained why there was overhead lighting and a large flat-screen TV tuned to ESPN.

Zacharias was at the far end of the table, standing next to his wife. Gage knew her from the tabloids. Barbara Townsend was tall, beautiful, and intimidating as hell. Both Townsends were clad in expensive outdoor clothing. Possibly L.L.Bean, but more likely custom made, Gage figured. Zacharias's eye patch made him look both dashing and menacing. Gage was glad he had his friends with him. For the first time, he realized he was in the deep end of the pool.

"I thought this was to be a private transaction," Zacharias said. He did not offer to shake hands, nor did he offer anyone a chair as they filed in. Gage's motley group remained standing, the table between them and the Townsends.

Zacharias looked them over and asked, "Who the hell are all of you?"

Before anyone could answer, his unpatched eye fell upon Jacob, betrayed in his effort to melt into the background by his spectacular, even by American standards, two-bath-towel beer belly. His gray wig and the one half of a fake walrus mustache protruding from the bandages on the right side of his face also drew the billionaire's attention.

"And what the hell is David Crosby doing here?" Zacharias asked, pointing at Jacob.

The visible half of Jacob's fake mustache twittered as he scrunched his mouth in confusion.

"He's not David…uh, he's the Una…I mean, well, uh, the Crapper is…" Gage stammered.

Bud Roy coughed and said, "Criminal Tourette's," into his clenched fist. Gage stopped talking.

Zacharias offered a thin, wintery smile. "I'm just screwing with you. I know it's not David Crosby. David Crosby's dead."

Barbara leaned over and whispered into Zacharias's ear.

He turned to her with a look of genuine surprise on his face. "Really? Hasn't he gone through, like, five livers? Guy looked like he was on life support ten years ago," he said. "I'll be damned. We oughta get the name of his doctor. That guy's a freaking miracle worker."

Gage attempted to redirect the conversation. "Mr. Townsend, these folks are here with me because we got a few new wrinkles in the deal."

Zacharias's good eye settled heavily on Gage. "The way you remove wrinkles is to apply a great deal of pressure and heat. I can do that."

"Just a few small things have changed," Gage said.

"They better not have changed too much," Zacharias said. "I have a quarter million in cash right here." He opened a large duffel bag on the table. "One-hundred-dollar bills. Two thousand five hundred of them."

Gage and his comrades gazed at the money as if they had stumbled upon a surf-and-turf buffet after emerging from forty days in the desert.

"But not a dollar more," Zacharias said.

"I ain't changin' the cash price," Gage said, resisting the urge to weep in the money's presence. "Thing is, we've got some, uh, logistical complications."

"Where's the arm?" Zacharias asked, noticing for the first time that neither Gage nor his friends were carrying any packages.

"The arm's in a safe place." Gage patted Rebel the Hound on his head. "Only me and Rebel know where it is."

The implied threat hung in the air between them like acrid gun smoke over a battlefield.

"OK. Let's hear what you want."

Before Gage could reply, McTane stepped forward. "Mr. Townsend, my name is Linus McTane. I represent Mr. Randolph in this matter."

"Oh fuck. A lawyer?" Zacharias asked, the distaste dripping off the words as he spat them out. "You sure sound like a lawyer. And you look like one. Got a kind of oily sheen. Jesus Christ. I hate lawyers. Even mine. Just the thought of talking to a lawyer makes me want to take a lobster claw and gouge out my other eye."

Barbara smiled at the joke only she was privy to while the others in the tent looked on with reactions ranging from mild concern to profound confusion. Zacharias took a seat but did not gesture for the others to do so. He looked at McTane. "Lawyers are—and I hate to generalize, Mr. McTane—everything that is wrong with America." Then he turned to his wife. "Barbara, can you be a dear and get me one of the guns I keep handy for shooting lawyers? A big one. This guy might be harder than most to bring down. Looks like he's been able to fatten up on gullible clients and frivolous lawsuits."

Bud Roy and Shelley nodded in unconscious agreement.

Barbara sat down as well. She did not require an invitation. "Hear them out, Zack. You know you want the arm. Let's at least discuss the terms before you shoot anyone."

McTane had been a practicing attorney in the South for many years. This was not the first time someone had threatened to shoot him. He took a seat unbidden. He knew theatrics and cheap ploys to establish dominance when he saw them. "Before we slap leather—and may I remind you, sir, you are in the South, and therefore rest assured, you are not the only one in this tent carrying a gun—why don't you listen to what we have to say?"

Zacharias changed the shape of his mouth into something that might have been a smile. "Sure. I'm done trying to scare you to death. Everyone sit down. Go ahead, Counselor. Confound me with your legalese."

As Gage and the rest eased themselves into chairs, McTane began. "No legalese. Just a simple quid pro quo."

"See, that's legalese," Zacharias said. "Anytime a lawyer trots out the Latin, I gotta add three fucking zeroes to the check I write.

McTane sighed. "Occupational hazard. We need a favor in return for the arm."

"Seems to me that giving you a quarter-million doubloons already is a pretty big favor."

"In addition to the cash," McTane clarified.

Zacharias waited quietly.

"Law enforcement officers up and down the East Coast, if not all over the country, are searching for two people. We know the whereabouts of both."

Zacharias tilted his head slightly to his right, but said nothing.

Shelley ran out of patience with the posturing and mannered foreplay of the two men. She dove into the silence and put the deal on the table. "Mr. Townsend, we got Jacob Kelley and Monica Bell in our, uh, possession. We need your help with, I guess, disposin' of them."

Jacob's fake mustache scrunched up with alarm. "'Disposin'?"

"Well, the problem you represent," Shelley clarified. "Not you in particular."

McTane frowned at Shelley's interruption, but Bud Roy shot him a look. Knowing what Bud Roy's fiancée was like when she got wound up, McTane remained silent.

"The fat guy here with the stupid mustache is Jacob Kelley, the Unacrapper. Monica Bell is bein' held somewhere else," Shelley said.

Zacharias had seen too much, and done too much, in his career as a software mogul to show surprise when encountering a felony. "Your photos in the paper don't do you justice," he said to Jacob. "Did you grow that mustache in a week? If so, it is a remarkable accomplishment."

"Nah. It's fake." Jacob unwound the bandages and took off the mustache. "And I ain't really this fat," he said, removing the bath towels from underneath his tunic.

"But you are the Unacrapper?" Zacharias asked.

"I prefer Jacob."

"Most people would. Well, Jacob, I have to admit I kinda like your style. I also hate the IRS. Not enough to do what you did, I guess. But then again, I don't have to. I'm rich and need not rely on the weapons of the weak." He turned back to the group. "So how did you end up with both Jacob here and Ms. Bell?"

"Monica, Gage, and the Unacrapper all ran into each other," Bud Roy said. "I mean that literally. They had a three-car pileup on some back road in Virginia. Gage was trying to help Monica but accidentally ended up kidnappin' her instead."

"If I had a nickel for every time that has happened," Zacharias said. "Oh, wait. I do." He suddenly had a thought. "I was listening to Sierra Darlin' dismember Monica Bell on the air when Bell got cut off. Was that what happened?"

"Yep," Gage said. "I ran into her. But our problem now is we need to get the Unacrapper here..."

"Jacob," Jacob said.

"Jacob," Gage continued. "We gotta get Jacob out of here and on his way to somewhere safe. We figure you can help with that while he hides out on *Freedomland*."

Before Zacharias could reply, McTane added, "We also need your help persuading Monica Bell not to press charges against Gage here."

"Just how do you think I can do that?" Zacharias asked.

"Offer her an interview. Maybe offer her money?"

"Christ," Zacharias said. "*More* money? Stonewall Jackson's left arm is gonna cost me more than Oscar Goldman paid for Steve Austin's right one."

Everyone mined their TV memories from the seventies to place the pop-culture reference in its proper context.

Zacharias required more incentive. "Why the hell should I do any of this?"

"It's not like you got a lot of choices," Gage said. "Besides, just how many of Stonewall Jackson's arms do you think are out there?"

McTane winced and Bud Roy sighed at the same time.

Zacharias looked at Gage the same way Babe Ruth looked at a hanging curve. "Well, I'm gonna go waaaay out on a limb here and guess that there are *two*. And I bet I know where to get the second one." He looked over the group and asked, "Again, why shouldn't I just call the police now and have you all arrested?"

McTane spoke up before Gage could dig the hole they were in any deeper. "A couple of reasons," he said. "One, we got the arm, and you want it. Not the one still connected to Stonewall, but the left one. The one that killed him. The one that changed the war." The lawyer was in his element. He was delivering a summation to a jury of one. "Oh, Mr. Townsend, you want Stonewall's left arm. Badly. If you're prepared to pay two hundred and fifty thousand dollars for a few musty old bones, then you are prepared to do more. Plus, keeping the police out of this is advantageous to us all. My guess is you don't want them poking around asking questions any more than we do."

"Now we're having a useful conversation," Zacharias said. "Let's say I agree to all of this. You said there were additional requests."

Shelley weighed back in. "Bud Roy and me want you to give us citizenship on *Freedomland* and help us fight the IRS. The Feds is tryin' to take two hundred thousand dollars of Bud Roy's money he got for gettin' shot in the clavicle…"

"Shot in the what?" Zacharias asked.

"The clavicle," Bud Roy, Shelley, McTane, and Gage replied in unison.

A curious man, Zacharias asked, "How does one get shot in the clavicle?"

"One gets the Jubblies Corporation mad at one by opening a bar and grill named Knockers," Bud Roy said, delivering a summation of admirable concision.

"And I thought Silicon Valley was cutthroat," Zacharias said, raising his visible eyebrow in appreciation of Jubblies's ruthlessness.

"Anyway," Shelley said, "we got clavicle money. The government wants to take it, and we plan to fight back by usin' ElimiTax. We want you to back us up with your lawyers. We want to be a test case for you, or somethin' like that."

"Story could be compelling," Zacharias said. "People don't understand tax law, but they understand being shot. And they really understand the government taking their money."

"I want citizenship, too," Jacob chimed in.

"Christ. Next you'll say you want that damn dog to be the *Freedomland* attorney general," Zacharias said, pointing at Rebel the Hound, who was snuffling around the floor of the tent to locate any stray food.

"Me and Rebel prefer to stay in Fayetteville," Gage said, hoping to sound reasonable. "Although I would 'preciate some help with ElimiTax when I report my Stonewall stolen-arm money to the IRS."

"Try not to refer to our deal in those terms when you enter it on your Schedule E," Zacharias said.

"Gage has got a criminal Tourette's type of affliction," Bud Roy explained. "We're workin' on it."

"Yeah, I got it bad. Don't I, Bud Roy?"

Zacharias's expression as he listened to this exchange momentarily made him look like a squirrel trying to perform long division. He blinked his good eye rapidly several times and then asked, "So what's the deal?"

"You get Jacob here off to *Freedomland*. Do that today. We join you tomorrow, bringing the arm, your new citizens, and Monica Bell," McTane summarized.

"What do you want out of this, Counselor? I haven't met a lawyer yet who didn't want a cut," Zacharias said.

"I am merely helpin' out some friends," McTane said.

Zacharias waited.

"But if you wanted to throw some legal work my way, I would be happy to take it on," McTane offered.

"Mighty Christian of you. Well, I will say this. You seem comfortable operating in the margins, and that is where I find myself these days."

"Oh, Linus is most definitely marginal," Shelley said. She still hadn't forgiven McTane.

Zacharias laughed. "OK. But no promises on either Bell or the American Pooper here," he said, pointing at Jacob.

"Aw, c'mon. It's Jacob."

"I'll do what I can," Zacharias said. "Jacob, there is no way in hell you are getting citizenship on *Freedomland*. We're not a penal colony like Australia."

Jacob protested, but Zacharias held up a hand, silencing him.

"We will, however, give you safe passage to somewhere else. I have more than a few government officials around the world on my payroll. We'll find someplace nice. You stay in here and leave with us after the battle. In the meantime, get your David-Crosby-the-morning-after-a-bender getup back on."

Zacharias stood up to signify their allotted time in his presence was ending. "As for the tax rebels, you have a compelling story we can use. For now, you're allowed to stay on *Freedomland*. The chopper will get you tomorrow morning. Early. My pilot says the weather will close tomorrow afternoon, and they'll be grounded until this stupid storm passes. We should have just enough seats. Let's work out a rendezvous point that's secluded, given the fame of one of your passengers."

"We gotta bring Howard, too. And he can't fly," Shelley said.

"Who the fuck is Howard?" Zacharias asked, growing exasperated by the ever-expanding citizenry. "*Freedomland*'s getting more crowded than Bangladesh."

"Howard is more a 'What the fuck' than a 'Who the fuck,'" Bud Roy said, explaining everything and nothing.

"Whatever," Zacharias said in a rare moment of not wanting to know, and control, every detail. "I got a guy with a boat. But it's gonna be a bumpy ride." He was quiet for a moment, considering the parameters of the deal he had just entered. "The wild card here is Monica Bell. You have, indeed, kidnapped her. She may not be willing to forgive so easily."

"Let's play it by ear," Bud Roy said. "Gage here says he has made some headway in getting her to see it was a big misunderstanding. Maybe an interview with you, or something like that, will be all the incentive she needs to let bygones be bygones."

"Someone kidnapped me; I would be after revenge," Zacharias said. "But I am game to mediate. I'm not, however, game to be an accessory."

"One more thing," Gage said. "Keep the Crapper here out of Monica's sight. She don't like him and wants him in jail. We'll tell her he drove off west. Got friends in Texas or somethin.'"

Everyone shook hands. Gage and his group, minus Jacob, moved toward the battlefield. After making sure Jacob donned his disguise and understood he was to remain in the tent, the Townsends followed. As the pair exited, Zacharias told the bodyguards not to allow anyone in or out.

"You caved," Barbara said as they strode toward the battlefield. "Not like you at all."

"They are an interesting bunch, and the Roemer couple could be just the case ElimiTax is looking for."

"And what if they become more trouble than they're worth?"

Zacharias looked at his wife and then took her hand. "The tree of liberty must be refreshed from time to time with the blood of idiots."

"Both bloodthirsty and condescending. Now, just how do you expect to take care of them?"

"It's a deep ocean, my dear. And if Monica Bell gets dropped in with the rest, so much the better." After walking a few steps farther, Zacharias Townsend added, "Might keep the dog, though. I like dogs."

CHAPTER TWENTY-THREE

James "Ponce" DeLeon sat in his rental car across the street from Knockers. Earlier, he had watched two men, one of whom he presumed was Jacob Kelley, leave the building in an old Ford Bronco. The pair wore Confederate Civil War uniforms and looked like they would be gone for a while. Regardless, Ponce waited an additional thirty minutes before crossing the street. *For all I know, these assholes dress up like this to go to breakfast,* he thought. He had spent little time in the South.

Once convinced their return was not imminent, he pulled his car across the street and parked it behind Knockers.

The front door was locked, as he had expected. He thought about breaking the glass but figured doing so would put Monica Bell in danger when the kidnappers returned.

Instead, he went around to the back entrance, trying various windows within reach on the way. None of them were open. But the rear service door provided something to work with. The heavy gate that added a further layer of security was unlocked. On the door itself, the kidnappers had neglected to throw the dead bolt, locking only the knob. DeLeon was pleased the door did not hold tight against the frame.

In his early days as a producer, DeLeon had worked two seasons on *Cops*. He had moved on from that assignment surprised at how easy it was for criminals, and the police, to enter supposedly secure structures. A lock was more a psychological comfort than an impediment to illegal entry.

This door would not be a challenge, as he had brought along just the tool for the job. He extracted an eight-inch plastic shim with a tapered edge from his jacket pocket. DeLeon put his weight against the door, slipped the shim into the space he created between the latch and the strike plate, pushed the tongue of the lock back, and was inside in less than ten seconds.

DeLeon crept into the interior. He proceeded down a long, dark hallway with an office and storerooms on his left and a large kitchen on his right. He moved with caution, but the brownish-red linoleum flooring, coated with a greasy residue that was the by-product of years of lard-based cooking and infrequent cleaning, stuck to his shoes. He made a sound like Velcro tearing when he walked. Unsure if there was another guard, he took two or three cautious but sticky steps and listened. Though he had taken on a few dangerous assignments in his career producing shows that were not quite news, James "Ponce" DeLeon had never been in a fight and assessed his chances at winning one as dismal.

He moved on but froze again when he heard voices. He stood there, puzzled over the conversation wafting down the hallway. *Did one of them just say, "Yippee ki yay, motherfucker?"* he asked himself.

"Well, I'll be damned," Monica Bell said out loud to what she thought was an empty room. *"Die Hard* is a pretty good movie."

James "Ponce" DeLeon crept into the room toward the sound of Monica's voice, unsure if she was alone. He thought he had heard at least one man who, strangely, sounded like Bruce Willis. DeLeon thought it unlikely that Bruce Willis had kidnapped Monica Bell.

DeLeon scuttled behind the bar on all fours, grimacing as his hands touched the grimy floor, and peered over the edge. He saw Monica, clad in a tight gray T-shirt and olive capri pants, sitting on the floor watching a movie on an old Dell laptop computer. DeLeon made a mental note that she should wear a similar outfit when broadcasting from the field. Ratings would double. Monica had a manacle around her left ankle. A cable led from the manacle to a pole anchored in the middle of a small stage.

He stood up to his full height behind the bar. "Monica?" he called softly.

Monica looked up. "Ponce! You came!" She moved across the room until the cable played out. "It's OK. They left me by myself."

DeLeon hurried over for a hug. He was ashamed that he was looking forward to it for reasons that had nothing to do with finding her safe. But not so ashamed that he abstained.

She let go first and stepped away. "How'd you get in?"

"Back door was easy to jimmy. How much time have we got?"

"Hours," Monica replied as she beckoned him to sit down at a nearby table. "They went off to reenact a Civil War battle. I bet they take a grits and cornpone break at midday. Maybe swill some White Lightning and bang a first cousin back at camp. Hell, I bet someone even volunteers to have a gangrenous leg sawed off so everyone can appreciate how hard it was in the olden days."

"Not a fan, I take it?" DeLeon said with a smile. "Good to see you haven't lost your spirit."

"Did you bring the phone?"

"A nice new iPhone. New account. I made sure it's in silent mode and turned the Find My iPhone function on. Hopefully, we can track your whereabouts. I programmed my number along with the police and the FBI."

He handed the phone to Monica Bell, who caressed it like it was the Holy Grail. "So what do we do now?" he asked.

"I don't know. But stay close."

"This crowd is whiter than David Duke's Christmas card list," Rebecca Aucoin told her husband as they walked through the throng of reenactors.

"Not a lot of African Americans need reminding about slavery," Sam Aucoin said. "Although if you ask the SOL guys, they'll tell you that slaves were happy to fight for the Confederacy. I guess by extension their ancestors should be happy to come out and pretend to be property for a day."

"Yeah," Rebecca said. "Black folks are missing a great opportunity to make white folks feel better about themselves."

The Aucoins stopped to watch a unit of reenactors march off to do fake battle. Sam thought they came by the grim looks fashioned to their faces honestly; their shoes, if nothing else, looked painful. He spied Hollis Turnbull, resplendent in a Confederate general officer's uniform, conferring with another group of reenactors in front of a large tent. He and Rebecca strode over to greet him.

"Hollis, you look dashing today," Sam said, sticking out his hand.

"Too old, too rich, and too fat to be a private," Turnbull said, returning the handshake. "General is the way to go. Ride around on my horse. Wave my sword at the Bluebellies. Curse them…politely, of course. Tell the artillery to fire, and then tell the poor bastards in the ranks to charge." He smiled and gave Rebecca a kiss on the cheek. "One hour of strutting around sounding like Foghorn Leghorn and then back to camp for a dram or two of Pappy Van Winkle."

Sam laughed. "Well, never let it be said you didn't do the least you could do."

Turnbull gazed at the units taking the field. The approaching storm was pushing forward a weather wall that made it a cold, overcast, blustery day. "Not an ideal day, although it's nice it ain't hot. The wind is gonna send all the black powder back in our faces, though. Might as well be smokin' unfiltered Camel cigarettes. 'Course, a lot of these folks already do that."

"When's the big show?" Sam asked.

"Soon," Turnbull answered. "Now, what you're gonna see is the Yankees over there"—he waved his sword toward the blue-clad reenactors in a grassy field—"who represent General Joseph Mower's Seventeenth Corps, reenact Mower's Charge."

"So the Union will attack?" Rebecca asked.

Turnbull nodded. "They will undertake a spirited push to the Mill Creek Bridge and overrun Joseph E. Johnston's HQ." He pointed to an encampment behind the still-assembling Confederate lines. "But then Lieutenant General William J. Hardee—that's me," he said and smiled, "will push him back."

"Where do Gage Randolph and SOL fit into this?" Sam asked.

"I forgot you had a proprietary interest. Gage will fall in the counter-attack." Turnbull pointed to where a group of Confederates were forming. "That's them over there. You gotta see Gage play dead. He bloats up like a corpse that's been rotting in the sun. Damnedest thing you ever saw. We even have a photographer here who uses the same techniques and equipment that Mathew Brady did. He's gonna try to produce an authentic-looking Civil War-era photo."

"Hollis, with all due respect, that is the stupidest thing I have ever heard in my life," Sam said. "What the hell does that prove? Or do? Or add?"

"I guess it's supposed to remind people that war was nasty and not some game. Remind 'em that people died," Turnbull said.

"Maybe," Rebecca chimed in, "the best way to do that is to *not* dress up in costumes and pretend it *is* a game."

Turnbull shrugged. "I know you think it's silly, but we are serious about our reenacting. It means somethin' to us."

"I know," Sam said. "We appreciate you taking time to show us around."

Appeased, Turnbull said, "Grab a good spot on the sidelines, and watch the South rise again." He put on his cap and mounted his horse, a big roan mare that clearly had done this before and seemed resigned to doing it again.

"Let's go watch Gage bloat," Sam Aucoin told his wife.

"Beats watching the South rise again," Rebecca Aucoin replied.

CHAPTER TWENTY-FOUR

Bill Spark believed he could see the gray ghosts of Confederates past interspersed in the audience gathered before *The Firebell*'s broadcast booth underneath a stand of oak trees overlooking the battlefield.

"We're coming to you live from the re-creation of the Battle of Bentonville in the beautiful state of North Carolina. This is just exhilarating," he enthused. "Watching men pretend to fight and die for what they believe in. The rattle of musketry and the roar of cannon. That, folks, is the sound of freedom. It's the sound of a million voices saying, 'Don't tread on me.'"

He let the audience soak in his eloquence and bask in his patriotism.

"Ladies and gentlemen, the smell of gun smoke hangs in the air. Mix it with the lingering aroma of the sweat of good men doing God's work, add in a dollop of fresh horse dung, and you have a veritable potpourri of liberty," Bill declared.

"That's right, Bill," Sierra Darlin' said. "I'm inspired by what I see here today. Watching these brave Confederate reenactors carry the day reminds me that some things are worth fighting for. Over and over again."

"Indeed, Sierra. As all of you fans of *The Firebell* know, we are taking our fight with Washington to the high seas. We're giving the middle finger to the IRS, but that is all we're giving them. The rest we're taking to *Freedomland*." He pointed at the Confederates on the battlefield. "The men these reenactors honor would understand what we are doing. They would agree with it."

179

"And they would support the fight our special guest of honor, and our new boss, is waging," Sierra said as Zacharias Townsend settled in beside them and donned a headset.

"Ladies and gentlemen," Bill said, "I want to introduce a true visionary and the most patriotic, freedom-loving man I have ever met. Zacharias Townsend." Gentle applause from the crowd drifted across the field.

"Thank you, Sierra; Bill. I'm glad to be here with you today. We are watching a reenactment of a battle fought long ago, but the war remains unfinished. The cause for which those men fought remains as pure and noble as it was when they fired the first shots in self-defense against a tyrannical government in 1861."

"You sure don't like Washington, do you?" Sierra observed.

"No, Sierra. I don't like them taking my money. I don't like them taking your money. I don't like them taking anyone's money. That is why I funded the creation and distribution of ElimiTax. That's why I back it with the finest legal team in the world, and that's why I am sponsoring the move of your show, and the wealth it generates, to *Freedomland*."

"Well, it seems like the only one who dislikes the IRS as much as you is Jacob Kelley. What's your opinion of his actions?" Bill asked.

"I have no idea where Mr. Kelley is," Zacharias replied. "No idea at all. But I wish him luck. I know why he took such direct and dire action. An oppressive government drove him to take such desperate measures. Our means may differ, but our objective is the same. We must reclaim our lives from Washington's despotic grasp."

"You are a noted collector of Civil War memorabilia. And in particular, you have an affinity for Confederate items. Why is that?" Sierra asked.

Zacharias looked at Sierra several moments too long, or so Bill thought, before placing his left hand on her thigh in a gesture that could be considered paternal only in a Greek play. "The government and the liberal elite prevent us from holding an honest discussion about states' rights and the overreach of imperial Washington by propagating all this politically correct blather about the Civil War being about slavery. The men who fought for the South were men of honor. They fought not to subjugate other men but to resist subjugation by Washington."

Zacharias, much to Bill's annoyance, kept his hand on Sierra's thigh. She did not seem to mind.

"Whaddya think about Stonewall Jackson's left arm?" Bill asked, his voice tight. "At the moment, that arm, and the hand attached to it, are not where they should be."

Sierra shot Bill a quick look. Zacharias smiled and removed his hand from her thigh before answering. "I can only hope that someone who appreciates its historical significance stole the arm to preserve and protect it."

"OK. Thanks, Zacharias. We look forward to our next show, which we will broadcast from *Freedomland*. In the meantime, we have a battle to watch," Sierra said.

"Yes, I'm looking forward to seeing the South strike a blow for liberty."

I bet it's not the blow you were hoping for, Bill Spark thought.

"Momma, is that man really dead?" Sam Aucoin heard a young boy ask his mother.

"No, sweetie. He's just pretendin'. Like you do when you play soldiers with your friend Tommy."

"I don't know. We never look like that when we play dead. This guy looks like Uncle John when we saw him in his casket after the tractor rolled over on him."

"Let's go get hamburgers," the boy's mom said.

Sam smiled as he turned to his wife. "I have to agree. I've fished bodies out of the Cape Fear River that didn't look as bad as Gage does right now."

Rebecca Aucoin looked over at Gage sprawled in the grass. "It *is* amazing. He's a good-looking man, but now he looks…well, I guess the word I'm looking for is *lifeless*."

Sam watched a photographer use an antique camera to photograph Gage as Mathew Brady might have during the Civil War. When the photographer finished, Gage resurrected himself. His features regained the animation of the living, and his stomach retracted as he rose from the dead. After acknowledging the smattering of applause, he moved off toward *The Firebell's* broadcast table. Sam Aucoin ambled behind him, holding Rebecca's hand.

CHAPTER TWENTY-FIVE

"**W**ell, what did you two think?" Hollis Turnbull asked as he looked down on Sam and Rebecca Aucoin from his horse.

"Always nice to have a war where no one dies," Rebecca said.

"Oh, that sometimes happens. Heat, weight, a bad southern diet based on great southern cooking. It can take its toll," he said. "No one dies from gunfire, but a clogged artery will take you out as sure as a well-placed minié ball."

"I see SOL has set up a recruiting booth," Sam said, pointing to a crowd around three long tables in a *U* shape and covered by green felt cloth. Behind the booth, a large Confederate battle flag and the SOL standard flapped and snapped in the steady wind. He noticed Bud Roy Roemer and Shelley DeWeese helping answer questions.

Turnbull made a sour face. "Not the kind of recruitment I think should go on here. They take advantage of the crowd's excitement to talk to people who are interested in reenacting. SOL starts off easy but then moves to indoctrinate them in political thought that would have been at home in 1857."

"Are they successful?" Sam asked.

"Not really," Turnbull replied. "There are always a few misfits wanting to blame carrying their virginity into their mid-thirties on blacks, Democrats, and entitlement programs that prevent us from contributing one hundred percent of GDP to the Pentagon. Meeting attendance at Marse Robert's spikes temporarily during reenactment season, but most drift away after a few weeks."

Still in character, Turnbull touched his hand to the brim of his hat, bade them farewell, and trotted off to indulge in a post-battle libation.

Sam shifted his gaze from the SOL stand to the crowd gathered around *The Firebell's* makeshift broadcast booth. A tall man ten pounds on the wrong side of heavy, with receding brown hair and a round face, was signing autographs. Doing the same alongside him was a beautiful, short, strong-looking blonde woman who radiated a combative intensity that, combined with her athletic frame, suggested she was a pissed-off gymnast. He presumed the two were Bill Spark and Sierra Darlin'. He had listened to them a few times and concluded that Bill was milking a schtick for all he could. Sierra, however, was a zealot.

Next to the two, Sam noticed, were Zacharias Townsend and a woman he presumed to be Mrs. Townsend. They were holding forth with a group of journalists. Bill Spark, Sierra Darlin', and Zacharias Townsend—that grouping Sam could understand. American patriots who somehow could square their fathomless love of the United States with their desire to remove themselves from it with all immediate haste. He didn't care about that. He was a cop, concerned with law and order and the safety of his immediate community. Treason was above his pay grade. As long as they didn't rob a 7-Eleven on the way out, it wasn't his business. He figured their petulant whining about taxes and personal liberty was, much like the reenactment he had just witnessed, nothing more than self-indulgent playacting. What Sam couldn't understand was Gage Randolph standing alongside media personalities and a billionaire several times over with the confidence of one who knew he belonged.

"What do you make of that?" Sam asked Rebecca. "Bill Spark, Sierra Darlin', Zacharias Townsend, and Gage Randolph. In the immortal words of the late Kermit the Frog, 'One of these things is not like the others.'"

Rebecca smiled at him. "Kermit is dead? My students will be devastated."

"Another victim of climate change," Sam joked. "Now, about Gage…"

Rebecca looked over to see Gage whispering in Zacharias's ear for a moment and then Zacharias replying via a whisper into Gage's ear. "I agree it's strange."

They watched as Zacharias ended his interview, collected Bill and Sierra, and moved toward a tent that was larger than the average American home. Gage caught the attention of Bud Roy and Shelley nearby. The three of them trailed in Zacharias's wake.

Sam and Rebecca mingled with the crowd for another twenty minutes until they heard Zacharias's helicopter come to life. A few minutes later, the Townsends, Bill, Sierra, and what appeared to be the world's fattest Confederate emerged from the tent, along with Bud Roy, Shelley, Linus McTane, and Gage.

"Christ, look at the gut on that fella," Sam told Rebecca. "If you could get it moving, that would be a formidable force in a bayonet charge."

The Townsends, Bill, Sierra, and their unknown Confederate friend shook hands with the others and then turned toward the helicopter, now kicking up a cyclone of dust and debris as it revved for takeoff.

"Looks like General Porcine McSlaveholder is going with them," Sam said.

Rebecca eyed the group for a long moment. "Not sure what's up with that," she said, "but there is nothing wrong with your cop instincts, Sam."

CHAPTER TWENTY-SIX

As his helicopter clawed its way into the sky, Zacharias Townsend introduced Bill Spark and Sierra Darlin' to their fellow passenger. "Folks, this is Jacob Kelley."

"The Unacrapper?" Sierra said.

"Jacob," Jacob said. He could not believe he was sitting across from *the* Sierra Darlin'. This, the single greatest moment in his life, justified the past few weeks of suffering. Thinking his odds with her might improve if he shed his disguise, Jacob removed his wig, bandages, and mustache, and extracted the bath towels from beneath his tunic.

"One of the, uh, conditions of employment, legal support, and *Freedomland* citizenship is that you overlook the occasional oddity," Zacharias told Bill and Sierra as he fixed them with a piercing gaze with his good eye.

"No worries," Bill said hastily.

"Jacob will spend some time with us until we can figure out what to do with him," Zacharias said.

"Sierra, I'm a huge fan of yours. You, too, Mr. Spark," Jacob said. "You both inspired me to take a stand."

"I suppose we can't interview Jacob?" Bill asked Zacharias.

"I don't think that would be wise until we have a plan of action worked out. Besides, we will have enough to talk about for your first show," Zacharias replied.

Forty minutes later, the helicopter settled onto one of *Freedomland's* helipads and the passengers disembarked. "You and Sierra are in the same apartment as before," Zacharias told Bill.

Jacob frowned when he heard that. He hadn't known that Bill Spark had a thing going with Sierra. But he had come this far, and he would not let the opportunity go to waste.

Zacharias looked at Jacob. "Follow Lila," the billionaire said, pointing to a crew member. "She will show you to your temporary quarters. I will drop by later so we can discuss plans for moving you along."

As the group moved their separate ways, Jacob caught up with Sierra. "Uh, Sierra…"

Sierra turned to look at him. Bill kept walking. "Yes?"

"Uh, would you like to meet for dinner? A place this size has got to have a Burger King or something. Maybe I could tell you my side of the story."

Sierra flashed a smile she had used countless times before to crush the hopes of those male fans who assumed an unwarranted, and creepy, familiarity with her. "Oh, aren't you sweet. I'm sure we'll see each other around." Then she turned and followed in Bill's wake.

He watched after her, deciding to find victory in her dismissal. *She didn't say no!*

Jacob Kelley turned and followed Lila, who was smiling after witnessing the exchange, thinking to herself: *I bet he doesn't understand she just said no.*

"I don't like it. That damn clavicle shooter was at the battle today," Bud Roy Roemer said while digging into a plate of ribs at a barbecue joint in Fayetteville. "He was watchin' us send off Townsend and Kelley."

Sauce dribbled down Gage Randolph's chin as he worked on a rib, and he wiped it off with his sleeve. He thought the sauce was too weak and the meat was clinging too tenaciously to the bone. "He don't have no proof, but he sure seems to have a suspicious mind."

"With good reason," Linus McTane said. "You two have done grievous injury to the North Carolina penal code."

"That's why we need to move Monica Bell ASAP," Bud Roy said while chewing. "Early in the A of fucking M. I don't want her seen coming out of Knockers."

"OK," Gage said. "I can handle moving her on my own. We should meet at the landing site. It's suspicious to have too many cars parked at Knockers, given that it's closed and all."

McTane pushed aside his empty plate and dug into an enormous piece of key lime pie. The third Mrs. McTane would not allow desserts in the house. Something about LDL and triglycerides. Whatever those were.

"Hell," McTane said, "there were never that many cars at Knockers when it was open."

"Gage," Bud Roy said, "you text Townsend and tell him we are moving up the, uh, extraction, to four a.m. We'll use a field on Linus's spread. It's far enough out of town that a helicopter won't wake anyone. Linus, can you be ready to go?"

McTane considered the money that might flow his way from even a sliver of Zacharias Townsend's legal work. "I won't like it, but I'll be there."

"Fine," Bud Roy said. "Gage, you sure you can handle Monica by yourself?"

"Me and Rebel have it under control."

"OK. It will be you three. I gotta help Shelley move our goddamn leopard. We're taking a boat. Fucking cat's gonna hate us."

McTane looked at Bud Roy. "Can't you get someone to, uh, leopard-sit?"

Bud Roy shook his head. "I don't know when we'll be back. Don't even know *if* we're comin' back. Even if I found someone, Howard would try to eat him. Then I would be back in court, this time on the wrong side of a lawsuit. I didn't get shot in the clavicle just to lose the money 'cuz someone got too close to my leopard."

McTane shook his head. "This is about the most complicated goddamn felony I have ever been involved in."

"We got a plan," Bud Roy said. "Now we just gotta pray Deputy Aucoin ain't staking out Knockers. If he is, we are most assuredly fucked."

McTane conceded Bud Roy's point. "It might be time to quit playin' defense. I know Sheriff Hawkins. I'll pay him a friendly visit to say Bud Roy here is feelin' put upon by Deputy Aucoin's general nosiness. See if we can't get him to back off."

Gage nodded. "Good idea. Tell him it ain't hypothetical, either. Lawyer it up."

Linus McTane smiled. "You bet, Gage."

"Sam, my boy," Sheriff Johnnie Hawkins said. "You are my best damn deputy and my biggest goddamn headache."

"Johnnie, I swear, I didn't shoot anyone today," Sam Aucoin said as he took a seat in Hawkins's office.

Hawkins leaned back in his chair. A big man and still solid despite closing in on sixty, his movements were precise—as if mapped out and planned well in advance—and executed with purpose and elegance. His .357 Magnum with a six-inch barrel—Hawkins was old-school and favored a dependable wheel gun over a semiautomatic—was holstered in a belt folded neatly on the corner of his desk. An African American sheriff who had won his last election in a majority white county with 63 percent of the vote, Johnnie Hawkins succeeded by harnessing great intelligence, discipline, and sheer competence to a tireless work ethic. As always, in addition to his gun, his desktop contained only what the task at hand required. In the early evening on a weekend, that was two mugs of coffee. He offered Sam one.

"Linus McTane called today. You know him, right?"

"How could I forget?" Sam said. His guard came up. He sensed where this was heading.

"He said you were harassing Bud Roy Roemer and Gage Randolph and that they have retained his legal counsel to protest said harassment. Said you were still upset about the shooting. You blamed them, he said. Linus told me you followed Bud Roy and Gage to the Cracker Barrel the other day and questioned them while they were eating breakfast."

Sam placed his mug on the coaster on Hawkins's desk. He sighed. "You know damn well I stop in there for breakfast twice a week when school is in session and I'm pullin' a night shift. Becks is out the door before I get home, and I hate to cook."

"I know," Hawkins said, holding both hands up in a placating gesture. "Told McTane that. Then he said you followed Gage to the CVS. Asked him if he was dating."

"Well," Sam observed, "Gage is a fine-looking man."

Hawkins grunted. "Sam, I need you to be careful. You have a hell of a future. You could go federal now if you wanted. And you could be the next sheriff if you wanted. But not if you get sued for harassment."

"Gage and Bud Roy are up to something. For God's sake, they were hanging out with Zacharias Townsend up in Bentonville today."

"That's another thing. Since when are you interested in Civil War reenacting? McTane told me you were up there, too. Hell, even I would be suspicious if I saw you that many times in a week."

"Man can't learn about his heritage?" Sam asked.

"Heritage?" Hawkins replied with a laugh. "For Pete's sake, your family came to America in 1926 and went to New Mexico. You said so yourself. What heritage are you looking for at a Civil War reenactment in Bentonville?"

Sam grinned. "OK. You got me there. I've been doing some digging around about Gage and that weirdo group called SOL. Wanted to see what all the fuss was about. Kind of an interesting day."

"Liked the battle, did you?"

"No. I thought it was stupid. What was interesting was watching Bud Roy, Gage, and McTane hang out with Zacharias Townsend and that radio nut Bill Spark."

Hawkins peered at Sam over his cup of coffee, which he held carefully with both hands as he sipped it. "Any crime being committed?"

"Most likely," Sam replied.

Hawkins smiled and leaned forward as he went for the kill. "Do you have any evidence that has been, you know, developed through dogged police work, of a crime being committed?"

Sam put his hands behind his head, leaned back in his chair, and sighed. "No."

"Then back off. I can't cover for you if McTane presses on this, no matter how much I might want to. He's connected, and he can definitely make trouble."

They looked at each other while Sam absorbed the message. Hawkins said, "Just let 'em be for a while. OK?"

"Sure thing, Boss. Anything else?"

Hawkins shook his head, and Sam headed out the door. The Sheriff swiveled in his chair and watched through the window as Sam left the building.

"Damn good cop," Johnnie Hawkins said to the empty room. "He ain't gonna leave it be."

"About time you got rid of that monster," Alma Spivey said as she watched Bud Roy Roemer and Shelley DeWeese wrestle Howard the Leopard's transport cage into the back of Bud Roy's Ford Expedition. "And not a moment too soon." She held in her arms Sprinkles the Second, a toy poodle of much smaller dimensions than his recently ingested namesake.

"Creative naming scheme you got for your dogs, Alma," Bud Roy said. "Why don't you chuck Sprinkles Part Two into Howard's cage? He just ate, but I bet he could use a Tic Tac."

"I detest you, Bud Roy Roemer. And I'm glad you're leaving and taking that horrible creature with you."

"We don't like you too much, either," he said as Shelley walked up to the front porch to lock the door. "But we ain't leavin' for good, and we ain't gettin' rid of Howard, either. We're just goin' to visit a rich friend is all."

"I hope you don't come back."

"Oh, for Christ's sake," Bud Roy said as he shut the tailgate on his SUV. "It was your fault Sprinkles Part One got turned into a Tender Vittle. Not ours. Besides, you'll never know if we come back. You got one foot in the grave already. I bet you trip over that damn fur ball and take a header down the stairs before the week is out."

"You are a foul man."

"We'll miss you, too, Alma. I wouldn't let Poodle McNugget out of your sight. There's some vicious field mice around here that will kick his ass."

Bud Roy and Shelley got into the Ford. He started the engine, and they pulled away without glancing back.

Alma Spivey stood in the driveway and watched until their taillights faded into the night.

CHAPTER TWENTY-SEVEN

"Well, did you win?" Monica Bell asked Gage Randolph as he entered the dining area at Knockers.

"It ain't about winnin' and losin'," he said as he sat down and let out a tired sigh. He removed his boots, which were as close to authentic as you could get, and therefore hurt like hell.

"Where's Kelley?" she asked.

"Part of my plan," Gage said with a smile and no small amount of pride, "was to get rid of him. He's on his way to Texas. Got friends there who want to help him."

"Texas?" Monica asked with a trace of disbelief. "Helluva plan, Gage. The Feds will never think to look for a government-hating, Jubblies-loving racist in Texas."

"Do you Democrats ever wonder why you don't win in the South?" he asked. "Anyway, you should be happy. Jacob Kelley is someone else's problem. Means more Jubblies for us."

"Can we please have something else tonight? Jubblies is killing me."

Gage looked at her and smiled. The stress of the past few days had driven him close to exhaustion. But he also needed her to trust him. The next day was going to be a long and difficult one.

"You know what? You've earned a treat." He stretched and stood up. "I'm gonna do some shoppin', and then I'm gonna cook a great meal for you."

Monica felt equal parts gratitude and trepidation as she considered his offer. "I'm not sure I'm up for grits and HoHos."

"I can manage better than that," Gage said. He stood and looked at his watch. "I should get going 'fore the stores close. I'm gonna change into something modern and then hit the road. Won't take long."

"And then we can talk about letting me go?"

"You bet."

As soon as Gage departed, Monica fished out her iPhone and called James "Ponce" DeLeon. He picked up on the first ring. "Monica, how are you?"

"I think we are nearing the end of this. Jacob Kelley is making a run for Texas."

"Texas? Does he know it's still a state?"

"Seems he has an actual friend. The friend is in Texas," Monica said. "You should call the police. A guy like Kelley…him we need to get off the streets."

"Not sure how I tell the police without getting grilled about how I know all of this," DeLeon said.

"Find a pay phone and make an anonymous phone call."

"A pay phone? Where would I find one of those? 1986? Maybe I could also send a fax."

"Funny," Monica said. "Check out Jubblies. If they don't have one, go to the bus station."

"I'm on it. I'll call the FBI rather than the locals."

"Oh my God!" Monica Bell said two hours later. "This is incredible." She looked at Gage Randolph. "You made this…what is it again?"

"Blackened salmon. A Cajun dish. And the salsa is Philippine mangos—those are the best—with onions, lemon, salt, coriander, and those little bitty hot peppers that spice up a bowl of pho. Those things really give it a kick."

"You sure you didn't buy this somewhere and then bang around a bunch of pots in the kitchen pretending to cook?" Monica asked.

Gage Randolph shrugged. "I told you I want to open my own restaurant. I like to cook. Always have. It's sorta like chemistry, which for some reason I was good at, too, back in high school. The key is to mix things together and make something greater than the sum of its parts...while avoiding accidental explosions, of course." He looked at her and smiled. "Kinda sexist to think a guy can't cook."

Monica returned his smile as she took a sip of a very good sauvignon blanc Gage had purchased, which proved to be an excellent pairing. "I stand hoisted on my own petard."

He shifted to a more serious topic. "Tomorrow, we're leaving here. Early. Three in the morning."

She looked up at him, unease written on her face. "Nothing good happens between midnight and six a.m. What are you going to do with me?"

He put up his hands. "Listen, nothing is going to happen to you. That I promise. I just need you to trust me on this one. We're going to meet someone who I can offer you something for your trouble these past few days. Make it very worthwhile. Maybe even give you a story."

"Gage," Monica said between mouthfuls of the salad he had prepared, "do you know how much I make? Do you know what it would take to make this week in paradise worthwhile? This guy would have to be richer than a Rockefeller."

He smiled. "Got it covered. Now finish up, put on your super-expensive face goo, and get some sleep. Helicopter's coming early tomorrow."

"Helicopter?"

Gage Randolph didn't answer. He cleaned up the dishes and moved off to the office to get some sleep. *Probably shouldn't have mentioned the helo*, he thought.

3AM?!? That's kind of early!

Monica Bell read James "Ponce" DeLeon's text and muttered, "Selfish asshole." She replied, *Sorry if my kidnapping is interfering with you getting a solid 8 hours, Ponce!*

He wrote, *I didn't mean it that way. But 3AM is not good. Lots of bad things happen at 3AM.*

She answered, *Which is why I want you to be ready to follow us when we leave.* Monica's thumbs tried to punch holes in the screen as she fought with DeLeon in a medium neither of them preferred.

He asked, *Why don't you call the police and end this? Because I want to protect this guy*, Monica replied. *Also he made me curious. Mentioned a helicopter and said we would meet someone rich and powerful. And that I would get a story.*

DeLeon's reply was quick and predictable: *If I wanted to lure you into the woods at 3AM, that is what I would say.* He's working off the Serial Killing for Dummies *standard game plan.*

Monica wrote, *Just follow us. But stay out of sight. Did you call the Feds about Kelley yet?*

Not yet, Ponce replied. *Wanted you to think it over again. I can have you free in 20 mins.*

She responded, *No! Call the Feds about Kelley and then get over here. We're leaving in a few hours.*

Monica Bell put the phone in her pocket and closed her eyes, willing herself to sleep.

"Boss, we got an anonymous tip that Jacob Kelley is on his way to Texas."

Special Agent Peter Carlson rubbed his eyes and looked up at the FBI agent poking his head into his office. Carlson was exhausted from the protracted manhunt.

How could someone so stupid be so elusive? he wondered. *I would have bet a week's pay we would've caught him at a truck stop eating meatloaf by now.*

Carlson didn't like to lose, and he certainly didn't like to lose to someone as dumb as he thought Jacob Kelley to be. Sadly, by day two of the manhunt, the FBI director himself had taken an interest in the case and had memorably told the press corps that Special Agent Peter Carlson would "flush out the Unacrapper" within twenty-four hours. By day five, Carlson had received 259 copies of a *Washington Post* editorial cartoon showing a befuddled-looking FBI agent standing over a toilet bowl with a plunger in his hand and a caption reading, *Flushing the Unacrapper is harder than I thought.*

"Great," Carlson said after a moment. "Do we think this report is any more credible than the many sightings of the Unacrapper on the summit of Mount Turdmore? Or the people calling in to tell us that Kelley was floating in a tiny boat in their toilet, like the Ty-D-Bol Man?"

"Possibly," the agent replied from the doorway. "Came from—get this—a pay phone. I didn't know there were any of those left. A pay phone at a bus station in Fayetteville, North Carolina, to be exact."

"Could be just a kid with a spare quarter who wanted to have some fun," Carlson assessed. "Did he say anything useful?"

"Well, there was one bit of extraneous information that seemed weird enough to be genuine. Caller said Kelley was disguised as a Confederate soldier."

"How is that a disguise? Wouldn't that, you know, bring attention to him?"

"Struck me as odd," the agent said. "I did a few years at the office in Birmingham. Alabama may be the last holdout from the Civil War, but even they don't dress like that day to day. So I took the liberty of using that computer thingy on my desk and connected to the interwebs. Turns out there was a reenactment of a Civil War battle in"—he looked at his notes—"Bentonville, North Carolina. Just a nine iron from Fayetteville. Even better, one of the units taking part was South of the Line."

Carlson perked up. "Kelley's group of neo-Confederate dipshits?" He stood up. It wasn't much, but it was more than they had. The FBI lab had pored over the tape of Jacob Kelley calling in to *The Firebell*, but the only thing they had learned was that there was someone else with him who was not happy about the phone call. And Fayetteville was in the vicinity of the wreck on that highway involving Jacob's last known stolen auto.

"Well, unless the Department of the Interior has managed to locate Mount Turdmore National Park, this is our best lead since Kelley called in to *The Firebell*. Want me to wake up the Charlotte office?"

"Yep. No reason they should get to sleep if we can't," Peter Carlson said.

"I thought my days of getting up at 3:00 a.m. to put to sea were behind me," Captain John Purdy muttered as he sipped his coffee and watched his crew load cargo and passengers bound for *Freedomland*.

From the pier, Bud Roy Roemer looked up at Purdy as he stood on the bridge of his vessel, coffee mug in hand, giving orders to his crew. Bud Roy then turned to the white crewman taking Shelley DeWeese's luggage off the pier and asked, "Are you Captain Purdy?"

The crewman pointed to Purdy standing on the bridge, looking every inch the captain to everyone but Bud Roy. Bud Roy stared up at Purdy for four long seconds but could not process information so at odds with his worldview. He was sure he had misunderstood. He asked the crewman, *"Who* is the captain?"

Taking in Bud Roy's struggle to reconcile his prejudice with reality, Purdy emitted a sound halfway between a grunt and a laugh. He was thinking of getting a sweatshirt with YES. I REALLY AM THE FUCKING CAPTAIN emblazoned across the front to help clients like Bud Roy overcome their preconceptions about what colors captains came in. But he didn't have time for Bud Roy to get woke—the sun would burn out before that happened—so he decided to settle for grudging acceptance. "Mr. Roemer," he called down, "I'm Captain John Purdy. Yes, that's me. Don't adjust your television; there is nothing wrong with the colors on your screen."

Bud Roy was about to offer a sheepish excuse that would have made it worse, but two crewmen, accompanied by Shelley, came into view as they manhandled Howard the Leopard's cage down the pier. They struggled to maintain a grip on the container while avoiding Howard's energetic attempts to dismember them with his claws. Now it was Purdy's turn to gaze with disbelief at what his eyes were telling him. Given his long career in the coast guard, he thought he had seen almost everything there was to see. And in his subsequent career as a charter boat captain taking rich nitwits after trophy fish, he thought he had seen the rest. But Howard the Leopard was a new one.

"What the fuck is that?" Purdy asked as he watched Bud Roy, Shelley, and the two crewmen lower Howard's cage onto his precious boat. "Please tell me the cage is locked."

"This is Howard," Shelley said. "He's an African leopard. But don't worry—he's tame and likes people."

Standing behind Shelley, Bud Roy caught Purdy's eye and shook his head side to side several times in a vigorous refutation of Shelley's assertion. He needn't have bothered. Purdy was not a cat person.

"It stays in the cage. And it stays on deck. For all I know, leopard piss smells like Old Spice, but I ain't taking the chance and putting him below. And, just out of curiosity, you know you're going to an oil rig, right? I mean, it's a nice oil rig, but still. It just doesn't seem like a leopard will, you know, fit in."

"Howard's part of the family," Shelley said. Purdy saw Bud Roy shaking his head again. "He'll be happy as a clam once we find a place for him to call his own."

Now Purdy shook his head. "Tie the cage down," he told the crewmen, "and let's get underway." He turned to Bud Roy and Shelley. "Get the rest of your gear on board. I hope you have sea legs; it's a mite rough out there."

Bud Roy grimaced and turned with Shelley to gather their remaining luggage. He would much rather have been in the helicopter. He glanced over his shoulder at Howard, who had a look of pure fury in his golden eyes and vengeance on his mind. For once, Bud Roy Roemer and Howard the Leopard were in agreement—they had both had better days.

Purdy watched Bud Roy and Shelley amble up the pier. "Weirdos," he said to himself. He turned to give Howard the Leopard an appraising look. The big cat returned his gaze with a baleful glare and then growled at him.

"Part of the family, huh?" John Purdy said. "Well, you still got better manners than that asshole congressman I had to take out there last month. Less likely to bite, too."

"Where are we going?" Monica Bell asked Gage Randolph as they cruised out of Fayetteville at three fifteen in the morning.

"Field outside of town owned by a friend," he said. "Helicopter'll come in and land; we'll get on it. Then we'll go meet a guy who should be able to make this all go away."

"Anyone else coming?" Monica asked as she absently stroked Rebel the Hound's snout. The dog, perhaps associating her with a regular supply of chicken, had taken a liking to her.

"Don't see how it hurts to tell you stuff now," Gage said as he turned off the two-lane and onto a gravel road. "Linus McTane, who has supplied, uh, legal advice, will join us. We'll meet the helo at his place. He owns a big spread. Linus is what you call a gin-and-tonic farmer. He has a gin and tonic, and watches other people farm."

The gravel road gave way to a long blacktop driveway, at the top of which was a large house with a commanding hilltop view of fields and pockets of woods. Before reaching the house, Gage turned right onto a dirt track that led down to a large grassy meadow bigger than a football field. He stopped at the far end and left his lights on.

There was a sharp rap on Gage's window. Monica jumped and looked over to see a heavyset man with a full head of silver hair atop a big moon pie face standing beside the driver door. Gage rolled down the window. It had been some time since Monica had seen anyone crank down a window in an automobile. "Mornin', Linus," he said.

"Not yet," McTane grunted. "I coulda used another five hours of shut-eye. The third Mrs. McTane was none too happy when the alarm went off. Come to think of it, neither was I."

"Linus, this here is Monica Bell. Monica, this is Linus McTane."

"Ma'am," McTane said as if greeting a client and not someone who had spent the past week chained to a stripper pole. "Please allow me to say you are even more beautiful in person."

"Gee, how nice," Monica said. "Why, that compliment alone makes up for being hog-tied to stripper pole at a bankrupt restaurant called Knockers and forced to endure the sub-thirty-seven IQ of Jacob Kelley."

"Do you even know what hog-tied is?" Gage asked. "If anything, you had a long lead and plenty of freedom. Most kidnappers would've said too much freedom."

McTane smiled. "You're a pistol," he said to Monica. "Look, you got lots to be mad at. I don't blame you. But we are honestly trying to figure out how to make this up to you in such a way that might keep Mr. Randolph here out of jail."

Monica sighed. "Believe it or not, Mr. McTane, that is a deal I will to listen to."

Linus McTane and Gage Randolph exchanged glances as the sound of a helicopter grew closer.

A hundred yards away, concealed in a copse of ash trees, James "Ponce" DeLeon watched a large helicopter land. He observed Monica Bell and her captors, including an enormous dog, get on board.

"Christ," he whispered to himself. "What do I do now?"

One hour later, Sam Aucoin found himself back in Sheriff Johnnie Hawkins's office. The gun belt was again on the corner of the desk, and two steaming coffee mugs were again sitting in the middle. Unlike Sam, Hawkins was wide awake, his uniform crisp and his face without a hint of stubble. No matter the time of day, he looked as if he had just arrived at work.

"Sam," he said as he handed the sleepy officer his mug, "looks like you might not be entirely crazy."

"Gosh, please make sure and include that in my next performance review." Sam gratefully took the coffee, which was nothing more than a caffeine delivery system at this time of the morning.

"I got a call from an Agent Johnson at the FBI field office in Charlotte. He said they'd received a tip that one Jacob Kelley, aka the Unacrapper, was in the vicinity and headed toward Texas."

"And let me guess: good old Agent Johnson wants us to shut down all traffic in and out of Fayetteville."

"I know, right?" Hawkins said. "I wasn't sure what he wanted me to do since the information was old. I told him it would be a damn busy day if I stopped every car in my jurisdiction driven by someone who wanted to blow up the Internal Revenue Service."

Sam smiled. Like many local law enforcement officers, Hawkins had no great love for the FBI; although, if pressed, he would admit a grudging but genuine respect.

"But," Hawkins said as he leaned back in his desk chair with his own mug, "then good old Agent Johnson said something interesting. He said the phone call came from a pay phone at a bus station here in town, and that the guy—not a kid, an adult male—reported Kelley was wearing a Confederate uniform."

Sam set his coffee down. "Now I'm awake."

"Thought that might get your attention."

"Son. Of. A. Bitch. Becks and I saw Gage, Bud Roy, and Linus McTane hanging out with Zacharias Townsend and them radio nitwits up in Bentonville. Townsend and his wife, Bill Spark, and Sierra Darlin' boarded a helicopter along with some big fat guy with bandages on his face wearing a Confederate uniform."

"Could be what we law enforcement professionals call a clue."

"I'm not feelin' too professional at the moment, Johnnie. I just stood there and watched America's most wanted terrorist escape. I didn't even have the presence of mind to shoot him in the clavicle. I should just change my name to Sheriff Fucking Lobo."

"I always wondered what his first name was." Hawkins smiled, stood up, came around the desk behind Sam, and clapped both of his big hands on the deputy's thick shoulders. "Don't be too hard on yourself, son. There ain't nothin' wrong with your antennae."

"You gonna tell Agent Johnson any of this?"

"Hell no," Hawkins said, releasing his grip on Sam and opening his office door to signify the meeting was over. "At least, not right away. Would be a nice feather in our cap, and a nice black eye for the Bureau, if we could catch the Unacrapper after they spent a week huntin' for him."

"So I got a little leeway on this?" Sam asked, standing to face Hawkins.

"A little. Not so much you can go around kickin' in doors. But enough to poke around in earnest. You're already way ahead of the Bureau on this one. But keep me up to speed, got it? Zacharias Townsend could buy and sell this whole county with the money he finds under his couch cushions. I want to know if you're gonna piss in his pool."

Sam moved toward the door. "Gonna do this without the uniform or the cruiser, if you don't mind. Just a badge and a gun. I'll bill you for mileage on my POV."

"Sounds like a plan. What's first?"

"A shower and then breakfast," Sam Aucoin said. "Whatever needs to be done, best it be done awake and on a full stomach. Doughnuts first. Then I'll let you know."

CHAPTER TWENTY-EIGHT

Monica Bell was impressed. She was wealthy, but buy-an-oil-rig-to-establish-your-own-floating-country wealthy was another story. After landing on *Freedomland*'s helipad, crewmen had guided the group to their palatial cabins. Now alone, she checked her phone and found she had zero bars. There was Wi-Fi, but it was an encrypted network. *Freedomland* was a dead zone. She tried several of the phones in her room, but they only connected her to an internal switchboard, which asked her to enter a six-digit PIN if she wanted an outside line.

"Cheap J. Paul Getty wannabe bastard," Monica muttered, slamming the phone down.

Soon after, she found herself reunited with Gage Randolph for a guided tour provided by one of the crew.

"So this thing can move on its own?" Monica asked as they entered the bridge, covered with enough electronics to make Captains Kirk and Picard feel at home.

"Yes, ma'am," the guide said. "It's a semisubmersible rig. Built to move around and drill exploratory wells. We can raise or lower it with ballast tanks as need be and move anywhere we want at up to seven or eight knots under our own power. She has great sea-keeping abilities, so we can ride out the biggest storms without even feeling them...too much," the guide qualified.

"So you're not worried about the storm?"

"Nah," the crew member said. "It won't turn out to be much. A weak hurricane already starting to break up. As you can tell, we're not feeling the ocean at all. Seas will get heavier, so in a few hours, we'll add more ballast and lower the rig to make her even more stable."

"When do we get to meet the owner?" Monica asked.

"How about now?" Zacharias Townsend said as he entered the bridge. "Ms. Bell, it is a pleasure to meet you."

Monica was, for a moment, speechless. Gage was right. An interview with Zacharias Townsend just might be worth it.

Quickly recovering both her poise and her attitude, she said, "Since I've been tied to a stripper pole for the past week, I suppose the pleasure is all yours."

"I heard about that," Zacharias said. "Mr. Randolph here has asked if I can help make up for any inconvenience you might have encountered."

"And how do you know Mr. Randolph? In my experience, billionaires don't run with, uh"—she looked at Gage, dressed in his usual faded jeans, work shirt, and Mack Truck ball cap—"hundredaires."

Zacharias laughed. Gage rolled his eyes. "Gage and I have a business transaction we will conduct later today."

"Stonewall Jackson's arm," Monica said.

Zacharias looked at Gage, who shrugged and said, "Lucky guess."

"You told me about it the first night we met," Monica said.

"Well," Zacharias said, "why don't we discuss things over breakfast and see if we can arrive at a deal that'll benefit all interested parties? I believe Mr. McTane is already in my quarters. He appeared eager to join us for breakfast."

"He doesn't look like he misses many," Monica Bell said. "Lead the way, Mr. Townsend."

"I don't think that poodle's sittin' right with Howard," Bud Roy Roemer said as he stood next to John Purdy on the bridge of the Hatteras Sportfish and watched Howard vomit on the deck below. Shelley DeWeese moved to comfort the leopard, who swiped his paw at her. Howard the Leopard was not feeling kindly toward anyone he associated with his present predicament.

"You fed him a poodle?" Purdy asked as he helmed his boat, searching for the best line through the rough seas.

"What? Oh, no," Bud Roy said. "Not intentionally. We would never do that. I love dogs."

"Oh, I'm not accusing you of anything or passing judgment," Purdy said, his eyes never leaving the sea. "I am agnostic about using poodles as a source of cat food. More research should be done. Just sounded to me like the leopard ate a poodle."

"Our neighbor's standard poodle got into Howard's pen," Bud Roy explained. "It ended kinda like you would expect."

"You oughta bring Howard to my house," Purdy suggested. He paused as he turned the helm a few degrees to starboard and added power, expertly surfing a large wave. "My wife has a yappy little dog. Thing's the size of a lima bean. Got a bladder to match. Needs to be walked every three hours or it detonates on the carpet. I swear that goddamn dog isn't more than four inches tall, but it pisses like it's fucking Man o' War."

Purdy positioned his boat to take the next wave. He had done this most of his adult life, and his actions were second nature. He talked to Bud Roy as calmly as if they were walking down the street rather than sailing into a boiling ocean. "The dog has to pee so much and so often I told my wife I was gonna name the little bastard Flomax. Luckily, I'm at the age where I gotta go three times a night, too. Still, it's a pain in the ass in the winter. I can't just let it out to do its business. It might blow away. Or maybe fall to its death in a muddy footprint. Wife insists I gotta put four little booties on the damn thing and then put on its little harness. Looks like I'm walking a fucking gym sock." He shook his head.

"A few days ago, Howard bit me on the ass while I was having sex with Shelley," Bud Roy confessed.

Purdy looked at him for a moment—reluctant pet owner to reluctant pet owner, although he thought Bud Roy was oversharing—and then said, "OK. You win."

"How much longer?" Bud Roy asked. "Howard ain't the only one a little green around the gills."

Purdy smiled. "You're doing just fine. Stay up here where you can see the horizon and feel the wind. You'll make it. Besides"—he pointed at a gigantic structure looming out of the surf and the gray, swirling mist—"we're almost there."

"How will we get aboard?" Bud Roy asked. "Sea's rough."

"Good question," Purdy noted. "I would never try to dock my boat against the rig in this sea state. We'd get the livin' hell beat out of us. But this rig is something. We're gonna pull in underneath, in the lee of the…I don't know what you call them; pontoons, I guess. This reduces the chop a good deal. We'll go into a submersible dock which will then lift us right out of the water. We can unload like it's a truck parked at a loading dock."

"Wow," Bud Roy said.

"It's good to be rich," John Purdy said.

"I shoulda guessed you two über patriots would show up here," Monica Bell said when Bill Spark and Sierra Darlin' joined them for breakfast.

"Oh, look who's quit hiding in shame after the beating I gave you," Sierra said.

"Dream on, Apartheid Barbie. Just because you're impervious to logic, reason, and facts doesn't mean you win debates. It means you're a fucking moron. It also means the only point you ever have is the one on your head that holds your Klan hood in place."

"Monica," Bill said before Sierra could reply, "I am glad you're OK. I was worried."

"Thanks, Bill. Seems like you've landed on your feet. Got a new investor in your radio show, I hear," Monica said, nodding at Zacharias Townsend.

"We see things the same way," Zacharias offered. "And Mr. Spark has a gift for condensing my politics into bite-size chunks for the masses."

"Yeah, well, blowing massive chunks over the airwaves is Bill's forte," Monica replied. "Speaking of the great unwashed, Bill, one of your most rabid fans is the Unacrapper. He couldn't get enough of your show."

Bill rolled his eyes. "Please. Mark David Chapman was a fanatic about *Catcher in the Rye*. Doesn't mean J.D. Salinger shot John Lennon."

"No. But you aren't J.D. Salinger."

"Who is?" Bill retorted.

Monica silently conceded the point.

"While I'd love to listen to this all day," Linus McTane said as he entered the room, "I'd rather eat."

"For once, I agree with a lawyer," Zacharias said. "After we eat, Bill and Sierra have a radio show to do. And Mr. Randolph and I have some business to conduct before we get down to the larger question of how to make it up to you, Ms. Bell, for the inconvenience you have suffered."

"Well," Monica said, "being tied to a stripper pole for a week was unpleasant. But it was better than flying commercial."

"You should get your own jet someday," Zacharias said from the buffet set up along the wall as he forked four pancakes onto his plate. "I have a Boeing triple seven."

"Let me guess," Monica said. "A simple G-VII wouldn't make the right statement."

"Exactly," Zacharias Townsend replied. "My guiding ethos. More is never enough."

James "Ponce" DeLeon had a problem. The problem was sizable, but not big enough to stop him from pounding down the four Krispy Kreme chocolate doughnuts in front of him while he searched for a solution. Doughnuts helped him think.

He ate his doughnut. It was a good doughnut. A little hoop of lard-based happiness. Eating it made him feel better. But he still didn't know what to do.

Monica Bell had gone off with her kidnapper and one other man on a helicopter. The helicopter had headed east, according to the compass on his iPhone. He hadn't heard from her since.

DeLeon was in over his head. He knew it. He knew he should go to the police. What he hadn't figured out, however, was what to tell them.

As he was pondering his next move, which was likely to buy another doughnut, a big, strong-looking man wearing jeans and a windbreaker came in. He had brush-cut blond hair and biceps you could see through his jacket, and he walked in with the assurance of someone used to entering rooms and then owning them. DeLeon's suspicions that the fellow was a cop were confirmed when the newcomer walked up to the counter and the hostess greeted him.

"Mornin', Deputy. What'll you have today?"

"Still not ready for my usual, Deb," the cop said. "How about two original glazed and a cup of coffee?"

DeLeon watched him pay for his meal and sit at a booth across from him. The cop looked over and fixed him with a stare. "Help you?"

"You're a policeman?" DeLeon asked.

"Deputy Sam Aucoin, Cumberland County Sheriff's Department. There a problem?"

DeLeon rarely took the direct approach. He preferred having an angle and leavening the truth with enough lies to create a favorable advantage. This made him one of the more honest people in cable news. But he figured the story was complicated enough. For the first time in a long while, he figured the truth was his best play.

"I'm Monica Bell's producer. You know—the missing TV star?"

Sam nodded. His doughnuts lay untouched, his coffee forgotten.

"Two guys kidnapped her and held her at a place called, and this is for real..."

"Knockers?" Sam said.

"Yes...Jesus...how did you guess?"

"I've been working on a hunch. The owner and I have some history."

"Well, Monica got hold of a phone and called me in New York..."

"When?" Sam asked.

"A couple of days ago."

"And you're just now getting around to telling the police?" Sam's green eyes bored in on DeLeon with a strength that pinned the man to his seat.

"Monica insisted. She wanted to work some things out with one of the kidnappers. The other guy, however, was that idiot...the Unacrapper."

"You have got to be kidding me." Sam moved into DeLeon's booth, leaving his breakfast on the other table. "You knew where America's most wanted domestic terrorist was, and you didn't tell us? You knew said terrorist was holding a missing celebrity hostage at said location, and you didn't tell

211

us? Let's see if you can further annoy me. Why would you withhold this from the police? What kind of asshole are you?"

DeLeon gulped. The truth, he had discovered, would not in the slightest set him free. "I...I'm a cable news producer."

"OK. That makes you a fair-size asshole. Am I to take it, Mr..."

"DeLeon."

"Mr. DeLeon," Sam repeated, "am I to take it that all the people you mentioned are no longer conveniently located at Knockers Bar and Grill for ease of arrest and incarceration?"

"Monica and another guy left this morning. She told me the Unacrapper left yesterday."

"And you're the guy who called in the anonymous tip about Kelley heading to Texas?"

"That's what Monica was told. She wants him caught. She asked me to phone it in."

"If she really wants him caught, you should have called it in immediately. We could've hit them at the restaurant."

DeLeon made a peace offering by getting up to retrieve Sam's doughnuts and coffee from the adjacent booth. He sat down. "We did let you all know he's on his way to Texas," DeLeon offered.

"No," Sam said. "You let us know Monica Bell had *heard* that he is on his way to Texas. In fact, you didn't even give us that much. Your information is much less sure than you communicated on the phone. I might point out there are a lot of ways to get to Texas, that Texas itself is enormous, and that we have no other leads."

"You don't think you'll find him?"

"Oh, we'll find him," Sam said. "It just won't be in Texas or on the way to Texas. But I know where to start."

"Where?"

Sam dispatched both doughnuts in a few large bites, drained his coffee, and stood up.

"All roads lead to Knockers. Come with me."

CHAPTER TWENTY-NINE

"Let me get this straight," Zacharias Townsend said as he stood with Bud Roy Roemer and Shelley DeWeese on the top deck of *Freedomland* gazing at Howard the Leopard, his one good eye transmitting images his brain was reluctant to accept. "You brought an African leopard with you to an oil rig? Where are we supposed to put him? What do we feed him? You see any gazelle on board?"

"Well, Howard is used to steaks now," Shelley said, addressing his question without alleviating his concern.

"I cannot stress enough," Zacharias said as he glared at her, "how much I hate people citing irrelevant facts to avoid facing a greater truth."

"He won't be any trouble," Shelley said, trying to placate the billionaire. "I swear, he's a good leopard."

"In what way is he good?" Zacharias asked. He harbored a fascination with people who indulged in anthropomorphic assessments of animals.

"Well, I mean, he don't eat people," Shelley said.

"Not all of 'em, anyway," Bud Roy muttered, rubbing his still-tender butt cheek.

Zacharias rolled his visible eye. "Well, I guess every country needs fauna. Howard's home is the tennis court until we can figure out a better solution. It's got a roof, so he won't be able to climb out. Make sure the door is secure." He snapped his right wrist up to glance at his watch. "Now that *The Firebell*'s producer is aboard, I have a radio show to attend. Get your leopard secured, and then a crewman will show you to your new quarters. After I'm done, we can discuss your beef with Uncle Sam, as well as the beef I now have to pour into this damn cat."

Zacharias Townsend turned and left before either could reply, leaving Bud Roy Roemer and Shelley DeWeese standing alone on a converted oil rig in the middle of the Atlantic Ocean except for their thoughts and a vengeful African leopard.

"You're listening to *The Firebell*, and we are coming to you live from our new home on the sovereign state of *Freedomland*. No income taxes. No rules about how much or how little I gotta pay Sierra Darlin' here, nobody yellin' at me for owning an SUV or being a white, heterosexual male. My friends, I am free. Free to tell it like it is. And freedom—let me tell you, there is nothing like it in the world."

Bill Spark looked around the state-of-the-art recording studio. His eyes settled on his stunning cohost, and he decided his journey from midmorning jock in Cincinnati to the voice of discontent for millions of frustrated Americans was complete. A few years living on this extravagant floating wedding cake, and then he would buy a place in Limón, Costa Rica, and spend his days imbibing on umbrella drinks and screwing any nubile Tica who would have him. He figured Sierra would have tired of him by then. She would want to take over the show anyway. Her priorities differed from his. Sierra Darlin' believed.

"What do you think of our new home, Sierra?"

She gave him a million-megawatt smile. *Not tired of me yet*, he thought.

"Bill, coming to *Freedomland* is the best decision you've made since you hired me. I am fired up. I never knew, never *could* know, what true freedom meant until I got here. In the brief time I've been in our new home, I have been reborn. This is what America should be. It is what America can be. And with the help of all of you out there listening, it is what America one day will be."

"You said it, Sierra," Bill said, annoyed she had just said what he was going to say. "We are going to bring the truth to all of you out there in Occupied America, and we will keep bringing it until we can return to a United States of America that is truly the land of the free. In a few minutes, the president of *Freedomland*, Mr. Zacharias Townsend, will join us. But for now, let's go to the phones and hear from our audience." Bill looked into the control booth and asked, "Who's on the line?"

"We got Phil from Toledo, Ohio," the producer said.

"Phil, how are ya today, buddy?" Bill asked.

"Not too good. For one thing, I live in Toledo."

"I've been to Toledo," Bill said. "I think it gets a bad rap."

"Well, I'm ready to move. Local taxes; county taxes; state taxes; federal taxes; sales taxes; taxes on alcohol, cigarettes; hell, probably even on porn, but no one I know pays for that anymore. You can see where I'm going, Bill, can't you?"

"I believe I can, Phil. You're feeling overtaxed and underappreciated. And you're feeling like you don't even know your country anymore. Do I have it right?"

"Yeah. Also, you know, I'm paying for all that stuff to make Toledo a better place to live. This shouldn't be too hard to do, what with the bar already being set so low. But trust me, it ain't working. And there are entire streets I walk down where I don't hear a word of English. So here's my question: how can I move to *Freedomland*?"

Bill laughed. "I guess Sierra and I did a good job of selling our loyal listeners on the benefits of our new home. I bet you're not the only one out there asking that very question. And there is no one better to provide an answer than the man who has just joined us in the studio, Mr. Zacharias Townsend."

Zacharias sat down next to Bill, donned a pair of headphones, and, because of his height, hunched forward to reach the microphone. Bill moved to adjust the mike, but Zacharias waved him off.

"Hello; Phil, is it?" Zacharias asked.

"Uh, yes, sir, Mr. Townsend. My name is Phil."

"And what is your question again?"

"Sir, I wanna move to *Freedomland*. How do I do that?"

Zacharias laughed. "Well, I guess the first thing you have to do is ask."

"Ask?"

"Yes. If you want to live here, you need to ask me. Nicely."

"OK," Phil said. "Uh, Mr. Townsend, uh, sir, can I move to, uh, *Freedomland*?"

"No," Zacharias replied. "You can't, Phil."

Bill and Sierra exchanged looks.

Phil from Toledo was confused. "You said all I needed to do was ask."

"No," Zacharias said. "I said the *first* thing you needed to do was ask, but I never said I would let you. It is the difference between a prerequisite and a promise. It is the difference between earning something and asking for a handout. It is the difference, Phil, between you and me."

Phil was tough. Or maybe he just really wanted out of Toledo. Either way, he wasn't done. "Why can't I move there?"

Bill and Sierra both winced. This had not started well and was going to end worse.

"Phil, tell me. What do you do for a living?"

"I'm kinda between jobs at the moment."

"Uh-huh. And what jobs are you between? Neurosurgeon? CEO of a major company? Pilot? What are you qualified to do?"

"Well, I was working in a glass factory, training as an electrician's apprentice. But it didn't work out. Then I was working construction, but that's kinda seasonal."

"So nothing," Zacharias said, "is what you are qualified to do. See, the problem is you don't understand what *freedom* means."

"Sure I do," Phil said. "It means doin' what you want to do."

"No," Zacharias replied. "It means having the opportunity to do what you are able to do. Phil, you are a loser. You're not talented, you're not smart, and you're not able to contribute. You need to stay in your little hole in Toledo, and you need to stay out of the way. Those of us who are smart, talented, and able to achieve great things will, when the mood strikes us, drop scraps from the table. Those scraps are for you."

There was a moment of silence as Phil from Toledo absorbed Zacharias's philosophy. Once he had, his response was predictable.

"Well, fu—"

The producer was ready for the expected reply and hit the kill switch. Phil's rejoinder remained confined to his small row house in Toledo, Ohio.

"That was one way to handle it," Bill said while cutting the microphones. "If we're lucky, maybe three or even four people are still listening."

"Put us back on the air," Zacharias said.

Bill reluctantly took his hand off the cough button and spoke before Zacharias could open his mouth. "OK, *Firebell* listeners, I'm sure you're all wondering what just, uh, transpired here between Phil from Toledo and Zacharias Townsend. I think Zacharias was practicin' some tough love on Phil—"

"I was letting him know the way things need to be," Zacharias cut in. "*Freedomland* is not about taking in the huddled masses. You can keep that slogan on that piece of crappy French art standing out in New York Harbor. I don't think America should try to lift all boats. That's socialism, and socialism doesn't work. In fact, I don't think America should try to lift *any* boats. Build your own damn boat. I know I did."

"Got that, people?" Sierra asked. "No free lunches, and you need to build your own damn boat. Mr. Townsend here did Phil from Toledo a favor by telling him to get moving and to stop lookin' to others for help. I'm sure Phil took his beating like a man and now is doing just like you said."

"No, Sierra, I don't think Phil is doing anything," Zacharias disagreed. "He was looking for a handout. He's not a winner. He's a loser. The rest of you, go out and be winners."

"Sounds good, Zacharias," Bill said. "Ya know, I think it's time for us to cut to a commercial. As he just said, we've all got to pay our own way. And one thing we're not free from here is paying the rent and the utilities. And speaking of that, here is a message from, uh, Concerned Christians for a Coal-Fueled Tomorrow." Bill raised his eyebrows in mild surprise as he double-checked the ad spot on his computer monitor. *Nut bags!* he thought. *But they are nut bags who pay the bills. I better sell it.*

"You know, God chucked an inexhaustible supply of gorgeous clean coal into the underbelly of the American continent," Bill said, leading in the spot. "He also put folks in the Appalachians who are born diggers to get that coal. Why, you look at the bottom of any hole in the United States, and you will find someone from West Virginia down there with a shovel in his hand and a grin on his face. Now, God didn't go to all the trouble of putting coal and hillbillies in the mountains so we could keep buyin' oil from Osama bin Laden or cheap solar panels from Chairman Mao. So listen to what these Bible-based climatologists have to say." He cut to the ad.

"Global warming. Climate change. These are terms straight from Satan's playbook," a male voice intoned. "In Genesis 8:22, God said, 'While the Earth remains, seedtime and harvest, cold and heat, summer and winter, day and night, shall not cease.' God promised the Earth would be fine. Do you really want to call God a liar like Al Gore does? God put coal in the ground for us to use. Are you comfortable telling God he made a mistake, like the loony-left environmentalists who would rather kill an unborn child than shoot a deer?"

Bill turned down the sound in the booth and swiveled in his chair to face Zacharias. "Did you really have to go after poor Phil like that? There are a lot of Phils in my audience. I'd kinda like to keep them."

"They won't go anywhere," Zacharias said. "Your audience is just looking for someone to blame. Someone to feel superior to. We can't come right out and tell 'em to blame the blacks, or the Mexicans, or women. Not anymore. Or at least, not directly. But we can describe character defects no one in your audience will see themselves as having. They will readily assign them to those who are different. Your audience has already made Phil black. Or Mexican. Or Asian. Or a liberal. You can crap all over as many Phils from Toledo as you want. None of the rest of the losers in your audience will think you're talking about them, even though most of them are Phil."

Zacharias looked at Bill and Sierra, fixing them with a gaze that betrayed nothing as they absorbed the depth of his cynicism. No feeling, no soul, and no empathy. He did what he did without reflection, just like an animal or a machine.

"People want to believe they can be rich, despite all evidence to the contrary. It's called the American *Dream* for a reason. There are only a select few who can make that dream a reality. The rest are too stupid to make it. They're cannon fodder for the rich."

Bill and Sierra remained quiet, wondering what they had bought into, as Zacharias pushed himself away from the console and levered himself out of his chair. He looked at his watch. "I need to go see if I can talk Monica Bell out of pressing charges against the guy who dug up Stonewall Jackson's arm," he said as if he was announcing merger talks with IBM. "Finish up here, then join us in my quarters."

"Wow," Sierra said as she watched Zacharias exit the studio. "He talks to us like he owns us."

"He does," Bill Spark said.

Jacob Kelley was tired of staying in his room. It was by far the nicest and biggest place he had ever spent any amount of time, but he already felt like a prisoner. No phone calls out. No computer to check the internet. No service for his cell phone. No Wi-Fi. The only thing he had been able to do besides gaze at the storm-whipped expanse of Atlantic Ocean outside his window was listen to the live feed of *The Firebell*.

Jacob was not at all happy with how Zacharias Townsend had smacked around Phil from Toledo. Jacob knew a thing or two about being between jobs. And he knew about rich assholes treating him like he wasn't good enough. He had never met Phil, but he knew him. It wasn't Phil's fault, Jacob reasoned. Just like it wasn't his. He knew whose fault it was. Them. The government. Liberals. Elitists. Minorities. God, there were so many of those now he didn't even know if the term *minority* was correct. He figured it was simpler when it was just the blacks he could blame.

He listened to Sierra Darlin' sign off from *The Firebell*. Sweet, beautiful, no-nonsense. She was both the who and the what missing from his life. She had called him a hero. And she had agreed to meet him for lunch or even dinner. Well, maybe not agreed, but she hadn't said no. And the absence of a no was likely equal to a yes.

Women are funny that way, he thought. *Still, there's only one way to find out.*

Jacob got up from the sofa. He strode to the door and pulled on the handle. Locked. He didn't like that one bit.

"*Freedomland*, my ass," he muttered to himself as he tried the door again. It didn't budge. He pounded on it.

After a moment, the door opened, and an Asian crew member blocked the doorway. Or tried to. He wasn't huge. But he had a gun on his belt. "How can I help you, sir?"

"I would like to go out on deck and get some fresh air."

"You have a balcony off your room, sir. Try that."

"I'd like to walk around," Jacob said. "I'm feelin' kinda cooped up."

"Sorry, sir. Mr. Townsend's orders. You are not to leave the room."

Jacob was in no mood to be told what to do by someone he figured was an illegal immigrant. The man didn't strike him as Norwegian. Jacob was upset that Zacharias didn't have the common courtesy to guard him with a proper white American. He figured the guy was doing the job for five bucks a day, too.

Something ugly flashed across Jacob's face. The guard saw it and took a step back while reaching for his sidearm.

Like most men, Jacob Kelley overrated his effectiveness in a fist fight by 6 billion percent. He wound up and threw a clumsy, looping right-hand punch that his opponent easily ducked, although doing so halted the guard's progress in drawing his weapon.

Jacob had, however, recently finished a book, the first one he had read in years. The novel had featured Jack Reacher, a former military policeman who had used the headbutt to great effect in several fight scenes. For the first time in his life, Jacob applied something he had read to a real situation. As his awkward follow-through on the punch carried him a step closer to the guard, Jacob used his momentum, snapped his head forward, and smashed his forehead into the guard's face.

The guard collapsed to the floor without a sound, unconscious.

Jacob followed him down but made a great deal of eloquently profane noise on the way. "Shovel fuck me with a spoon!" he howled. "Jesus, that hurts! Goddamn Lee fucking Child, or whoever wrote that fucking book. Never mentioned how much this fucking hurts. Which is a lot!"

Jacob rolled over on his side in the fetal position. He stayed curled up for a few more moments, feeling sorry for himself. He then looked at the guard, who was breathing through his mouth, his broken nose already beginning to swell.

Jacob stood up. He grabbed the guard under the arms and pulled him into the doorway, using his body as a doorstop. Jacob looked at the door and noticed the lock was a card-swipe mechanism. He checked the guard, found a key card in his jacket pocket, tested it, and then put it in his own pocket. Jacob placed a chair in front of the door to keep it from locking them both inside.

My guess is he's gonna be kinda pissed, Jacob assessed, looking at the guard's face. With the chair in place, he dragged the guard, who was slowly coming around, to a spot near the sofa.

Jacob Kelley took the guard's gun, a 9mm Glock 17, and stuck it in his waistband. He also took a two-way radio from the guard's belt and made a quick lap of his quarters, ripping every phone he could find out of the wall. No sense having him raise the alarm so soon. Key card in hand, he nudged the chair back into the room and stepped into the hallway. The door behind him gave a satisfying click as the lock snicked into place.

Alejandro Fernandez was about to make a serious mistake.

An assistant food preparation specialist working for a renowned chef, he was slowly climbing the hierarchy of *Freedomland*'s kitchen. He loved food, and working for this chef was an amazing, if brutal, education. One day, Fernandez wanted to run a kitchen on a big cruise liner, and this apprenticeship was an important step toward realizing his dream. However, he was still a ways down the kitchen pecking order. His low status made him the perfect man for filling the ridiculous order Zacharias Townsend phoned down to the kitchen.

"Take these steaks, and feed the cat living in the tennis court on the top deck," the chef said, handing Fernandez the tray of raw meat. A busy man, the chef walked away before Fernandez could ask several important questions that might have equipped him with critical, need-to-know information.

Fernandez's English was more than passable. Zacharias Townsend insisted that English be the national tongue of *Freedomland*, at least when he was within earshot. But Alejandro Fernandez was not a native speaker, and he did not pick up on the chef's use of a singular noun. Had he done so, he might have wondered just how big a cat had to be to cause the cook to give him nine steaks. *Feed the cats? How many damn cats did those people bring that I need to feed them nine steaks?*

He stepped out onto the upper deck and leaned into the strong wind and stinging rain of the storm churning up the East Coast.

Howard the Leopard was not happy. He didn't have the vocabulary to express his feelings, but it was true nonetheless. His stomach was still queasy from the boat ride, and he missed his enclosure and his tree. He might have missed the humans who fed him steaks, but he now associated them with the very upsetting recent events that had brought him to this uncomfortable place.

Howard squirmed deeper into the makeshift enclosure that had been hastily erected at the request of Shelley DeWeese as he sought shelter from the frigid wind and rain pummeling the tennis court. His ears caught the sound of a gate being opened—he knew this sound, and he associated it with food. Despite having an upset stomach, it was not in Howard's cat nature to miss a meal. He peeked out of the enclosure and saw a chubby human carrying food.

Not one given to dawdling, Howard the Leopard sprang into action and loped toward dinner.

At first, Alejandro Fernandez's brain could not process the imagery transmitted by his eyes. His brain was, along with the rest of him, expecting twenty to thirty kitties, weighing maybe five or six pounds, who would rub their bodies around his legs and meow with excitement when they caught sight and smell of the bounty he had brought them.

What he saw, however, was one gigantic cat, with paws the size of frying pans and teeth the size of a paring knife. This was not what Fernandez had expected to see, nor wanted to see, coming toward him. After one long second spent adjusting to a new and unwelcome reality—one in which he was, for all intents and purposes, prey—he reacted as anyone would.

"Aaaaaah! Aaaaaah! Aaaaaah!" Alejandro Fernandez screamed at an octave usually reserved for tween girls at a Justin Bieber concert. He threw the platter of meat at Howard, who had stopped running when the human emitted the high-pitched squeals. The meat scattered on the tennis court, but the tray hit Howard on the head. This did no lasting damage. His skull was designed to take a zebra kick. But neither did it improve his deteriorating opinion of humans.

Shaking off the impact of the tray, Howard grabbed the nearest steak and began working on it.

Fernandez, shouting curses in his mother tongue, ran out of the tennis court, slamming the gate behind him. The gate, instead of locking, bounced back open. Fernandez, in headlong flight, didn't notice.

But Howard the Leopard did.

CHAPTER THIRTY

"**W**hy are we going to Wilmington?" James "Ponce" DeLeon asked Sam Aucoin from the passenger seat of Sam's Honda Pilot as he tore down Highway 87 toward Wilmington, North Carolina.

"That's where the information points us," Sam said as he settled the Pilot in at 95 miles per hour. A search of Knockers had turned up undeniable proof that Monica Bell, or someone, had been chained to a stripper pole. But nothing more. A subsequent breaking and entering of Bud Roy Roemer's house and a cursory examination of his computer produced a phone number and pier-side address for the *Marlinspike* charter craft; John Purdy, Captain; in Wilmington. Given *Freedomland*'s presence off the coast, Bud Roy's odd friendship with Zacharias Townsend, and Purdy's line of work, Sam thought Wilmington the logical next stop.

"Well, why do I have to go with you?"

"Because I haven't decided whether to arrest you for being an irresponsible asshole," Sam said. "Perhaps you can redeem yourself and spare me the trouble of filling out a lot of paperwork."

Upon hearing this, DeLeon remained quiet for the rest of the trip, which had been Sam's intent.

Forty minutes later, Sam pulled into the parking lot of the marina where Purdy berthed his boat. They both exited the car, and DeLeon followed Sam into the office.

"Cumberland County Deputy Sheriff Samuel Aucoin," Sam said, flashing his badge at the skinny young man behind the counter wearing a long-sleeve pullover with an elaborate *Legalize Weed* logo on the front. The clerk looked stricken until Sam said, "I'm looking for Captain John Purdy. Can you tell me where I can find him?"

Relieved, the clerk turned around to look out the window. "That's his boat there," he said, pointing toward a slip on a pier running out on the left side of the marina. "The new Hatteras. Man, that thing is sweet. He got back in a few hours ago. He makes a lot of runs out to the rich dude's oil thingamajig. Far as I know, Purdy is still on his boat."

"Thanks," Sam said as he headed out the door, DeLeon trailing in his wake.

"I'm surprised you didn't arrest him for wearing that shirt," DeLeon told Aucoin as they made their way to Purdy's slip.

"Freedom of speech," Sam said. "His pot, however, is likely in a small bag behind the counter. Did you see the way his eyes shifted when I showed him my badge?"

DeLeon was impressed. "But you won't do anything about it?"

"Why?" Sam said. "Clog up the court system with that shit? Besides, much bigger fish to fry today."

They came up to the side of Purdy's boat. Sam called out his name, and Purdy appeared in the cockpit at the stern, a squat, silver-haired, competent-looking, African American man. He was holding a rag and a large wrench.

"I'm John Purdy," he said. "You looking for a charter? Don't recommend a run today. We can do it, but you won't enjoy it. Weather'll break in a day or two. Why don't we set you up for later in the week?" He was looking forward to doing something besides milk runs to *Freedomland*.

"We need to ask you a few questions," Sam said. "Do you mind?"

"Not at all. Come aboard."

Sam and DeLeon stepped into the cockpit as Purdy closed the hatch to the engine room, hidden behind a bench seat.

"What can I do for you gentlemen?" Purdy asked as he took a seat and beckoned for them to do the same.

Sam pulled out his badge and introduced himself. Purdy nodded and waited for more.

"I understand you make runs out to the Zacharias Townsend oil rig, *Freedomland*," Sam said as he sat down.

"Yep." Purdy waited for him to ask the question he wanted to ask.

"Did you make a run out there today? And if so, who did you take?"

"Yes, I did, as a matter fact. And seeing as I doubt the law recognizes anything like captain-passenger privilege, I will be happy to tell you, especially since they had the bad manners to bring a leopard on my boat."

"Bud Roy Roemer and Shelley DeWeese," Sam stated.

Purdy leaned over to a cooler and took out three Sprites. He passed a couple to Sam and DeLeon. "And don't forget Howard," Purdy said. "I know I won't."

"I imagine the leopard was not happy to be on a boat."

"You ever seen *The Exorcist*?" Purdy asked. "It was sorta like that. But worse. Things were coming out of every orifice on that animal, and many of the substances I believe he produced out of sheer spite." He sighed and pointed to a mop, rags, and various cleansers in the corner. "Been cleanin' this damn boat for three hours, and it still smells like the inside of a leopard."

"Did Roemer or DeWeese mention why they were going to *Freedomland*?" Sam asked.

"Said they were working on a deal and that they already had a bunch of friends out there."

Sam knew what he needed to do. "We want you to take us out there. To *Freedomland*."

DeLeon looked up at the dark sky. "What about the storm? No offense, Captain Purdy, but this boat seems tiny."

"The *Marlinspike* is a helluva boat," Purdy said.

"*Marlinspike*," Sam said. "Is that a fishing term?"

"Nope," Purdy said. He looked at Sam and appeared to approve. "But most people just assume it is. It's seaman lingo. Refers to a tool sailors use for rope work, splicing…that kind of stuff. I named her *Marlinspike* because I never want to forget that sound seamanship skills are what will bring me back every time."

"That sounds a little rehearsed…"

Purdy grinned. "A tad. Sometimes customers find the concept of going out on the ocean better than the reality. So I gotta deploy the hard sell. But that doesn't make it any less true."

"Well," Sam said, "if I have to go to sea in anything smaller than the *Queen Mary*, you're the guy I want behind the wheel."

"She'll make it just fine," Purdy said. "And at a good clip, too. The storm won't amount to too much more. Still, it'll be rough, and the boat will take a pounding. So if you don't mind, can you tell me why we need to go today?"

Sam stood up. "This is gonna sound crazy, but I believe Roemer kidnapped Monica Bell and they are both now on *Freedomland*. I aim to go get her back. I expect, while I'm at it, that I might find the Unacrapper out there, too, and possibly Stonewall Jackson's missing arm."

Purdy was unfazed. "Maybe before this morning, I would have doubted you. But since I just hauled a spitting-mad leopard out there, there's no reason to think those other folks you mentioned aren't there as well."

"So you'll take us?"

Purdy slapped the gunwale of the Hatteras affectionately. "We get some fuel and she's ready to go. Who's paying?"

"Me initially, and then Cumberland County. I hope."

"As long as someone does."

"OK," Sam said. "I need to get a few things from my car and make a phone call, then we can get underway."

"Get your gear, and make the call from the bridge," Purdy said. "We don't wanna waste daylight."

"How about I wait on shore until you get back?" DeLeon offered.

"Nice try," Sam said. "But you're comin' with me. The whole damn reason we even have to go out there in the first place is because you didn't call the police when you should've. C'mon; you can help get my stuff from the car."

"What stuff?" DeLeon asked as they walked up the pier.

"Shotgun. Ammo. Body armor."

"Is there an extra bulletproof vest for me?"

"No such thing as a bulletproof vest. Stay behind me when we get on the rig," Sam said as he used the remote to open the rear hatch of his Pilot.

"Remaining here would be very far behind you," DeLeon observed.

"And me dropping you in jail for aiding and abetting a wanted felon and obstruction of justice would put you even further behind me yet," Sam Aucoin replied. He grabbed a shotgun and thrust a Kevlar vest into James "Ponce" DeLeon's arms. "Carry this and follow me."

Rommel Carlos Vergara stood behind the control panel in a small room off the bridge of *Freedomland*. Like many of the crew, he was Filipino, hailing from a tiny fishing village in northern Luzon. And like most Filipinos, he had a nickname. Everybody called him RomCom.

RomCom had come to *Freedomland* from Carnival Cruise Line. He had jumped at the chance for better pay, better hours, and better living conditions, which allowed him to send even more money back to his wife, kids, and extended family. While all of Zacharias Townsend's promises had not quite materialized—the pay was better, although Townsend clawed some of that back by what RomCom thought to be exorbitant charges for room and board—RomCom was still making more than enough. A couple more years working on *Freedomland*, and he would have money for a new house and a new fishing boat back on Luzon.

Absorbed with increasing *Freedomland's* ballast to lower the rig's center of gravity to better ride out the gathering storm, RomCom didn't notice the control room door swing open. He had begun flooding ballast tanks on the port side and was about to initiate the procedure for the starboard side when he heard a low growl.

RomCom looked up to see a full-grown tiger—at least, that's what he thought it was—crouched atop the table opposite him. Although not a big-cat expert, he assessed this particular feline to be one of ill disposition, his snarl displaying for RomCom the largest teeth he had ever seen.

RomCom experienced a range of emotions—mild surprise, incredible surprise, fear, denial, rationalization, and fear again—in three long, terrible seconds. He stared at the cat. The cat stared back.

He tried screaming but discovered he had lost his voice. The cat hunched as if preparing to strike. RomCom's brain accessed the atavistic fight-or-flight data bank regarding giant cats that had been embedded in human DNA twenty thousand years ago. Quickly crunching the numbers, RomCom concluded that flight would end in his likely consumption. Having settled on fight as his best option, he reached below the control panel and brought out a fire ax.

This did nothing to change Howard the Leopard's mood, nor his own feline calculations about the odds of winning the imminent altercation. Cats are arrogant bastards, and Howard the Leopard was no exception. He took a swipe at RomCom with one giant paw and moved to the control panel.

RomCom parried with the fire ax, then launched his own attack. Unfortunately, his large backswing smashed the ax into the backup control panel on the wall behind him, which erupted in a shower of sparks. Fueled by adrenaline and panic, RomCom wrenched the ax from the panel and sent the blade straight for the leopard's flank. The big cat was much quicker than RomCom and deftly moved inside the arc traveled by the ax. The vicious blow missed Howard and hit the main control panel instead, eliciting another shower of sparks. A cloud of acrid smoke arose from the ruined controls.

Howard the Leopard hit RomCom in the face with a lightning strike from his powerful forelimb. The blow, worthy of a heavyweight boxer, knocked RomCom's head up and backward into a low stanchion. He sank to the floor, unconscious.

Howard, sated from his steak dinner, lost interest in the human as soon as he dropped to the floor and stopped trying to hit him with the ax. Disturbed by the smoke and the arcing electrical panels, Howard the Leopard padded silently out the door, looking for a quieter, more comfortable place to sleep before hunting.

With his gear stowed and Captain John Purdy helming the *Marlinspike* to sea, Sam Aucoin called Sheriff Johnnie Hawkins from the bridge.

"Say that again?" Hawkins asked.

"We believe Monica Bell, and possibly the Unacrapper, are on *Freedomland*," Sam told him. "Oh, and Stonewall Jackson's arm, too."

"Well, shit. Say hi to Jimmy Hoffa and D.B. Cooper while you're out there. What, besides temporary insanity, has driven you to this conclusion?"

"I have Monica Bell's producer with me. He was in touch with her and even visited her at Knockers where she was being held captive by the Unacrapper and either Bud Roy Roemer or Gage Randolph. Or both. Likely both. And somehow, Linus McTane is involved. Monica Bell got in a helicopter with him when it landed at his farm, and they flew off east."

"Well, if you have an eyewitness and the story is strong, bring him in so we can get a warrant."

"Oh, c'mon, Johnnie. Townsend will throw an army of lawyers at us. None of those people will be on *Freedomland* by the time we're able to get out there with a warrant—if we even *can* get a warrant after he lawyers up. Could be none of them would even be alive. This is the best way."

"Sam, if you're caught or if this fails because you're wrong, we will both be out of a job…and likely never able to get another one."

"Johnnie, I'm sure of this. Trust me. They're on *Freedomland*. And I bet Stonewall Jackson's arm's out there, too."

Hawkins sighed on the other end of the line. Sam knew he had won. He knew he would go even if Hawkins denied him permission. And Hawkins knew it, too.

"OK, Sam. What's your plan?"

"Well, I thought I would go out there, snoop around, and see if I can find any of these folks."

Hawkins let out a snort. "Oh, as long as you've got a plan. I know most plans don't survive contact with the enemy, but yours didn't even survive being spoken out loud. For all of our sakes, please try to come up with at least a bullshit reason to explain why you're out there in case you get caught."

"Don't worry. I have a cable news producer with me. I can produce bullshit by the barrel."

"Good luck," Hawkins said. "Keep me in the loop. If anything goes wrong, shoot the cable news guy so at least one good thing comes out of this mess. I'm going to update my LinkedIn résumé in the meantime."

"We'll call you when we've arrested the Unacrapper and rescued Monica Bell," Sam said with much more confidence than he felt.

Hawkins's reply was a grunt as he hung up.

Sam Aucoin placed the phone down on the bridge console and braced himself as the *Marlinspike* slid past the seawall protecting the marina and into the storm-roiled Atlantic.

CHAPTER THIRTY-ONE

"You prefer cash, then?" Zacharias Townsend asked Gage Randolph.

"Mr. Townsend," Gage replied, "we've been over this. As you've said, you are a software billionaire hacker, genius-type guy. I'm just a back-woods nobody with a high school education. And truth be told, the high school wasn't all that good. So yeah, I'll take cash."

"That's a lot of money to carry around," Zacharias said as he handed over a duffel bag containing $250,000.

"Rebel will watch my back," Gage said, giving his friend a pat on the snout. Rebel was still eyeing Stonewall Jackson's arm, which now occupied a place of honor in a customized, climate-controlled glass case behind Zacharias's desk.

Zacharias turned to the others in the room. "Now that we have that transaction out of the way, we need to explore how we keep Mr. Randolph free to enjoy his newfound wealth."

All eyes but Bud Roy Roemer's turned to Monica Bell. Shelley DeWeese was not pleased that Bud Roy's gaze had been fixed on Monica the entire time.

Monica smiled at Gage. "Congratulations. Two hundred and fifty grand will keep you and Rebel in Jubblies hot wings for years. I suggest you put some aside for your angioplasty...and colostomy bags for Rebel."

"I got plans for it," Gage said.

"Well, before you blow it all investing in an animatronic re-creation of Pickett's Charge or something, why don't we discuss how to get me much less pissed off at you four," Monica suggested, pointing at Gage, Bud Roy, Shelley, and Linus McTane, "for chaining me to a stripper pole at a two-bit bankrupt titty bar for a week? Even in North Carolina that has to be at least a misdemeanor."

Bud Roy frowned and pondered defending his establishment against Monica's harsh description. Sierra Darlin' saved him the trouble. "Why do you always have to tear down the South?" she asked. "The South has a code and morals. The South has laws. And we respect 'em."

"What's this 'we' stuff?" Monica asked. "You're about as southern as Orville Redenbacher. You're from Lindstrom, Minnesota, for Christ's sake. Admit it: you were on the high school curling team." She gave Sierra an icy smile. "Rumor has it you were conceived when Ann-Margret lost a drunken bar bet to Bo Svenson."

"Nice to know you can use Wikipedia," Sierra said. She glared at Monica for suggesting she was more Swedish than southern. "I don't even know who those people are. I guess only old people like you have heard of them."

"I always liked Ann-Margret. She's stunning," McTane said. "And Bo Svenson was great in those *Walking Tall* movies."

"I thought that was Joe Don Baker," Bud Roy said.

"Just the first one," Gage said. "The other two were Bo Svenson movies."

"Christ, how could they make *three* of those?" Shelley wondered. "Bud Roy made me watch 'em on video. All in a row. They were awful. And then The Rock remade it. That was not a good idea."

"Look how many *Rocky*s and *Rambo*s there were," McTane said, rising to the defense of the fictionalized memory of Sheriff Buford H. Pusser. "Admit it. Only the first one of each was any good."

Zacharias slapped his hands on his desk. Everyone jumped at the sound.

"I swear, I am going to put every last fucking one of you on Adderall. Jesus Christ. Can we please focus on the task at hand?"

All eyes remained on Zacharias. They nodded and remained mute. He returned the gesture, back in charge, as he expected to be. "Monica, you have suffered an, uh, inconvenience over the past several days."

Monica raised her eyebrows but said nothing.

"So the question is, how can we make it up to you so you leave Mr. Randolph here…"

"And my friends," Gage added.

"Right, and his friends," Zacharias repeated, pointing to Bud Roy, Shelley, and McTane, "out of this."

"Let's not forget you," Monica said. "You're involved in the kidnapping, or at least the coverup. And let's not forget your, uh, jones for bones," she said, pointing to Stonewall Jackson's arm resting in its place of honor behind Zacharias's desk.

Zacharias turned for a moment to look at the relic and then faced the group again. "Oh, I'm big enough to take care of myself. But for the sake of simplicity, let's keep me out of it, too. So what would it take?"

"I've been thinking about that," Monica said.

Everyone leaned forward, keenly interested in the answer. Gage, who knew her the best, thought it a fifty-fifty proposition that she told Zacharias it would take even more money than he had.

"I want two things."

"Go ahead," Zacharias said. "What are they?"

Monica held up an index finger. "Number one: I want an exclusive with you. I want a camera crew out here, and I want them given the run of *Freedomland*. And then I want to sit down and discuss with you on camera why you love America so much you can't wait to leave it."

"Done," Zacharias said. "I look forward to educating your viewers on the proper role and the proper size of government."

"Great. I bet your explanation of why a multibillionaire thinks he is above paying taxes will resonate with the working class. Now for number two." Monica took a deep breath.

Uh-oh, Gage thought. *This one's gonna hurt.*

"I want them," Monica said, pointing at Bill and Sierra, "sent back to the mainland."

"What?" Bill exclaimed at the same time Sierra said, "You bitch!"

"Hoo, boy," McTane said, easing his bulk into a chair. "I knew it wouldn't be easy."

"What the hell do you mean trying to get us kicked off *Freedomland*?" Bill asked.

"Well, Bill, if you and Daisy Mae Brownshirt here," Monica said, winking at a furious Sierra, "want to take a stand against the tyrannical government, do it on dry land."

"We've just announced we're moving here," Sierra said. "You'll make us look like idiots."

"You *are* idiots, but yes, this will cause some embarrassment. That's why I'm insisting on it. I'm sure you can explain it away, though. You all want to make a stand? Stand on your own, just like you always tell your audience to do."

"Well, we already have an arrangement with Mr. Townsend here," Bill said. "He's got the lawyers and the resources to crush you and crush the IRS."

All eyes in the room shifted to Zacharias.

"Deal," he said.

"You can't do that!" Bill erupted.

"Sure I can," Zacharias said. "Look, this is easy. We can spin it any number of ways. You decided to return to, oh, let's call it 'Occupied America' like you did on your show this morning, to battle on the front lines. You'll still get legal support, and I will advertise generously."

"That's not the point!" Sierra said. "She's out to destroy our credibility in the eyes of our audience. This is not about dollars and cents. This is about who we are."

"Well, who you are," Zacharias replied with finality, "are my guests. You are also employees. You'll do as you're told."

"See? Easy." Monica smiled and winked at Bill and Sierra.

"I will not let you destroy everything I've built," Sierra seethed.

"*You've* built?" Bill said.

"Shut up, Bill." Sierra glared up at her partner, the force behind her gaze more than overcoming the disparity in stature. "All you do is mouth a bunch of stuff you don't believe. I'm the one who made *The Firebell* what it is."

He glared back at Sierra. "You were just a—"

"I've got to agree with her, Bill," Monica interrupted. "Before you brought Sierra Goebbels here on board, your show was aimless, silly, and only occasionally did you find your voice. She's made it what it is—a vicious, unprincipled forum for intolerance and ignorance."

Bill and Sierra talked over each other in a bid to retort, but before they could sort out who would go first, the door to Zacharias's office opened. Barbara Townsend walked in, a taut look on her face. Zacharias smiled. He had been expecting her.

His smiled faded when he saw Barbara followed by the crew member who had been standing guard outside, his hands in the air. Behind the guard was Jacob Kelley, sporting a pistol in each hand and an epic bruise on his forehead.

Jacob pistol-whipped the guard, who fell to the floor and didn't move.

Rebel the Hound growled. Gage reached down and took a firm grip on the dog's collar. "Easy, buddy."

"I heard yelling," Jacob Kelley said. For the first time in his life, people had noticed him when he had walked into a room. He liked the feeling. He turned to the woman who had inspired him to take the action that had brought him to this place. "Sierra, is there a problem?"

Rommel Carlos "RomCom" Vergara opened his eyes to find the craggy face of his boss, Marvin Stevens, peering at him from six inches away. This was only slightly preferable to staring at the tiger again. At the thought of the enormous cat, he gave a start and spun around, an action he regretted a moment later. His throbbing head told him he was concussed.

"RomCom!" Stevens screeched in a treble voice utterly incongruous with his gargantuan body. "What the fuck happened here, son?"

"Cat," RomCom croaked, his voice barely audible.

"What? Cat? Have you been drinking, son? Are you telling me a kitty cat came in here and sharpened its claws on the ballast controls?"

RomCom did not shake his head. He wouldn't be doing that again soon. "No," he said. "Big cat. Huge cat. Angry cat. Tiger. Attacked me." Summoning a reserve of pride, RomCom smiled. "I fought back, though. With an ax. Drove it away."

Stevens stood up and looked down at RomCom. "I don't see no jumbo feline anywhere around. All I see here is you, passed out next to an ax. And I see the ballast controls are destroyed. Both the main and the backup. That ain't good."

RomCom saw where this was going. "I swear, I'm sober. And there was a cat. It attacked me."

Stevens looked at him. He motioned to two men standing behind him. "These two are gonna take you to the infirmary. You better be tellin' the truth."

The crewmen moved beside RomCom and helped him to his feet. They made their way slowly to the door.

"Hold on," Stevens said. "In all the excitement about you being attacked by a giant tabby, I forgot to ask the all-important question: were you able to start the flooding process on both ballast tanks?"

RomCom closed his eyes, trying to remember. "No," he said. "Port side only."

"Well, that explains the list to port," Marvin Stevens said. "Mighta been nice if you hadn't shredded both sets of controls."

Jacob Kelley was enjoying having every eye in the room on him for once. It had all been worth it. The long days spent making his unique brand of explosive. The terror of being on the run from the law. The helplessness he felt while being mocked by Monica Bell. All of it had served a purpose. The journey of pain had brought him to this moment. For the first time in his life, he mattered.

The years of humiliation inflicted upon him by a series of low-paying, unappreciated jobs and the accumulated stress of constantly being one missed paycheck from bankruptcy melted away as he looked into what he thought were the adoring eyes of Sierra Darlin'. He was here to rescue her. He was here to claim his prize. He shifted his gaze to Monica Bell.

And to exact vengeance.

"Well," Zacharias Townsend said from behind the desk, "you appear to have our attention." For an unarmed man facing another man with a Glock pistol in each hand, he appeared preternaturally calm.

"First things first," Jacob said. "Gage, lose the iron. I know you're carrying. You always do."

Gage Randolph released his grip on Rebel, slowly opened the denim jacket he was wearing, put his hand inside, and extracted a .357 Magnum with a four-inch barrel. He placed it on the floor.

"Step back away from it," Jacob ordered.

Gage did so.

"Call Rebel over to you. I don't want him gettin' any funny ideas, and I don't want to shoot him."

Gage called Rebel, who had moved off after discovering a new smell in the office. Rebel came over, wagged his tail, and sat by Gage, who took hold of the dog's collar again.

Satisfied, Jacob turned to Bud Roy Roemer and Shelley DeWeese. "I expect you two are carrying also. Since I will search you if you deny it, you better be honest with me. You first, Bud Roy."

Bud Roy reached behind him under his untucked shirt and extracted a Colt Defender 45ACP.

Gage let out an admiring whistle. "Nice pistol."

"Thanks," Bud Roy said as he placed it on the floor under Jacob's watchful gaze and then stepped back from it.

"OK," Jacob said, pointing the Glock in his left hand at Shelley. "Now you."

Shelley opened her small handbag and removed a 9mm Ruger LC9s and placed it next to Bud Roy's pistol. She then took a few steps back.

"Now you, Legal Eagle," Jacob said, turning to Linus McTane. "Your turn. I know you carry. You said so yourself back in Townsend's tent in Bentonville. Be nice like your friends and give it up."

McTane sighed heavily and stood up. He reached his right hand inside his navy-blue blazer and extracted a chrome-plated 38SPL Colt Cobra with a two-inch barrel that he carried butt forward on his left hip. He laid it on the floor with the other firearms.

"Kinda teeny tiny, ain't it, Linus?" Bud Roy asked.

The lawyer shrugged. "If you're shooting from over three feet away, you're doing it wrong. It'll do the job, and then some."

Monica watched the disarmament process with increasing dismay and amazement. "Jesus Christ," she said, looking at the small arsenal on the floor in front of her. "Did you people stop off at a gun show on your way here?"

"Just how we go about our day," McTane said. "Would no sooner leave the house without my gun than I would without my pants."

"Go about your day?" Monica said. "What the hell happens during an average day in North Carolina? Do you honestly think you're gonna have to shoot your way out of the Costco?" She shook her head as she surveyed the firepower on display.

"Oh, look," Bud Roy said. "Monica Bell, bringin' liberal outrage to a gun fight. How's that workin' out for ya?"

"About as well as you bringing a gun to a gun fight," Monica said. "A helluva lot of good your gun is doing you now, lying on the floor. Unless maybe you trained it to shoot all by itself."

Bud Roy shrugged. He had to admit his gun was not doing a damn thing for him at the moment.

"Well, how about me, Crapper?" Monica asked. "You want my gun, too? Or theirs?" She pointed to Bill and Sierra. "Or theirs?" she asked, moving her finger toward Zacharias and Barbara Townsend.

"I don't care if Sierra is carrying," Jacob said. "I trust her, and she won't let Bill hurt me, even if he had a gun, which I doubt. And as for these two," he said, pointing to the Townsends and then nodding at the guard on the floor, "they pay someone to carry for them." He looked back at Monica. "And you. I've heard your rant on guns. Unless you're a hypocritical bitch, there ain't no way you carry. You're too much a liberal wimp."

Monica said, "My flamethrower clashed with this top, so I left it home today."

"Very funny." Jacob paused and looked her up and down, his gaze obvious, heavy, and violating. "But you never know. Maybe I should pat you down just to make sure."

She looked him in the eye, her jaw set. "Sport, you touch me, and, guns or no guns, you'll be eating through a straw for months."

Jacob flushed red, and Monica turned to Zacharias. "I should've known you were mixed up with this asshole. Deal's off. You helping the Crapper," she said, pointing at Jacob, "is something I cannot abide. When I get out of here, I'm going to fry your ass."

"Get in line," Sierra said. "Bill and I are gonna make sure everyone knows you're an elitist fraud."

"That true, Bill?" Zacharias asked. "You willing to give up my backing and risk my wrath just because you don't like how the deal is going?"

"Looks like we gave up too much just by coming here," Bill said. "Time to claw some of it back."

Barbara let out a loud sigh. "See, dear? I told you this would be too messy. I applaud you for trying, but now it's starting to bore me."

Her husband smiled. "Me too, sweetheart." His left hand dropped to an open drawer in his desk, and he pulled out a Glock handgun identical to the two Jacob had in his hands.

"Don't move," Jacob said, bringing both guns to bear on Zacharias. "I'll shoot. I've got nothing to lose."

"That's for damn sure," Zacharias replied. He raised the handgun.

Jacob pulled the trigger on the gun in his right hand, his shooting hand, first. It wouldn't budge. He pulled it again. Nothing. Ever the optimist, Jacob tried the pistol in his left hand. Again, nothing happened.

"Lower your guns," Zacharias said, pointing his Glock at Jacob. "Or keep them up. I don't care. They won't fire."

Jacob looked at both guns. He noticed a small device on the magazine of each pistol and peered at it curiously.

"Why don't they work?" Monica asked with mild interest. She was learning a lot about guns today.

"Fingerprint-enabled safeties?" McTane asked.

"Yes," Zacharias said. "Keyed so only three people can fire any one firearm here on *Freedomland*. The guard assigned the weapon, my wife, or me. I can fire them all."

"Gee," Monica said, "it doesn't sound like the NRA would approve of your national firearms laws here."

"The NRA's insane," Zacharias said. "I don't want people like Mr. Kelley here to have the right to vote, much less to bear arms. Poor people with guns never ends well. They tire of poverty at some point, but are too stupid to get rich. So they try to take what isn't theirs. It's fine when they just shoot one another, but eventually they turn on their betters."

"I used to have a hard time figuring out your politics," Monica said. "You seemed to be all over the map. But now I get it. You've taken the worst the right and left have ever come up with and warped it to fit with your dystopian, Ayn Randian worldview. You're not right or left, Republican or Democrat. You're an asshole."

Now it was Zacharias's turn to shrug. He motioned with his gun. "I need you all in front of me, please. Tighter grouping. My eye patch limits my field of vision. And move farther from your guns. Barbara," Zacharias said, nodding at his wife, "why don't you take that lovely Colt Defender there and help me cover our guests?"

Barbara moved three steps forward and retrieved Bud Roy's pistol. She nodded as if she approved, switched off the safety, and pointed the pistol at the group. It was clear to all she knew her way around a gun.

Jacob moved to Sierra's side. He reached down and took her hand. "Don't worry, Sierra. I'll get us out of this."

Sierra jerked her hand away as if she had touched a live wire. "Don't touch me, creepo," she spat. "Was that the hand you used to stuff your own shit into a pipe?"

"I wore gloves," Jacob said.

Sierra stepped away from him and closer to Bill, who put his arm around her. "Get us out of this?" she said, incredulous, giving Jacob a venomous stare. "You moron. You're the one who disarmed everyone in the room except for the bad guy."

"That's true," Zacharias said. "I was wondering how to do it myself, but then you came along and did it for me."

Sierra glared at Jacob. "We had more guns in here than the entire First Infantry Division. And now we don't. You're the fucking Alamo, Custer, and Pearl Harbor all rolled up into one greasy, low-IQ, shit-bombing wad of stupid. Don't come near me or talk to me. Ever."

She stepped to the other side of Bill, putting his bulk between her and Jacob, glaring at Jacob as she continued. "Fucking stalker. I read about your search history on the internet. If I catch your eyes on me, I will kick your nasty, pathetic ass all over this room."

Jacob reeled under the force of her verbal assault. His brief hope that he could have a life with meaning crashed to a close. Sierra would never be with him. He was Jacob Kelley, a sporadically employed loser. In fact, he realized, he wasn't even that. Not anymore. All he would be was the Unacrapper. All he would ever be was a joke.

I am so fucking tired of this, Jacob thought. He took a quick step toward Zacharias, who shot Jacob in the upper right shoulder.

Bud Roy thought it looked like a direct hit to the clavicle. "Ouch," he said.

Jacob collapsed. Shock was first, but the pain would come, as Bud Roy well knew.

Despite seeing a man shot and the assault on the senses produced by the thunderous gunshot in the enclosed space, McTane's lawyer instincts whirred to life. "I got experience with clavicle-based lawsuits," he told Jacob, who was writhing on the floor as the pain introduced itself.

"Yeah," Shelley said as she emerged from her own stunned silence, "experience losing them."

Zacharias laughed. "There will be no lawsuits, Counselor. There will be no anything." He looked at Jacob squirming on the floor, trying to stanch the flow of blood, with no apparent concern. "Interesting. I've never shot someone before. I've had it done. Sometimes startups in the Valley just don't want to sell for any price. You'd think it would be upsetting. But it isn't. Kind of like stepping on a bug. But easier. Gun doesn't require any emotional involvement. I didn't put that bullet in his body. The gun did."

He looked at Barbara. She nodded and told their hostages, "You will all now do as we say."

Just then, a red phone on the wall by Zacharias's desk rang.

McTane looked at Bud Roy Roemer standing protectively near Shelley DeWeese. He shifted his gaze to Gage Randolph, who was doing the same for Monica Bell, while his hand still maintained a firm grip on Rebel the Hound's collar.

"Does anyone feel like the floor is tilting?" Linus McTane asked.

CHAPTER THIRTY-TWO

"**I**s it just me, or does the thing look like it's tilting?" Samuel Aucoin asked as John Purdy helmed his boat closer to *Freedomland*.

"The nautical term is *listing*," Purdy said as he throttled back the engines, "and yes, she's definitely tilting. May be a problem with the ballast tanks."

The *Marlinspike*, now moving barely faster than a drift, wallowed in the rough sea as Purdy crept closer to the oil rig.

James "Ponce" DeLeon came up from below, looking wan. "What's the matter? The boat slowed down and it's getting, uh, tippy."

Purdy ignored him. "We got a problem."

"What's that?" Sam asked.

"We're not sinking, are we?" DeLeon asked, panic in his voice.

"Shut up," Purdy and Sam said in unison, neither looking at DeLeon.

"Problem is how I get you on board," Purdy said. "Normally, we pull up under, in the lee of the pontoons, and into a hydraulic dock that lifts the whole boat out of the water. With this list, and it seems to be increasing while we sit here, I don't think that will work. And I don't want to risk it."

"Well, I gotta get on," Sam said.

"I know."

Purdy took a pair of Fujinon 14x40 marine binoculars from a niche in the console and studied the structure for a long moment before speaking again.

"OK, here's the good news. The whole damn thing is made of ladders. They are everywhere, and they all lead up, as a good ladder should. The one I am looking at is on the pontoon riding higher in the water." Purdy pointed, and Sam set his bearings along the man's index finger until he saw what Purdy saw.

"The chop isn't too bad there," the captain continued. "We'll put out the fenders, and I'll pull up close. You both jump to the ladder and up you go."

"Jump?" DeLeon asked with alarm. "What if we miss?"

"You'll fall between the oil rig and the boat," Purdy said. "The boat weighs well over one hundred thousand pounds. The oil rig, close to that in tons. You get caught between the two in this chop, you'll end up nothing more than a wet slick on the ocean surface."

"So what you're telling us is, don't miss," Sam said.

"Yep."

"OK," Sam said. "I don't think I want to be wearing body armor when I jump. I go in the drink, I'll go straight to the bottom. And we can leave behind the shotgun as well."

"Why don't we just call for help?" DeLeon asked.

"I'm gonna do that anyway," Purdy said. "I can't tell if they can fix this or not, but the rig is top-heavy, and a few more degrees is all it will take to roll."

"OK," Sam said. "I'm as ready as I'll ever be. Get us as close as you can."

"I'm not ready," DeLeon said.

"And you never will be," Sam replied. "But you're gonna go first. You're the reason I have to go hunt these people down on what appears to be a sinking oil rig. Had you been a responsible citizen instead of a cable news producer, we could have surrounded them in Fayetteville while you prayed for a shootout as you filmed the whole thing."

Purdy directed the crew to put out the fenders on both sides. He goosed the engines as he gauged his approach. Sam joined him on the bridge. Purdy handed him a radio. "I preset it to a private channel, compatible with this unit," he said, showing Sam a twin of the radio he just handed him. "Consider me your seagoing Uber. Tell me when and where, and I'll be there to pick you up."

Sam gave Purdy a clap on the shoulder. "Thanks, Cap'n."

The deputy moved to the bow along with DeLeon as Purdy brought his precious boat closer to the underside of *Freedomland*.

"Why do I have to go first?" DeLeon asked.

"Because if I go first, you'll wimp out." Sam gauged the distance between the bow and their target ladder. "Get ready."

Purdy's superb seamanship was apparent as he nosed the *Marlinspike* as close as he could to the pontoon, taking advantage of the windbreak provided by *Freedomland*'s structure and holding the boat in place with a dexterous use of the throttles.

DeLeon spent a few seconds timing the rise and fall of the bow with the ladder. He then reached out, grabbed the lower rung, and kicked furiously until his feet gained purchase. He scrambled up a few feet and waited for Sam.

Sam reached out at the crest of the next wave, grabbed the lowest rung, and moved up the ladder via a series of effortless chin-ups until his feet found the bottom rung. He was grateful for the time he had put in the gym.

"Showoff," DeLeon said.

"Get moving toward that hatch," Sam ordered, pointing at an opening over fifty feet up.

As soon as Sam had made his jump, Purdy maneuvered his boat back toward the open sea. Sam's radio chirped, and Purdy's voice said, "Good luck and be careful. Call when you're ready. We're not going anywhere, and I'm calling for the cavalry."

Sam Aucoin paused for a moment to wave to John Purdy and then disappeared into the hatch.

"What do you mean we're sinking?" Zacharias Townsend bellowed into the phone.

His hostages looked at one another, fear and surprise showing on their faces.

"Not sure I can be any clearer than that," Marvin Stevens said. "A freak accident in the control room fried both the main and backup ballast controls. The cocks on the port side are wide open. I've sent two men to close it down manually, but I've lost contact with them. For all I know, it has something to do with the tiger that's running loose."

Zacharias was stunned. "What's this about a tiger?"

"The crew member in the control room working the ballast operation said a big-ass cat attacked him. A tiger or something. The controls got damaged when he was fighting it. Or so he says."

"Jesus," Zacharias said, giving both Shelley DeWeese and Bud Roy Roemer a murderous stare. "Can we save her?"

"The tiger?" Stevens inquired.

"No, goddamn it!" Zacharias shouted. "*Freedomland*."

Stevens was quiet long enough for Zacharias to guess the answer before Stevens said the words.

"It's too late. She's at thirteen degrees and the cocks are wide open. Even if we got a team in there, a manual shutdown would take too long. At seventeen degrees, for certain, she's going to fall on her side."

"How long?"

"Maybe an hour. Maybe less. The sea state ain't helping. She was designed to take up to an eighteen-degree roll. But she's heavier up top since the refit. She could roll at seventeen. Maybe even sixteen."

Zacharias slammed his fist on the desk. An almost $1 billion mobile sovereign state, *his* sovereign state, brought down by a fucking tiger. No, even worse. A leopard. That was—what? One-sixth of a tiger? Goddamn it. A fucking leopard. The puniest of the big cats.

Fuck me, Zacharias thought. *Might as well have been a goddamn civet or something.*

It wasn't fair. But fairness wasn't something Zacharias spent a lot of time considering.

"Get the crew off," he told Stevens. "Abandon ship."

"Copy," Stevens said. He hung up and activated a klaxon. A loud-speaker announcement gave the order to abandon ship, reinforced with the message: "This is not a drill."

Zacharias looked at his prisoners. Monica Bell, showing compassion that surprised even her, had stripped off her sweater to make a compress and sling for Jacob Kelley. He was too numb from shock to react. Bud Roy and Gage Randolph helped get Jacob to his feet.

"Bad news, good news, and more bad news," Zacharias told them as he and Barbara covered them with their weapons. "The bad news is that *Freedomland* is sinking. It seems the engineers who designed her left her vulnerable to leopard attacks." He shook his head. "I don't blame them. None of us saw that one coming."

Shelley took in a sharp breath. "Howard got loose? Is he OK?"

"I sure fucking hope not!" Zacharias screamed, his voice rising a full octave, his customary icy reserve depleted. Then he took a breath to rein in his emotions. There was a lot to do and a short time to do it.

"The good news: I have equipped this vessel with a small fleet of state-of-the-art lifeboats. The crew and, most importantly, Barbara and I, will be just fine. Lloyd's of London won't be too happy, though."

"And the other bad news?" Linus McTane asked, knowing the answer.

"Ah, yes," Zacharias said. "All of you are going to die today, for various reasons. Monica and Bill and Sierra because they have threatened me. Bud Roy and Shelley because they brought that fucking cat here. Gage because he screwed me over during a business negotiation, and the rest of you because I don't want any witnesses to the aforementioned killings. But no killing here. Start walking, or I start shooting body parts, like I did to Mr. Kelley. I'm going to take the lead. Barbara will bring up the rear. Don't try anything. She's an excellent shot. And so am I."

The group headed toward the door, following Zacharias, who was walking backward with his gun leveled at them.

"Tell your dog to stay, Gage. I like dogs, but I'll shoot him if you don't."

Gage bent down and gave Rebel a kiss and told him to stay. Rebel did as Gage asked of him. That was their way.

"What about him?" Gage asked, pointing to the pistol-whipped guard, who was just starting to come around.

"I'm sure he'll wake up and start moving soon," Zacharias Townsend said. "Good thing he was unconscious when I decided to kill all of you. Saves me from having to kill him, too."

"Abandon ship," James "Ponce" DeLeon said, repeating the announcement blaring over the loudspeaker as he and Sam Aucoin stopped to get their bearings. They were still working their way topside. "Shouldn't we get off this thing?"

"Seems that way," Sam said. Walking down the corridor reminded him of being in one of those amusement park houses with the tilted floors. "But we're not going anywhere until we find Monica Bell and the Unacrapper. They're here. I know it."

"How about I abandon ship? I'm just holding you up. Besides, although people say I'm brave, I'm not brave. I'm scared."

Sam stopped again and looked at DeLeon. "Who says you're brave?"

DeLeon thought about Sam's question for a second. "Well, I guess no one I know says I'm brave. I just imagine a lot of viewers who saw me on TV shows where the crew went on ride-alongs with the police and stuff would think I'm brave."

"They don't think you're brave, Ponce. They think you're ridiculous." He gave DeLeon a light tap on the shoulder. "Let's get moving."

"How are you going to find them? This place is huge." To DeLeon, it seemed that all they had done since entering the superstructure was walk down an endless stream of linoleum-floored corridors lit by harsh fluorescent overhead lighting.

Sam spied a large man making his way down their current corridor from the opposite end and started off toward him.

"Easy. I'm gonna ask directions."

Marvin Stevens stopped as he saw Sam and DeLeon coming toward him. He let them get closer and then asked, "Who're you two?"

Sam thought divulging the truth to be the most advantageous course at this point. Despite a voice an octave too high for his size, the big fella looked like he would be a handful if he objected to their presence.

"Cumberland County Deputy Sheriff Samuel Aucoin," Sam said as he produced his badge and ID. "I'm looking for Zacharias Townsend. I suspect he's harboring Jacob Kelley, also known as the Unacrapper. And you are?"

"The chief engineer. Marvin Stevens." Stevens looked at Sam for several long seconds. "A bit outside your jurisdiction, ain't ya, Sheriff?"

"Not today."

"And how do I know you are who you say you are? Anybody can get a badge and claim to be a cop. Maybe you two are the guys who sabotaged this rig."

"You think the damage is deliberate?" Sam asked.

"It sure as hell didn't decide to go ass over teakettle on its own," Stevens said. "Now I ask again—just why should I believe two strangers who show up on an oil rig thirteen miles offshore right after it starts to sink?"

Sam put his hands on his waist, pushing back his black North Face windbreaker, revealing a new M&P .40-caliber pistol holstered high on his right hip. "Why would I go through this rigamarole pretending to be a cop? If I was a bad guy, I could've just shot you."

DeLeon stepped away from Sam. As big as the deputy was, he looked almost frail next to Stevens.

Stevens glanced at the gun and then at Sam. "Gun'll buy you a little with me, but not too much. I been shot before."

"I'll bet you have," Sam said. Then he grinned. "But not by me."

Stevens looked at Sam for a moment and then grinned back. "Fair enough," he said in his peculiar voice. "We both got better things to do today than find out who's tougher. 'Sides, what can Townsend do to me? This thing is gonna roll over inside an hour, and then I'm out of a job."

Sam and DeLeon waited for Stevens to make up his mind.

"Keep heading topside," Stevens said. "They'll be coming from the other end. Where his quarters are. The side that's sinking. Crew'll be grabbing those lifeboats first since they're easiest to launch. Whatever you do, get to the top. If you're stuck inside when this thing rolls, you're screwed."

"How about you?"

"Making sure everyone is moving out. Not the first time a ship I was on went down. There's always a few who think it's a drill and remain in their racks." Stevens looked at his watch, doing the math. "I better get moving."

"We have a friend out there in a charter boat. He's called the coast guard. Help is on the way." Sam put out his hand. Stevens locked his enormous paw around it.

"Good luck," Stevens said. He turned and they parted company.

After a few steps, Stevens stopped, turned back, and called after Sam and DeLeon. "Couple more things," he said.

Sam turned.

"You find Townsend, you'll likely find the Unacrapper. And the cable news gal who's missing. I seen 'em both."

"Thanks," Sam said, elated to have his hunch confirmed. "What's the other?"

"Watch your asses," Stevens said. "I'm pretty sure a tiger is running around loose somewhere. Already attacked three of my men, I think."

"Leopard," Sam said.

"Huh?"

"It's a leopard. Not a tiger."

Stevens shrugged. "I doubt that matters when it's trying to eat your face."

"Good point." Sam Aucoin turned and headed up the corridor, James "Ponce" DeLeon trailing behind.

"I am amazed," Monica Bell said to Zacharias Townsend as she labored to keep her half of Jacob Kelley ambulatory, "at how lightly the concept of taking several lives seems to weigh upon you. You ignored several off-ramps that could have defused this situation and went straight to killing. I guess the question is whether you were born evil or acquired it during your ascent to overlord of Silicon Valley."

"*Forbes* tried the same bullshit line of questioning when they wrote that cover story on me last year," Zacharias said. "I told them I had what it took to get to the top, and I have what it takes to stay here. The tech business ain't for the faint of heart."

"It's more than that," Monica said. "Gates and Bezos aren't pushovers, I'm sure. I think it's about power. You haven't been told no in so long, you don't believe there is anything you can't do."

"Sounds to me like you are describing someone with confidence and willpower. Guilty as charged."

"No," Monica said. She paused, shifted the burden that was Jacob Kelley, and then began moving again. "I've read that being in powerful positions for a long time can affect the brain. I believe you're brain damaged."

Zacharias snorted a short, derisive laugh. "Ah, just the sophisticated, nuanced diagnosis concerning a matter as complicated as neuroscience that I would expect from a cable news pundit."

Gage Randolph, listening to the exchange, added his unique perspective, shaped via a passion for movies. "I've figured out who you are," he told Zacharias as he struggled with his own half of the semiconscious terrorist.

"We've been through this. I'm a computer genius multibillionaire."

"You're Karl Stromberg."

"Who?" Zacharias asked along with Monica.

"Karl Stromberg. The Bond villain. From *The Spy Who Loved Me*. Played by Curd Jürgens. Had a big undersea lair. Was a fearsome asshole. A lot like you."

"*The Spy Who Loved Me*?" Monica said. "Jesus, Gage. Are you the sole remaining member of Fayetteville's Blockbuster Video store? Did you watch that on VHS or Betamax?"

Gage smiled. "It's on iTunes."

"Nice to see you have something in your playlist besides *Die Hard*, I guess," Monica puffed as they half dragged and half carried Jacob down the companionway. She had refused Bud Roy Roemer's offer to spell her. Jacob was the proprietary burden she shared with Gage.

Zacharias didn't mind a little idle conversation to pass the time before he killed seven people. It kept them from thinking of ways to fight back. "So what happened to Stromberg?"

"Bond killed him," Gage said. "Gut shot him."

Linus McTane joined in. "I thought Bond dropped him off the Golden Gate Bridge."

"Nah. That was Christopher Walken in *A View to a Kill.*"

"Christ, that movie was awful," McTane said. "Roger Moore was about seventy-five when he made it. No way a guy that age was getting laid that often by that many young women before Viagra."

"Well," Sierra Darlin' said, "maybe he was, you know, just there for them."

Bill Spark, who had been listening with mild interest in an unsuccessful attempt to take his mind off his imminent death, laughed. "Bond? No way, toots. James Bond would never propose a merger unless he could seal the deal."

"James Bond never gave one woman an orgasm," Monica said.

"What?!" all the men said in unison, including the semicomatose Jacob, who found the assertion as much a jolt to his senses as smelling salts.

"He's James Bond," Bud Roy said. "Of course women enjoy sex with him."

"He's a selfish bastard," Monica asserted. "Bond has sex the way a man thinks a woman would want a man to have sex if a man were a woman."

Barbara Townsend, Shelley DeWeese, and Sierra nodded their immediate agreement with Monica. The men in the group were silent for a moment as they processed the algorithm in Monica's statement.

"You're losing us," McTane said after a few seconds. "There was an awful lot of, uh, whaddya call it? Fluid gender identity in that sentence."

"I surely don't like them trannies," Bud Roy announced.

"This ain't about trannies, dummy," Shelley said. "Shush. You might learn something useful, and then you won't have to have Howard help me get off."

Everyone looked at Shelley. And then at Bud Roy, who kept looking at Shelley.

"Who's Howard?" Barbara Townsend asked with a little too much curiosity to suit her husband.

"Howard's our leopard," Shelley said.

Bill Spark let out a low whistle. "You have threesomes with a leopard?"

"No!" Bud Roy shouted. "And I don't need no help from Howard. And neither does Shelley." He turned again to Shelley, who remained—to Bud Roy anyway—distressingly silent.

The group let that sink in for a moment as Zacharias led them through a door to a staircase. "Up we go."

"So what the hell did you mean about all that man being a woman stuff?" Gage asked as he and Monica labored under the load that was the Unacrapper.

"Well," Monica puffed, "rarely have I seen a love scene in a movie and thought it reflected what a woman wanted in bed."

"Well, in the movies I seen, the women seem to enjoy it," Bud Roy said.

"They were *acting*," Sierra said. "Women become good at that."

"What's that supposed to mean?" Bill asked, looking at Sierra.

Sierra remained quiet.

Bud Roy looked at Shelley. "Are you sayin' you've been fakin' it all these years?"

"Not all the time, Bud Roy. Of course not. I just want us to be open about stuff so we can have an even better relationship."

"Jesus, Shelley. We're about to die. And you lay this on me now? You couldn't just, you know, keep fakin' it and let me die a happy, confident man? Christ, women have a gift for bringing up seriously upsetting shit at the worst possible time. Couldn't you have waited until I was sitting down to watch my favorite TV show like you usually do?"

"All I'm saying," Monica said, the words coming between breaths as they reached the top of the staircase, "is that you men shouldn't take your cues from James Bond. Or porn."

"It's a moot point now," Zacharias Townsend announced as they all stepped onto the sloping deck of *Freedomland*. A blast of wind, rain, and salt spray greeted the group. "There is no secret agent coming to save you."

CHAPTER THIRTY-THREE

"There they are," Sam Aucoin said to James "Ponce" DeLeon as they made their way across *Freedomland*'s increasingly precarious deck. He pointed at a small knot of people exiting a hatch and heading for another section of the deck in the direction that was now downhill.

"Where are they going? To the lifeboats?" DeLeon asked.

Sam stopped, watching the group. "I don't think so. All the boats in that section already launched. The crew didn't need to be told twice to get the off this thing. It's deserted except for those assholes."

"And us," DeLeon mumbled.

Sam ignored his complaint. He pointed at the group. "That tall guy is Townsend. Looks like he has a gun. And the woman behind them, I think she's his wife. She's got a gun, too." As he said this, Sam drew his M&P.

"Can you shoot them from here?" DeLeon asked, taking shelter behind a concrete outcropping.

"Not with a handgun at this distance. And not in this weather. We need to get closer. Follow me."

"Where's *my* gun?"

"Still at the gun store, I hope. The last thing I need is you blasting away like Dirty Harry. We need to wait for our moment and then hit them. If we do this right, no one has to fire their weapon."

"And if we don't do it right?" DeLeon asked.

"Stay low and follow me," Sam Aucoin ordered.

"Where are you taking us?" Linus McTane asked Zacharias Townsend.

"Down into the machinery spaces. You're going to perish trying to find your way out of *Freedomland*. At least, that's how the story will be told. A terrible misfortune."

McTane stopped in his tracks. "Why should we march willingly to our deaths?"

Zacharias pointed his pistol at McTane's crotch. "Because if you don't, I'll shoot you in the groin. See, I'm wagering that all of you would rather play this out and take a chance some miracle will save you. However, if you'd rather get shot in the crotch…"

"Trust me," Bud Roy Roemer advised McTane, "you don't want to get shot in the wang. Getting shot in my clavicle was bad enough, and it ain't nearly as important as my penis."

"Seems to me your girlfriend begs to differ," Monica Bell offered.

"Oh, fuck you," Bud Roy retorted.

"Only if Howard the Leopard is around to help," Monica said.

"Quiet!" Zacharias shouted as Bud Roy turned beet red and Shelley DeWeese studiously studied the slate-gray sky. "Jesus. You people are annoying."

McTane looked at Bud Roy and then back at Zacharias. "My friend here makes a good point about the value of not getting shot in the hoo-ha. Still, why don't you just shoot us and end it? Over quicker for all of us."

"Well," Zacharias said, "bodies with bullets in them generate questions. Bodies floating in a flooded compartment are just unfortunate victims."

"What about the Crapper?" Gage Randolph asked. "He's got a bullet in him."

"Oh, Mr. Kelley won't be going with you all. The authorities will find his body back on the mainland. A suicide, after having snapped under the pressure of the manhunt."

"He committed suicide by shooting himself in the clavicle?" Gage asked.

"Yeah. Whuh da fuggh?" Jacob Kelley said, emerging once again from his semiconscious torpor.

"The guy tried to blow up the IRS building with twenty-five pounds of his own shit," Zacharias observed. "It'll be in keeping with his general law enforcement profile of being dumber than dirt. No one will question it. The FBI won't work it hard. Another case all wrapped up. The Bureau always gets its man."

Everyone but Jacob nodded in grudging agreement at Zacharias's assessment. He didn't disagree. But he had discovered, as Bud Roy had some months ago, that the clavicle seemed to be attached to a great many body parts, and it was wise not to move any of them.

McTane played his last card. "Appears we are at what they call a crucial juncture in our little drama. You can't shoot us because it would be too hard to explain. So maybe we won't go any farther."

Zacharias's mouth formed the thin, upturned gash that passed for a smile. The eye patch did not soften the expression. "Nice try, shyster. I said, 'Bodies with bullets in them generate questions.' But I've got lawyers on top of lawyers." He smiled again as he thought about the outcome. "The next time I'm in negotiations with someone, they will sit there wondering if I killed people. That reputation will put everyone across the table from me at a disadvantage. Probably worth five percent on any deal. But it won't matter to you because I will give you a nine-millimeter circumcision," he said, again pointing the Glock at McTane's groin.

"OK," McTane said. "I believe you."

"Now let's keep moving, shall we?" Zacharias said. "Almost there."

They struggled another twenty-five feet through rain driven sideways by the wind to a gray steel door, dogged shut by a large wheel. Zacharias stepped to the side. He gestured with his pistol at Bud Roy and McTane. "You two open the hatch."

Bud Roy and McTane spun the wheel to undog the hatch. Once done, they struggled on the sloping deck to lift the heavy door against both gravity and wind. As they did so, they had a quiet discussion.

"We gotta do somethin' soon," Bud Roy whispered. "I ain't gonna drown. I don't like the water. You wouldn't be carryin' a backup piece, would ya?"

"Jesus, Bud Roy," McTane whispered back. "Of course I ain't carryin' two guns. One gun is prudent. Two is weird."

"I used to think so, too…until today."

"Good point," McTane allowed as they wrestled the door open. It fell against the bulkhead with a heavy clang.

"OK, everyone," Zacharias Townsend said as he stepped into the hatchway. "Line up and follow me. Barbara will shoot anyone who doesn't comply."

Sam Aucoin and James "Ponce" DeLeon used the cover provided by equipment, fencing, a concrete wall, and foul weather to mask their approach and close the gap with their quarry. They paused behind a wall thirty feet away and watched Linus McTane and Bud Roy Roemer muscle open the large hatch.

"OK," Sam said, whispering loudly into DeLeon's ear to overcome the combined cacophony of the pounding surf, howling wind, and lashing rain. "Here's how we do this. I bet the hallway is like all the others on this thing: long and straight. I'll take the lead and come up fast behind Mrs. Townsend. If I hit her right, she'll go down without a sound."

"Jesus…"

"Ain't gonna help us," Sam said. "We have to do this. You and me. Once I put her out of commission, you take her gun and cover the hostages. Remember, some of the hostages are bad, too. I'll work my way forward to get Townsend."

"What if he starts shooting?"

"I'll kill him. Or they will, if they think they have nothing to lose. Get ready. Once she steps through the hatch, we move up fast." Sam looked at him. "You better be behind me, or this will be the worst day of your life."

"Already is."

Once everyone was in the companionway, Zacharias Townsend walked backward, leading them toward an engineering space that Marvin Stevens had reported was flooding. He would herd them in, seal the hatch, and watch them die. Maybe he would have to shoot a few of them, but he would toss the gun in with them and then let the police make up their own story if *Freedomland* were to be salvaged.

"OK, people. We are just about there. If you're gonna pray, do it now," Zacharias said.

Linus McTane was tensing himself to put up a fight, even though he was fat, past fifty, and unarmed. Going quick would be better than drowning.

Just then, a low, guttural growl emanated from the shadows of the hallway.

"Uh-oh," Bud Roy Roemer said, unconsciously moving his hands over his butt. "I know that sound."

"Howard?" Shelley DeWeese asked.

Zacharias heard it, too, and risked a quick glance behind him to see Howard the Leopard in the hallway, fifteen feet away—ears flattened, fangs bared, coiled, ready to strike.

"Jesus!" Zacharias yelled. With reflexes many would have described as catlike, he whirled to snap off a shot at the leopard. Despite his admirable reaction time, he was not, in fact, as quick as the actual cat in the hallway.

Zacharias was only halfway through his pivot when Howard the Leopard hit him with all the force a very pissed-off apex predator in full flight could muster. His headlong assault drove Zacharias against the wall. The billionaire screamed and beat at the leopard with the gun in his left hand. Howard locked his powerful jaws on Zacharias's left arm just below the elbow and bit savagely through flesh and bone, twisting his strong neck and removing the forearm with the speed, efficiency, and ferocity of a Civil War surgeon performing an emergency amputation.

Zacharias screamed and sank to the floor, looking at the gun, still in the hand of his severed forearm.

The immediate threat eliminated, Howard the Leopard bounded through the stunned group and toward the open hatch.

Sam Aucoin and James "Ponce" DeLeon were in the middle of executing their plan, closing in on the back of an unsuspecting Barbara Townsend, when something growled, someone yelled, and then someone, perhaps the same someone, screamed.

Both men kept running, intent on closing the distance, when Sam yelled, "Fuck!" and dove to his left, leaving DeLeon as the lone and not very formidable obstacle between an angry 137-pound death delivery system and the exit. DeLeon was merely a speed bump on the road to Howard the Leopard's freedom. The big cat smashed him against the wall and atop of Sam on its way out the door. Howard wanted nothing more than to find a nice, quiet, dark space to hide. He had had a very bad day.

Barbara spun around to shoot the escaping cat but spied Sam struggling out from under DeLeon, who had been knocked senseless when bulldozed by Howard the Leopard. Seeing Sam reach for his pistol on the floor, she traced her sidearm over to him and prepared to fire.

Sierra Darlin' dissuaded her from doing so by sucker punching her on the side of the head.

Dazed but not out, Barbara hit Sierra with a vicious backhand, knocking her into the wall. Sierra sank to her knees, trying to clear her head.

Before Barbara could deliver a coup de grâce from her pistol, Monica Bell stepped in and drove a powerful right-hand punch into Barbara's stomach, following it up with an expert open-palm strike from her left hand to the tip of Barbara's nose, putting the weight of her body into the follow-through. Barbara screamed as blood spurted from her broken nose. Her pistol clattered to the floor. Monica lacked the killer instinct, however, and backed off. Barbara took advantage of the pause and lashed out with a kick that caught Monica in the ribs, doubling her over.

Barbara's follow-up blow was interrupted by Sierra rejoining the fray. She grabbed Barbara's hair, twisting and using all of her weight to yank the taller woman viciously backward and off her feet. Sierra kneeled on Barbara's right arm and punched her in the face with frightening speed and ferocity.

Monica leaped on top of Barbara's left arm and weighed in. She and Sierra established a brutal rhythm as they pummeled their nemesis until Barbara ceased to struggle. She lay there dazed, covered with blood oozing out of her broken nose and cracked lips. Barbara appeared to be missing at least two teeth, and her eyes were swelling shut. She was no longer a threat.

Monica and Sierra helped each other up, standing over their conquest together, hands on knees, panting from pain and exertion.

"Jesus, she was tough," Monica said between breaths. "Someone needs to check her for an Adam's apple."

"What a bitch!" Sierra said.

"Got that right," Monica agreed. "But nothing compared to us." She put out her hand, and Sierra gave her a low five.

They looked up to see that the men—including Jacob Kelley, wobbling against Gage Randolph—had formed a semicircle around the combat area, gazing at them openmouthed.

"Thanks for the help, guys," Monica said as she struggled to recover her breath.

"We were kinda unsure what to do," Gage mumbled.

"Lemme guess," Monica said. "You didn't want to hit a woman?"

"Well, yeah," Gage said, having propped Jacob against a wall.

Monica straightened up. "This might have been, you know, one of those exceedingly rare cases in which it would have been acceptable…prudent, even…to do so. What with her being a murderous psychopath hell-bent on killing us and all."

"I dunno," Linus McTane said, "it was also kinda…" He scratched his head and started over. "Watching a bunch of, excuse me for saying so, attractive women go at it like that—it was kinda…well…uh…distracting, I guess, is the right word. I don't think we had the time to get beyond that and realize we had to do something."

"Oh, for God's sake," Monica said, exasperated. "Really? Is there any set of circumstances, under any condition, at any time or place, at any stage of life, or," she looked at McTane, "at any degree of corpulence where *somehow* a guy isn't thinking with his dick?"

"Jesus, Bill," Sierra said, squinting at her paramour through a heavily watering eye. "Do you have an erection?"

"It's due to fear," Bill Spark said as he covered his crotch and the other men stepped away from him. He mustered what dignity he could and rallied science to the defense of his poorly timed tumescence. "You know…scared stiff. That's where that comes from. It's a real thing. It's…it's a fear boner."

"That's an urban legend," McTane said. "All you are is horny."

Sam stepped forward, intent to take charge and renew the group's focus on survival. "I'm Cumberland County Deputy Sheriff Sam Aucoin. Jacob

Kelley," he said, looking at the Unacrapper, "you are under arrest for…well, you know what you did. As for the rest of you…well…some, maybe all of you, are also under arrest. But we'll sort it all out later, although I recommend y'all exercise the right to remain silent so we can get the hell off this thing before it goes belly up. We got wounded we need to…"

A piercing scream from Shelley DeWeese interrupted Sam. Zacharias Townsend, forgotten by everyone either partaking in or observing the epic Amazonian struggle, had harnessed the legendary willpower that had enabled him to amass a fortune, turned his belt into a tourniquet, and stanched the flow of blood from his shattered arm. He had recovered his pistol from the left hand of his severed forearm and was now aiming it unsteadily at his foes.

Gage stepped in front of Monica, shielding her from Zacharias's gun. Sierra did the same for Bill, not covering very much of him.

Sam bulled his way past McTane, brought his pistol up into a steady two-handed shooting stance, and sent three rounds downrange into Zacharias's chest so fast it sounded like one shot.

Zacharias Townsend was dead before he hit the ground.

A deafening silence followed the thunderous gunshots.

Sinking oil rigs. Amputation by leopard. Epic fistfights. Zombie billionaires back from the dead. It had been a long day. Everyone was immune to surprise, inured to further shock. No one did more than blink at the latest act of violence.

"Nice shooting," McTane said.

"Three dead-center mass," Bud Roy observed. He looked at Sam. "What, no clavicle this time?"

"He seemed kind of hard to discourage," Sam said.

Behind them, James "Ponce" DeLeon, once again conscious, struggled to a sitting position. He looked at the odd gathering of men and women, many of whom were bleeding.

"Did I miss anything?" he asked.

CHAPTER THIRTY-FOUR

Sam Aucoin's progress guiding his herd of actual and potential arrestees to the nearest lifeboats hit a snag that would have made PETA proud.

"I'm goin' back for Rebel," Gage Randolph announced.

"Gage, if you think I'm gonna let you out of my sight..."

"Deputy Aucoin, my best friend in the entire world is waiting for me to come back and get him. I know where he is, and I know he hasn't moved, even though he's likely gettin' scared. He believes in me. I won't let him down."

"I'm pretty sure I need to arrest you," Sam said.

"You can do that after I get Rebel. Hell, what with the criminal Tourette's Bud Roy says I got, I'll probably confess all manner of things."

Bud Roy Roemer and Linus McTane rolled their eyes at Gage's suggestion he had crimes to confess but said nothing.

"I'm going with him," Monica Bell said.

"Now, wait a second..."

Monica looked at Sam. "Deputy, you need to get these folks off this thing. Gage and I have been through a lot. I'm going to help him out one more time, and then the three of us—Gage, Rebel, and me—are going to get in a life raft and leave for good. Then we can all talk about what may or may not have happened."

Sam sighed. He had wounded to care for. He had America's most wanted terrorist and an evil billionaire wannabe murderess—beaten to a pulp and still in shock over the violent demise of her husband—in his custody.

"OK. Go. But we still have questions for both of you."

"Thanks…Sam," Gage said. He and Monica headed off toward Zacharias Townsend's office at a slow jog.

Now it was Shelley DeWeese's turn. "Well, if he's gonna go get Rebel, Bud Roy and me are gonna go find Howard."

"The hell we are," Bud Roy said. "Did you see what that fucking leopard did to a guy worth several jabillion dollars? Imagine what he'll do to us."

"Howard was protecting me," Shelley said.

"Howard had no idea who we were. That cat killed Townsend because he was first in line."

"I'm afraid Howard won't get off in time!" Shelley wailed.

"And I'm afraid he will!" Bud Roy yelled.

"We're going," Shelley said as she stomped off. "Bud Roy, c'mon. Deputy, if you want to shoot us, do it now."

"We're not done, Bud Roy. But go ahead," Sam said. "My advice is don't look for Howard too hard. He doesn't seem to be in a good mood."

"God, tell me somethin' I don't know." Bud Roy shrugged and moved off after Shelley.

Sam looked at Jacob Kelley, Barbara Townsend, Linus McTane, Bill Spark, and Sierra Darlin'. "OK, time to go. Radio guy and gal, you take Mrs. Townsend here. One on each side. Linus, you and me got the Unacrapper."

"Jacob," Jacob said.

Sam ignored him and keyed the radio John Purdy had given him. "*Marlinspike*, this is Aucoin. Do you copy?"

"I'm here, Deputy," Purdy responded immediately. "Where do you wanna be picked up?"

"We're headed for a lifeboat on the, uh…hell, I don't know. I'm all mixed up. If you're lookin' at the damn rig and the side going down is on your right, we're going to launch from the uphill corner closest to shore."

Purdy took a moment to translate Sam's description into a compass heading. "Copy, Deputy. We'll be waiting off the northwest corner. Good luck."

"Thanks, Cap'n." Sam Aucoin signed off. "Guy must have a compass implanted in his brain," he said to Linus McTane.

They moved off toward the lifeboats.

Gage Randolph and Monica Bell believed they were finally in the right hallway after having gone down a series of dead ends.

"This place is a maze," Gage said. "But this looks familiar. Carpeting. Paneling. Seems like a hallway the guy who owned this thing would use."

Monica said nothing. Her ribs hurt from the kick Barbara Townsend had delivered. It was enough just to keep up with Gage's pace.

Gage looked over at her. "You OK? You're movin' kinda stiff and all."

"I'm fine. Just sore."

They heard frantic barking coming from a room at the end of the hall. "That's Rebel," Gage said. He broke into a run.

Monica followed at her own pace. This was a family reunion, and she wasn't family.

As she reached Zacharias Townsend's office, Gage and Rebel the Hound were in the middle of a joyful man-dog greeting. Gage was bent over so Rebel could place his forepaws on his shoulders. The dog was joyously lapping his face.

"OK," Monica said. "Are we ready?"

"You bet," Gage said. He headed toward the door, Rebel the Hound right behind.

"Uh, Gage," Monica said. "Aren't you forgetting something?"

"What? Stonewall's arm?" Gage said, pointing at the relic, still in the glass case, smeared with Rebel's nose prints from his industrious attempts to get at the arm during his time alone. He looked at it one last time and then looked away. The arm was less a Civil War relic than a gruesome reminder of ZachariasTownsend's demise.

"I don't think I want that," Gage said. "Would be kinda hard to explain what I'm doin' with it."

Monica smiled. "Rebel really was all you wanted to come back for, wasn't he?"

"Well, sure," Gage said. "He's my dog."

"How about the money?" she asked, pointing at the duffel with $250,000 in it.

"Dang it! I was so worried about Rebel I forgot about the money." Gage walked back, picked up the bag, and slung it over his shoulder. "Well, I guess Townsend won't be missing it. And I did give him the arm."

"I think it's yours. You taking money paid to you for stealing a severed arm by a man now deceased from a leopard attack is, remarkably, about the closest you have been to the right side of the law in the past week."

"Damn it. One more thing: I gotta get my gun, too," Gage said.

"Gage," Monica said, touching his arm and stopping him from moving into the room to collect his Magnum.

"Yeah?"

"You and I have navigated our time together guided in part, and for reasons I still don't quite understand, by the movie *Die Hard*."

Gage smiled. "See, I told you Helsinki syndrome was a thing."

Monica laughed and then immediately regretted it when her injured ribs protested. "Yeah, I guess it is. But let me give you some advice drawn from that other cinematic bible for men, *The Godfather.*"

"And that is?" Gage asked.

"Leave the gun. Take the money."

He smiled and made a you-first gesture at Monica Bell toward the door. Gage Randolph followed her out of the room, Rebel the Hound at his side.

"Shelley, we got to get off this thing, hon. It's gonna roll any minute now," Bud Roy Roemer said. Creaks and groans emanating from the superstructure punctuated his words as it protested the stresses being placed on it. *Freedomland* almost seemed to come alive as it was dying.

"Howard's all alone and scared, Bud Roy. We gotta find him," Shelley DeWeese said.

"If that damn cat is all alone, it's because he's killed everyone he's come into contact with today."

"Bud Roy, I know you hate him, but I've grown to love him."

"Shelley, if there is one thing I've learned from watching all of those *Chomp!* TV shows about them African cats with you, it's that leopards like Howard have an amazing survival instinct. Sure thing he's already off this rig and killed anyone who got in his way."

Bud Roy gazed around the deck. Garden terraces full of carefully cultivated plants and trees had collapsed, resulting in mini mudslides that made negotiating the sloping deck treacherous. Cranes and other equipment had snapped their moorings, creating a jumble of steel and cable that proved almost impossible to penetrate.

Howard could be anywhere. They would never find him in time.

A light standard crashed to the deck forty feet to their left. Shelley jumped at the sound.

"OK, Bud Roy. You're right. He's gone. Let's go, too. But if we don't find Howard, you gotta promise to buy me another leopard."

He grunted. "Can't we get something smaller? Don't they have something similar to dogs? Can't we buy a, uh, whaddyacallit? A teacup leopard? Do they have those?" he asked hopefully.

"No," Shelley said. "A leopard. Full size."

"Fine. I promise. Maybe we can find one that hasn't gained a taste for human flesh."

Bud Roy grabbed her hand and pulled her with him toward the one remaining large lifeboat he could see. The boat was bright orange, about twenty-five feet long, and built to survive a hurricane. It had sheer, sloping sides rising to a small structure that looked like a conning tower. To Bud Roy, it looked less like a boat than a miniature submarine.

"You have any idea how to work this thing?" Shelley asked a minute later as they clambered onto the derrick holding the boat in place.

"This type looks different from the other ones we saw earlier," Bud Roy said. "They were on a big slide and just dropped into the ocean. This one here's on a davit."

He located the control box for the electric winch and pressed the button. Nothing happened.

"Figures," Bud Roy said. He looked around. There had to be a backup. He located the manual winch arrangement.

"Looks like we lower it by hand. One of us on each side guidin' the rope. We gotta move at the same time, or it'll snag."

Bud Roy looked at the antiquated setup. "You know, I bet this was for Townsend. A more dignified way to abandon ship if he had the time."

He looked down. They were still at the low end of *Freedomland* and only had about sixty feet to the water.

"OK," he said to Shelley. "You got a winch on your side, and I got one on mine. We work together and she'll settle right down. Then we'll cast off the line and float off pretty as you please."

Shelley studied the winch with Bud Roy. She was conversant with machinery and understood at once how it would work. She went to the bow and prepared her winch. When Bud Roy gave the sign, they both turned their cranks, lowering the boat slowly to the water. They took their time, doing it right, and in five minutes, the keel of their lifeboat kissed the ocean. The pair cast off the lines.

Bud Roy moved to the hatch in the small conning tower on top of the sheer hull. He noticed it was already open.

"OK," he told Shelley. "I'm gonna go in first. You follow. I'm sure this thing has an engine. We'll get her started and head for shore. Or the coast guard. Whatever we find first."

Shelley clung to the side of the conning tower as the ocean tossed the boat in several directions at once. "Hurry," she ordered. "It's hard to hold on."

Bud Roy swung his leg into the hatch and lowered himself in. He dropped into the main compartment. It was long and narrow, with rows of bench seats facing each other. He was about to call for Shelley to come down when he heard a low, familiar growl.

Oh, shit, he thought.

Not wanting to lose precious time confirming what he knew to be true, Bud Roy scrambled up the ladder toward the hatch. He might have made it, but he rammed his head into Shelley's foot as she was beginning her descent into the hull.

"Get the fuck out, Shelley! Get the fuck out! I found Howard!"

In his blind panic to escape, he pushed Shelley, who was already reversing course and had one leg out of the hatch. Shelley lost her balance and tumbled off the conning tower. She reached out for a handhold but found none as she slid down the side of the lifeboat and into the ocean.

"*Buuud Roooy!*" she screamed as a ten-foot wave carried her away from the craft.

Bud Roy was in no position to help. He had his torso out of the conning tower when Howard the Leopard struck, pulling him back down the ladder and into the main compartment.

Fighting for her life in the ocean, Shelley thought she heard Bud Roy scream. She tried to swim back toward the craft but another big wave caught her, lifted her like she was a small toy, and slammed her into one of *Freedomland*'s steel pontoons.

Shelley DeWeese's demise was mercifully quick.

Bud Roy Roemer's took a little longer.

Once Gage Randolph got Rebel the Hound, his money, and Monica Bell safely aboard the lifeboat at the taller end of *Freedomland*, he studied the instructions.

"Looks like we're in for a carnival ride," he said. "We need to strap in, hit this here release button, and hope this fucker floats. It's over a hundred-foot drop."

"I hate roller coasters," Monica said as she buckled the three-point harness in the seat next to Gage.

"Not crazy about 'em myself, but I guess it beats dying."

Gage strapped the bag containing the money into the seat across from him. He then manhandled Rebel the Hound into his lap to secure him for the journey. "You surely ain't no lapdog," he said.

Rebel licked Gage's cheek in response. His unwritten checklist of life's essentials consisted of Gage. Gage was there. All was well.

Monica took half of Rebel into her lap. "Damn mutt needs to go on a diet," she said.

"Ready?" Gage asked.

"You bet."

Gage Randolph hit the release button, and woman, money, man, and dog plunged toward the ocean.

"I'll be damned," Sam Aucoin said from the helm of his lifeboat. "Looks like these things drive themselves." He had been surprised when, after the terrifying free fall from *Freedomland's* top deck to the roiling ocean, the engine had started and the helm had turned over on a heading for the Port of Wilmington.

Sam radioed John Purdy. "*Marlinspike*, this is Aucoin. Over."

Purdy's voice came back. "Sam, we got you visually. Saw you take the Nestea Plunge off that damn thing. Must've been quite a ride."

"Terrifying," Sam said. "Listen up. As soon as we hit the water, the boat's engines kicked in automatically, and now it appears to be steering a course for the Port of Wilmington."

"That is correct," Purdy said. "I just got off the radio with a guy named Marvin. Got a voice that sounds like he sucked helium before speaking. Anyway, he says Townsend spared no expense on the lifeboats. They're like self-driving cars. They're programmed to head for the nearest port."

"So we just sit here?"

"Yep. Coast guard is on station. A couple of big cutters will monitor the rig and keep a lookout for survivors and strays. I'm working with the smaller patrol boats to ride herd on the, uh, Great Orange Fleet. Just sit back and enjoy the ride."

Sam looked at his fellow passengers. "Not likely," he said. "By the way, don't let Marvin's voice fool you. The guy's big enough to go five rounds with a Buick and come out on top."

"Copy that," Purdy said. "Speaking of wantin' to go five rounds, this Marvin fellow said he has two injured crewmen, one with a busted nose and one with a concussion from bein' pistol-whipped, who want a piece of the Unacrapper."

"Tell 'em to take a number," Sam said. "Everybody get off the rig?"

"We're tracking all but three. Two crewmen who we think met the tiger..."

"Leopard," Sam said.

"Whatever. And then Townsend himself."

"You can put him down for dead."

Purdy didn't press for more information.

"Did you hear from the other two I told you about? Bud Roy and Shelley?" Sam Aucoin asked.

"Nothing. And *Freedomland* capsized a few minutes ago. If they're still on it, they're in a bad way."

"I got somebody on the radio," Gage Randolph said. "He says the boats are all programmed to run back to Wilmington, and..."

Monica Bell looked up at him from her seat. While Gage had turned his back, she had removed her sopping-wet clothes and wrapped herself in a survival blanket. A sodden mass of T-shirt, bra, capri pants, underwear, socks, and shoes lay at her feet.

"...he instructed me not to touch a damn thing."

Monica smiled and motioned for Gage to sit beside her. He did so. Rebel the Hound, not one for sharing attention, put his head in Gage's lap. Gage patted him absentmindedly.

"I asked about Bud Roy and Shelley, but they haven't reported in yet. Hope they're OK."

"Me too."

Gage looked at her for a long moment. "So where do we go from here?"

Monica knew what he meant. And it surprised her that she was more than a little sad that he did not imbue the question with additional meaning.

"Gage, you are the reason I survived all of this. Granted, you're also the reason I was in it to begin with. But you did your best. And your best, as I have discovered, is damn good. If the Crapper tries to drag you into it, it will be my word against his. And I'll win."

"I believe you. I've known you were on my side since you made that phone call to your friend. Actually, I knew it before then, which was why I left my phone there for you."

"You knew?"

Gage laughed. "Ms. Bell, you don't know southern men at all if you think some hot wings and Jim Beam will give us the squirts."

"You must have some faith in *Die Hard* if you let me have your phone."

"I had faith in you." He smiled. Once again, Monica thought the smile a good one. She smiled back.

He looked at Monica. Unknown to her, a gap in the blanket had opened. Gage sighed inwardly and gently reached over to pull the blanket shut. Monica never flinched as he did so, which surprised them both.

Gage put his arm around her, and she leaned against his shoulder.

"I think this is the beginning of a beautiful friendship," he said.

"Your movie references are getting better," Monica said as she nestled into his shoulder.

"Yippee ki yay, motherfucker," Gage said.

They both laughed.

For the next six hours, devoted Son of the South Gage Randolph and New York limousine liberal Monica Bell talked and laughed, and argued some just to make things interesting. They interspersed their conversation with bouts of seasickness and throwing up in a bucket. Looking back, Gage Randolph maintained it was the best night he had ever spent with a woman.

Because it was his best night as a man.

CHAPTER THIRTY-FIVE

Sheriff Johnnie Hawkins, FBI Special Agent Peter Carlson, and an army of cameras, producers, and reporters from every network were on hand to greet the surviving citizens of *Freedomland* and Cumberland County Deputy Sheriff Samuel Aucoin as their small flotilla arrived at the Port of Wilmington.

Video of the wreckage of Zacharias Townsend's confection of avarice, ego, and oil rig played continuously on the news as anchors competed to find the best biblical allusion to explain the vessel's demise. Several expanded beyond the Bible and quoted Percy Bysshe Shelley's *Ozymandias*, while others went with the lyrics to "Money" by Pink Floyd.

Broadcast and cable news showed Sam leading a badly beaten and disheveled Barbara Townsend, in handcuffs, to a patrol car. Initially, anchors reacted with outrage, appalled that Deputy Aucoin had, apparently, used excessive force against Barbara Townsend when placing her under arrest. This led to many impassioned panel discussions on abusive law enforcement officers and the need to have more women in the profession to give it a civilizing influence. When, sometime later, it became known that Monica Bell and Sierra Darlin' had administered Barbara Townsend's beating, the same experts launched into equally impassioned discussions about the increasing masculinization of women, the blurring of gender roles, and the danger this posed to females who entered male-dominated career fields such as law enforcement.

Conservative pundits believed Sam Aucoin's arrest of the Unacrapper confirmed the superiority of small local government over the inefficient, expensive, and incompetent federal government. Liberals found it to be a consequence of unconscionable attacks on the federal government by those intent on destroying proud institutions such as the FBI, thus leaving everyone in the country vulnerable to terrorists, Russian hackers, Nigerian scam artists, and angry white middle-aged male virgins.

With the spreading debris field bubbling up from *Freedomland*'s grave serving as a background, many commentators pointed out that the coast guard, funded by US tax dollars, had saved the lives of almost the entire crew. They then pointed out the irony, given that *Freedomland* was the manifestation of Zacharias Townsend's utter hatred of taxation and his rejection of even the most basic tenets of citizenship.

The same video also provided incentive for others far removed from responsible journalism to speculate on *Freedomland*'s destruction. Ignoring the lack of supporting evidence, wild theories spread rapidly across the internet. The most prominent accused the Deep State of sending a message to antitaxers by ordering the United States Navy to torpedo Zacharias Townsend's floating rejection of the IRS. The popularity of this canard forced mainstream journalists to debunk it, thus giving the rumor even greater credence in the darker corners of the American psyche.

While a good portion of the American public raced one another to the bottom, Jacob Kelley, against all odds, seemed to discover at least a fragment of his moral compass. As he was being led to an ambulance to take him to the hospital, he spied Monica and Gage Randolph in the crowd. Somehow, Jacob knew what he had to do and was pleasantly surprised to realize it might even be the right thing to do.

"It was all me that done it!" Jacob cried out as the cameras rolled. "I tried to bring down the IRS. Then I kidnapped Monica Bell. I'da gotten away with it, too, if it hadn't a been for Gage Randolph." He caught Monica's eye. She nodded faintly in thanks.

Somewhere deep inside, Jacob Kelley felt better about himself than he had in a long time.

"Now, that is a raging case of criminal Tourette's if ever I seen one," Gage said to Monica.

She reached over and gave his hand a quick squeeze. "Looks like he caught it at just the right time."

Linus McTane was holding court in front of a bank of microphones, announcing his intention to both defend Jacob, whom he termed "a misguided patriot, but a patriot nonetheless," and to sue "the ever-lovin' shit" out of the estate of the late Zacharias Townsend and his heir apparent, Barbara Townsend.

Deputy Sheriff and man of the hour Samuel Aucoin walked over to Monica and Gage. "I have my suspicions about what happened," he said. "But that's all they are. And I don't think anyone is in the mood to press. This story has good guys; bad guys; rich, scheming women; and smart, resourceful women who are tough as nails. Everyone is likely to run with that."

Sam looked at them both for a while. They knew he knew. That was enough for him.

He delivered his assessment: "The right people are going to jail and the right people aren't."

Monica reached out to touch Sam's forearm. "You have good instincts, Deputy. You could be a cable news producer."

Sam smiled. "While I'm sure you meant that as a compliment…"

"Yeah…Not everyone takes it as one."

Sam said, "People are gonna want to talk to you both. I assume your stories will correspond."

"We both know what happened," Monica assured him.

Gage stuck out his hand. Sam took it. "Gage, I'm sorry about Bud Roy and Shelley. We can hope, but it doesn't look good. The conditions don't favor a recovery of any sort."

"Thanks, Sam," Gage said. "They weren't by no means perfect. But they were my friends. And they stood by me."

"Well, Bud Roy and I had our differences. But when he made a friend, he stuck. I'll give him that."

Sam Aucoin moved into the crowd, parting it with the easy confidence all big men have. Gage Randolph and Monica Bell watched after him.

Several hours later, Bill Spark and Sierra Darlin' sat in their hotel room in Wilmington, North Carolina. He wore a bathrobe after having spent close to an hour in the shower trying to wash away everything bad that had happened to him in the past day.

Sierra practically disappeared into her bathrobe. Bill loved the way women looked in robes. They were perfectly designed for the garments. Conversely, he thought he looked like a big, fuzzy sausage.

"What do you see in me?" Bill asked.

Sierra spoke slowly, her tender jaw and black eye trophies from her fistfight with Barbara Townsend.

"Sometimes I'm not sure, to be honest."

"I really wasn't much help out there, was I?"

"There wasn't much occasion to be," Sierra said. "You rolled with the punches. You always do."

"You fought back."

"I always do," Sierra said. "I always have."

"I know I like you. After yesterday and today, I might even love you. You were amazing."

"I like you, too, Bill. And who knows where that could go."

Bill got up to pour a drink. He had bought a fifth of Johnnie Walker before checking in. He poured one for Sierra, too. She took it and washed down four ibuprofen. She would hurt for a while.

"I think you need your own show; you're too big and too good to be my sidekick," he said.

"Not yet," Sierra said, surprising herself and Bill.

"Really?"

"I don't know if you noticed, but I was kind of working out some issues on Barbara Townsend's face."

"We all noticed."

"Well, you sure did." Sierra giggled. "Fear boner?"

Bill joined her. "OK. Truth is, you make love like you fight: with every fiber of your being. That's what I was thinking. That's what got my motor started."

"I'm not ready to talk about my issues, although Lord knows I have 'em," Sierra said. "But I will tell you this. There are things I believe and things I thought I did but have realized I don't. Does that make sense?"

Bill shrugged and took another slug of Johnnie Walker. "No. But I'll keep drinking until it does."

"I'm a conservative, Bill. A true, dyed-in-the-wool, don't-tread-on-me, small-government, keep-your-hands-off-my-guns-and-my-money conservative. I was born that way. Pretty sure liberals and conservatives are born rather than made, and we argue to persuade the ten percent of the country that either wasn't born one way or the other or are smart enough to think for themselves." Sierra took a drink. "What I am not, however, and what I do not want to be, is an asshole. No one is born an asshole. We have a choice."

"You think we've been assholes on the show?"

"I think we've been clowns. Maybe assholes, too. We are right. I deeply believe that. But we're talking about this stuff in the wrong way. Christ, I saw a man killed tonight. And if he hadn't been, he would have killed me.

Over what? Taxes? The size of government? Jesus." Sierra shuddered as she recalled the night's events. "I need to work out what I want to be before I tell others what they ought to be. And when I'm ready, I will engage in a conversation and not deliver a diatribe. Talking is better than yelling." Sierra hugged herself. "I've had too much yelling in my life."

Sierra got up stiffly to get some more Johnnie Walker. Bill watched. He knew when to offer help and when not to. Sierra was clear about those things.

"It's there when you're ready," Bill said. "And so am I."

Sierra lay down on the bed and loosened her robe. "I'm ready, Bill." She reached up, grabbed the lapels of his robe, and gently pulled him down on top of her.

"You sure?" Bill asked. "It's been a long day for both of us. And you took a few big shots to the beezer. Hell, I'm not sure *I'm* up to this."

"We could both use a little tenderness after the day we've had," Sierra said. She smiled—a stiff smile, but still a world-class one. "And if you're having trouble, just think of me kicking Barbara Townsend's ass."

"Oooh," Bill said. "I think pitchers and catchers just decided to report. Batter up!"

They both laughed. Then Bill said, "OK. I'm ready to go. But on one condition."

Sierra looked at him.

"No acting."

She pulled his face close to hers. "No acting. You just do *exactly* what I tell you."

Bill Spark and Sierra Darlin' laughed again.

But only for a moment.

CHAPTER THIRTY-SIX

Howard the Leopard's boat didn't take him and Bud Roy Roemer's body to the Port of Wilmington because no one ever shut the hatch, which was required to activate the self-piloting mechanism. So Howard drifted for three days. He survived on rainwater that came down the hatch, the bounty that was Bud Roy, and the amazing ability cats have to shut down and wait out the bad times.

When Howard's lifeboat reached shore, he happily reacquainted himself with dry land. Something in him told him to head south.

Three days into his overland journey, Howard stalked and killed a feral pig. He found it far more agreeable than the fare on his lifeboat and logged the tastiness factor into the vast majority of his brain assigned to keep track of such things. That was an animal he hoped to see more of.

On day six, Howard and a black bear had a difference of opinion over who would dine on a small deer Howard had killed. He decided, in his own cat way, not to mess with those mean fuckers ever again.

He kept moving south, urged on by a climate he found increasingly comfortable.

On day seventeen, Howard crossed a highway at night. Something told him this was a place where a leopard could make a good home. Howard the

Leopard couldn't read, but if he could have, the sign he strolled past would have confirmed his assessment.

Welcome to Florida.

Two weeks later, Deputy Sheriff Sam Aucoin was sitting with a cup of coffee in his hands in Sheriff Johnnie Hawkins's office.

"They found what was left of Bud Roy Roemer in a lifeboat drifting off the coast," Hawkins said. "Damn gruesome. Just a head and Bud Roy's left thigh remained. And gulls had worked those over." He shuddered and then indulged in a little of the mordant humor cops are known for. "It looked like Bud Roy booked a cruise on the SS *Jeffrey Dahmer.*"

"Howard was partial to saving the thighs for last," Sam said, remembering Sprinkles the Dog. "So I take it they suspect Howard the Leopard?"

"Leopard fur. Leopard scat. Leopard paw prints," Hawkins said. "Even the FBI is fifty-six percent sure this is the work of a leopard."

"Well, statistics don't lie. If you keep a leopard in the house, it's way more likely to eat a member of your family, or you, than to ward off an intruder."

Hawkins grinned and drank some coffee.

"Are they putting out a BOLO for Howard?" Sam asked, using the acronym for a Be On the Lookout order.

"There have been sporadic reports of leopard sightings in Florida. Along with a Tasmanian devil sighting"—Hawkins fished his notebook out of his shirt pocket and flipped it open—"a capybara sighting, a pygmy hippo sighting, a king cobra sighting, a puma sighting, and a zebra sighting." He flipped his notebook closed. "Howard made it to the Promised Land."

"Oh my," Sam said. "If he can find something to mate with down there, they'll be up to their asses in leopards inside of five years."

"Not our problem." Hawkins took a sip of coffee and set the cup back on his empty desktop. "How about you? I suspect you could hook on with any federal shop or any police force in the country."

"Becks and I talked about that. I like it here. She likes it here. And I hear you might just be thinking of hanging up the spurs next year."

Hawkins smiled. "You heard right. And if you want my job, I will do everything I can to help you get it. After that, I'm goin' fishin'."

Sam Aucoin stuck out his hand. Johnnie Hawkins took it. "Johnnie, if you're serious about going after some big fish, I know just the boat captain for you."

CHAPTER THIRTY-SEVEN

Eighteen months later, Cumberland County Sheriff Samuel Aucoin pulled his cruiser into the jammed parking lot of Twelve Gage Southern BBQ, across the street from where Jubblies used to be.

He walked in and found Gage Randolph at his customary station behind the bar, monitoring every detail. Rebel the Hound kept him company, resting between patrols for brisket dropped by diners.

Sam looked around. The place was packed, the band was hot, and the barbecue even hotter. Somehow, against the odds, Gage had found his calling and bottled lightning.

"Sheriff," Gage said, sliding a cup of coffee down the bar to Sam. "Nice of you to drop by."

"Well, Gage," Sam said, "ever since you ran Jubblies out of town, where else am I gonna go for hot wings?"

Gage smiled. "Best in the state."

"That's what I hear. I also hear you're opening another restaurant in Durham."

"I've got an angel investing with me."

"She is that," Sam said, raising his mug to the TV behind the bar, tuned to *The Monica Bell Show*.

"You like her?" a fat man seated next to Sam said. "Why? Commie bitch. She's a goddamn liberal." He used a thick forefinger to push at his glasses, which were too small for his bucket-size head.

"That she is," Gage said. "Possibly the most infuriating person I know. Correct in her opinions maybe two percent of the time, and that has been achieved only after repeated interventions. But I'll bet you five bucks she could knock you on your ass. And I'll bet you ten I can if you talk about her unkindly again."

"Sheriff, you gonna let him threaten me like that?" the customer asked.

"Only if you keep runnin' your mouth," Sam said. "Be civil and you'll be fine."

The man heaved himself off the stool and waddled off.

"One battle at a time," Gage said.

Sam looked at him. "Speakin' of battles, I hear you quit SOL."

Gage smiled. "No time now that I got this place up and runnin'. And I think I was leanin' that way regardless. Some stuff didn't sit right."

He shifted his gaze from Sam and looked over the crowded room and packed tables brimming with every flavor and hue of humanity. He found reassurance in the scene; at least for the moment, his customers were bound to him and to one another by a shared experience and the special joy that only food, friends, and family can provide. Gage appeared to be soaking in all that had been missing from his life. Etched on his face was the cost.

Gage returned his attention to Sam. He was quiet for several seconds, as if he had more to say than he had words to use. Finally, Gage shrugged and said everything he needed to: "Hell, I sell barbecue to everyone."

Sam nodded.

"And truth be told," Gage said, jerking his head in the direction of Monica on the TV, "maybe she's convinced me of a few things. Don't tell her that, though."

Sam gave Gage a look of genuine friendship. "We're all a work in progress."

"I'd like to think so. You know, now that I got the best ribs in the state, I still see Linus all the time. Hell, he represents half my profits. I hope there's a Linus in Durham."

"One thing America has plenty of," Sam said. "Fat lawyers."

He put out his hand, and Gage took it. The sheriff then moved off to meet Rebecca Aucoin, six months pregnant and ready to indulge a massive craving for barbecue, at their customary table.

Sam Aucoin gave his wife a kiss and held the seat out for her. Feeling a pang of loneliness, Gage Randolph watched Monica Bell on the TV until she signed off.

Then he picked up the ancient cordless phone on the counter—a reminder of both how far he had come and those he had left behind—and dialed the only number in New York City he knew by heart.